TRAVIS RANDALL

HOUNDING

A TALE OF THE HEAVING SKY

Burrow & Grim

Burrow & Grim Press

ISBN: 979-8-9866561-0-6
Library of Congress Control Number: 2022948141

Cover design by Gianna Rini.
Edited by Rossa Crean.

Disclaimer: Crossed Crow Books, LLC/Burrow & Grim Press does not participate in, endorse, or have any authority or responsibility concerning private business transactions between our authors and the public. Any internet references contained in this work were found to be valid during the time of publication, however, the publisher cannot guarantee that a specific reference will continue to be maintained. This book's material is not intended to diagnose, treat, cure, or prevent any disease, disorder, ailment, or any physical or psychological condition. The author, publisher, and its associates shall not be held liable for the reader's choices when approaching this book's material. The views and opinions expressed within this book are those of the author alone and do not necessarily reflect the views and opinions of the publisher.

Published by:
Burrow & Grimm Press,
An imprint of Crossed Crow Books, LLC
6934 N Glenwood Ave, Suite C
Chicago, IL 60626
www.crossedcrowbooks.com

To those who have wolves of their own.

PART

ONE

THE WORLD IS TOO FULL

---

*"It is a chalice
held out to you in
silent communion, where gaspingly
you partake of a shifting
identity never your own."*

-Reflections, by R.S. Thomas

CHAPTER

1

TRANSITION

They set his trial for midday. Greydal didn't know if he would last the hour. The truth then undeniable—it may be his last day under open sky. In a cruel way, this was the fulfillment of old dreams, wasn't it? Nightmares he had suffered as a child about the end of the world now come a-choking.

Crouching by the side of the road, he tried to fill his lungs as the sapphire wings of the distant 'cada bugs produced a horrible screeching, a rural ensemble of anxiety. In contrast to those frantic refrains, the rain. It increased its pattering, becoming a steady and cool comfort. Yet, quickly, the scorching heat of the valley reduced that to mere sweat. He wiped his brow and scanned his surroundings again.

There: a miniature apocalypse on the other side of the stone path. Tiny figures scurried in their alarm as Greydal approached the anthill and stooped to examine the creatures. Their waving antennae gave an impression of dire panic. Run! They fled before him.

For a breath, he allowed himself a grim satisfaction. Then his conscience gained the upper hand, and he searched the grass for something to help the crimson things. As the rainwater pooled, he collected a handful of twigs before crouching to set them next to the dirt tower, hoping the creatures were smart enough to grab hold. The wind-carried water pelted a few as they fled toward the scraps. One ant was braver than the others, or forgot something important and turned to its burrow, only for the rising torrent to wash it into a crack. He lost sight of the straggler and turned his focus on the survivors. Several now clung to a leaf, the water lifting it just as the ants' tower collapsed in a dramatic tumble.

An entire population struggled silently in the stream, the visible members of the colony dwindling as they were ferried to the grass. Soon, the crew cleaving to the now twirling leaf were all that remained, each of them shiny from mist.

He watched them for a moment, wondering. Greydal leaned in to give one a boost with an ignored twig as the ant struggled to pull itself onto the leaf's rosy face.

"Ah, looks like the rain is doing away with the vermin."

The vague shadows squatting under the speaker were almost circles. "Hello, Ster Finch," Greydal sighed. A droplet rolled from his forehead to his nose, tickling it.

"Ster Finch, he says. You know it's just Marro, don't you, boy?"

He looked up, but said nothing. The man who loomed over him stroked a damp, pocked face, eyeing Greydal's. "Sure you do," Marro murmured. Greydal kept silent as he dropped the twig and stood, wiping his forehead with his other hand. He wished the doomed colony well.

"Say, are you already on your way to the Rings? I'm headed that direction myself." A slurry of sunlight from a part in the clouds fell across the man's face and turned him glowworm as a breeze picked up the red leaf between them and sent it spinning away.

"Sorry," Greydal replied as he shielded his eyes from the indiscriminate rainfall. "I'm— I have to meet a friend."

"Suit yourself, boy, I'll be sure to tell your pa hello. See you at midday."

Greydal had already begun striding away from the gargantuan man. He was unsure how long Marro's eyes followed him as he waded through the cone stalks. To be safe, he walked until he knew the field's machined walls hid him. Once there, he leaned against one and glanced at the sun's face, which hid in anticipation behind the clouds, peeking through their breaks. Taking a few breaths, he counted down from ten.

Can't go around it.

Greydal pushed himself off the wall and stumbled over a hidden crumble of substicrete, spitting at it before continuing towards the south road. The sun ignited the faltering clouds and was all the hotter for the dampness on Greydal's brow, under his dusky tunic. He slid the garment over his head and tied it around his waist as he marched through a field ever-erupting with weeds. Coming upon a low, wooden fence, he slid underneath and managed to avoid its snagging splinters. On the other side, he eyed his surroundings.

There was no sign of Marro. All the better—the man wouldn't be around to pester Toshi as well. Greydal's friend would be rounding the bend soon, surely. How long had he been waiting, though? It was hard to concentrate. His thoughts congealed, and all he heard was the parched singing of the 'cada bugs.

"It's been a day, and it's still morning," he whispered.

Was it, though? Rainy days *did* make it hard to tell the time. Had he missed Toshi somehow? No, he felt sure he would have spotted the boy passing him at the crossroads. He had to keep waiting. He glanced around for another loitering spot and decided on a low tree which strained away from the stone path, half-heartedly offering shade.

Approaching it, he rubbed his hands across its trunk. Rough and moist. He turned and leaned against the tree. After a beat, he gazed across the fields, picking absently at the wet bark. His eyes ached from the soft glare.

The heat was almost as bad as the anticipation. Maybe he should have just waited in the barracks—at least the spot wasn't boiling. But no, that low, cool space was occupied, bloated with the glaring absence of his father. The road was the best spot to while away what may be his last hours under the unobscured light of day. He shook his head and relaxed his jaw after he discovered it clenched tightly enough to make his temples ache. Then he paused to focus again on his surroundings. He needed to breathe. It wouldn't do to walk into his trial a jittering mess.

Uncrossing his arms, he took a shaking breath before allowing the sounds of the world to re-introduce themselves. At first, he couldn't hear anything aside from his racing mind and the far-off screeches. Thankfully, their owners would go back to their deep, insect sleep within days as the mating season withered.

After (or rather, if there *was* an after), he would only have to contend with his own solitude. Realizing he had already lost the thread, he returned his awareness to the world. Soon, he became conscious of the light pattering of rain on puddles. The mournful sounds of birds hooting beyond the tree line. After a time, he made out the croaking of some newt or frosk. It all continued in spite of his fear, and he nearly smiled. Now, he made his awareness scour the tree under him, and then his body. His consciousness roved his toes to his scalp, and he fell into the sensation, a hush settling on the road. Soon, there was only himself, floating in the darkness behind his eyelids. He leaned there, the thumping of his heart the sole sign time continued to turn.

What came next was a dream brought on by stress.

In the dream, he crawled. On hands and knees, he shuffled infantile, pouring between mossy trees towering beyond a field

|5|

older than it had any right to be. He crept after a peculiar scent, now halting as he spotted its source: a boy—skin the color of a rose petal, well-muscled and coiled as if about to spring into flight.

But no, the prey slept, propped against a leaning cousin of the surrounding evergreens. Smiling, Greydal pushed his hands into the wet soil and inhaled to take in the young thing's aroma. Strange, there was no odor of illness, no sickly sweet notes. All the better, he reasoned impressively. He paused to listen, squatting deeper among the fallen vines. The rain would mask his approach, though he was already silent as death. His muscles slid into place as his eyes rolled into his head. Now, he navigated by scent alone to crawl through the undergrowth towards the low tree and its occupant. Rain and sweat dripped from his flanks.

Greydal woke an eye at a time, an uncomfortable knob in his back. He leaned from the trunk and rubbed his shoulders as nervousness squeezed him but...he couldn't remember why. Had he been dreaming?

Looking around, he realized he was still on the south road, waiting for Toshi.

Toshi.

What time was it? A glimpse skyward told him the rain clouds had gone. More than that, the sun's light appeared as though it was well past midday. Rising, he stumbled towards the crossroads, glancing behind once more for a sign of his friend. There was nothing, only puddles that would disappear within hours. Whether he had missed the boy or not, Greydal was late.

The oncoming road was kinder to his worn feet, yet he took care, sidestepping the spined mushrooms which squatted in the cracks, each waiting eagerly for an uncareful footfall. Those tiny, luminescent hazards were a constant nuisance in this part of the valley, and he expected to find more on his return journey that evening, should he be granted such a mercy.

Thinking this, a strange feeling emerged, as though he were unnaturally exposed. As the flesh on his back prickled, he untied his dyed tunic from around his waist and pulled it over his head. It didn't help. The sensation of nakedness increased, and then mutated, becoming a lurching twist in his stomach as he tried to continue onwards.

That's not good, he thought briefly before bile surged from his lips onto the hot stone. In the harsh light, it looked nearly black, the spew. He panted for several breaths, leaning over his knees. Spitting before wiping his mouth, he released a panicked laugh. He had never vomited from stress before. He shook his head and hurried on.

After several minutes absent of more disruptions, he allowed himself to tentatively mull over the events ahead. If the Humble Array found him complicit, he was dead. There was also the possibility they would decide he was canny to his father's crimes but had been forced, as it were, to obey him. Greydal wasn't sure what the judgment for that offense must be, but he didn't imagine it would favor him. He loathed to let himself think of the possibility the elders would find him altogether innocent. After sidestepping another thorny toadstool, he mentally explored that future. He would be released and likely granted most of his father's belongings. But there would be stigma, he knew that. Once a pariah, always a scapegoat.

Greydal obviously preferred to live and would advocate for himself if he could, yet he doubted the Array would give him the chance to speak at all during the proceedings. His account was already in one of the sheriff's sable books, and the elders had all they needed or cared to know. What he truly resented was Marro judging him. Marro, with his falsely apologetic eyes and sweaty hands, *always* sweaty. He spit again, but the taste of bile remained.

The foliage nearer the Rings was desiccated, in sad contrast to the heady verdancy of the forest hemming the crossroads. Spire-like trees gave way to gravel and shrubs, which hatched from the stone. No moss here. The air itself was dry, and Greydal imagined that as he closed with the first aperture, he transitioned to a different time and place.

Great bubbles of glass rose from the approaching crater, so large he could spy them from several thousand paces. A faint buzzing tickled his inner ears, and the world smelled of ozone. At least he didn't have to share this journey with anyone from the village, though he would have liked Toshi's company and hoped to find the boy at the entrance to the Rings.

That series of structured metal and glass was far, and it was a while before he passed under the entrance arch. As he did, the heat of the day evaporated, and he felt cool air on his scalp. His friend wasn't in sight, just the sun's light turned to muted rainbows as it filtered through the translucent ceiling. The burning, oily scent was mostly absent as well. Across the wide chamber, he spotted the secretary. The man stood with his arms folded at the waist near the doors at the distant end of the room. Greydal's footsteps echoed as he approached.

"Good...well, I shouldn't say 'morning.' You're late." The voice sounded hollow in the empty space. "I know, I—" Greydal's own voice trailed off. It didn't matter.

"They're waiting for you inside the third Ring." Your father is there as well, the man didn't say. Greydal knew it, regardless.

"Thanks, Alom." He displayed a crafted smile, meant to re-assure, and moved past the man to open the doors. Out of the corner of his eye, he saw Alom reach out, only to drop his hand at the last moment.

Greydal forged ahead. The doors were made of retrofitted ferrous wood and hard to push. For a panicked second, he thought they would never budge, and he would have to ask for help. Then they slid apart with a moan, and the sight of a huge, empty space greeted him.

More pale, curved glass enclosed the vastness from far above. To Greydal, it appeared the platform on the other side of the doors simply ended, a cliff for him to plunge into nothing. He knew metal steps hid on the far end of the platform, of course, ones leading down to the second Ring, the first within the crater itself.

But he allowed himself another second to memorize the sight of the illusory cliff in case it was the last peaceful image of his life. Dust in the air tinkled in front of his eyes as a distant, scintillating wall cascaded. The light was beautiful. Alom cleared his throat, and Greydal smiled in embarrassment, nodding at the man before moving onto the platform. Then he made his way towards the stairs.

They creaked when he put his weight on the second step, which didn't inspire confidence. His breath came heavy as he leaned, carefully as he could, on the see-through railing before beginning his descent. The spectrum of lights from the ceiling seemed to disappear as his view changed, and after fifty steps, he stood directly over the center of the yawning gap. He spied what he assumed were Rings Five through Nine far below. Did the builders of this place not have a better way to travel into the crater? They must have been crafty enough.

He was stalling. Gritting his teeth, he closed his eyes and continued into the depths.

*** *** ***

Elsewhere, the drying air shuddered. Newly formed clouds undulated in glee as they made way for an unreality, part of that thing which all of life instinctively recognizes, the dead having infiltrated our dreams to whisper its mystery.

Below, bald-headed birds picked nervously at a glistening meal, stashed without care in the canopies. But their banquet was soon forgotten. For these fearsome citizens of death were now witness to a miracle, a suspended fountain of cosmic ichor blooming in the smoldering sky. And, behind it...yes, behind it...the crashing source.

Love is the sea, as the poet said.

In a forgotten hollow, flute music erupted, and was heard by none.

RULING

He had anticipated a crowd yet encountered a private affair. Only five attended, excluding himself and his half-entombed father. As he entered, Greydal discovered to his shame he had missed the opening proceedings.

The elders waited in silence on his approach. They must have already heard the evidence from the sheriff and his sable book. At least Greydal wouldn't have to listen as his own words condemned him. He stepped on the pedestal, which sat below the Humble Array's bench, looking up at Crawl Quymora, who gazed at him with soft eyes.

Crawl's voice was a flute. "Ah, Greydal, welcome." Greydal tried to bow. Crawl ignored his poor attempt and continued, "Now that you have arrived, we may begin with the, ah, latter half of the judgment. Is that alright with you?" He nodded, and the old man replied, "Thank you. Please, ah, announce yourself for decorum's sake."

"My name is Greydal. Greydal Duinn."

"Thank you. And tell us why you are here, eh?"

"I-I'm here to answer for a crime," Greydal recited.

Crawl nodded and replied, "Quite right, thank you. The rest of you, I will again call out for attendance." He cleared his throat. "The man previously known to the law as Tier Duinn."

After a silence, Greydal's father whispered, "I am here," from his makeshift sarcophagus. Crawl bobbed his head in response, and then called on the others.

"Sheriff Calahurst." The sheriff nodded.

"Ster Marro Finch." Marro smiled and waved his hand before him like a benediction.

"Ster Jon Grime." After a beat, Jon gave an assent.

"Dame Maizy Hawker." Maizy announced herself with a hum and said, "I'm here, Crawl."

"And I, Crawl Quymora, am present as well."

A hollowed-out skull, which sat in front of the old man, stared mindlessly. Crawl added, "Is there anyone...I missed?" The room was quiet aside from one of its occupant's ponderous breathing. The skull said nothing.

"We've, eh...heard from Sheriff Calahurst and Tier Duinn, and we've read the accounts of others." Crawl glanced alongside the towering bench to his right and left. "It is rare indeed we folk meet in this place, to judge the guilty, and, ah, innocent." Crawl turned his attention to Greydal and peered at him from the lofty officiant's chair.

"If we discount Tier Duinn's judgment, this trial is the first in seven years to be held in the Ring." He paused. "Do you know why that is?"

Greydal took in an unsteady breath. "Yes."

When Crawl didn't reply, he sighed and added, "It's because Ring trials are kept for decisions that affect the whole of the village."

"Precisely, ah, quite right. Smart young man. The last trial here, again excluding your father's, was for Orman's decision to involve bandits in the protection of the, ah, town. You were there with your father if I recall." Greydal nodded, unsure if he was agreeing he had been at Orman's trial or in the village during the attack.

He remembered little of the trial except the previous sheriff had made some sort of alliance with a foreign crew of killers to sweep the roads of dangers. The endeavor failed or went sour, and the gang turned its lethal attention on the valley's inhabitants. The village defeated them...barely. From what Greydal understood, the elders—Crawl in particular—wanted to make an example of Orman. They decided to both punish him and warn villagers against trafficking with outside forces in a single judgment. Ironic then, that Greydal was on trial for what was almost certainly a similar charge. He noticed himself smiling and forced the grin off his face. He was just nervous.

The Maer continued, "For that reason, we called you here today. Feud. Feud is the most dangerous thing with which a small collective of people can grapple, eh? We've proven time and again we are capable of standing against adversarial agencies, beasts, and, eh, others..." He trailed off, then looked at Jon, who tapped the wood of the bench. "Jon, please."

Jon appeared to become aware of himself and mumbled, "Sorry, go on."

Crawl cleared his throat and began again. He furrowed his brow as he attempted to recall his rhythm. "The beasts, yes." His shoulders drooped. "We are capable of defending ourselves, eh? What we cannot withstand is infighting. Feud, as I said. It is a fundamental truth small colonies of people who struggle with one another perish. We must be a-ah, unified front at all moments, in all times.

"From corner to corner, the world is...well it is, er, dangerous, and that is as true here as it is in the west."

Greydal attempted to appear rapt, but the anxiety that clutched his stomach like a vise made it hard to concentrate on Crawl's droning. He thought about what the man said, or rather, what he didn't. Of course, murder occurred in the village—it was rare—but it happened. He could guess what Crawl failed to suggest with his roundabout speech.

"The conclusion. The decision we make today in this place won't set a legal precedent alone, it will tell our people what is acceptable, eh? Conduct is key. It's, ah, survival." The Maer took a breath and sat back. "Sheriff, if you please."

Sheriff Calahurst nodded and stood. The man's black, broad-brimmed hat looked like a halo from Greydal's perspective. It was surprising the man wore anything on his head at all during the judgment. He had thought the village considered the Rings sacred, though Greydal supposed it was possible that Calahurst didn't much care.

"Ster Duinn. Your father killed a man." Calahurst didn't spare a glance at Jon, who reddened. "That murder is not why you're here."

There it is, Greydal thought.

The sheriff's countenance was grave as he turned to the others. "You all know what Tier was hiding." He stared at each one of them in turn. "Even should we declare Greydal naive of his father's actions, he mustn't be allowed rejoinment. Accidental contact with the Interloper's handicraft is contact enough. He's poisoned." Calahurst let his words hang in the air. Maizy appeared as though she was about to interrupt, but Crawl shook his head at her.

Calahurst looked down at Greydal. His eyes were dark.

"A wolf in lamb's skin." He pointed. "That's what this boy will be, whether he intends it or not. If we welcome him back, it'll destroy us." The sheriff paused. Then he nodded to himself and added, "That's my official recommendation. Please, consider it." Calahurst sat and placed his hands palm down on the bench. The sheriff's scarred face was a pale olive beneath his pitch-colored hat, unreadable. Greydal was stunned. Calahurst had acknowledged his innocence in one breath and declared it immaterial the next. The man doomed him.

"Hmm. Thank you, Sheriff," Crawl nodded. "You've, ah, put it plainly the danger we face here." Crawl then peered again at the rest of the bench, frowning at Marro, who barely suppressed a smile.

"Greydal, I will go over the facts again before we vote. You, ah, witnessed your father kill a man and told no one, not a soul. You slept in the same room your father hoarded forbidden items. This you kept silent through ignorance or contempt. You attacked Ster Finch, directly after the murder.

"You've pleaded guilty to two of these charges, eh? But you denied, ah, said you didn't know, and are innocent of, the items stored under the floor of the north machined building. The barracks, I believe some call them." Crawl steepled his fingers and sighed. Then he dropped his hands and held up a quill before dipping it in a well of ink. "This," he raised the wet pen, "is my judgment."

He spent several anxious moments writing on something Greydal couldn't see. Then Crawl picked it up and dropped what turned out to be a slip of parchment into the hollowed-out skull on the bench.

"Whatever is decided here today, the true results rest on me." He gestured at the skull. For an odd second, Greydal thought the old man identified the dead thing as himself.

"This judgment is now written. It is, ah, done. If you are guilty, the penalty is within. Likewise, if you are innocent. Today, we vote on the charge of corruption, the artifacts, eh? The other charges, not worth a vote in the Rings. We determined as much already." Crawl smiled but looked sad.

"Sheriff, your, ah...vote please."

The sheriff stood again. "Guilty."

Greydal expected Calahurst's decision but felt sick to hear it voiced. Crawl looked at Maizy. She drew herself up. "Oh, for Dawn's sake, look at him. Innocent."

Crawl nodded, "Thank you. Ster Jon?" Greydal looked up at Jon. The man rubbed his head. "Guilty."

Greydal's eyes widened. Jon *knew* he would have never knowingly—

"Ster Marro?" Crawl interrupted his panicked thoughts. Marro smiled to himself and seemed to waft in his own silence. When it became awkward, he announced, "Innocent."

"It is my vote, then," Crawl sighed. Greydal held his breath.

"Innocent. By all, ah, accounts, the boy did not know of his father's hoard, and no evidence pointed to the contrary, eh?"

Greydal blinked. Had he heard correctly?

Crawl wasn't finished. "I said *hoard* just now, but truly, it was less than three items as you all, I'm sure, heard during the testimonies. Easy to hide. The murder itself. Greydal, your behavior after the crime...the irresponsible actions of a boy. Now, you will be called upon to live as a man."

Crawl snatched the skull before him and dumped its contents into an outraised palm. Setting the skull down, he held aloft the sheet of red ink.

"This is the judgment, eh? I placed it upon you already. As you have been deemed innocent, I will read from that side." He turned the paper. Greydal's head was light as Crawl read the parchment aloud, "The boy...the man, Greydal Duinn, now Greydal Alone, is to be granted the belongings, which were, eh, seized by the village of Harlow Valley. This includes a sum of fifty-five minted shavings, a metal woodsperson's axe, and the various sundries found within the home. The barracks will likewise become his property. The artifacts...and other, ah, suspicious items, won't be returned."

Crawl set the paper down. "You will owe Ster Marro a week of labor for the bite you delivered, ah, forcefully, upon his arm— Jon, sit down."

Jon had stood, causing his chair to topple sideways. From Greydal's point of view, Jon's height was only narrowly improved. He could see a vein throb on the man's corded neck. Jon's voice was shaky as he sputtered, "Avel's dead!"

Avel. Odd how after death the man's name had taken on a new weight, one never achieved in his life. A cheat and a thief, but he had been well-loved by Jon.

Maizy reached out a hand and replied, "Jon, we spoke on this. Who here can say what the *right* course of action was? I'd be frightened out of my damn wits!"

Jon wasn't dissuaded. "He could have saved him. He could have told someone." Jon's voice was strained, and Greydal knew the man well enough to see he was close to crying.

Then the sheriff interrupted, surprising him. "That's not the case, I'm sorry. Avel died with Tier's hands on his neck. It didn't take long."

Jon stared at the sheriff, and then, intimidated or not finding what he sought, looked around. Maizy glared back while Marro inspected something on his nails. Jon glanced again at Calahurst and said, "Then what about the blight, huh? That boy's been playing around my son for years. What about all you said of him being spoiled by the things his father was keeping?"

The sheriff held Jon's gaze. "I stated my case on the matter. He was declared a free member of our fine hamlet, as you just heard." The sheriff looked calm as a summer day. Jon slumped. After a moment, he turned and descended from the platform, ignoring Greydal's pleading eyes, and marched from the chamber. The sheriff's cool gaze found Crawl's.

"Oh, he's fine. Let him go. This thing is almost over anyway," Maizy looked irritated as she spoke.

Crawl nodded his agreement and said, "She, ah, Dame Hawker, is right. It is almost over. He can leave." The sheriff settled wordlessly back in his chair.

Crawl turned his scrutiny to Greydal. He continued, "As I said, you owe Ster Marro a week of labor. It will be at his convenience, eh? I expect you to not, ah, 'stir the pot,' as they say."

The order repulsed Greydal, but he forced himself to nod.

"I want you to fully understand what we did here today. Comprehend it. Your father forfeited himself, his *personhood*, when he handled and hid the things he did." Greydal nodded, and the old man went on, "As you walk out of this Ring today, you will have proved you don't deserve to join him, eh? You will henceforth be Greydal Alone. The family Duinn is wiped from the slate.

"Once your father is executed, that will be true not only in the legal sense. Do you understand me? Were you listening or just pretending to, ah, hear when I spoke of the dangers of feud? Of schism?"

Greydal looked up and held the old man's watery gaze for what felt like the first time. He knew what the man implied. He said, "Yes, Ster, I-I get you."

Crawl Quymora nodded, content, or pretending to be content.

"That's the bit then, eh? You will go first. We will follow."

Greydal realized he was dismissed. Was it over? Had he really survived the judgment? He stood rooted to the podium and looked to each of those seated. The elders, which made up the Humble Array, appeared willing to let him walk from the room. Maizy nodded at him and smiled. No, something was wrong.

A profound knot twisted in his gut, a surreal dread uncoiling, like the sensation of picking up a shining rock to uncover a sopping multitude beneath. As Greydal backed from the podium, his heart thudded an uncertain beat. He had dreamed this, hadn't he? That was why it felt so familiar.

For the first time since he entered Ring Three, his eyes found his father's. Not much of Tier was visible behind the brick sarcophagus. The small hole where the town shoved victuals left only room for the upper half of a face, and his father's gaze was a shadowy glimmer, though Greydal saw Tier shared his fear. Without speaking, his father told him that it, whatever *it* was, wasn't over.

Greydal paled. He turned and left the hall with his heart in his throat. He wouldn't see his father again until the new moon two weeks later.

*** *** ***

As Greydal passed the ferrous wood doors to Ring One, he found Alom looking at the encasing dome above, a thoughtful expression softening his features. Greydal put on a brave face as he approached and said, "Well, I'm out."

Alom glanced down in evident surprise. "Ah, Greydal. Yes, you are. I'm pleased to see it."

"Did you not think I'd come out alright?"

"That's an unfair question, and you know it," the man said as he momentarily looked back to the glass.

Greydal shook his head, following the man's gaze. He thought for a moment. "Did you spot Jon? I need to tell him—" He struggled to find the words. "You know I'm not dangerous," he finished after a beat.

The secretary spoke, "I don't presume to know what happened in the Ring, but I know you're innocent because you're standing before me. I also know you're a man now for the same reason. That means," he locked eyes with Greydal, "you'll have to grapple with the struggles of men." Alom turned and crouched so the tall man's gaze became level with his, causing him to notice the man's hazel skin sported a collection of extremely fine wrinkles. How old was he? Greydal always assumed Alom was just wise before his time. Now, he wondered if the man simply aged well.

Alom's warm eyes intimidated him but he couldn't look away. The man continued, "Jon is angry, and rightly so. But he's also afraid. Don't seek him. If you see him, well…"

"Why? He should know better than almost anyone—"

Alom held up a finger. "There may come a time where he finds understanding, if not forgiveness. Until then, you will only do him and *yourself* harm by trying to clear your name. Your name is cleared already."

He straightened and placed a warm hand on Greydal's shoulder. Alom gave it a light squeeze, and then dropped his arm as the sounds of Crawl Quymora's labored breathing echoed from the stairs beyond the platform.

"It's best you leave. Go home and get some rest and let me know if you need anything. And no, don't tell me now."

Greydal swallowed his next words and nodded before hurrying across the dusty floor to the arch. The moment he passed under the aperture, the humidity of the world resumed with a viscousness. Though, he was thankful the morning's rain had lessened the sun's heat. In just a few hours, it might be cool. Now, the fear of awkwardness drove his gait as he hurried along the stone path. He didn't want Crawl, an old man, to catch up with him, much less the others. The elders had intended this walk of his to be solitary, after all.

He wondered again where Toshi was, ill at the thought that boy's father might have forbidden them from fraternizing. Wouldn't his friend have stood up for him? Granted, Jon was an intimidating presence at the best of times. Greydal thought of when Toshi and he were young, to a time when they had snuck into the boy's kitchen and stolen several pink apples, which his mother often used in baking. Jon found out and hunted the boys down to a nearby barn where they had erected their headquarters. Jon had trampled through the 'No Kluddes Allowed' sign, crushing it into the mud. After, Jon beat Toshi and marched Greydal the not-insignificant distance to his father's. He remembered following Jon out of the village and towards the barracks before trying to run. Jon had shot his hand out like a viper and caught Greydal by the sleeve.

Of course, Tier had acted concerned upon having his son delivered to his doorstep. He promised Jon he would discipline Greydal and so on. Although, once his father closed the door, he had turned to Greydal and said, "*That* was over three apples?"

"And a winter berry, but he only knows about the apples."

Tier wiped his forehead. "You know we have food, Greydal."

"I know," Greydal had replied, just before removing a purple berry from his pocket and popping it into his mouth.

He came to himself. He was on the road, walking towards a vacant home. For the first time since the turmoil began, he cried, his tears coming fast and hot. They blinded him, and it was a time before they slowed. By then, he had passed the crossroads and the fields. He trod the phosphorescent mushrooms and blindly stepped over the night vines, which reached in their growing corpulence across the stone in preparation for the moon's light. Farther, beyond his tear-stained vision, a weed-throttled village huddled in the growing darkness, perhaps in wait.

*** *** ***

Great happenings were afoot, reflected in the creaking heavens. The beast panted in silence as it considered. How was it that it had found itself in this valley of all places?

It had been called. There was no doubt, not after...

In the grizzled, old wolf's life, little changed. Whether pluck-ing men screaming from their hunting lodges or piling infants on the rocks, the mission was the same: eat and eat filthily—wet the haircoat, sate the thirst. Coat it all in a blanket of glinting gore.

But earlier, when aged light burned the sky through a mask of rain, something had shifted.

Two of the wolf's hands grasped the flimsy trunk of the great evergreen as another reached out towards the boy's carcass, pulling him higher. Such a small thing. The beast eyed the incomplete body, hardly large enough to fill its massive palm. In some ways, the corpse looked like *him*—the young one by the puddled road that morning. Shining eyes blinked beneath the beast's long tresses.

Things would be different now. After all, True Meaning had coalesced again, to upend this putrid garden.

*** *** ***

He walked south as signs of habitation asserted themselves. A small roadside shrine to the Legate peeked from the weeds, its wood old and dim next to the ever-bright red and gold figurine. A cultivated bed of twisting flowers coursed from where Greydal knew a stone house hid on the hill to the west. As he drew closer to the village, the sounds of young night drifted through the valley. He passed the stables with the huffs and snorts of the razorbacks greeting him. The place smelled of musk and manure, even from the road.

He arrived at the small path, which branched a hundred yards north from the town gate. The overgrown track twisted westward, towards home. He paused at the junction, which was near invisible in the approaching gloom, and stared into it for a breath before he shook his head and entered the thicket.

The walk was quiet, and shadow cloaked the path. Luckily, the patches of feeble light from the dying sun and the glow of the few mushrooms huddling beneath fallen leaves provided some illumination. But when Greydal spied the shine of the oto-lantern through the trees, he smiled in relief, then rounded the bend to approach the painted metal portal. A cloud of insects orbited the light, and his swats caused the door to slide open with a squeal. As he crossed the threshold, he heard the village's bell ring once to announce the evening watch.

He woke several times in the night, his mattress damp with sweat. Greydal didn't think his perspiration came from nightmares. His dreams, barely remembered, gave him a strange thrill or black comfort. He sat up for a moment in the dimness until an overhead light waxed as it reacted to the room's vertical occupant.

He laid back and struggled to remember his most recent dream. As he reached for it, it slid from him and all he could recall was a sunless orb, suspended in ink, and a terrible sense of vertigo. Was he underwater in the dream? Or was it someone else? Occasionally in his nighttime fantasies, he played the parts of others, like an actor on the Vermillion Stage. Sometimes, the actors blended in with the set. Greydal furrowed his brow. Was he thinking about his dreams or the village theatre now? He couldn't remember.

As he drifted to sleep, his fuzzy gaze roved the darkening cabin. Not his father's. It was his now. His slumber slowly resumed, and he believed for a moment he could hear his own mumbling carry into the next dream.

Outside, the night birds and animals quivered. In their way, they hoped beyond hope the thing crouching beside the low, gray building wouldn't notice them. Silent breath fogged the narrow, inset window behind Greydal's sleeping head.

UNKNOWNS

It filled Greydal's room like a stench upon his awakening, a background sliding of the sediment of existence, bearing on him with the weight of dreams. He woke with a scream, in the moment unsure as to what terror or pain he vocalized. There was a period, sweat-covered as his flesh tingled, where he hoped that whatever he had seen in his sleep didn't follow him out.

After he collected himself, he rose and took great care to ignore his nascent dread (or at least enough to keep its nameless source from materializing). He dressed before blinking his eyes against the growing light.

"Off," he muttered. Despite his words, the light remained. Belatedly, he realized it was only the sunlight streaming from the ancient, thick-paned window.

He left his room, but as he entered the hallway, he had to fight the traitorous urge to run. But, of course, he didn't run. There was nothing to run from—a fact he told himself, under his breath. He squeezed through the corridor, weaving past the familiar rubble to the kitchen. Not for the first time he eyed the faded markings above the steel table.

Wish I knew more about the previous occupants of the quarters, he thought to distract himself and wondered what the original owners would have made of him. Did the Old Folk imagine that a boy would have the run of a place clearly designed to house guards? At that thought, he blanched. He had the run of the place.

Ah, yes, it was already fading, the dream-fear, replaced by the sober air of unhappy reality. He stopped eyeing the old writings and turned to search for anything approximating a morning meal. It took some looking, but he was able to uncover the last of his and his father's stores: three jars of fruits and meats, preserved in jelly.

In days, he would be without food. He had made no attempts to plan for the long term before his judgment, and now he registered clearly for the first time he would have to work to provide for himself. Frowning at this unwelcome knowledge, he replaced the top to the meat jar and contented himself with an apple, which he dug from one of the other glass canisters. Its sweetness was a balm as he ate at the metal table, mind churning. He sat there for a time, chewing on the fruit of his restlessness.

He stood, then slunk down the hall, past the collapsed entrances to other cabins to re-enter his own lodging. Across the room, pausing in silence for a moment, wondering why he tried to make no noise as he bent to lift the rug. Now, his father's cache grinned beneath, and he lifted the alloy plate with more ease than he anticipated, almost dropping it.

Greydal stared into the small hole where his father had stored the alleged contraband. The last time this hatch was open, he hadn't had the chance to peek inside despite what Jon and the sheriff believed. What had Calahurst called it? The Intruder? Interloper? The others at the trial understood the meaning of the term, that was clear. It sounded like a title. Like the Legate. He puzzled over this scrap of information as he stared into the dark of the empty hiding place, now a home for mud and spiders. At a loss, he replaced the alloy plate and the tattered rug, coughing as dust tickled his throat.

He knew the world wasn't boundless, but it was wide. At least that's what his father had told him. There were other lands and other hamlets. Larger towns, even. He suspected the Interloper, if it was anything, was a local name for another village's religious icon. That was what the word sounded like in the sheriff's throat. There was veneration or dread there.

But why would his father have kept something associated with another land's legends, not to mention the other items his father was supposed to have ferreted away? Greydal wished he could ask, though what good could it do? As he thought this, the walls quivered, and a surge of anger rose like vomit in his throat, surprising him.

Was he angry at his father for his lies? Or was he ashamed of himself for his cowardice? The sheriff had been wrong at the trial. Greydal was certain Avel would be alive if he had acted instead of hiding.

The cabin was altogether too enclosed. Grabbing his boots, he went to the hall and paced to the barracks entrance, but stopped as he neared the door, sighing and walking back to the kitchen to grab a second apple. Holding what he feared might be his lunch, Greydal returned to the exit.

He waited as the metal door squealed open, preceding the orange morning light, which splashed across his face. He shielded his eyes until they adjusted and he stepped forward, almost dropping his fruit as he tried twice to shove it into a pocket with fidgety hands. After successfully stowing the apple, he inhaled and reveled for a moment in the coolness of the early day, struggling to release his temper.

A bird, partially concealed by the broad leaves above the barracks, squawked in alarm as he stepped further into the sunlight. He didn't hear it flap away and assumed it to be watching him. Looking, he soon spotted it, its aqua coat standing stark against a yellow beak. A tenderbird. That surprised him. They normally didn't migrate from the canopies.

"Are you lost?" he asked. The tenderbird stared at him with fearful black eyes. "Suit yourself, I was just trying to be friendly." He stooped to pull on his boots, one on before he spotted the paint. One-booted, he pressed his way through the tall grass near the path to get a better look.

"You've got to be winding me," he muttered in near perfect imitation of his father. Greydal moved to a patch of shade and looked in shock at the vandalism. *AGUE LEAVE US* leaped in bright, crimson paint across the side of the building, the sight of which closed his throat as a memory lurched, unbidden: old women and decrepit children praying to a red figure, scraps of parchment clutched in their hands. Greydal's father kneeling next to him, larger than life. He holds Greydal's hand so hard it hurts.

Greydal shook his head and dispelled the old thoughts. After pondering for a moment, he determined there was no use in trying to remove the defacement. The paint had set, and he wouldn't give whoever authored it the satisfaction of scraping at the wall for the hour or so it would take to remove the words.

When had they done it? The vandals must have arrived during the night or early dawn. It didn't surprise him that he had heard nothing. The walls of the barracks were almost a third of a foot thick.

He looked up at the tenderbird watching him.

"Figures, doesn't it?" He slipped out of the underbrush and pulled on his other boot. "My name is *cleared already* my ass." Greydal paused. Of course, he had cursed before. Almost all the boys of the village made a sport of it. But now, the act tasted more mature in his mouth. "Fuck." That was a new one. His father would have glowered at him had he overheard. But Greydal was an adult, wasn't he? He was free to talk how he wanted. Encouraging? No.

The reality of his predicament settled further over him. He needed to find work, and fast. The Maer hadn't sent anyone by with the shavings Greydal was told he owned, judging by the lack of a chest full of items outside his door.

He smirked. Maybe Crawl was just being true to his name. Regardless, those fifty-five shavings wouldn't last more than a month if he meant to save any of them. He trudged the shadowed trail as these and other thoughts swarmed, the tenderbird squawking after him in an accusatory tone.

"If you're going to be like that, go back to the treetops!" Greydal yelled over his shoulder.

He paused at a spot along the path and stood in silence for a breath. Then he took several steps off the trail to look at his tree. As a child, he often ran to this spot when his father was harsh with him or others were rough, and he would hide deep within in its hollow. Now, the cavity was filled with toadstools, which festered among the old nest of some animal, long abandoned.

He fingered the carved symbol above the hollow: an arrow or sword with horns sprouting from its middle. It was an image Greydal had conceived as a younger boy, though he had never decided what it meant. With the passage of time, he could no longer recall if he had truly invented the symbol upon carving it. The thing had acquired a kind of retroactive familiarity that made him wonder if he hadn't seen it somewhere first. Either way, he long ago adopted the horned arrow when communicating with Toshi. He scratched the symbol on walls to denote meeting spots and scrawled the image on sheets of parchment in place of his name. It was supposed to preserve secrecy. Now, he doubted it had done anything other than appear self-important.

Standing in the shade of his tree for a moment longer, Greydal watched as an iridescent beetle rounded the trunk. Realizing belatedly the bug was of a sort that pinched, he dropped his hand from the bark. He had to give up childish things like secret codes and tree hideouts.

He moved onto the dried mud of the path as a small rodent scurried from the underbrush on his leaving. Soon, he arrived at the road and turned south towards the village, walking past five men on their way to attend the cone fields. At their passing he notice they carried small bows and had both quivers and long knives slung on their belts. Hunters, then. They spared him no glances as they headed north. He looked at himself, an apparent vagrant, aside from his boots, which were the most expensive items he owned.

The road widened. The mutilated trees by the north gate of the settlement stared, unseeing. From each, the town had hewn cruel, carved faces, which sneered as he approached. Making to pass the guardians, he stopped to blow out the glowing eye of one a villager must have missed, leaving the smell of wax drifting in the wind.

Greydal left the vine-encrusted scowler and rounded the bend to the north village entrance. Sidling up to the wall and the heavy wooden gate, he eyed the flowery carvings that wormed across the old timber. He didn't need to try and press against the wood to know the doors were sealed on the other side by a golden locking mechanism as he glimpsed its shine through the seam of the gates.

Before he decided to yell out for passage, a blurred shadow overcame him, and a face peered down from the direction of the sky. Greydal started and glanced up, but it was only someone who leaned from the platform behind the gate's right upper hinge.

"Ho, pretty boy!"

The woman was hard to see from the sun, but Greydal recognized her voice. "Ida, the gate?" he asked.

The guard appeared almost horizontal as she leaned from the wall. "It's not for me to say, but there's been some trouble. You'd best get inside before the other watchman's back." She disappeared, and then rattled open a side door carved into the gate, waving him in. She was wearing her blue guard's jacket half-unbuttoned—a fashion choice, not a sign of disregard.

Greydal passed under the doorway and inhaled, making a face. "Eugh, isn't that a little strong?"

Ida looked dour, her short-cropped blonde hair falling over her eyes. "I have a date tonight."

"I hope she doesn't have a nose." He grinned and ducked as Ida made to cuff his head.

"You'll understand when you're older."

"*Older?*" Greydal asked incredulously.

The girl looked offended, her freckled brow furrowed. "There's plenty of difference between a sixteen-year-old squirt and a lady of eighteen. If you don't know that, I don't have any hope for you."

Greydal rolled his eyes but halted as Ida wasn't looking at him any longer. He turned to follow her gaze. Marston was leaving a nearby street, stomping towards the gate.

"There's the other as I said," his friend whispered and added, "Best you leave."

Greydal didn't argue and cut towards the market, hissing to Ida as he left, "Since when is *he* a watchman?" He glimpsed her smirk, and then straighten as the boy neared.

Greydal left her to her fate and jogged from the exposed thoroughfare to slip through an adjacent alley, thick with a graffiti of mold. The wetly thriving backstreet spit him out near a collection of market stalls.

A tall merchant he recognized by face alone barked at him and followed with a "Shit!" as Greydal quickly apologized for almost toppling the merchant's bin of cone stalks.

He weaved through a series of ramshackle shops. Listless farmers' wives barely saw him as they staffed the stalls under the dreamy morning light. Where was everyone? Normally at this time, the village should be busy with people about their early tasks. Come to think of it, he hadn't spotted any farmers on the road. Perhaps there *was* some kind of trouble as Ida mentioned.

He crossed the path of a dusky-skinned woman and her companions as they carried bundles of chopped wood to nearby drying racks. Their muscled arms shone with sweat. As he traveled farther, an older man down the lane chatted to a young lady in whom the man held an embarrassing abundance of interest, straining his smile towards her.

The woman, or rather girl, lounged on the rotting sill of a second story window and appeared as disinterested as the man wasn't. So, people still attended to business, it seemed. But then something else presented itself, a commotion in the distance, faint but unmistakable. It was the sound of many people trying to speak over one another. For the second time that morning, he shook off an unwanted memory.

Jogging to a nearby street exit and peering around the corner, he found the shuffling backs of several large men, who defeated his view of the crowd beyond. People were gathered at the square, though, that much was obvious. He doubled back to the previous street and scaled a knobby tree that groped a neighboring home, sliding from the mossy bark onto the clay shingles to creep to the roof's summit. It gladdened him it was a dry morning despite the previous day's rain, for he gained the height of the roof with ease. The village stretched before him.

He saw the western wall first, a natural cliff of jagged stone towering over the hamlet. Its white and pink rock was a monumental slab of raw meat from a distance. The only activity that disrupted the illusion was the spattering of downward shadows cast on the wall, which fell from its face in various places, sprouting from the handful of small homes carved into the stone and infrequent ledges peppering the rock.

He broke his gaze with the wall and glanced to the square below. *Legate!* Half the valley seemed to be in attendance. The villagers packed around the theatre and the statue of the First Maer, which looked like a glob of chiseled marble.

Thinking of Maers, Greydal searched for Crawl, but there was only the sheriff. The black-garbed man was atop the theatre's stage, which sprawled at the far end of the square. Greydal could barely spy it for the throng, but he saw that next to Calahurst leaned a makeshift podium. Were they planning on some sort of announcement?

He tried to listen to the congregation below to make sense of the spectacle, but it was all noise. He returned to his watch and found he was just barely close enough to spy (if he squinted his eyes) at how the statue of the First Maer mirrored Sheriff Calahurst's uninterested gaze.

Greydal shook his legs, and then sat down on the roof to wait patiently alongside the agitated crowd. Again, he tried to make out what the people nearest to him said, but the only words he caught were "missing" and "animal" from an arm-locked couple directly underneath his perch. His eyes drifted to the western wall again as an old wish reemerged. He was confident he possessed the ability, though maybe not the stamina. But the thing that always kept him back was that, if he failed, he'd never be able to try again.

As a rule, Greydal was keen on climbing the giant stones in the forests and practiced with them often. The western behemoth on the other hand was intimidating in the extreme despite its beauty, that last aspect being why the few wealthy Harlow Valley inhabitants lived in compact homes nestled into its face. Aside from the wall's stark charm, it served as an incredible natural defense.

As a child, he hadn't experienced much of the assault of the Kluddes mercenary gang. Frantic adults stashed him in the second, southern barracks for safekeeping. This one was a pristine copy of the ruin to the north, though sadly lacking beds and other furnishings.

Greydal had since come to understand the village normally used the southern barracks to house thieves and drunks. Of the attack, he had only mental images of the spare, dark interior and a vague memory of a red-faced tulka, wearing Kludde leathers, peeking in through the thick-paned window. Though, that memory was likely false, as no Kluddes ever made it into the village itself. Alive, that is. During the attack, some of the mercenaries had allegedly tried to sneak into the hamlet from the cliff instead of targeting the southern gate. The bandits' reasoning was supposed to be that the trees atop the western wall concealed any movement. Because of this, they had crept to the brink and tried to climb down. They fell to their deaths, of course. Greydal knew from bitter experience it was one thing to climb up stone. It was something altogether different to descend it.

Was Ida the one who had claimed that story? Or was it Toshi? He couldn't recall any longer.

Coming to himself, he looked around. The town was still anxiously milling in the square. It was too bad he couldn't while away the time with Toshi. He and his friend were due a conversation, he decided, and then frowned like someone much older. He pulled out his rationed apple and bit into it as he ruminated, already forgetting he was to save it for lunch.

He needed to ensure there was no bad blood between the two of them. Since the murder, he had only encountered his friend twice. Both times, Greydal had been too deadened to act as a conversationalist. Looking back, he couldn't remember how Toshi had behaved—reserved or supportive?

Movement to his right caught his eye. There was a mouse on the roof near his hand. Greydal grinned. "How'd you get up here, fella? Or are you a lady?" The mouse wiggled its nose and scurried closer. "Here, you want some apple? It's sweet."

He bit off a piece and took it out of his mouth.

"Don't try and eat it all at once." He set it down in front of the gray creature. It hopped closer, and after a moment, nibbled on the apple chunk as Greydal chuckled to himself. But the sight of a small, reddish figure pulled him out of his enjoyment.

He turned in time to witness Crawl, dressed in his officiant's robes, approaching the podium. The crowd hushed in an expanding wave as words drifted from the couple beneath the roof, "More? Why would you think there would be more? Oh—" The man's companion silenced him with a nudge. Greydal watched the Maer look at the size of the crowd and gesture to the sheriff. Calahurst bent and pulled an item from behind the podium, a horn. He handed it to Crawl, who raised it to his lips.

"Hello. Eh, hello! My friends and family." He heard the old man clear his throat through the horn. "Please, settle down." Greydal felt the crowd had behaved remarkably well for that statement. "I will treat this first as though no one here knows what happened last evening, as I'm sure many do not. Let me say, too, that anyone who does not wish to be...discomforted...is welcome to leave. You will, I'm sure, be told the story later by those who can bear to hear it."

Crawl cleared his throat for the second time. No one moved as an awkward silence fell on the square. The sheriff inspected his boots.

"Ah, yes, well, I guess I'll get on with it, eh?"

No one answered.

"At some point last evening, or maybe yesterday afternoon...we are not sure...several children of the village were, eh, taken."

Greydal sat up straight. What did *that* mean?

"Four to be exact." The crowd rippled with voices but stopped when it almost drowned out Crawl's next words. "Some were taken from different, eh, locales. All outside of the village walls. We think it was four..."

Even from the distance of Greydal's perch, the Maer looked tired. The sheriff appeared as though he prepared to seize the horn before Crawl raised his voice.

"Two of the children were found. They are dead. They, eh, died, were killed it seems. An animal, we believe." Another silence, which turned to murmuring.

This time, the sheriff reared behind Crawl and laid a hand on the old man's back. Crawl surrendered the horn without protest and sat next to the podium.

Calahurst did not clear his throat before speaking, "All of you here, heed me."

There is a dangerous boy beyond our walls, Greydal thought.

"There is a dangerous creature beyond our walls." Hearing the sheriff nearly quote his thoughts made him reel. "It took three children yesterday, and we suspect it took a fourth the day before. All of them were attacked outside the village and were between the ages of seven and fourteen. Two were known friends and may have been with one another when the animal struck."

The sheriff's words roused a dizziness, causing the roof to sway, and then spin. Calahurst continued to speak, but the sound of rushing liquid soon muffled it as Greydal lowered his head, holding it in both hands. But there was no awareness of his body at all and the sound of the coursing blood in his skull changed, becoming a rhythmic crashing. Waves.

If he had lost his body at first, now he lost his sight, and the square faded. Without eyes, Greydal perceived himself from a long way off. The boy was small, like an ant, sitting on the roof with his head in his hands. As he wondered whose vantage he held, Greydal spun and fell, the sense of motion like swimming in the deep streams which clawed the valley. He tried to follow the current but became lost and collided with himself. Greydal shook his head, stunned and confused.

"—don't know if the animal's nocturnal, but I'm taking every precaution to preserve lives. Please, find me or a watchman if that causes you problems. Thank you." The sheriff dropped the horn on the podium as the stunned silence of the square ended in tumult.

The first one to shout was a man Greydal recognized as Yorn. But the sheriff was already escorting Crawl from the stage towards two grim-looking watchmen.

Greydal rubbed his eyes, and then slowly turned to the mouse, who sat beside him. The little animal appeared to have been observing the proceedings.

"Gotta go," Greydal said and turned before sliding down the roof to the tree and hopping to the worn cobblestones below. He landed on the balls of his feet but almost tumbled.

It wasn't dizziness but a sort of numb detachment, as though he didn't have full control of his body. Dream-movement, like some fantasy had found a way to invade the world, coating everything around him in unreality. It caused the streets and deteriorating patchwork cottages to appear far away, viewed through a pinhole. In fact, the proceeding he just witnessed had been passing strange as well. There was a sense of lost time, coupled with vertigo.

These odd concerns disappeared entirely once he spotted Marston. The older boy's dark blue watchman's jacket stood out from his pale countenance and the dark-dusty street, which extended ahead. Greydal watched as the new guard ordered a child out of his way, somehow appearing both self-pleased and unhappy at the same time.

Taking a deep breath, Greydal gritted his teeth and stepped into Marston's line of sight, waiting for the older boy to close the distance.

Almost immediately, Marston called out, "If it isn't the cold-blood's son! I thought I saw you slip in earlier. Didn't you hear no one's allowed in or out?"

Greydal waited for him to get closer before saying, "You sure I don't have sheriff's approval? I saw him yesterday. Did you?" Greydal's voice was shaky already, and he silently cursed himself.

Marston sneered and walked close enough to touch, the older boy ready to pop while a blue vein on his neck throbbed. The watchman spoke, "I want you to listen to me very carefully, *Ague*." Greydal's breath caught. Marston lowered his voice to a whisper, "Me and my friends know what you did. They don't hold Ring trials for the kids of criminals."

Greydal clenched his fist. "You don't know anything."

"You were part of it. We know, even if the old man and the others decided not to stomp you out."

Marston's proximity made him uncomfortable, but he forced himself to not back away or look down. The golden sickle icon woven into the collar of the watchman's jacket sat level with Greydal's nose as he struggled to speak, but adrenaline and anger made his body tremble.

Before he could produce a retort, Marston raised his eyebrows and added, "Oh, I found something a while ago but never had the chance to hand it to you in person since you live like an animal out in the forests." Marston reached in his pocket, but paused as if a thought had just occurred to him. "Come to think of it, maybe *you're* the one who put those kids in the trees. I'll make sure to bring it up to the sheriff."

With that remark, Marston pulled out a crumpled piece of parchment, wrinkled with age. He threw it at Greydal's feet and shouldered past before turning and adding, "Oh, I'm watchman blood now, so address me properly. *Ster* will do fine."

The watchman spun and continued towards the town square as the crowd spilled onto the street. Greydal watched the back of Marston's head for several moments as he fought the urge to attack the older boy. A dozen half-cooked responses raced through his mind, but as soon as he found his voice, a wall of villagers had already hidden his enemy. He shook as he looked down, eyeing the ball of parchment. Instantly, he knew he should leave it in the street.

A breath, and he bent to retrieve it. Greydal didn't have to unfold the thing to recognize the canticle but did so anyway. *Ague Leave Us! A hymn to the Bishop and His Envoy the Holy Red Legate* played dully across the sheet. Soot faded the rest of the text, but he knew it by heart. Tears swelled to blur his vision, and he clutched the bridge of his nose as he tried to forbid them from flowing. Then he turned and stumbled deep into the nearest alley until he was sure no one could see him. It hurt to breathe, and so he crouched for a time, ragged. Minutes passed, and then so too did the haze.

He left the hymn balled up atop a pile of clay and leaves when he finally sought the street. Though upon exiting the alley, he froze. A horrible thought had occurred to him, worse than the memories surging, seeking to overwhelm. Breaking into a sprint he hurdled towards the east end of the village. Greydal crossed two lanes, and his feet skidded on a pile of manure. A soot-shaded razorback lounged feet away, one he quickly suspected belonged to the sheriff as the beast stood larger than the ones he knew from the stables, and its tusks weren't blunted by rounded iron. He looked down and cursed at the state of his boots but gave the animal a wide berth before bending to examine the damage. The razorback huffed, and Greydal scraped his feet on the stone as he dogtrotted away. He passed a small barn, and then the tavern, which now sat almost empty. But the words on the tavern's sign mocked him, and he increased his pace.

He arrived at Jon Grime's low cottage, his heart thrashing in his chest as he closed with the door. He steeled himself before knocking. No response. Taking a deep breath, he imagined, somewhat embarrassed by his own whimsy, that he stood at the entrance of some devil's cave. But he told himself he couldn't leave until he knew.

A silvery windchime hung from the roof and swayed in the wind, tinkling. Greydal took a larger breath and knocked three times with more vigor. A moment later, the door opened. Toshi looked out from the dark hallway.

"Oh, thank the Dawn. Tosh', you idiot, I thought you died."

Toshi flashed a meek smile. "Not dead."

Greydal eyed his friend. The boy stood in the doorway to Jon's house, but didn't make any move to step onto the rough porch or to let him inside. Greydal thought he heard Jon or Toshi's mother clanking pots in the kitchen.

"What happened? Is that why you turned back yesterday? I didn't know about this animal until Creepy Crawly announced it to half of Harlow just now."

The boy looked embarrassed. "Oh, that. I learned about it from my pap last night. He's one of the men they sent out to look for the— Well, he said he's searching for the missing children, but I think they're already, you know..." He made a slicing motion across his throat.

"Ah, Tosh', I'm sorry. Your dad's one of the scariest men in the valley aside from the sheriff, no offense. I'm sure he can handle some cat or whatever it is." A pause lingered between them as Toshi waved away his apology. After a beat, Greydal said, "But you're right, I think. Crawl said the children were killed, all four of them."

Toshi nodded.

The ensuing quiet made Greydal brave. "You weren't at the crossroads yesterday."

His friend looked down and took a shallow breath. "I was gonna. Honest. But my pap..." Greydal waited. "He doesn't— He won't let me right now. See you, I mean." The words were a physical blow. "I know you had nothing to do with what your da did," Toshi hurriedly continued, "but...mine's just angry is all, and he wants me to be careful."

Greydal didn't know what to say, but shame and anger made his face hot. Seeing his expression, Toshi added, "I can't begin to think about how awful things are for you right now, Grey, I just— You're not the only one struggling, you know? An' now with these other killings, I just want to take a load off him." Greydal shook his head, and Toshi rushed to say, now close to babbling, "I'm sure stuff'll change soon, now that it's all over for you."

At that, Greydal's vision swam, and the windchime gave a tinkling laugh.

The moist wind drew dust across the doorstep, and his next words came without warning, "Fucking rodent. I would have—" I would have stood up to my father for *you*, he didn't finish. His throat had closed. "I can't believe how much of a coward you are," he managed to grind out through the emerging lump behind his tonsils.

Toshi looked taken aback. The boy began, "C'mon, you know—"

But Greydal interrupted him, "You and your pa think I'm dangerous? Again?" He knew he burned from his spat with Marston. It was why his voice sounded like a growl.

"What?! No, I'm just trying to look out for my family..."

Greydal knew he had already crossed a line but couldn't stop himself. "You weren't there. That's all that matters. I was so scared, Tosh'." Greydal pointed a finger in the boy's face as he glimpsed Toshi's mother in the hall. "I hope you kept our writings because that's the only proof you'll ever have," he snarled.

After a beat, there was another tinkle from the windchime, and Toshi replied, "...Of what?"

Greydal blinked and realized he hadn't said. "Of our friend-ship!" he yelled, even in the moment knowing how drastically silly he sounded. A hush swam between the three: Greydal, Toshi, and the boy's ever-silent mother.

Before he could succumb to embarrassment from his outburst, he turned and left them standing in the tumbledown doorway. Not looking behind him, he retraced his path and stalked the roads on his way to the western wall.

He thought for a moment about how the Ring trial was sup-posed to have made him an adult, while all it seemed to have done was reinforce his own childishness. He cursed himself as he passed the tavern for the second time that morning. The sign advertising *The Last Goodbye* above the door seemed ironic now. Though, in future memory, the joke would be a grim one.

EVIDENCE

He was more comfortable knocking on Alom's silver door than on Jon's wooden one.

"Greydal Alone. Come in, please."

Greydal stepped across the threshold into Alom's floral-scented abode, a home tunneled into a pink strip of the western wall that remained constantly cool, despite the many candles standing on every free surface. He didn't know how Alom maintained them all. He hadn't called on Alom at his home for several months, but the only noticeable change was the position of several stacks of ink-stained papers.

"I'm glad to know you made it inside the village walls. I was concerned for you and the others outside the gates."

Greydal smiled. "That's almost a quarter of the valley, I think."

"Thirty-eight percent, if the census is accurate," Alom said, pleased with himself.

Greydal rolled his eyes and ambled through the man's recessed living room, gliding his fingers over the marble statue of a dog as he passed it.

"Calahurst missed you," Alom told him.

Greydal shook his head and asked, "What are you going to do if the sheriff ever hears you call him that?" The man shrugged and smiled. Looking around, Greydal added, "Where is Cal, anyway?"

Alom whistled, summoning a clacking of claws on the stone floor. The long canine loped around a corner and jumped at Greydal, who laughed. The dog dropped to a squat after a stern look from Alom.

"It's okay, I don't mind," Greydal said.

Alom wasn't placated. "The young man is to learn not to jump on guests, whether they mind or not," he replied and scratched Calahurst under the chin.

Alom then gestured to the seats arranged near an artificial hearth. Greydal picked one and waited as Alom retreated to make coffee. Calahurst plodded dutifully behind the man. Greydal sunk into the soft chair and eyed the great painting, which overlooked the room. It was the most complicated piece of art he had ever seen. Although, he allowed he only could compare it with the paintings hung in The Last Goodbye and to travesties like the statue of the First Maer. Nevertheless, he could tell it was of quality.

The piece was almost abstract, full of indistinct blues and golds, except for a handful of identifiable structures mingled across the work like half-forgotten mistakes. Somewhere, the outline of a man stood behind a red figure, but Greydal always had trouble spotting the two. The longer he gazed, the more he noticed, and each time he visited Alom's home, he felt sure he saw a different painting, but he knew that was absurd.

"What do you spy this time?" Alom's voice shocked Greydal. He turned to see the man bending over the back of his chair. Self-conscious and smiling, Greydal accepted the icy coffee and took an immediate sip. It was delicious.

He swallowed and replied, "I hadn't noticed those statues before." He pointed at the tiny, humanoid shapes standing erect within one of the vague, lavish rooms. "I always saw them as columns."

Alom smiled and seated himself. "Maybe they were. The Mansions are supposed to be a curious place."

Greydal rolled his eyes. "Sure, but that's just a painting, not the thing itself."

Alom didn't look convinced and replied, "You know, the man I purchased this from hinted he'd been all the way west. Maybe a little of that realm rubbed off on his stock?"

Greydal thought about that and said, "But he couldn't have actually visited the Mansions, if they exist. You're supposed to have to die to do that."

Alom smiled. "Maybe he did?" Seeing Greydal's expression, he laughed, "No, you're quite right. I'm not sure why the painting has the effect it does. My *belief* is that it is so cunningly wrought, it tricks the minds of those who spy it. The statues you see now were always there."

"That's maybe more impressive than magick."

"Well...creation holds much that is fantastic without being sorcerous."

"Like the horn the Maer uses, right? Heard he got it from—"

"Like the horns, as there are two of them in the village, but yes."

Greydal smiled at the man as a comfortable silence descended while they drank their coffee. Calahurst weaved from behind Greydal's chair and laid his large head on his lap. Greydal absently scratched the long-haired mutt. "Did you see the commotion this morning?"

"Hm," Alom frowned. "I've been awake since just after midnight working with Crawl and the others."

"What happened?" Greydal asked. "I heard the speech but...an animal?"

Alom grimaced and replied, "It appears that way. We've done an exceptional job of keeping the valley clear of some of the more horrendous lifeforms I'm sure populate the four corners of the world, speaking of the wide breadth of creation, but this time, something slipped through."

"I've never heard of that happening before."

"You haven't." Alom eyed him. His words were phrased as a statement, but Greydal could have almost mistaken them for a question. When he didn't reply, the man sighed and said, "Well, we aren't often in danger because we don't present much of a target. We're armed to the teeth and—"

"I'm just surprised is all," Greydal interjected. "I've never heard Creepy Craw— The Maer, talk like he did today. I know there were times when a forest cat grabbed a kid or a razorback trampled one...but that's different." Greydal sipped more coffee.

Alom held his gaze. He asked, "How many people do you think live in the valley?"

Greydal calculated for a moment and replied, "Several hundred?" Alom answered with an expectant look, and he corrected, "Five hundred?"

"It is nearly one thousand. As I said, just about forty percent of those do not reside within the safety of our walls. These are the less well-to-do farmers, loners, hunters, and young men like yourself who make their living out there," he pointed at the northern wall of his home, "or up in the hills," then pointed behind him. "Much of our wealth and protection is because of those who reside outside the gates, even if some won't admit it."

Greydal understood and completed Alom's thought, "It began with kids near the village, but what if it gets spooked and decides to terrorize the rest of us out in the valley?"

Alom inclined his head and set his coffee aside. "I'll be frank with you," he said, "I am no hunter nor expert in animals, Calahurst excluded." The dog wagged his tail. He continued, "I've been told they found tracks near the two children's partial remains. The tracks do not look like a cat's, nor a dog or wolf's, or any other animal with which our best hunter was familiar. It can climb trees, but we don't know how long it lives, whether it migrates, whether it gets full, nothing."

"Everything gets full."

Alom tilted his head.

Greydal rubbed his neck and said, "I need to find somewhere to stay then, since I can't leave the village. The sheriff locked everyone in."

The man waved his hand and said, "Oh, please, sleep here. Crawl's probably going to keep me up until this is over, and Dawn knows Calahurst needs the company. He thinks I'm too strict." Calahurst wagged his tail again.

"That means a lot." Greydal wasn't lying.

"Was that the only reason you looked like a moldy peach when you arrived at my doorstep?"

"No." Greydal contemplated telling him about his fight with Toshi but recalled the man's admonition against seeking out Jon.

"There's a boy, Marston. Do you know him?" Alom said he didn't, and Greydal continued, "Well, he's a watchman now. He vandalized the barracks, *my* barracks. Last night."

Alom frowned. "That's...May I ask how?"

"I woke up and found 'Ague Leave Us' painted on the outside. He must have done it in the night." More softly, he added, "Assuming he could have left the village."

Alom's face froze for a beat before resuming its natural gentleness. "I'm sorry, truly," he said after a moment. "For them to bully you about—well, you had no control over it. It's unseemly. I'll speak with the sheriff. This boy needs a sit-down at the least."

Greydal's pulse spiked and he frowned. "I appreciate it," he began, "But you don't— I didn't tell you to squeal." Plus, it would likely only serve to rile the watchman.

"Nonsense. I'll speak with the sheriff," Alom repeated.

"But—"

He could tell the man had already decided. A newt materialized in his throat. Alom hadn't even asked him how he knew it had been Marston.

"Are you hungry? I have leftover fowl. It's been hard to eat since..." The man paused.

"I'm starving," Greydal offered.

"Good," Alom replied, relieved. "It's in the kitchen, help yourself. I have to go see Maizy, pardon me, Dame Hawker. One of the victims was her niece."

Greydal's eyes widened. "Ah, why did you let me keep you?"

"I let you keep me because I enjoy your company."

Alom gestured for him to follow to the kitchen. They exited the living room and entered the room serving as the cooking space and connected larder. It sported a makeshift island of imported granite and a cornucopia of culinary knickknacks. Greydal watched Alom prepare a basket of wine, sweetbread, and soap from the supply.

"Why did you call me by my new name? Alone," Greydal asked.

"Why shouldn't I?" Alom countered. Greydal began to ask for clarification when the man added, "It was for the same reason I told you to keep yourself from Jon." Greydal tilted his head. He didn't follow.

The man sighed and explained, "I expect there will be others who hold what Tier did against you, since you were his son. The same way our enlightened Ster Grime does. You won't be able to defend yourself to their satisfaction, and you shouldn't try."

Greydal recalled his outburst at Toshi and grimaced.

Alom mistook his meaning. "That's not to say you don't deserve to defend yourself," he said as he switched out the wine he had placed in the basket for a different, redder one. He continued,

"It *is* to say you will never acquit yourself more than you have already."

Greydal sighed and moved aside as Alom carried the basket out of the kitchen, then following the man as he walked towards the front door. Alom whirled on him. "You *are* Greydal Alone. Don't let Tier's decisions disrupt you more than they have already."

The man's intensity embarrassed him. Perhaps becoming self-conscious, Alom placed a hand on Greydal's shoulder. They stood at the door.

"Thanks again," he told the man.

"Please, I'm glad you're here. Anyway, if you decide to leave, please lock up beforehand. Here's an extra." Alom reached into a pocket and produced a thin, metal blade, handing it to Greydal. After a breath, he went through the doorway and let the breeze close it behind him. With that, Greydal and the dog stood alone in the man's beautiful home.

Without much consideration, he wandered to the kitchen in search of the fowl Alom had mentioned, Calahurst trotting happily behind. There it was, a plucked and roasted jungle pheasant sitting under a glass case. Greydal's mouth watered as he retrieved it. He found it still warm. Greydal fought the urge to dig in at once. He needed to find a fork or some sort of utensil (just because his father was absent didn't mean he would feel good acting like an animal). Besides, the bird looked greasy with some sort of glaze. He rummaged around Alom's kitchen for several minutes, discovering the man kept all his ironware within an old, wooden box, stored inside a chest-height cabinet. Greydal tossed aside two long, wooden sticks, which were the first items retrieved. He couldn't imagine why they were in a utensils box.

There, a fork.

He hurried to the table and retrieved a flat blade, which dangled from a magnetized strip on the wall. "Don't look at me like that.

It's been a while since I've had pheasant, that's all." Calahurst's fuzzy face exuded condemnation as Greydal tore into the bird.

His father called these animals jungle pheasants, but he was positive they had a different name. Tier called lots of things by strange names, come to think of it, though he was unsure where his father obtained half his knowledge. Yet, it was true his father knew a great deal, despite living his later years out of a rundown edifice hidden in the woods.

Greydal wondered if perhaps the barracks had at one time held more than dust. His father was the man who had uncovered the method for opening the sliding doors for both the north and south barracks, and was the first to set foot in those places. From what others had intimated, the village previously viewed both buildings as simple extensions of the Rings. To them, they were places an older, wiser people had built, but sites that didn't require much other than reverence. It was possible the barracks had contained pieces of history. Might his father have taken those for himself? Greydal wondered if it was possible that either the north or south buildings had been where his father obtained the items Avel James found. Something made him doubt it. The sheriff was supposedly almost as well-traveled as Tier. Yet, he had acted appalled at the things Greydal's father was supposed to have hoarded.

He wiped his hands on his pants, smiling in guilt at Calahurst, who eyed him with reproach. He reached forward and retrieved a chunk of meat before throwing it at the dog. Calahurst deftly caught it in his wide jaws. The animal bribed, Greydal stood and spent time cleaning the kitchen before he moved to the living room.

Once there, he gazed again at Alom's painting. This time, he spotted a tiny mound or island, topped with a whitish triangle. He interpreted it to be some sort of settlement or shrine. Thoughtful, he resumed his place on one of the cushioned chairs.

"Alright, Cal. Here's my dilemma. How can I find work? It seems useless now that the place is in a panic." He was silent for a moment. "Do you think Maizy would take me on as an apprentice? Leatherworking could be useful."

When he glanced at his audience, Greydal found Calahurst's body pointed like an arrow away from him.

"Are you listening?" Calahurst didn't react. The dog's snout was aimed at a darkened hallway adjacent to the room.

"What are you doing?"

The dog growled, low, almost beyond hearing.

The hair stood on Greydal's arms and the nape of his neck as he glanced at the hallway. The corridor glared, empty, but the dog backed, and then retreated to where Greydal sat. Ignoring the animal, he pulled his feet up and crouched in the chair to turn fully and peer over its back, straining his eyes towards the shadows pooling there.

He glanced to the chair's side and noted Calahurst's tail was now turned towards the floor as the dog's growls gained in volume.

"Shh it's okay...quiet," he soothed the mutt in a strained voice. For some reason, he didn't want Calahurst to make too much noise. "What's back there?" he whispered, and slowly put his feet towards the floor. The dog whined as Greydal fully dismounted the chair and stood. He petted the hound as he passed.

Despite his feigned bravery, he tried not to make any noise as he slunk forward. Then Calahurst chuffed from near the chairs, causing him to realize the dog wasn't following. Greydal forged ahead and stepped into the hallway, his first footfall causing the wooden flooring to creak. He held his breath to listen.

The only thing he could hear was the dry panting of Calahurst in the room behind him. At least, he was sure it was the dog, though he forced himself not to turn around and check. Fists now clenched, he continued along the corridor, a span with just two doors at the end. One gaped open and led to an elaborate restroom while the other, old and iron, sat shut.

He approached the first and glanced inside, but, seeing nothing unnerving, moved on to pause outside the second. Only silence filled the hall.

No! His ears caught the faint sound of footsteps coming from beyond the iron barrier. Now, shadows twisted before his feet, reaching from beneath the crack at the bottom of the door. Someone moved there in that unseen space. For a moment, he considered trying to look beneath the crack but was too afraid to place himself in a position where it would be hard to run. Instead, he approached the iron, his hand shaking as he gripped the knob. He twisted. It was unlocked, and the door swung open with more ease than he anticipated.

An empty study greeted him, the light of two red candles forcing upon the place an aspect of old comfort and mystery as sheets of old paper and older tomes hunkered in dark, wooden shelves. A well-used quill and inkwell sat in the center of a carved desk, but aside from its hulking presence, there was no one.

He checked down the hallway at the lounge and saw Calahurst looking worried, now slumped by the chair. Well, the candles accounted for the shadows he'd detected, but the footsteps he'd imagined discomforted him. Taking a deep breath, he entered the study. No specters leaped out.

Satisfied he was free of danger, he examined the shelves on the walls. Many of the volumes within were shiny and in a language that, at first, he didn't recognize. He almost gasped when he realized it was the same as the kitchen wall of his barracks. The language of the Old Folk, a thing rarely encountered outside of the Rings. He pulled a book at random and found it was slick with the substance his father called plastick. As a boy, Greydal had found the substance surrounding a piece of tan matter within a sealed container, half-buried beneath a tree. His father had said the cache was probably a type of ration, and the plastick served to keep it fresh. This seemed plausible enough.

Do books of the Old Folk need to be kept fresh, too?

He leafed through the volume and found it almost incomprehensible, the ancient tongue being notoriously hard to parse and requiring time to read correctly, even for the initiated. He looked through five more before he came across one of any interest, containing gray and white diagrams of a fold-out variety.

He spent several minutes attempting to divine their nature, but the only thing he learned was the Rings to the north were supposed to, or perhaps used to, contain what looked like plants, arranged in rows. He found a second image of a glass bubble, this one clearly a half-built Ring based on the confusing text. The image itself contained a series of structures like beds or hollowed logs set against a wall, something like a tree or bouquet of snakes reaching out to each cylinder. He wondered if these beds sat somewhere in Rings Five through Nine. The town had never explored those.

But...Alom collected the writings of the ones who built the Rings? Greydal wondered at the knowledge as he replaced the books, then realizing the diplomat had one missing. Each tome displayed digits on its side, but Number 03 was gone. Poor Alom. Greydal imagined the jump in numbers cruelly vexed the man.

Shaking his head, he turned to leave the study. Before he could exit, he glimpsed words in his own language and wandered to the desk. A blank piece of parchment half-covered the writings of an open journal, which lay on the wood. No, the thing wasn't a journal. It was a tearaway book, meant to allow the drafting of multiple, identical letters. He lifted the parchment, and a pregnant silence descended on the room as he read the message. When he finished, he took a moment to ensure the study looked as it had when he found it, setting the blank sheet of parchment down in its previous, haphazard position. Then he backed, giving the space one more glance before leaving.

Study exited, he gently closed the door and walked to the living room as his jaw unclenched. Searching, he noted the dog had vacated his spot near the chairs. As Greydal peered around for the animal, he heard a sound he knew was impossible: footsteps *running* from the study he had just left, towards the living room.

Greydal yelled and whirled. But there was nothing racing to greet him, just the darkened hallway sitting empty. Panting, he put his hand on his chest as Calahurst bounded from the kitchen to investigate the shout.

INCIDENT

Early evening crept like a thief through the home's sole window as Alom returned. "Ah, Greydal," the man huffed as he carried in a large chest. "Why in the world is the chair turned backwards?"

Greydal stood to help Alom get the chest inside. "I was playing with Calahurst. Throwing him pheasant bones," he lied.

"The young man doesn't need any more encouragement to come after my dinner."

"Sorry."

Alom waved off his apology and said, "I have your effects. It turns out they failed to deliver it to your home with everything going on. That suits you just as well, since you can't leave the village."

"They still haven't killed the animal, then?"

Alom shook his head. "After Hawker, I went to see the sheriff to inquire about that very thing."

"Oh, um, how is Maizy, by the way? I feel sick thinking about her daughter. I've known her since she was a baby. The daughter, of course, not Maizy."

Alom stared with a bemused expression. "Dame Hawker is about as miserable as you probably suspect. Looking back, I shouldn't have brought her red wine. Also, I would choose your words with more care, at least around less enlightened company."

Greydal's eyes widened when he realized what he had exposed. He hurried to say, "I'm sorry. I meant to say niece."

Alom nodded and replied, "It's okay, but if you feel as terrible as you say, then you should make sure you maintain her privacy as she grieves."

Greydal nodded. He felt stupid. "What's in this thing? It's heavy as the Dawn."

Alom barked a laugh and said, "I saw an axe in there, and some other items. There's also a bag of fruit and some pig jerky courtesy of Dame Hawker." The man smiled and added with barely suppressed mirth, "She wouldn't let me leave without some food for you."

Greydal stared for a moment at the metal chest before unlatching and opening it. Lifting the huge jerky bag inside, he asked in surprise, "Is this razorback?"

"I believe so," Alom said. "Maizy's stables have too many of those monsters as is. I'm glad she's finding other uses for them."

Greydal chuckled, and then registered the man had used the woman's first name. "They're pretty scary," he agreed.

Greydal set the jerky down and continued to dig through the chest. There was his father's axe, which he had never witnessed being used—Tier had kept it stuffed away. He lifted the implement, and its heft surprised him. "This weighs more than the bag!" he exclaimed.

Alom raised his eyebrows but didn't comment. Greydal then peered into the chest and recognized his father's books. Most, he knew, were treatise on other lands, their flora and fauna particularly. He'd skimmed through them as a boy and sometimes when he was older and bored, now noticing that amongst the collection one was missing: his father's journal. He turned to ask Alom about it but quickly thought better, assuming the journal must be evidence of some sort.

"Where did you find my chest, by the way?" Greydal asked.

Alom paced across the living room and replied, "I'll tell you in a moment. Let me get you some blankets."

Alom went into the kitchen and opened the door to another room before returning with silken sheets, laying them on the turned chair and clearing his throat. Greydal watched the man absently tap fingers against his leg.

"After I left Maizy's, I went to see the sheriff, as I said. I wanted to find out if there was news about the children." Alom paused and looked down. "He had a visitor when I arrived, and I wasn't able to speak long with him." Alom didn't so much seat himself as collapse into the opposing chair. Greydal raised an eyebrow before the man added, "He gave me your chest when he found you were staying here tonight."

"Wait," Greydal said, "so have they found the other children?"

Alom's face grew grave. "They were very high up, which is why no one spotted them sooner."

Greydal remained quiet for several heartbeats. Marston had intimated something similar. He asked, "What do you think it is? I've never heard of something dragging kids into the canopies before. The cats just took people into the bushes or the easy-to-reach branches, the few times they attacked people."

Alom sighed, "I don't know. I haven't heard anything of its like either, although it has a name already. I overheard some calling it the *Calf-Ripper*, like for a baby cow or razorback. I suppose the Child-Ripper was too obscene. As for what the thing is, I'm sure it's some animal from the lands above the valley."

Greydal nodded and asked, "What does the sheriff think?"

"One can only guess." Seeing his expression, the man added, "Oh, he *says* he believes it's possible some other town ran the beast out of its habitat, which could be why it came here."

"You don't sound like you believe him. Actually, wait...how do you know?"

"Pardon?"

"I just meant you seemed to have learned a lot from being turned away because of a visitor."

Alom's expression became crafty. "I did at that. I'm good at acting the nuisance when I need to. It's necessary if I want to be effective," he explained.

Greydal smiled. He could admire that. "Who was his visitor, anyway?"

"I'm not certain, but it was someone from beyond the valley."

Really. That was news. "How could you tell? His clothes? Old man Crom in the stone house my way looks like he belongs in a stage play."

Alom laughed and said, "Greydal, dressing with eccentricity is not a telltale sign of being foreign, in case you were confused. In that event, I'd be from beyond the valley, too."

Greydal smiled and told the man, "You don't dress that weird. You just like clean clothes."

Over the next several minutes, Alom went on to explain how he knew the sheriff's visitor was an outsider, saying the individual he had spotted at Calahurst's house was a tulka, one of that hardy, ruddy-skinned race. Greydal responded by pointing out that many of the tulka from the village were initially outsiders. "Like me," he added.

Alom replied, "You're right. Most aren't from here. But I know them all, native or not. Though none as well as you, I'll admit." Then he added, "But you see, my logic is sound. The visitor must be new."

"I always wondered if the Kluddes left one or two behind. My father thought so and said they were part of a larger force," Greydal mused aloud.

Alom gave him an odd look, possibly considering his words. Then, after a beat, he said, "Well, the town did a fine job of hunting down the ones who fled after the attack, but I suppose one or two could have escaped. Although, I doubt our sheriff would be seen conversing in the open with an ex-Kludde. He's much too smart for that." Alom leaned back. "That theory about the renegade Kluddes, though...It's possible the ones we dealt with were some sort of rogue faction of another land or a nation's fighting force. Each of theirs fought like three of ours, unequivocally. They were trained." Alom's voice was breathy.

Something about the words made Greydal pause until, at once and quite out of nowhere, he discerned what was off. Alom was drunk. In fact, he had been for a while, perhaps before Greydal arrived at the man's front door earlier that day. His eyes widened at the revelation, unsure what had clued him. The change was hard to spot, and he didn't think someone who wasn't familiar with the man would have noticed. Or perhaps it wasn't drink. Something else? Greydal had heard of herbs and fungi that made people feel drunk. He was curiously certain that was it, almost laughing at the revelation.

Of course, he wasn't a complete stranger to substances. His father had given him beer on several occasions, and Greydal had stolen from the back of the tavern with Ida when they were both younger (Toshi had sat that particular excursion out). But to stay drunk or on some herb for the better half of a day was a feat. Alom must be exhausted.

Greydal eyed the man slumped in the chair across from him. *Alom, why did you say the sheriff was too smart to be seen talking to a Kludde?* That's what he wanted to say. Instead, he asked, "Is your home haunted?"

The man raised an eyebrow. "Is it—"

"Haunted," Greydal finished.

"Why would you ever ask such a thing?"

Silence.

"Greydal?" Alom asked softly.

*** *** ***

It was two days before Crawl and the sheriff allowed the people of the village to come and go as they pleased. Despite some odd reports about strangers in the hills, there had been no further killings as far as anyone could tell, and the farmers had become restless, feeling that the sheriff had given those who lived outside the walls an unfair advantage.

Fortunately, Greydal had been able to stay at Alom's both nights, but he had not remained a freeloader or tried not to be one. He helped Alom where he could, including carrying parchment bundles to and from the man's various meetings. Greydal had been surprised at how busy the life of the town's sole and self-appointed diplomat could become in the midst of a crisis. Although, he suspected Alom took on several responsibilities that probably used to belong to Crawl Quymora.

During this time, Greydal resolved to charge his fear head-on and go straight to Marro. The morning after his first night at Alom's, he tramped to the south end of the western wall and knocked on the giant man's door. The brass knocker stared at him with one eye and the other looked as though it searched for something just off his right shoulder, giving it more than a passing resemblance to its owner.

Upon answering the door, Marro surprised Greydal and told him a full week of work wasn't required, only help lugging some old furniture stored in a nearby barn. Of course, once Greydal had moved all the dense chairs up the steps to Marro's home, the man changed his mind.

"Oh, would you believe it, boy? They don't match the rug. Return them, would you? I'll have another task when you get back. Wouldn't want Old Crawl thinking I went against his word too much." The man winked.

A series of meaningless and complicated tasks followed, which Greydal knew were Marro's way of avenging himself. Finch was a wretch, and the jobs grated Greydal's nerves, but at least he was confident the man had learned his lesson about trying anything strange. Greydal considered telling someone (namely Alom) about his suspicions. After all, the secretary had believed him right away about Marston. But he dropped the idea. He had just that, suspicions. Even if Alom believed him, what could he do? Marro was as influential as anyone in the valley. Greydal decided he would simply keep an eye out for something that could be wielded in the light of day against the corpulent man and leave it at that.

It was after midday when he finished. Passing under the doorway, Greydal was exhausted but free, now having no reason to force himself into further interactions with the man. As he took a breath upon exiting the domicile, Greydal found that the air outside was foul. Though, he thought, perhaps that was just the result of opening the door to Marro's so frequently that day.

Greydal smiled to himself before taking another, deeper breath. He looked at the sky to find the clouds were low and freighted. Fast, too. It seemed the heat had returned, lending the heavens the illusion they were the rippling underside of some swelling beast. He peered from horizon to horizon, but no part of the sun's wide face was visible. The village now mirrored the vagueness of the sky, and he descended the steps to continue onwards, inheriting the overcast.

As he walked through town, Greydal watched several flocks of birds overhead, fleeing the hills. As with some others he had seen, these flew in large quantities to the east. What could it be that they sought out there in the wastes?

The people of the valley had long since discovered there was quite literally nothing in that direction for leagues and leagues. After exiting the valley and following an overgrown stream, a traveler would find that the water trickled thinner and thinner until it dried. Farther on, the ground was desiccated and acidic, worse than the gray space surrounding the Rings. His father had once told Greydal that if one were to travel east by razorback or cow for five days, the ground would turn black, like tar. He asked his father if one's feet would stick out there. His father had never answered, and as Greydal watched the flocks swarm east, he decided they probably went out there to die. Maybe they dove off the Edge, plummeting from the end of the world.

Putting the doomed things out of mind, Greydal spent the rest of that day looking for gainful labor and successfully returned to Alom's that night as an unofficial employee of the tavern, which Greydal thought must be an irony, him having stolen from the place, on occasion. Before he swore off alcohol, before his father berated him into a state close to weeping one day. Tier had found him passed out in the woods.

Yes, gainfully employed. It was thanks to Ida that he got his foot in the door. When he had arrived at The Last Goodbye, the older girl popped from behind the counter. "Greydal! Out of the cradle and into the tavern!" She smirked at her rhyme.

"Do you just do every job in the valley?"

Ida stopped wiping the rough counter. "Only the two. I pick up some work here now and again. That's when I'm not staring blindly north or south atop a gate, I mean."

"The village has never been safer."

"Oh, hush your snout. You try sitting for eight hours at a time with no company but Rulf or Marston. This is practically a luxury." As if to prove it, she pulled a swig from a small metal flask hidden under the bar.

"Oh, no thanks. I'd rather jump off the west wall."

"You and me both."

"How did your date go? Did she vomit when you tried to kiss her?"

Ida huffed and turned up her nose. "Do you think any lady wouldn't jump at the chance to kiss this mug? She and I enjoyed a nice, romantic stroll, and she kissed me first, I'll have you know. We did more than that, too, but a lady doesn't smooch and tell."

Greydal raised his eyebrows in mock surprise. "I think you just did. Either way, if you ever need someone to lie about your merits, I'm happy to."

Ida threw a rag at him, and he caught it before tossing it on the bar. "So?" She gave him an expectant look.

Greydal shook his head. "I need work. I've got some of my father's— *Tier's* money, but it's barely enough to keep me fed." He didn't add he had received a chest full of food. Better to not press his luck.

"So, you want to work at this fine establishment? Well, it's not up to me, but I'll talk to Dame Sofya and ask if she'll look you over. Handle the bar for me will ya?" Ida scooted out of sight. The wooden door to the rear swung at her passing as Greydal stayed where he was. He shrugged at an old soak who soon wandered up looking for nourishment.

The following interview, if he could call it that, didn't take long. Ida ushered Greydal into a back room where Sara Sofya dealt cards to three others. The heady aroma from her pipe hurt Greydal's head as she looked him over.

"You a Kludde?"

"I'm sixteen."

She looked at the exposed skin of his lower neck, near his collarbone. "You sick?"

Greydal shook his head.

"Alright, come around here in the evenings, and I'll put you to work. Mostly chopping dried wood, cleaning, that sort of thing. Can you handle that?" Greydal said he could. "Bring a hatchet. If you don't have one, ask Ida to lend you hers."

With that, Greydal found he was dismissed.

"She's a hoot, isn't she?" Ida asked when he returned to the front. "I've always been curious if she's like that to everyone." He laughed with her but wondered.

*** *** ***

Greydal worked almost every night at The Last Goodbye until the day of the new moon and his father's execution. The lack of further killings didn't soothe the populace as he had anticipated. Instead, the fear of the village shifted from a targeted agitation to a generalized suspicion. He guessed it was difficult for people of action like the sheriff—the man had looked tired and harried the few times Greydal came across him. It must have frustrated Calahurst he couldn't just drag the Calf-Ripper to the Rings for a judgment.

The rest of the valley wasn't any better. Villagers saw Kluddes in the trees and omens in their morning food. One man even claimed his dog had flown up into the sky when he took it to urinate, though he had been drinking and no one could remember whether or not he even had a dog.

Greydal worried that their overactive imaginations would cause them to turn on him, a perfect effigy of their woes, real or imagined. But perhaps cooler heads would prevail. Upon thinking this, Greydal acknowledged that should include himself. He owed his friend an apology, yet he hadn't run into Toshi inside the town or beyond its walls since their argument and couldn't bring himself to return to Jon's house.

He thought about what to do as he swung his father's axe. Sofya wasn't lying when she told him that she would have him chop wood for the tavern. It was almost all he had done for her over the previous week and a half. When he asked after its purpose, she had stated rather plainly that the wood went to replacing barrels in the basement, yet the thin planks didn't look like they were suitable for barrels. Ah, well.

The axe made a humming sound as it cut the humid air. The tool itself...

It was unusual. When Greydal first fingered the edge, it was dull. Yet it proved capable of slicing through the wooden blocks like it would air, but only when he put his full might behind the swing. Not for the first time, he stopped to examine it. The axe didn't appear different from any other elongated hatchets he had seen, and the only peculiar aspect of its design was that it was all metal, aside from a wooden inset in the handle. He shrugged. Another of his father's mysteries.

He continued chopping. If nothing else, the work gave him some needed exercise where he could vent his frustrations. These had built without end since—

The murder.

Constantly, Greydal's mind was drawn to it. Even the axe in his hand was a tie to his father, and therefore, that day, that moment. It was inescapable. His father had killed a man, and he had watched.

There was a *thwunk!* sound, and Greydal looked down. He had split the stump upon which the blocks were meant to be chopped, and he paused to take a breath. The axe was his now. He needed to stop thinking of it otherwise. As soon as this idea drifted through his mind, a second followed, and he went inside the tavern for a moment. He returned with a short knife from the kitchen. Eyeing the axe's handle, he decided on the upper part of the wooden inset and carved, lightly at first, and then with vigor when he discovered it had less give than he expected.

It took several minutes, but he finished, admiring his handiwork under the filthy light of the waning moon. The tool now sported Greydal's sign, the arrow with horns. That was better.

He went back to his axe work and thought about the tavern as he swung (more carefully now). It wasn't a bad place as far as he had seen, despite its reputation. If nothing else, Greydal found he enjoyed the brief moments of company with Dame Sara Sofya, a woman whom he had met several times as a child, though she hadn't remembered. There was a refreshing honesty to the proprietress.

So many people in Greydal's life presented only abstractions to the world, himself included. They were like the gold mechanisms on the north and south gates of the village. Inside those mechanisms, small gears and tumblers fit together and turned to allow the removal of a solid alloy bar. But the gate guard operating one of those golden locks didn't necessarily know about these things. Just move the lever and watch the bar slide. So, it was with most people, gold casings hiding the inner workings. But not Sofya, Greydal thought. She was all gears and tumblers, displayed in the open.

He hoped to be more like her one day. Though, he worried he might be too inherently private. In his mind, that quality was his most developed trait.

*** *** ***

He spent his free time alongside Ida when the girl was not atop the gates. They threw darts and played cards inside The Last Goodbye before most patrons arrived. When the evening crowd showed, Ida hopped behind the bar, and Greydal went to work cleaning or cutting wood. He never got the chance to check the basement—though he had been curious what all his labor was for—and nothing else notable occurred at the tavern...with one exception.

It was a slow night, and Greydal had completed his work, so he re-entered the establishment to badger Ida before heading to the barracks. A drunk farmer leaned over the bar and was in the midst of telling what sounded like a ghost story. Approaching, Greydal noted Ida gazed at the old man with concern.

"Paule, what do you mean a face?" she asked.

"I knows it sounds madder than a hare, but I's seen it!" The man leaned over the counter to wave his hand at her. Greydal cleared his throat, and the man turned. The sight of Greydal seemed to reinvigorate him. "You there, young-un! You'll believe me when's I says that it leaned down from the sky! Like a cloud! But it weren't no cloud! It was real, killed a bunch o' birds!"

Ida gave Greydal a sympathetic look before replying to the man. "Paule, just take a breath, my son. So, you saw some spooky lookin' clouds. That's nothing to yell about."

"You'd be hollerin' if you's seen it! A cloud, *but it opened its eyes!*"

Greydal stepped nearer and made to put a hand on the old man's back. When he got close, the man screamed and fell over. "That's it! That was the damn face! Yours!" He howled like a cat in heat and scrambled away before fleeing through the open door.

Greydal dropped his hand and looked at Ida, who shrugged.

*** *** ***

An altogether different sort of disturbance occurred the next night on his way to the barracks. He would later imagine he might have stood a chance against the three if he hadn't gotten surprised.

As it was, his head hit the stone of the road before he knew what collided with him. For a horrific moment, he thought it was the Calf-Ripper. Then someone kicked or punched him in the face, and his head bounced off the stone a second time, sending stars across his vision. His fingers went limp and his axe rolled from his grip. They dragged him from the road. As they did, Greydal's eyes glanced across one of the guardian faces hewn into a nearby stump. It looked afraid.

The assailants threw him against a tree. Then someone punched him in the stomach. That had been Marston, he was certain. "You fucking rodent," the older boy inadvertently quoted. "Where's the fight, Ague? Pink-skinned *cunt*." Another punch, and Greydal slumped.

Someone pulled him off the bark and grabbed at him to hold him straight. Greydal saw his chance. He stomped on the assailant's foot and bit the fingers prying at his face. He knew the boy's voice through the ensuing howl. It was Rulf, one of the other gate guards.

Then Marston punched Greydal in the nose, causing him to release the other boy's hand from his mouth. He recognized that response as a mistake when they threw him to the dirt and three separate kicks connected with his side, almost cracking his ribs.

Greydal's thoughts were fuzzy as someone crouched next to him. It was Marston again. The boy whispered, "I know it was you. You should have taken your lumps and moved on. I'm not a watchman anymore, but my boy Rulf here..." He spit. "We'll tell everyone you jumped me. Luckily, my friends were here."

"I'll kill you." Greydal's voice sounded wet, and he tasted blood.

Marston, pale face reflecting the feeble moon, stood and kicked him again. "What's that, whelp?"

Greydal coughed. "I'll kill..." he took a breath, "all three of you."

Marston laughed. His voice was greasy as he said, "Not if we get you first."

There was a silence, and then Greydal heard Rulf whisper, "No. This is just to teach him a lesson."

"Who would know? We could say the Ripper got him."

Another voice Greydal didn't recognize chimed in and said, "Look at him. He's barely with it."

As they bickered, Greydal's hand found a stick in the dark. He didn't know if it was strong or sharp, but he clutched at it with his life.

Time drifted uncertain (minutes? hours?) before he registered they didn't plan to attack him. He sat up with difficulty and peered around, head swimming. There was no one. Had he passed out? A glance at the stick in his hand told of its sharpness, its outline stark in the thin moonlight. Greydal let it fall to the dirt and tried to stand so he could go home.

*** *** ***

He woke after midday in the hallway of the barracks, covered in his own vomit. Dried blood caked his face. When he stood, the world churned, and dizziness almost drove him to the floor. Mastering himself, he successfully stumbled from the building, but had to crouch near the path when the pain in his skull became too much.

After a time, he stood again and headed towards the trees to spend an hour in the stream to the west cleaning himself. A naked trudge to the barracks followed, him having left his torn clothes in the water. He kept his boots, though.

Later, he discovered they had taken the money he held on his person, only twenty-five or so shavings, which had sat in a small satchel carried to and from the tavern. One of the assailants had apparently embedded his axe in a tree, next to the dirt track. He wondered idly if they had considered using it on him as he had lain unconscious.

After returning to the barracks, Greydal got dressed in his father's clothes, all too large. Then he sat in the sunlight and brooded, his nausea rearing its disfigured head to torment him as his vision swam in concert.

Legate! His head ached! He tried to breathe and spent some time clearing his nose, the pressure in his skull lessening with the removal of a cork of bloody phlegm. He inhaled and frowned, catching the scent of early decay. Greydal looked for its source and soon found it, a lump of aqua sprawled in the grass.

The dead thing sported small flies like a necklace of jewels, crawling it with an ancient intent. It was a tenderbird. He couldn't tell if it was the same one he had encountered the day after the Ring trial because he couldn't locate its face. No, its head was missing altogether. That was it.

He inhaled. Then, slowly as he dared, he looked to the green above, but there were only the undersides of towering trees. They moved gently.

It was the wind.

The other trees weren't moving as much, but that was just because his were taller.

Had to be the wind.

Greydal abruptly stood and limped away, to the lesser tree which held his axe between its bark, retrieving the weapon with little difficulty. He did not look back as he trudged the path to the road.

CHAPTER

6

HAVOC

On the day of the new moon and his father's execution, the hamlet erupted. The news: Jon Grime and his family were missing. Not just that, hunters had found an older boy in the trees to the southwest. From what Greydal could gather, the Calf-Ripper had killed Erl Wardosh, a seventeen-year-old. Now, fear made the air heavy, so much so that it was almost a solid substance, covering the village's alleys and thoroughfares in a sludge of suppressed panic.

For Greydal, between the murder of Avel James, the Calf-Ripper killings, and Marston attacking him, the chaos was wearing thin. But the news about Toshi's family troubled him in a different manner. He felt responsible in a way he couldn't articulate.

As he pondered these recent troubles, he fingered the axe sling. Maizy had made it just like he asked. While his busted lip and nose had shocked her, he was able to lie about the previous night's attack since the old woman couldn't see the dark bruising on his spine and ribs. After she clucked over him, Greydal described to her what he needed and gave her the required shavings.

When he left the stables two hours later, he had stopped at the exit and looked over his shoulder, Maizy waiting behind him. The orange lamplight spilling from the opening lit her. A breath taken, and he gave his condolences about her daughter before thanking her for the food she had given him. She produced a sad smile and small wave as he left her standing amongst the low snorts of the corralled beasts she tended.

Now, the axe hung low behind his back and could be quickly retrieved by unlatching the leather tie. He didn't know if its purpose was to ready himself for another assault of Marston's, or prepare for whatever killed the tenderbird. No, not *whatever*. It was the Calf-Ripper. He knew it in his bones. Greydal suspected the beast nested somewhere near his barracks, or at least frequented the location. But what had become of Toshi and his family? That hadn't sounded like the work of an animal. Resolving to go by their home and see what he could find, he crossed the village and neared the east wall.

Soon, Jon's cottage lurched into view. It looked dead, an empty husk. Though, perhaps that was just because Greydal knew no one currently dwelt there. He approached, and then rounded the cottage. The rear window was broken, the one that faced the east wall. He recalled Ida had mentioned something along those lines when she first told him the news.

"Burglar, I hear. Guess he burgled the whole family?" she had said.

This in and of itself was strange, because Greydal heard from a different neighbor that the front door was discovered unlocked when the sheriff and several watchmen arrived to investigate. Apparently, the neighbor saw them walk in without any to-do and nail it shut on their exit.

Deciding there was no point in waiting outside, Greydal approached the window. Then his foot crunched something in the trampled hay and dirt. He looked down to find a piece of glass. He pursed his lips as he searched for others, finding none.

Reaching towards the sternum-high window, he pulled himself up to sneak within. He made short work of the activity, but came close to cutting himself on an opaque shard that caught at his sleeve. He released his shirt, and as he lowered himself to the hallway floor, held his breath to listen. Silence. Greydal smiled to himself before straightening, taking a deep breath as dizziness swelled.

He felt like a thief. The house was warm and dark, but sunlight streaming through the windows left islands of illumination by which he could navigate. He searched for any broken shards on the ground. There were none. Did that mean they were wrong about the break-in then? He briefly imagined Toshi smashing the window to escape some unknown pursuer before being dragged into darkness. But then, who collected the rest of the glass outside?

He entered the main area of the dwelling. There was nothing immediately significant to see, aside from a turned over chair. Passing it, he went into the dusty bedroom where Toshi and his parents slept.

An amalgam of familiar scents coated the place. It was surreal to note things he associated with his friend and the boy's parents: ink, fruit, and wood. A combined musk specific to the family. He inhaled, his eyes scanning the room. Curious, there was a stack of papers stuffed under the dresser. They peeked out like an unkept secret. Greydal bent and picked up a sheet, only to see his own handwriting. This was one of his, a message sent to Toshi at one time or another—it even had his mark.

Upon reading, he discovered that the correspondence was three or four years old. In it, he pretended to speak as a swordslinger from the Sect of the Mist (he had repeated to Toshi one of Tier's stories from far-off lands, and it took root, becoming part of their personal mythos). He continued reading. On the paper, a younger Greydal was telling Toshi that he had been forced to slay an assassin who ambushed him on the mesas. In reality, Greydal had never seen mesas, and the text seemed childish now. He crumpled the paper and let it fall to its final resting place on the wooden floor.

Greydal strode from the dingy chamber and stopped again in the main room, standing next to the fallen chair, and closing his eyes to attempt a recollection, to envision what he had seen the last time he had been inside Toshi's house. That had been at least a month before. But he knew the place almost as well as the barracks.

Yes, there was the leaden chair where Jon would recline and carve wooden figurines. The hearth was where Toshi would sit and draw or write by its glow. There were the plants, dark ones grown wild and mean within the valley's hollows and dales. Toshi's mother liked them because they looked mysterious, and she kept them housed in painted clay pots lining the rotting timber of the walls.

Running through this list, Greydal thought again of the old correspondences he had found. It gave him an idea. He opened his eyes, and sure enough, Toshi's main stack of writings and the bin that stored them were gone. They should have been next to the hearth. The boy wrote for the love of it, and Greydal doubted he would have stopped after their fight. Why would anyone take the writings, though? Parchment was valuable, but he knew Jon wasn't nearly as poor as the cottage indicated. He moved a few steps to the right and saw the man's alloy hunting spear, which Greydal had examined on numerous occasions, was still near the front door. Worth hundreds of shavings, not to mention the actual silverware in the kitchen. The forks and knives were an heirloom of the grandmother. He peered into the kitchen to confirm they were present, neatly arranged in a shallow, wooden container.

There's a sensation that may come upon a person in places wide or empty. Some children feel it when they rise to retrieve a glass of water in the middle of the night, while all others sleep, the cool and stale air an uncanny contrast to the warmth of blankets. Others recognize it when returning to sites once bustling with life, now poised and vacant. It's the quiet understanding of arriving at the cusp of a hidden peril, of stumbling into a world less forgiving of accidental trespasses. That uncomfortable awareness leaped up his spine, and he shivered, a response which might have only been his body's attempt to dislodge the feeling.

The windchime outside jingled. It sounded close through the busted window.

Out of ideas and unnerved, Greydal left the way he had come. As he approached the window, he made time to break the sharp glass off the frame. Then he tried to maneuver through. As he did, his ribs sent a jolt of pain through his body, and he yelped, tumbling from the aperture. He hit the dust harder than he anticipated and was forced to gracelessly roll to mitigate any further damage to his bruised body.

Now, fully outside, he falteringly stood, and then paused to steady himself before ambling to the front of the cottage. His ribs seemed to be intent on expelling all the air in his lungs. In response, he sat on the ground to catch his breath, ignoring the stares of two men who lounged on a porch connected to a nearby home. The heat had returned, which may have been why the two men were shirtless, their tanned torsos appearing as a kind of leather from Greydal's distance.

He quickly forgot about their vacant stares. Something about the home had bothered him, maybe the front door. Why had it been unlocked when the sheriff arrived? Come to think of it, why had Calahurst and several guards been on the scene before anyone else? By all rights, it should have been any one of Jon's multiple neighbors (who were almost *all* known busybodies). And again, who had cleaned up the glass? Was it one of the neighbors being neighborly, or someone about a nefarious erasure?

An idea bubbled up, half-formed. Greydal wanted to test it against Alom, suspecting the diplomat could tell him much if the man could be convinced. Unfortunately, any sly questioning would have to wait until after the execution that evening as the secretary would be at the Rings with Crawl until the sun gave way to the freshly dead moon.

It was odd to think about. Tonight, Greydal's father would die, and he would watch. What he knew was coming numbed him and he wondered if he was simply finished with it all, out of emotional stock. He had run the gamut since the murder. Logic said he would come to grieve his father's death, but it felt less real now than it had when he first heard the verdict of Tier's trial.

Greydal's ribs seemed to have calmed somewhat, and he was ready for a more pleasant distraction, so he stood and decided to head to The Last Goodbye. Maybe Ida could take his mind off the oncoming night.

As he strode away, he heard behind him the sound of the cottage's windchime, curiously muffled.

*** *** ***

The dense gloom of an evening without moonlight came heavy, and the air itself grew rapidly stale and thick, though no one mentioned it. In the dust of Ring Three, Greydal stood with the others. He wished Maizy was present.

When they had stopped at the woman's house, and then the stables, she had been absent, and a protracted search had revealed nothing. Marro and Alom were the only members of the Humble Array present (and Alom barely counted) as the sheriff and Crawl were apparently unavailable, likely busy with the Grime family disappearance. Greydal looked around at those assembled.

In the murk, they became ghouls, their expressions unreadable and malformed by shadows.

Maybe he was only stressed. He had never been in the Rings after twilight, nor attended an execution. Would it have been easier if he had witnessed one before? Likely not.

He watched as burly men broke the bricks housing his father. His father fell to the ground before them, but Greydal didn't recognize the man, hunger and trauma being the famous wasters that they are. Was he dead already?

His father's bare, olive skin was stretched taught over his broad frame, and he was much paler than Greydal remembered. But the red diamond tattoo on Tier's forehead stood stark against his grimy skin, now looking almost painted on. His father's breathing was ragged—Greydal's throat closed at the sight.

Like the last time he was in Ring Three, the proceeding sped by. Alom, standing in for Crawl, commended the soul of the man formerly known as Tier Duinn to the Mansions of the Dawn, should he be judged worthy by the Bishop and his holy representative, the Red Legate. Alom lowered his arm and nodded at no one in particular.

And like that...

Greydal watched the killing squad of masked men skewer his father, the spears going in like shards of moonlight and coming out, muted by a darkened slick. One spearhead had something fibrous clinging to it.

He may have blacked out then. When he returned to himself, he, Alom, and the others walked along the main road. Vague mumblings turned into speech. "—and they will stay to attend to the body. When we return, I will inform the Maer of the punishment's conclusion," Alom's voice said.

Greydal struggled for his own and couldn't find it. He was so tired.

They walked in silence for a while. Maybe it was a leftover trick the dark of the Rings had played on his mind, but Greydal soon came under a frightening illusion, one making each person beside him featureless. Or rather, they all looked the same, like cloudy water. He couldn't tell who was Alom or Jon or Marro or any of the other villagers.

He shook his head. No, Jon was missing, he remembered that.

Greydal wondered if maybe he was losing his mind when the hallucination departed. He approached the stables with seven others, who all wore the faces they were meant to. But something was wrong. It wasn't supposed to be dawn yet.

"*Fire!*"

"Oh, no..." someone gasped, covering their mouth with a hand. The southern horizon glowed.

Alom sprinted past him in the direction of the village.

Then Marro loomed to his right and turned to Greydal, saying with a seriousness he had never before exhibited, "Boy, help where you can." Then he too was off as fast as his large frame would allow, followed by three others.

Greydal stood for a moment, then ran. He caught up with the group quickly and passed them, eventually coming to the carved guardians. Their faces were moving in the waning shadows. He cut right into the trees to save time on his way to the barracks. The absence of the moon's light would have made navigating through the underbrush a terrible task, but the furious burning to the south lit his way.

Something stabbed him in the arm. A tree branch, he suspected. He kept running and soon arrived at his home, now able to smell smoke wafting from the village. He ignored it and waited for his door to squeal open. Once inside, he hurried to his room and rifled through his father's things, coming away with a torn tunic. It was the one his father had worn when he fought and killed Avel.

Tying it around his face, Greydal grabbed a half-full canteen of water from the kitchen before hurrying to the front door. As he exited the barracks, he looked south. The glow was brighter now. He ran to the road as fast as the waxing light would allow, and a thick night vine almost tripped him. No, it was a new moon. There would be no vines groping the open ground tonight. A body, then.

He nudged it with his foot in the dark and heard the jingle of metal and a faint sloshing. Greydal shuddered but didn't waste time to learn who or what it was and continued towards the road as the smell of smoke ballooned. As he arrived at the village wall, he saw the front gates were closed, but someone had opened the inset door. There were people on the other side, within the burning village. He rushed to it, and entered, coughing as the smoke stung his lungs through the makeshift mask.

The blaze wasn't half as bad as the haze and the gleam across the clouds indicated, but it was spreading. A man in a watchman's jacket and an indigo mask yelled at him and pointed at a nearby cottage. Its roof blazed, and there were two others trying to kick down the door. Greydal sprinted to them and motioned them aside before releasing the axe tied to his back from its sling.

Greydal's first strike caused the axe to go through the wood, and he almost lost it. Trying again, he turned his next swing downwards at the last second, and the door nearly split in half. Two kicks, and it was in pieces. The two to his left and right ran inside only to drag an unconscious man and child from the home.

Greydal yelled to them, "Are there any others?" He pointed inside, but they didn't hear him. Someone rang the night watch bell over and over. He ran, returning to the guard from before, finding the man pouring water on someone's eyes.

Greydal slapped him on the arm and yelled in his ear, "Is it the Kluddes?" The man said something in reply, but Greydal couldn't hear it.

"What?!" he said and coughed.

The watchman took off his mask, and Rulf replied in a weary voice, "Not Kluddes. Someone else. Go help, but watch out—" He coughed. "They're wearing gold." Greydal nodded and handed Rulf his canteen of water.

The next few minutes were hectic. He made his way towards the center of the town, helping one man break open a water barrel, and soon after, watching over a confused child until she spotted her father. Greydal handed the girl off, and then tried to determine what direction the center of town lay, where the fire was thickest.

Despite the blaze, or because of it, he quickly became lost in the dirty air and so wandered towards the nearest glow. Everywhere he looked there were bodies. Some displayed gruesome wounds across their necks or stomachs, gaping splits and tears. As Greydal paused to examine one corpse, someone yelled his name. He spun to see Alom approaching through the haze. Incredible that the man had spotted him from so far.

Greydal left the body but halted when Alom waved him back. Putting a hand over his makeshift mask, Greydal waited. As the man drew closer, he saw Alom bled a fountain from a wound in his chest.

"Alom!" Greydal put his hands on the man, who didn't quite collapse, but dragged him stumbling towards a nearby alley. Alom batted his hands away. "Let me help you!" Greydal raised his arms to remove his mask, thinking he could use it to try and stanch the bleeding, but Alom grabbed him.

"Listen to me," the man's voice was hoarse, "you *have* to leave the village. They're..." he wheezed, "they're after tulkas."

At first, Greydal didn't say anything. Then he asked, "Who are they?" Alom only heaved in reply and slid against the wall. The smoke had thinned in the alley, yet Greydal could barely see. He realized he was crying.

"Alom, what do you need me to do? Where's Calahurst?"

The man clutched at him. "Run."

Despairing, he asked, "Which way?"

Alom pointed a curled hand towards the opposite end of the alley. The man slumped, and Greydal knew he was dead. He yelled, but the collapse of a nearby roof muffled the sound as he watched the secretary's body slide down the wall, a red smear signifying his passage.

More than anyone else in the valley, Greydal trusted Alom. So, he ran.

It was the wrong direction for anyone who wished to leave the village. He jogged for nearly a minute before the western wall reared above him in the smoldering dark. He mistook it for a cloud, but he soon could spy its pinkish base beyond the last houses. Greydal cursed and turned to head the way he had come when someone collided with him. It was Rulf. Rulf brandished a long knife, and Greydal thought for a terrible moment that the older boy meant to kill him.

Then Rulf coughed and yelled, "Get back!" Greydal looked behind the watchman. Figures approached in the smoke. No, just one. It was the sheriff. Greydal started to yell for the man, but Rulf forcibly covered his mouth. They backed towards the rock wall as the figure with the broad-brimmed hat neared.

"Rulf. Move." The sheriff's voice was horrible, and the man's breathing troubled. Greydal had inhaled the smoky air for maybe less than five or six minutes, yet could barely stand it. How long had the sheriff been exposed?

Calahurst covered his mouth with an elbow and drooped like a wilted flower as he trudged towards them. Rulf pushed Greydal back and brandished the knife. "You motherfucker!" the older boy roared over the flames.

What? Greydal's mind spun.

Despite his bravado, Rulf continued to retreat towards the wall, and Greydal copied him. They were close to Marro's place, a calm thought told him. Then the sheriff replied with a wheezing command, "Move, now. Last chance." He drew a weapon that looked like a bouquet of daggers at the end of a perpendicular handle. Then there was a report like a loud whine, and something sliced Greydal's ear.

Without thought, he and Rulf charged. There was another whine, but he didn't feel anything enter him as he closed with the man. Rulf reached Calahurst first, barely. The watchman planted his long knife in the sheriff's side as Greydal arrived and pulled his axe free from its sling in a fluid motion, raising it high. Greydal brought it down. The axe head hummed as it opened most of the sheriff's head vertically.

Hot blood flecked Greydal's eyes and he blinked.

The man's hat fell in half to float towards the ash-blanketed ground.

Greydal fought a violent cough as he pulled the axe free from Calahurst's jaw. The dark-suited body crumpled, hitting the dust.

What had they just done?

Not giving him time to think, Rulf grabbed Greydal and yanked him away from the corpse.

"They're still coming!" Rulf croaked.

He stopped to wipe his eyes before he looked, seeing what the older boy meant. Other figures in the haze were visible again, their elongated shadows playing on the smoke like actors backlit on the stage. A dreamy stillness settled on him then, and Greydal replaced his axe in the leather sling before waving at Rulf, who had moved away.

Greydal gestured at the wall, and then wiped his hands in the ashy ground, telling the older boy to do the same as fast as he could. Rulf looked like he was about to argue, but then nodded and complied. Gasping, they both stumbled up the steps towards

Marro's home. Greydal's eyes burned as he stepped off the side of the stairs and mounted the crooked stone. He was lucky there weren't many flammable structures on the western edge of the village as he wouldn't have the breath to do this otherwise. Without much further deliberation, he climbed.

From the hundreds of times he had analyzed the western wall, Greydal knew he and Rulf now started at arguably the worst point possible, the stone smooth and providing little purchase. The *positive* part of this section was that, as the pair gained altitude, the wall would become easier to climb, much more than in any other spot. However, the ascent required they didn't waste their energy before the halfway point, something he didn't know if they could reliably manage.

Greydal looked down and saw Rulf successfully following him. He mimed to Rulf how to splay his foot out to the side and plant his hips into the wall to preserve friction and his center of gravity.

Then below the watchman, near the last of the houses, he caught sight of figures in gold exiting the swirling smoke. He could tell they were foreign despite what Alom had said. Though, Greydal doubted these were anything like the visitor the sheriff had earlier entertained. These beings' great, globular helmets gleamed in the firelight, and the myriad cavities dotting them did the opposite. The holes gaped, graves for light. The strangers' coats tinkled just within hearing, sounding strangely like windchimes. One of the foreigners appeared to be backwards. It traveled with its gliding fellows, but shambled in reverse, its heels facing the rock wall.

As Greydal tried to understand this, his head filled with fog and his stomach churned from an unannounced nausea, forcing him to fight for a moment to stay glued to the rock until it passed. Ignoring the encroaching figures, Greydal looked up. From his angle, the western wall appeared larger than it ever had. He motioned to Rulf, and they continued to climb.

After a minute, the pink rock transitioned to a white strip. These parts were the tricky ones. With a free hand, he waved at Rulf and pointed to the north, across the white strip. Greydal climbed horizontally along the bottom of the white rock. Once he reached a more rugged section, he made sure the older boy saw him cut across and continue to ascend by using a double-handed grip. He used it on a larger, exposed stone to allow his feet to switch positions.

Now, he could plant his right hip against the wall. He ascended and looked down to watch the other climber. Rulf was doing far better than he would have expected, but even in the low light, he could tell how the watchman's hands bled. He mimed wiping his hand on his tunic and saw Rulf copy him. They continued to ascend, and the smoke got worse, despite a growing wind swelling as they climbed. It soon became difficult to breathe.

Looking down, he found he could no longer spy the golden figures that had stepped from the haze. Perhaps that was because his vision swam from the height. In spite of the circumstances, they were nearly halfway to the top, and Rulf had managed to remain within feet of him.

Fortunately, the climb was about to become less physically demanding, yet, they were both exhausted. Surmising they wouldn't make the full climb if they kept going, Greydal searched as he climbed for a spot where the pair could rest, but didn't identify one until they were another third of the way up the wall. Here, the stone became more jagged, with pieces of it jutting out at right angles. Greydal pulled himself up onto a ledge and sat half-off to make room for Rulf, now close to passing out as his ribs screamed at him. Somewhere else, a rhythmic throbbing threatened to deafen him as time grew muddy, the beating in his skull serving as an aimless, wet metronome.

He abandoned thought until several moments or an eternity later, he watched the watchman's hand grope for the ledge, and

Greydal grabbed it to help him up. After they were both seated, he shifted his axe in its sling and took off his tunic to wipe the blood from Rulf's hands as they gulped the fresh air. He noted the wind had turned east and pushed the plume of smoke in that direction.

Thank the Legate for small miracles, he thought dreamily. His exhausted fingers let the breeze take his tattered, bloody shirt.

***　***　***

The last of the ascent was a blur, but one thing was clear: Rulf's ability was astounding, the older boy proving himself to be a born climber. When the two reached the height of the cliff, it was the watchman who gained it first and pulled Greydal over the edge onto the rough ground. Rasping breaths and sweat, they stared up at the underside of the low, leaning trees.

"Holy—" Greydal coughed, "shit." His voice sounded like someone else's. Rulf laughed like a crow. Then they crawled towards the foliage, and both sat against the nearest tree while gazing out over the twisting cloud of smoke.

The sounds of the crackling flames and isolated screams were all that filled the night for a time, aside from the two's ragged gasps. At some point, Greydal realized the bell had stopped ringing, and unrelatedly, he had lost all the hair on his arms and hands.

His hands. They ached beyond measure. In a similar fashion, his muscles were as soft as jelly, and he was sure a rib had slipped out of place. But he had done it. He had climbed the western wall. A strange giddiness overcame him, out of proportion to the accomplishment, and he started laughing as tears streamed down his face.

Rulf looked over with an unreadable expression. "I hadn't figured we got you so bad." the older boy murmured. Greydal didn't know what Rulf was talking about and continued to giggle.

"I guess you'll be glad to know Marston's dead. Just like Erl, though maybe not that bad."

Greydal stopped laughing. Rulf's breathing was burdened, sounding more like a wounded animal.

"What happened?"

"Well, Erl—" Rulf coughed, "killed by that thing, the Ripper. Got him right outside the south gate. Marston had a beam fall on him tonight, though, as he was helping a family. Split his skull." Greydal stayed silent. He didn't know what to say. Rulf added, "Looks like I got away with only some ripped up hands. Even if I almost lost my fingers." He wagged the ones Greydal had bitten the other night.

"Marston cracked me in my nose. I hadn't—" Greydal coughed, "I hadn't planned on letting go."

Rulf sighed. "Well, count me fortunate."

The quiet that settled over them stayed unbroken for several minutes until Greydal asked, "What happened?"

The watchman shook his head as he stared at his hands. "I was at the north gate when someone—" He hawked and spit. "We were attacked. It was a wash. Most of the watch died up front, I think. So much for all our spears and shit. I saw Calahurst shoot Ida with that knife thrower of his."

Greydal cut in, "Ida's dead?"

Rulf only shrugged. After a moment, he added, "I saw her go down."

Greydal lowered his head and rubbed his neck with his hand. "But why? We were at my father's— We were at the Rings. Alom said they were going after tulka." His eyes widened. "Alom! He knew." He turned to Rulf and coughed. Clearing his throat he said, "Alom had...this note about the sheriff." He recalled what he had found in Alom's study. "I think he meant it for Crawl. He said Calahurst was— He had kept the things seized after Avel's murder. Do you know about that?"

Rulf shook his head. "Not really," the watchman replied.

"My father didn't just kill him out of the blue. Avel broke into our barracks to rob us but stumbled across something. Under the floor. We came home and caught Avel as he was digging around. I only saw the tail end of it because I was a few minutes behind." Greydal coughed again, this time from deeper within his chest. Prolonged talking made his throat ache, and he tried to summon spittle to continue, but his voice was almost gone. Rulf waved his ensuing explanation away.

"Doesn't matter now. The man's dead."

Greydal didn't know if Rulf referred to Calahurst, Tier, or Avel.

"Whole village is dead," the older boy added, and Greydal felt as though a knife had prodded him.

Greydal tried to stand and said in a weak voice, "We have to go south. That's the quickest way down. We can take the slope. Others will have seen the smoke by now and come running."

"Greydal. Stop and listen."

He ignored the older boy and pushed off the tree. "We have to help. If we go south, we can meet up with anyone else who—"

Rulf interrupted, "You hear any shouts?"

Greydal paused. He held his breath, but all he heard was the dying roar of the flames and the whisper of the wind. The trees creaked high above. He sighed and sank to the ground. After a moment, he crawled towards the lip of the cliff and peered into the smoke. The fires dwindled, and he could just glimpse tiny bodies, unmoving. They looked like ants.

CHAPTER

7

ANTECHAMBER

They fought each other during the westward trudge. Greydal had tried to sneak away in the dark, but Rulf tackled him and made him swear to follow. "You can't help them," the watchman insisted. Greydal struggled underneath the boy, but Rulf was bigger and much stronger. "Get it through your skull," Rulf whispered and shook him.

Greydal reluctantly followed once the boy let him up, but the duo soon found it was too dark to navigate. They had tried following the upward slope as a guide, but nearly tumbled into a stream. After identifying its course, the pair felt their way to the flowing water and drank greedily as several mushrooms ignited a nauseous, green phosphorescence at their presence.

To Greydal's mind, the hill water was the best thing he had ever tasted. He drank until he was full, and then swallowed some more, softening his parched throat somewhat.

"I can't smell the water," Greydal told Rulf in between sips, "but I can taste it."

The watchman wiped his mouth. "I think we're nose-blind right now. Blind-blind, too. We need to wait until the sun's back."

"Tell me why you want to leave the valley," Greydal demanded as he laid back against thick ferns which curled lightly around him. They tickled his bare chest, and he swatted them away. At his rough touch, they released a noisome perfume: wax and spoiled milk.

He made a face.

Rulf folded his arms and replied, "Listen, you don't burn down a village and kill *everyone* to just sit on your thumbs after. You said they were going after you tulkas? Well, they didn't seem picky to me. If they want somethin' in the valley, fine, but I don't want to be in it until they're gone. Maybe ever."

Greydal thought about that and remained silent. The two sat at the bank of the hill spring and listened to the sounds of the forest, what few there were. He was surely addled, but the night was hushed, almost like it had been listening to their arguing and now waited for some third participant to speak. Greydal peered into the darkness, finding the trees surrounding them curved like snakes in the gloom. He followed the bends of their vague trunks, which twisted upwards for almost a hundred feet. His vision had mostly adjusted, and looking through the canopy, he saw that beyond the trees, stared open sky. "We're sitting next to an exposed glade," he informed Rulf.

The boy didn't reply, so Greydal changed course. "If we have to leave the valley, it'll be a day's hike west."

Rulf sighed. "No."

"What?

"Point. You want to get got strolling the western road? We need to hoof it."

That was true, Greydal supposed. He asked, "Have you ever been outside Harlow before? The valley itself, I mean. I haven't, aside from as an infant, supposedly."

Rulf took his boots off and stuck his feet in the stream before replying. He said, "When I was younger, my parents took me to see the Grandfather. He's right near where the road splits." He pointed in a direction Greydal was certain wasn't west. Greydal nodded anyway. The Grandfather was a carved stone rock which some of the less-religious villagers prayed at for guidance. His father had taken him to it, once.

A dense silence descended on the pair, and they sat for a time, enjoying the stream.

"What's that? Is that a house?"

Rulf said he didn't see anything and continued to bathe his feet.

"No, look, up and to the right on the other side of the glade," Greydal insisted. An umber wall of stone or some other substance broke the pattern of foliage roughly fifty yards away. Greydal sat up from his bed of ferns and pointed. "We shouldn't sleep out here tonight if we can help it."

Rulf cursed under his breath and pulled his boots back on as Greydal stood, head swimming. He allowed the vertigo to pass before nodding to the older boy in the dark. They bounded the stream and climbed to the glade. Its grass stood long and twisted, and as they cut through it, the blades caressed them. Greydal pushed them away, now wishing he hadn't given his shirt to the wind, bloody as it was. Although, he considered it was possible the blood from his garment might have made the grass more persistent. The foliage in this part of the valley was known to be opportunistic when it came to nourishment.

As they drew closer to the structure, Greydal found he had been right. The place was a house, an old one. A chimney jutted from a tall, triangular roof, which splayed from a high, central point and was just long enough to scrape the ground on either side. There was no window or opening facing them, so the two parted the leaves to the left of the overgrown domicile and walked through the underbrush.

They passed a crafted gap in the angled roof and spotted a window that looked out into the wet thicket. Greydal approached first and discovered that it was too dark to peer into the home, or else the window had frosted glass. He backed and continued searching for an entrance or clue as to the nature of the place, following Rulf, who forged ahead.

The older boy almost tumbled from a hidden edge before Greydal yanked him back. "Legate!" Greydal glanced at where Rulf had nearly fallen. It was some sort of cliff. Creeping forward, they both stared into the abyss, but it was difficult to tell if the swirling emptiness was only a short drop or some inexplicable chasm.

"Why in the Four Corners would anyone build a house on the edge of a pit?"

Greydal shrugged in the dimness. "Erosion?"

They backed and circled the house in the direction they had come, but found the other side identical. Another black window leered at them from beneath the thatched roof.

"Where in the valley is the damn door?" Rulf spit and reached around on the ground.

Realizing the watchman meant to find something dense to break the glass, Greydal said, "Wait, see?" He motioned Rulf to where he stooped. Greydal ran his hands over the discolored, straw-like substance of the roof and found what he was looking for. A hidden handle. He pulled, and a square section of the angled roof opened outwards.

"How did you see that?"

"I didn't. You can feel it's a different kind of material from the rest." They peered inside. The interior of the house was utterly without light, like a cave entrance.

"You first," Rulf said. The older boy grinned in the dark.

"Aren't you the watchman?" Greydal replied but entered the house anyway. The inside smelled damp and musky, similar to dogs when they got wet. "Well, there's no Calf-Ripper in here," Greydal called to him. After a beat, Rulf followed him inside. Greydal continued, "Don't shut the door. It's worse in here than it is out there. See anything we could light?"

"With what? Do you have a fire starter on you? Flint?"

Greydal got down on his hands and knees and padded his way towards where believed he had seen the chimney poke out of the roof. For a moment, his questing fingers found something unexpected: a long strand, thick and rough, but flexible like hair. *Some creature's quill?* he wondered, supposing the house *would* make a fine nesting place. In the dark, he let his palm run the strand's length, and when it proved greater than the span of his arm, he paled. But no, it couldn't be from something living then. Likely instead, it was a piece of fishing twine or something similar. Then his hands brushed stone, and he explored right and left.

"Found the fireplace. I don't— No, there's nothing here."

"Shit."

Greydal looked at where he thought Rulf was. "Why don't we just lie down? We'll figure this place out in the morning." Silence pervaded the house, so Greydal added, "Even if we could start a fire, I don't want to shout our presence to the rest of the valley."

That convinced Rulf, and Greydal spotted his profile crouch towards the floor. He heard the boy's hands pat the ground and could tell Rulf was trying to find somewhere to lay out. Then the sound of a hard object hitting the ground echoed through the blackness.

"What was that?" he hissed.

"Nothing, I just dropped something."

"What'd you drop?" Greydal asked.

"Don't worry about it. I'm lying down."

Greydal shook his head, and then stretched out as well, scooting away from the fishing twine and leaving his axe and sling in easy reach. He found to his distaste the thatch-covered floor stuck to his sweaty back. *Probably molden,* he thought. From where he lay, he could see the outline of Rulf's reclining body to his right in front of the square of brighter night that was the exit.

He turned his head and scanned the darkness beyond his own feet, where he surmised the apparent cliff hid on the other side of the currently-invisible northwest wall of the house. Greydal stared and tried to make out the rest of the interior. It was impenetrable. He heard Rulf shift.

The older boy was the first to break the stillness. "Whose house do you think this was?"

Greydal cleared his throat. "Was? For all we know, the owner is just out. Or crouched over there in the dark."

Rulf spit. "Don't start with that shit. This place is empty, and the house is swallowed by the trees. Trying to give me bad dreams?"

"I think I'm going to have bad dreams for a long time. Like when—" He paused. Rulf wouldn't care about his childhood fancies, but Greydal knew what he had said was the truth. He'd seen things today that went beyond the pale. Alom was dead. His father was dead. He had killed a man, with an axe.

"Stop. I know what you're doing, and you can't dwell. It'll drive you crazy, and we have to keep it together," Rulf whispered. Greydal didn't answer, so the older boy added, "You understand me? Now, get some shut-eye." Rulf turned over. "No more ghost talk. I'll take first watch."

Greydal couldn't resist. "I never mentioned ghosts."

The night deepened, but the pain of his torn ear kept him awake. Greydal reached a hand to inspect the wound but quickly withdrew it. The split there made his stomach turn. He would have to wait for the light of day to let Rulf examine the damage.

As he thought this, he became aware Rulf's breathing had turned slow and soft.

So much for first watch, he thought.

In the ensuing minutes, Greydal discovered he was discomforted most not by the day's violence, but by what he had heard over a week before in Alom's home. In the light, it was easy to dismiss the visitation as some sort of delirium. But huddling in the curdled dark of the old house, the experience was both imminent and visceral. The blackness beyond his feet continually drew his eyes, and he was more and more sure someone else looked back at him. Perhaps like a child would have, he forced his eyes to close and allowed exhaustion to take over. He was asleep within minutes, despite the pain.

There was a time where he didn't think at all until, abruptly, he was aware of himself. In his dream, and he knew it to be a dream, he lay sprawled on the floor of the old house. Light had never known this place, but he could still see. He gazed down and noted he was shirtless and lying on a primitive, thatch floor. He looked over to where Rulf slept, but there was only a shadow of the older boy, as if he was not entirely present.

The sound of footsteps drew his eyes towards the darkest part of the house. There was a door there, at the far end where the home faced the cliff. Greydal knew in the way of dreams the footsteps he heard approached from a long way off. But soon, they became louder, more excited. Sensing they must be warded off, Greydal tried to speak and sound brave, but his voice came out a weak mumble.

The house creaked, and the gleeful tread grew louder. Someone was out there. They were looking for him.

He tried to sit up but his body was as heavy as stone.

They neared. The steps sounded just beyond the door.

A primal panic seized him then. He didn't want to see what was on the other side. Some part of his mind screamed at him to wake up! Wake up! But it was too late.

The door wrenched open.

Later, Greydal would try to explain the dream to himself, to make sense of it. But it didn't make sense. In his memory, the door gave way to mundane darkness. It was as though there had simply been another part of the old house now revealed. But what was strange was that his dream-self had screamed as if *he* could see something the remembering self could not.

Greydal had woken from that screaming, scaring Rulf half to death. His companion had jumped up and yelled from his stupor, matching him. Ignoring the watchman's panicked gaze, Greydal stumblingly exited the old house, and the startled Rulf soon followed, finding him near inconsolable.

After a bewildering few moments, the older boy attempted to convince him to return to the inside of the house. Failing that, Rulf tried to pry out an explanation. But what could Greydal say? Besides, the dawn was just arriving, and the world appeared to glow after that night of total darkness.

Eventually, Greydal calmed and managed to mumble, "Bad dream."

Rulf blinked, and then inclined his head, his features softening. "Me too. Last night was rough. You ready then?" Greydal nodded, and Rulf said, "Good. I'm gonna stick my head in real quick and poke around. I wanna know what this place is."

Greydal didn't reply and watched as Rulf re-entered the house. The older boy didn't stay inside for long. From within, he called out, "Hey! I can kind of see in here now, you won't believe this. There's a *door* here, right near the back. Frame around it looks busted."

A small, choking noise emerged from the back of Greydal's throat, and he turned away to hide his face.

*** *** ***

They hiked in a frenzy all day and rarely spoke. Once, as they crested a ridge, they turned to see the specters of smoke drifting from the southeast. "We're going further north than we need. It'll bring us too close to the road," Rulf muttered.

After that, they tried to angle south as they hiked. Greydal quickly became exhausted and complained to Rulf. "If we go any further west, we'll bump into the Mansions," he half-joked.

The watchman turned as he walked and smirked. "I thought you were a forest kid. What'd you do all that time playing around under the boughs and vines? Didn't you have to run from big cats?"

Greydal shot him a rude gesture and replied, "Cut me some slack. I'm basically an invalid, or didn't you ever listen to Marston?"

Rulf was silent a beat before he said, "You're not an infirm, even if he called you Ague." Another quiet moment, and then he added, "The only thing you're sick with is self-pity."

That stung and felt unwarranted. "Why, just because I'm exhausted of being reminded about the damn thing?"

Rulf stopped hiking and turned around to look at Greydal. "That's what I'm talking about," the watchman replied. "Listen, because we've got to keep moving, I'm only going to say this once. Your life isn't easy, but so what? You're not the only one with troubles. And you survived—the Ague sickness, your father, the village...and Marston and Erl. You wanna trade places with someone lying back there?" Rulf stuck a thumb towards the faint tower of smoke in the distance. "I'm sure plenty of them would switch with you."

Greydal didn't know what to say and so lowered his head to stare at the ground. He heard the older boy continue his trudge through the undergrowth, which was turning rocky. After a breath, Greydal followed. "You talk like you know me."

Rulf looked behind. "Do you think Ida and I just stood mute the two years we manned the gates? She worried about you, the week running up to Duinn's execution. We talked."

*** *** ***

That night was almost as lightless as the one before. Timid slivers of moonlight trickled through the leaves of trees that desperately clung to the sides of the massive stones, all sprouting like mold from the hillside. The pair mounted one boulder and spread out on it. "We've got to find some grub, and soon. I could eat a tree."

Greydal nodded. "I've been keeping an eye out for other dwellings. But the valley's huge, and most people are near the roads," he replied. He looked over to see Rulf chewing on the stem of a leaf. "I thought you were joking."

"This is just to keep my brain tricked. I was hoping we'd find some considerate hermit and his beautiful daughter up here, but no luck."

Greydal turned over and thought for a moment. "We're about a half-day away from the western road and probably about the same to the lip of the valley. Maybe we could angle north?"

Rulf spit and replied, "We just got done leaning south for the whole day. The road's further than the rim would be. I think."

Greydal nodded and asked, "Okay. What do we know about the area beyond this part of the valley?"

The watchman sat up. "Well, when I went to see the grandfather, I asked my ma something similar."

Greydal's eyes widened, and he silently cursed himself. "Your mother—" he interjected, and Rulf grew still. Greydal cleared his throat and continued, "I should have asked before. Is she...?"

The older boy was quiet for a moment before answering, "The western road is supposed to split like the branches of a tree. That's what she told me when we visited the Grandfather. It's—" Rulf sighed and said more quietly, "It's what all the missionaries are supposed to travel along."

Greydal held his breath. Then he nodded and replied, "My father had some books that said the same. There's supposed to be some sort of trading post along that road if I'm thinking of the right one."

The night continued to deepen, waking nocturnal insects. For several minutes, neither boy said anything as they listened to the swelling chorus. In the distance, a bird called to another, but it went unanswered.

"Okay. So, besides the main road and a merchant spot mentioned in an old book, what else have we got?" Rulf asked.

Greydal furrowed his brow and replied, "I've never heard of any nearby villages, so they must all be pretty far or we'd be trading with them. The few traveling tradesmen *I've* heard of came from far out west as well—" He caught himself and corrected, "No, sorry, I might be wrong in that. Just because they didn't trade with us doesn't mean they aren't there. It's not as though Harlow would have rolled out the welcome rug." He picked up a small stone and felt it between his fingers. It was rough.

Rulf said, "I think we're goin' about this—" the older boy spit out the leaf, "the wrong way. Let's step back while we have the time and think."

"Well, our forests stop and stay gone for a while, right? Though I've heard there are real jungles farther out. And like you said, there's the main road that splits like a tree."

Rulf interjected with a hand and said, "Exactly, and why would there be roads unless they led somewhere?"

Greydal threw the rock into the darkness. He heard it hit a tree. "You've never heard of a dead end?"

"Huh." The older boy paused before continuing, "Well...not all gonna be dead ends, if there are any. We know there's supposed to be that monastery out west, on the way to the Mansions."

"You believe in them? The Mansions, I mean."

Rulf sat back in the increasing murk, his face hard to read.

After an awkward silence, Greydal added, "My father would tell me tall tales about villages and bigger towns, but never where they actually were. He'd just say *west* or *south* or *far*, what have you. But, regardless, once we pick a direction, we should stick to it so we don't waste energy."

"I wish I'd thought to bring a bow. It'd be nice to flash some animal while it's busy with a mouth full of foxglove"

"You can shoot?" Greydal asked.

Rulf nodded and replied, "I'm decent."

"I had you figured for a bash-them-over-the-head type."

Rulf looked at him. "I still could be."

Greydal threw his hands up. "Fine, if you had it your way, where would we head now?"

"Just where we've been heading, west. Once we crest the ridge, we can angle one way or another based on what we see."

Greydal shook his head and replied, "That's fine provided we see something. I don't want to have to turn back just to go track down some farmer and beg for food. I can hear your stomach already, and I haven't eaten since yesterday morning."

"Worst case, we lose a little belly fat. You remember Yorn? He went five days without when he got his leg caught under that log a couple years back."

Greydal rubbed his head. "People can go longer if they have water. That's not what I'm worried about. You were right earlier. We don't know who those people were or what they want."

"Okay. So, what's your point?"

"We need the energy to run or attack if we get caught. What if those golden men are combing the valley?"

"Fair," Rulf snorted and spit. He continued, "Here's the deal then: we angle northwest, staying far enough away from the road, so we aren't likely to get picked up or spotted. But once we hit the ridge, if we don't see what we want, we'll be close to the road and can burglarize some recluse."

Greydal laughed. "I think that's how you get cursed, but fine."

Rulf nodded and laid out on the rock. He whispered, "Wake me if we're getting eaten by the Calf-Ripper."

Greydal let his companion fall asleep. He wanted to use the relative alone time to think anyway. The area beyond the valley was a total unknown. His father, Tier, was the only person Greydal had known personally who had left the valley more than once. Calahurst had only come to the village late in life. If he discounted them, Greydal could count on one hand the people he knew who had willingly gone beyond the rim in his lifetime. He and Rulf were about to add to that list. That thought...

Stirred or disturbed? Or was there a difference?

CHAPTER

8

VELD

The next afternoon, just after midday, they arrived at the lip of the valley. It might as well have been the Edge of the world to Greydal. They mounted the final, mossy rocks at the margin and stood gazing over the vastness. He had never seen the sea, but the expanse of grass swaying in the warm wind could have been one.

"Oh."

"Yeah."

The two were silent for a moment as the breeze's whispering whipped past their heads. The grass spoke, too, a choir of dry mutterings.

"I don't see any towns."

"I don't see much of anything," Greydal countered. "Just that." He pointed a finger at the grassy plain below them.

Rulf nodded and peered at the northern horizon to the right. "Where's the road?"

"Just there. You're looking too far," Greydal said. He pointed at an ash-colored line snaking farther down from the ridge. It was hard to pick out, so immediately did the grass consume it.

"We're closer to the road than we should be," Rulf said.

Greydal replied, "I'm glad we are. We need to find a farm."

He studied the landscape for signs of habitation, but saw only a rundown structure, a shrine maybe, near where the road crossed into the valley. His eyes traveled west, and he thought he could spy the beginnings of some other terrain in the distance, a forest or rock wall.

Rulf turned and said, "I'll be clear with you, I'm hungrier than I've been almost my whole life, but I'm not going back. You only saw them golden things from far off when we were on the wall, right?" Greydal nodded, and Rulf continued, "Then you didn't see what they do when they get a hold of someone." He shivered.

"I think I saw the bodies."

"Yeah. Well, it's worse to watch it happen. I'd rather starve."

Rulf descended into the field. The western side of the ridge had higher elevation than the valley-side, and it only took them several minutes to climb down. Greydal hadn't anticipated how tall the grass would be. It had looked less towering from atop the ridge.

Once they reached level ground, Greydal said, "I'm not sure how we'll spot much of anything now. Look at that." The grass was nearly his height.

"Just stay close to me. I can see over it fine."

Greydal spared a look to the north, where the structure he had thought was a shrine sat in its dilapidation. Closer now, he could tell it was a kind of grave he had never seen before. Even from the distance, he could tell it had likely once been painted a lively green. Who would erect a thing like that out here?

The silence of the plains seemed ominous instead of serene as he followed Rulf inwards.

They walked for what felt like several hours, yet the sky was just as bright by the time they paused to rest. When they continued, Greydal sent a glance upwards to make sure the two were heading in the right direction. The indistinct lines of the heavens threaded almost perpendicular to their current orientation, which meant they were trudging westward. He gazed at Rulf. The back of the older boy's short-cropped hair stood barely above the grass, which seemed to grow higher the further in they went. Rulf's large arms pushed aside the stalks, and his legs trampled the rest underneath. Greydal followed in his wake, and occasionally, looked down to examine this new world. The ground beneath his feet was nearly black, and the atmosphere inside the grass potent and wet.

"If we find wildlife, how are we going to cook it?" His voice was muffled.

Rulf glanced back. "What?

"If we find— You didn't hear me?

"You think you or I are fast enough to run down an animal?"

"I think we can surprise one. As long as it's northwest of us, we'd be downwind of it. Can't you tell by the way the grass is waving?"

Rulf nodded but never answered his question. They kept walking. Greydal's stomach growled, and his awareness returned to his body, noticing how faint his head was, how fuzzy his thoughts seemed. Was that the result of hunger or a concussion? He hoped it was the former but suspected his injuries simply dizzied him.

His sliced ear pained him, too. Greydal reached up to touch his wound, and he winced, lowering his hand when his fingertips grazed the torn flesh. He suspected that when it healed, he would have a V-shaped chunk missing.

Gritting his teeth, he tried to scrape the dried blood off with his fingernail but cursed and gave up when the pain grew severe enough to make his eyes water. He sighed and let his mind drift to the previous night. A kind of creeping self-awareness had settled on his thoughts, starting as soon as they left the house. He struggled for the right description of the sensation. Was it the feeling of being watched? No, he was doubly aware, as though there were two of him, one overlaying the other. The feeling was distinct, but he couldn't understand it.

The blades of grass rubbed together in the wind and created a subtle rustling like the noise he had heard from the ridge. The sound drew his attention away from himself to the surrounding landscape. Something occurred.

"I don't remember spotting any rivers to the north or south when we were on the ridge."

"What's that?" Rulf didn't turn around.

"I was just thinking, animals would be near water, right? Well, the valley was full of streams, deep ones sometimes. So, where's the river that supplies all that water?"

"I dunno, north maybe? It's probably hidden by all this." Rulf waved an arm.

"Maybe."

It was around dusk, when the light of the sun faded, they found they were too tired to continue. They chopped and pulled at the grass to make room to lie down, and the ensuing circle looked like something giant had put its foot down in the endless field. As he settled, Greydal examined the clearing. He was surprised he hadn't spotted any insects. The things normally adored dense vegetation. He reached over and picked up several discarded blades, slurping the dew from them. Then he said, "There's a river to our south."

"How do you figure?" Rulf trampled the widening circle of open space.

"If it was north of the road, we'd have crossed it before hitting the lip of the valley. The stream near that abandoned house...the stream angled up and to the left, so southwest." Rulf didn't reply. Greydal rubbed his neck and added, "We could go to the road, but we don't know how far it is until there's any habitation. For all we know, we've missed it already. But we *do* know there are animals here." The older boy was still tearing away at grass. "Rulf, are you listening? *Something's* eating this grass." Greydal held up a blade to show the tear marks. "These are from teeth. Not insects."

Rulf turned to him and wiped sweat from his brow. "You know, sometimes it's best not to dig too deep. Can't you just lie down?"

"What?"

"This place... Look. Haven't you ever seen movement out the corner of your eye?"

"I don't—"

"When you're alone, I mean. Happens to everyone. You're alone and something maybe moves off to the side. You know what the smart thing to do is when that happens?"

Greydal said nothing, and the older boy finished, "Smart thing is to *ignore it.*"

They ignored each other for a time until Greydal clicked his tongue and insisted, "I'm telling you, these are teeth marks."

Rulf sighed. "Alright, fine, there are animals, but one more day."

"But—"

"We can make it. If we see nothing, we see nothing. Then we can turn south to your river." The older boy stopped and laid amongst the torn grass.

The grass was a bed, and Greydal could feel the cool, damp ground under his hands when he pressed them through the discarded blades. He realized he hadn't replied to Rulf and said, "Alright. One more day." He turned over.

"Get some sleep," the older boy commanded.

"First watch?" Greydal ventured, but Rulf didn't reply.

Exhaustion made his thoughts crumble into nonsensical vagaries, but he was apparently too hungry to sleep, and his stomach turned into knots as he found himself imagining food. In his mind, it looked abstract and beautiful, glistening with flavor.

An hour later, Rulf asked, "You awake?"

"Are you?"

"I feel exposed out here."

Greydal gazed at the wall of grass surrounding their tiny clearing and found he didn't agree, his mind now returning from the depths of half-sleep. "I don't know. It's kind of like a fortress."

"What's that?"

"A fortress. A village, only more defensible."

Rulf looked at him in the dark. Greydal asked, "What?"

"You make that up?"

"Not that."

"Ida said you know a lot. Where'd you get it all, then?

"Most of it's from talking to Alom—" The image of Alom dead in the alley. "Other times from my father, his books and tales."

"Guess I missed out."

"You didn't. A lot of my father's stories were nonsense." Greydal's back was wet from the ground, and he shifted to pull more stalks of broken grass beneath him. "I could tell you one," he added. The older boy didn't answer at first, but Greydal saw him nod in the dim light. "Alright, then. Well, I'll stick with the one about the fortress. My father called it the *Tale of the Excondalt*, or sometimes the *Wizard*. It's about the end of the world." Rulf was quiet.

Greydal fidgeted in the silence. He continued, "I'll probably mess it up, but here it is. A long, long time ago, or maybe a long, long time from now, there was no sun or moon. There was no sky, too. Only stars—"

Rulf interrupted, "Stars?"

"I'm getting to it. The story has to have a flow if I'm going to do it justice." Greydal shifted on his bed of grass. "So, there was no sky. Instead, there was an infinite shadow, filled with tiny fires. They were called stars."

Rulf interrupted again, "How did anyone see without the sun and moon?"

"Well, that's a different story. But, as it happens, there were two bigger stars that shined on everything. Anyway, I'm getting off track. Those tiny fires in the dark looked over a bunch of strange places, all floating like islands. You know islands, right?" Rulf said he did, and Greydal continued, "One spot was an open plain, like this one." He gestured his hands to the grass. In truth, his father had said the location in the story was a rocky one, with massive hills that reached high above the tallest trees.

"There was a war there between two enemy factions. It doesn't matter why, because at that time, it had gone on so long no one knew the original cause. Part of the reason it *kept* on, though, was that one faction, we'll call them the Brains, had a great and terrible base of operations. A fortress.

"It had walls that reached towards the dark and roots that drove into the ground. Every time the other faction—we'll call them the Shanks, because they never stayed in one place—every time the Shanks tried to attack the Brains' fortress, they failed. All their arts and wiles were nothing. The fortress defeated them."

Greydal sipped some dew from the bending stalks near his head and continued, "The Shanks despaired, were close to giving up. One of them, though, the Shanks' chief, refused to surrender. He sent out a call for help: 'Anyone who can stop the Brains and end their reign of terror will have earned the right to marry my daughter.' Well, that lit a fire under the warriors of that long and wide world. The Shanks were known to be a strange and beautiful people, and the daughter of that chief more so."

He sipped more dew. "One hundred killers and fighters threw themselves against the Brains' fortress. All died, one after the other. All seemed lost...until the Excondalt came."

At this point in the story, his father would pause to let younger Greydal ask who the Excondalt was, even though he knew it after so many retellings. Rulf said nothing, and Greydal looked over at his companion. The older boy's chest rose and fell in a slow rhythm. Greydal smirked. Oh well, he could finish the tale another time, maybe once they got somewhere safe. He closed his eyes and drifted. At some point, he entered unconsciousness, though it was a dreamless slumber. His last thought was that he imagined he could hear a tinkling sound across the wind, like trickling water or laughter.

The next day in the grass was much like the first. This time, it seemed they had only walked for several hours before a bleary gloaming overtook the light. A paranoid whisper told him the grass had ruined his perception of time. Had they gone anywhere at all? Maybe they would be stuck there, arguing and half-drunk with exhaustion until the sun died permanently.

Then the sudden urge for a glimpse of road, or tree, or any-thing other than these long, waving stalks seized him, and he jumped to try and see over the grass. But they had grown too tall, the stalks. Surely, they weren't straining towards the sky to block his view.

If there was an explanation aside from his own starved mind playing tricks, none registered. As night swallowed the plain, they were forced to create a clearing, the same as before. Spreading out under the darkening sky, Greydal struggled against his mounting panic.

Time passed. As his body's fatigue dragged at his unraveling thoughts, Greydal whispered to Rulf, "Tomorrow. You said." There was no response.

Afterwards, his sleep was pale and fitful as his stomach and dizziness kept him partially anchored to wakefulness. A nascent dream rose, half-formed. Silence drifted like a cloud across the plain as tiny fires in the sky of his mind wheeled, and then went out, one at a time, then altogether. Something slid against Grey-dal's back.

He woke to Rulf trying to slip his axe from its sling. His breath caught, but he managed to headbutt the older boy from his prone position. Rulf fell backwards as Greydal rose. The night was close to over, and the first red hues of dawn coated the artificial clearing. He shook himself further awake. On the ground, Rulf rubbed his face.

Though groggy and crazed, Greydal spoke with as much authority as he could muster, "We're not doing this. Do you understand? We'll—"

He halted his speech and punched Rulf as the older boy tried to stand. Greydal furrowed his brow as something shifted in his chest, snakelike. He put a hand on his axe.

"Tell me you understand before you try and get up again. I'll open you."

A silence.

"Tell me!" Even a yell sounded muffled in the stifling grass.

"I understand you're going to get us killed," Rulf spat. "We know nothin' about this place." Greydal gripped the axe tighter but said nothing. The older boy continued, "Those animals, the ones you're sure are by a river just south of here? They're more liable to kill you than the hunger."

Rulf had lost his mind. "Why?" Greydal removed his axe from its housing as he asked the question, preparing to swing. "Why take this?"

"I knew you were leaving at dawn. I couldn't let you throw it away."

The adrenaline and hunger shook him, but he forced himself not to crouch to steady himself. The older boy added, "I wasn't going to leave you. Just make you follow me."

"Rulf, shut up."

"Listen—"

"No, do you hear that?"

There was a crashing in the distance, like a large man running through the grass. It grew closer.

They locked eyes. Greydal said, "You distract, I'll swing."

Rulf nodded and hurriedly stood and then backed away, taking off his shirt to wrap it around one hand, creating a half-formed flag. There were several seconds of heavy breathing between the two, and then it was upon them, a behemoth of horn and hide.

The thing's protrusions were twisting roots, and eyes stared from the sides of its elongated head. Greydal saw its nostrils flare in a moment that seemed outside of time. He swung and heard the bellow of the creature. Its tongue lolled from a jaw that contained teeth like a person's. The beast stumbled, and then righted itself, bolting through the underbrush. He looked down and found the axe gone from his hands.

"After it!" Rulf ran towards the fleeing animal, and Greydal followed. His weapon was lodged in the thing's side, so deep only half the handle was visible.

The ensuing hunt was breathless. The pair lost sight of their prey four times, but used the trail of dark blood and splayed hoof marks to give chase. The animal continually ran in a dizzying zigzag, and after a while, Greydal lost all sense of direction. Twice they cornered it, and Greydal tried to rip his axe from the beast's side. Both times, it swung its horns, and he was forced to throw himself to the grass. Near the end, they followed it via its keening wail. Was it calling for help? Greydal clenched his teeth as he jogged.

Finally, the thing collapsed. Greydal reached it first and slowed, panting and lightheaded. The animal sprawled on its side and gasped as he imagined a drowning victim might.

"Careful," Rulf's voice was somewhere behind him, "it could still slice you."

He ignored the older boy and approached. The animal's eyes were a grayish blue, like his own. Reaching for the axe, he withdrew it with little effort, and the beast moaned as blood pooled on the thirsty ground between the stalks of trampled grass. With a swing, he separated the animal's head from its body and slumped to the ground, covered in draining vitality. His heartbeat was thunderous as he looked at his victim, close to vomiting the empty contents of his stomach. Then he smelled it.

He tried to stop himself. He did.

The blood, he licked it, first from his hands, and then his arm.

If the hunger in his belly was fierce before, now it was a furnace. He glimpsed Rulf approach out of the corner of his eye, and so he jealously hacked off a chunk of flesh with the axe, squeezing the blood from it one-handed, letting it pour down his throat. It tasted like water, like honey.

"Greydal, stop. Stop!" The older boy pulled his hand away. Greydal looked up to his companion and whispered desperately, "We have to cook this. We have to find something to burn—" Then their eyes widened at the same time. They both could hear it: windchimes.

The heady atmosphere of the tall grass, congealed solid with tension as the duo waited in silence. They listened to the tinkling sound of metal drift between the stalks. Slowly, Rulf raised a finger towards his lips. Greydal inclined his head and set down the chunk of beast-flesh as lightly as he was able. He rose then, standing next to Rulf to strain his ears. There was nothing. Where had the windchimes gone?

Rulf whispered, "Let's—"

Several golden blurs burst from the grass. Greydal fell over himself as he and Rulf scrambled from the space. *How?!* His mind whirled.

The hunters didn't chase like men. They almost ran on all fours, their helmeted heads close to the dirt. As he and Rulf hurdled through the grass, Greydal tightened his hand on the bloody axe, somehow still in his grip. He looked over his shoulder and spotted two of the things in pursuit. Both were less than ten feet behind.

One of them was running backwards. It was the one he had seen before on the rock wall. Unlike its fellow, this one's movement was troubled, its arms contorted at unnatural angles to grasp the wet air. Its fingers were bent towards the back of its reaching gloved hands, forming ugly, reversed mitts. But the dark chasms dotting its helmet were the same as its compatriot's, threatening something Greydal didn't want to contemplate. He was falling behind Rulf's pounding tread. Fear overcame exhaustion, and he drove his feet into the soil. That fear turned to blind hysteria as he recognized the things in the scaled, goldencoats gained, despite his exertion. They made a sound like a hundred voices talking at once. No, that was the sound of—

Water.

Both boys tumbled almost simultaneously into a river coursing through the grass. Greydal had a split-second view of the other side of the bank where short trees stooped. Then he was underwater, and the current carried him for several airless moments before his head broke the surface, and he gasped—just in time to glimpse three golden shapes crash into the water near him. Fighting to maintain hold of his axe, he tried to right himself, only to spin. His eyes glanced across the framework of the sky far above, and an insane thought struck him then, that the river must flow from the south and *split* to the east and west. *That* was why they hadn't run across it. Then pain lanced up his body. Something had his leg, dragging him under.

In the murk, he spied an object, vibrant and red, wrapped around his calf. Greydal kicked, but his body wouldn't respond. Whatever reached like crimson mucus out of the holes in the attacker's helmet twisted into his limb with a violent strength. He tried to scream, and his mouth filled with water. At the sound of his gurgling cry, the mucus *flared.* Between the bubbles, he glimpsed what looked like spines or worms extend from within the goop. They coiled into his exposed muscles as blood filled his vision.

Greydal fought and twisted. He couldn't breathe, and an ugly horror struck him as he saw the muddy shapes of the other two attackers rise from the low riverbed, curling towards him. He expelled the last of his air as he gurgled a yell, swinging the axe. It cut through the water just like it did everything else.

Bubbles obscured his vision, but he felt movement. He was coursing down the river again. He had one last look at the attackers before his head broke the surface of the water, showing him that the axe had cleaved two of the monsters' helmets in half, including the backwards one, now all open like a bit fruit. Something awful spilled from the creatures into the encompassing stream.

*** *** ***

It had been a grueling effort to escape the current. Greydal pulled himself through the mud onto land and collapsed, his blood soaking the riverbank. He could smell it, pungent and nauseating. He knew that he was dying.

Somehow, his axe was with him. He tried to let go of it, but his hand refused him. Then he coughed, water spilling from his lungs. He was unconscious before his head hit the wet clay.

EXHAUSTION

In his dream, he was in the house at the edge of the pit with its door that led to nothing. He inhaled once, the mold and musk filling his lungs as the darkness parted to reveal the truth of things: he was alone. But this time, he could move. When he tried to sit up, he slipped, gasping in revulsion at the state of his right leg. It was gone from the knee down.

The emotion that filled him then didn't have a name. He reached a shaking hand to his stump, a sheared puckering of furious tissue. He couldn't make himself touch it, instead quickly retracting his hand and turning to drag his maimed body to where he remembered the side hatch in the roof to be. He neared it, reaching upwards, only to find the side door missing. A carved block of wood woven into the inner roof replaced the exit. The block bore a mark in the shape of an arrow, bisected by squirming horns.

Greydal slowly turned towards the other door, the door at the far end of the empty house. This didn't feel like a dream.

The steps began. This time they came heavier and faster, uneven, as if borne from the bristling protrusions of some lopsided, galloping person. A thing between a gasp and a scream clawed its way up to his mouth. Far, near, now *close!* The steps were right outside the house. Greydal crouched in the darkness, a hunted hare waiting for death's door to open.

Wait, it was open. The door was already open. When had it—

A familiar face, upside down with wide eyes, stooped towards him from the darkness to his left. In its nearing gaze, he witnessed...

What?

The nightmare crumbled violently, giving way to a grimy, half-sleep. Greydal stirred. He could hear someone clanking something metal. There was the taste of smoke on the crisp air.

Then the face returned, rocketing from the depths to follow him into the cruel light of awareness. In these final moments, he sensed the seed of what hid behind the thing's insane eyes. There was once something wrong with the world, all of it. An image of a worn blanket, painted with the colors of life, rose into view. A writhing knuckle of dying tissue hid beneath, the true shape of existence. Something about the sight caused Greydal's mind to revolt. He woke fully with a gasp into what felt more like a dream than the place before. He was lying on his back, and he was freezing.

There was something on fire to his left, causing him to think for a moment he was back in the village. But then, it was too small to be a cottage ablaze. Trying to move, he found he was too drained to lift a finger, his fuzzy vision only showing him coiling smoke and the underside of dense firs. Parting his lips, he tried to speak.

A dark shape appeared at his left, and he strained away from it, thinking it was the presence from the old house. The shape cupped his chin and poured a cool liquid into his mouth. He coughed, but swallowed most of it.

Someone said, "That's enough for now." Greydal tried to glimpse who spoke but immediately fell back into unconsciousness.

He wasn't sure exactly when next he dreamed, but he was positive a long time had passed. In the dream, he, Rulf, and Tier all sat around a fire. His father was dead, but didn't appear to mind. He was telling the two boys a ghost story, which ended with the revelation that there was a wolf behind them.

Greydal replied, "I know, but I can't get it to leave." He looked over to Rulf, who was dragged into the dark beyond the trees.

Looking at his father, he said, "You're dead. It's my fault." Tier only shook his head and pointed. Where Rulf had sat, there now crouched a man, like an older version of Greydal. He wore Greydal's face, but a foul expression twisted it. "Who are you?" he asked his doppelganger.

The other's face became a parody of a grimace.

"You're not me. I don't know what you are," he told it.

Someone else's hand reached out of the dark behind the doppelganger and crushed it before tossing it away. He now saw that his discarded copy was made of mâché, like the puppets on the Vermillion Stage. Greydal peered at the hand, but couldn't see to whom it belonged. As he strained his eyes, steam emerged from the darkness and coiled around the hand's fingers.

"Greydal, don't look at it."

He glanced at his father, but found the man now bore the features of Alom, who smiled, but looked sad.

"You're going to have to wake up soon. Don't be afraid."

Greydal looked towards the sky, and tiny fires filled the night. He fell towards them, and then flew through the void. The fires winked past him as he hurdled through the cold, and he perceived he approached something in the emptiness. A black marble. He knew he would have to land on it, but how? It was so small.

Someone shook him awake. No, they were making him sit upright. He wished they would go away and let him sleep. The someone said, "You need to eat. Open your mouth, darling." They shoved a warm sludge between his parted lips, and then held his jaw closed as he choked and swallowed. "Again," they whispered.

This time, he parted his lips and allowed the stranger to feed him. The mixture burned on the descent, but was wonderful and warm in his stomach. The hands on his face were soft.

Another voice said in a rough tone, "How's he doing?" Greydal looked and saw a great shape in front of a multi-colored wagon. The light was weak, or his eyes were bad, but Greydal could tell it was a tulka, the wine-colored face shining in the firelight. He tried to speak but couldn't find his voice.

The one who fed him purred, "Shh now. If you're smart, you'll rest. Just one more bite, and you can lie down. He's doing alright." This last remark seemed to be for the giant near the wagon.

Greydal nodded anyway and looked up at the woman, who raised a spoon to his lips. All he could identify was shaggy hair and deep, watchful eyes. He consumed the contents of the spoon, and she lowered him onto his bed. The sound of clanking pots drew his awareness before he felt himself being lifted, bed and all, as he slipped into unconsciousness.

*** *** ***

Several days passed, all more of the same. He would learn that his captors or caregivers called themselves Marcos and Roan. He also found to his incredible dismay the dream about his leg had come true. He prodded the stub below his knee with his right hand when he woke one morning and almost passed out from the shock. When the woman he came to know as Roan re-entered the wagon, he leveled an accusing glare at her.

"Did you—" his voice was raw. "Did you have to?"

Her tone was sardonic. "Lucky."

"What?"

"It was you or the leg, I'm afraid."

Greydal furrowed his brow. "I...believe you," he lied. There was no reason to antagonize her in his weakened state. She nodded, apparently satisfied, and grabbed a pot before exiting the cart.

He rested his head on his makeshift stretcher, as that's what it was. His eyes traveled the interior of the wagon where he had been deposited. It should have been roomy but was cramped with objects stacked on every shelf and surface, many tied down with blue twine. There were glasses, cooking utensils, ropes, clothing, and other items. The blanket, which he'd earlier kicked to the floor, was scratchy and sported a peculiar floral pattern. Some might have considered it a kind of finery if the thing wasn't covered in his sweat and stink. Outside, Greydal heard laughter and the accompanying grunts of an animal. A razorback, maybe. He looked towards the open door of the wagon and noted a sword and other implements, which could only be weapons. They hung from hooks to the right and left of the aperture. Who were these people?

He tried to tell in what kind of place they camped, but he could only spy immense tree trunks and a ground covered in needles through the opening. The air tasted dry, though. That meant they must be far west or north, if his father's books were anything to go by. Greydal wondered how long he had been in a state of semi-consciousness. It only felt like days, but he suspected it might be closer to weeks. They had been feeding him the same gruel for every meal, and the times he had eaten blurred together.

With the embarrassment of a teenager, Greydal grimly surmised someone would have had to clean him when he fouled himself. His cheeks burned. He resolved he would take care of such matters moving forward, even if he had to drag his carcass from the wagon.

He flexed his remaining foot, and then his leg. His body weighed as much as a house, but he *could* move. Bracing himself on the wooden panels to his right, he tried to set himself upright, but his head swam as black spots covered his vision. After taking a deep breath, he tried again, and this time, succeeded in righting.

From his new vantage, he noted that stranger items than he had glimpsed before also filled the wagon. There were two lenses, like spyglasses connected by hinges. He spotted a silver ball suspended in the clear liquid of an unmarked bottle. The ball sported writings that wiggled when he caught them in the corner of his eye. There was a taxidermized animal, like a dog, but small enough to fit on a plate. It had a toothy grin and had been shoved in a corner near the roof of the wagon.

There were stranger items still. Above him hung a small, woven web like a spider's. It was braided with knotted twigs, and its velvet (if that's what the material was) shimmered in the light. The spaces between its lines didn't look like they belonged to the wagon, though. The longer he gazed, the more his head hurt, and the painful feeling forced him to avert his eyes.

Were these people witches? Treasure hunters? He tried and failed to arrive at an assessment of the two who had kept him alive since his tumble in the river. *The river.* That brought unpleasant memories, and he suffocated them before they could draw him into a dark rumination.

"So serious."

He turned to see the wild-haired woman leaning in from outside the wagon. "Don't be afraid of us. We wouldn't save you just to kill you," she said. Greydal looked her over and decided she probably wasn't much older than him. He asked her, "Was it you? I saw someone else." He tried to sound calm.

"King Marcos. You want to hear a lark? He did it with your axe." Greydal didn't see the humor and scowled. She then told him,

"Once we caught on as to what you carried, we knew it was the cleanest way." Her smile was large and genuine.

When he didn't respond immediately, the girl shrugged and added, "I fixed you up afterwards, though, and tended the wound. You were dead when we found you, or close to it. Half-starved and mostly out of blood. I'm surprised you didn't freeze to death on the way to our camp."

"Thank you, then. For saving me." Greydal's voice cracked, and her smile widened.

"It's alright, little warrior. Just be careful. Not all of these knickknacks in here are trifles."

She pulled herself into the wagon, black dress brushing torn around the ankles. She crouched near him, producing a steaming bowl of soup. He hadn't seen her carry it in.

"King Marcos decided you could be done with the medicine, though I disagreed. Here, he made it himself." She pulled a spoonful out of the bowl and blew on it. Her breath raised goosebumps on his arms, and he tried not to let her see how vulnerable he felt.

He accepted the mouthful of soup and swallowed before coughing. "Is this all spice?"

She laughed. "Would you stop if I said yes?"

He accepted another sip and said, "Where are we?"

"Why, are you thinking about running?"

"I don't think I'll be able to run any time soon." He refused to look at his leg. Instead, he gazed at the bridge of her nose since her eyes made him uncomfortable. He continued, "It's not safe to be around me. I think a boy that was traveling with me might..."

She set the bowl on the wooden floor and leaned towards him. Her face was a foot from his, and he smelled wildflowers on her hair. "We," she soothed, "are perfectly practiced with defending ourselves. Don't worry your little head. As to your question, we're on a nameless track within the Owl Barrens."

"Owl barons?"

She smirked. "Bare-rens," she enunciated.

"I don't know where that is."

She picked up the bowl and offered him another spoonful of the soup, which he accepted. She explained, "Well, we dragged you out of Small River about two weeks east of here. So, not far from the Whisper Veld." They sat in silence for a moment as she helped Greydal finish the broth. He nodded to show he understood, though he patently did not.

"It didn't feel that small," he said.

"Deceptively deep, it." She put a hand under her chin. "Alright, what do we call you?"

"Greydal."

"Greydal what? Do you have a family? Or did you run away?" She smirked. Did she think that was funny? Setting the bowl near the door, she ran a hand through her tangled hair.

Greydal thought for a moment and said, "Greydal Alone."

Her smile became impish. "That doesn't sound like a real last name to me. Maybe the epithet of an overly romantic child."

He glared at her and said, "My father's name was Duinn. Alone is what we call anyone who's forced to become the first of their line."

Her eyes widened. "Ah, not a runaway then. He kicked you out, did he?"

"He's dead."

All was quiet in the wagon for several heartbeats. She broke the silence. "It sounds like there's a tale there."

"I guess there is."

"Then I will wait for King Marcos before I make you tell it." She rose to leave, empty bowl in hand.

He spoke to her back, "Wait. What's your name?"

She turned and said, "Since you did me the courtesy of being honest, I'll do the same. You can call me Roan." She bowed like a stage performer and added, "At your service."

"And King Marcos?"

She glanced left and right as if she and Greydal were con-spirators. "He's my father." Then she disappeared through the opening.

Greydal laid back on his stretcher. Who in the Four Corners were these two?

He fingered the wooden sides of his stretcher. Sigils he didn't recognize spread across its surface. Someone had engraved them into the wood.

The wagon was quiet as he sunk into the fabric of the bedding.

After a beat, he clenched his jaw and reached his hand down to the stump of his leg. It was warm, though covered in rough ban-dages. He encountered the unexpectedly profound urge to jerk his hand away, but he made himself explore what remained of his limb. There was a dull ache that intensified where he touched. As he investigated, he flexed and found he could move it just below the knee. The understanding dawned that, not only would he no longer run, he was now a cripple, just like Yorn from the village after his dire rendezvous with the tree. Climbing as a pastime was over. So, too, was any chance of escape if the golden things found him again. This revelation made him sick, and for the first time in his life, he considered what it would be like to take it.

Rulf's words came back to him with a viciousness. The older boy was probably dead now, and Greydal had survived him. As he had survived his father, Alom, and the rest of the village. Would he shame himself with self-pity? *Now?*

He lived and had full possession of his wits. He had lost his leg, true. That only meant he would have to be that much smarter in the future, wilier. Furthermore, Greydal needed to know who had orchestrated his attack and why. At once, it consumed him, giving him a kind of fevered purpose. Those things in the golden helmets had gone after tulka, according to Alom. Greydal was one, so was that why they had followed him from Harlow and into the grass? Roan and Marcos, whoever they were, appeared to know more about the lands outside of the valley. The girl even had a name for the river which had nearly drowned Greydal.

He didn't know the intentions of the two, but resolved to draw whatever information he could from them. After that, he would decide his next steps. *Steps.* He smirked in spite of himself.

Turning over, he winced as his ear connected with the bedding. He reached up to touch it and found it covered with the same type of bandages as his knee. It felt glued to his skull. He shook his head and tried to get settled despite the wound. After several buzzing minutes, he approached a state much like sleep, though he pondered fuzzily. He would need his energy and all his faculties if he wanted to go toe-to-toe with Roan, he mused. She was quick and knew it. But he was curious what this Marcos was like. *Was* the man a king?

As if in response, Greydal heard a booming laugh in the distance.

Later, the wagon moved.

*** *** ***

It was night. Greydal wasn't sure how he knew. The door sat closed, and the interior of the wagon gave no signs of the surrounding wilderness aside from flickering lights creeping under the doorframe. The crickets. That was it. He heard their cries trickle in through the wood. The surrounding forest must be a home for the insects, then. When he had been young, crickets would arrive on hot nights and fill the valley with their chirping pleas. Greydal remembered catching several in a jar and asking Tier why they made the noises they did. Tier had told him a ghost story in response, and Greydal let the crickets go after that.

He didn't want to think of his father right now. If only Roan had left him a candle. Earlier, he had noticed a stack of books, some in his language, and he now yearned to read. The titles he glimpsed were tantalizing, curious names like *Riddles for Animals* and *The Whites of Your Eyes*. There were others stacked elsewhere.

One stood out, a dusky tome with striking, gold text on the spine: *Killer of Witches - Combatting Agents of the Interloper.* That one merited investigation. He resolved the next time there was light to read, he would try to reach it. As he thought this, the door opened, allowing moonlight mingled with the fulgent glow of a fire to fill the wagon. A wild head of dark hair, face wreathed in shadow, peered in at him.

"Looking around, are you?"

"Hello."

"King Marcos wants to speak. Do you think you can stand? I'll help."

He nodded, and then, unsure if she could see him, said he could try. She approached, and he smelled smoke on her hair and dress. Sitting up with an audible grunt, he felt her arms reaching to his sides to clasp his back. He swallowed.

Her face was close to his, but he could only see the halo of her hair. "Ready?" The voice was right next to his ear. He nodded.

She lifted, and he stood with his left leg at the same time. He wanted to show he wasn't an invalid, but was forced to lean on her as she helped him stumble from the wagon. Extreme lightheadedness threatened as they descended three wooden steps to stand on the dirt outside. A blaze greeted them, large enough to send licking flames at least six feet in the air. Around the fire, huge trunks restrained what appeared to be dense forest spreading in all directions. Greydal had never come across trees so wide nor so tall. They plunged into the night, towards the grimy, skywide face of the moon. And their bark—Greydal's eyes widened slightly. The bark was split as if peeling, but beneath it, something shifted.

"What kind of firs are these?" He breathed a sigh as Roan set him on the ground in front of the fire. Her face shined in its light.

"These are old trees, from a place where everything grows tall and lives for a long, long time."

"They're not from here?"

A deep voice crackled, from the fire itself. "Lad, nothing is." A great shape rose from the other side of the blaze. It was the tulka from before.

He was the largest man Greydal had ever seen, including Marro. But where Marro had been all flab, the man now circling the fire was muscle, like a razorback had decided to put on clothes. The man's outfit was strange, buttons and swirling patterns woven into the outer jacket. His pants were tight, though that may have just been because of his size. Regardless of his dress, he didn't look like a king. Though, Greydal allowed he had never met a real one.

"Are you Marcos?"

The giant grinned, his teeth barely visible behind his curling beard. "I am, indeed, lad. Welcome to my court." He waved a cudgel of a hand towards Roan, the wagon, and the outline of a grazing bovine through the trees. Greydal raised his eyebrows. King Marcos strode forward and squatted in front of him. He spoke with a conciliatory tone, "First, let me apologize about your leg. Like I'm sure Miss Roan here has informed you, it was you or it."

Greydal nodded. The man smelled like the fire itself and was closer than he would have liked. The skin under the man's brow and around his eyes sported tattoos of spikes or rays. They spun onto his cheeks, forming sharpened tears.

"Second, Roan intimated to me that you may not know where you are, is that right?" Greydal didn't feel like it was time to speak yet. The man only sought an affirmative. He nodded. There was no point in lying when he had already told Roan as much. The man closed his eyes and inhaled.

"As I thought. Roan?"

Greydal heard a whistling hum through the air. Marcos caught his axe with a lazy swipe. Greydal turned to the girl and glared. She had thrown it right over his shoulder but didn't look as though his anger perturbed her, and so he turned to King Marcos.

Before he could speak, the king said, "Last of the preliminaries. Can you tell me what this is, yes or no?" The man pointed a huge finger to the mark Greydal had carved on the wooden portion of the handle.

He nodded and answered, "That's mine. I carved it." Marcos' eyes flicked over his shoulder, presumably at Roan.

The man looked at him. "I need you to tell me where you learned to do something like that."

Greydal fell still. "Sorry. Why?"

"It's important."

When he made no sign of answering, the king said, "Lad, this is no time to play coy."

"I'm not playing anything. That mark is just a symbol I made up," Greydal answered. Why were they so interested in the image on his axe? King Marcos nodded at Roan. The woman came over to Greydal and crouched beside him, putting a hand on his shoulder.

"Little warrior," she soothed, "I know you're tired and afraid, but we're here to help, I promise."

He looked into her shadowed eyes. They seemed to draw in the darkness around her. After an uncomfortable silence, he answered, "I have questions, too." Roan turned and nodded at King Marcos.

The king replied, "Aye, lad, we may be able to answer them. Here, let the mark rest for now. Tell us something else. Where are you from?"

Greydal clenched his jaw. "I'm sorry. I don't know either of you. Do you know about the things that did this to me? How do I know—" *you aren't with them?* he finished in his thoughts.

They exchanged glances, and Roan said, "Yes, we saw the Friars. Their corpses tumbled in the foam upriver from where we found you. I can assure you we have no love for the mendicants of the Wyrm."

Her words meant nothing to him. He fidgeted for several breaths before admitting to himself they were at an impasse. A gamble then, on the two's trustworthiness. "Alright, I'll tell you what I know." Then he hurried to add, "But you need to do the same in return."

King Marcos nodded. "Aye, we can do that. You go first."

"Wait, why do I have to go first?"

King Marcos grinned. "You are in *my* court. So, it is my prerogative to do as I like. Therefore, you start."

Greydal looked into the man's eyes. Alright, if this king wanted to know, he would tell him. But he wouldn't give the man everything.

King Marcos read his thoughts. He said, "Be forthcoming, be honest. I can see your eyes, lad. You want to hold back information to keep yourself safe... or to have something to bargain with. But trust you me, I can sniff out lies like a hound."

Greydal's face flushed in response.

"Now, start."

Greydal looked at Roan, who stared at him. She would be of no help. He took a deep breath and tasted the smoke from the fire. The scent of the fir trees mingled, introducing a richness. He put a hand on his wasted leg and cleared his throat.

He asked, "Can I have some water? This will take a bit." Marcos nodded, and Roan crouched next to Greydal and handed him a canteen. He took a swig and began.

He told the two nearly everything he knew. He told them about Harlow Valley, about his father's crimes, even why he was called Greydal Alone. King Marcos was interested in what he had to say about the sheriff's remarks at the trial.

"And this Calahurst, he never said anything else about the things your da' was hiding?"

Greydal shook his head but frowned.

King Marcos saw his expression and said, "What is it, lad?"

"I'm not— It's just that, I haven't gotten to the attack yet, but the sheriff was involved in an assault on my village. Before, the man had seemed dedicated, fanatically so, to protecting us. Even at my trial. So, why would he turn traitor against Harlow?"

"Keep spinning us your story. Something tells me I might have an answer. Was the sheriff born in your village?"

Greydal replied, "No one ever told me for certain, but I'm positive he was one of a handful of outsiders like my father and me." Marcos nodded as if he had expected the response.

After this interruption, Greydal went on to explain the events just after the trial. He spoke of the Calf-Ripper and what he knew of the creature. He told the two how pieces of children had been found high in the treetops surrounding the hamlet. "We'd never encountered anything like it."

"Maybe some beastie that rolled into your valley."

"That was the running assumption, I think. Maybe it's tied to the attack on the village I'm coming to...but I'm not so sure."

Roan spoke up. "Why is that?"

Greydal shrugged. He didn't know how to phrase his suspicion without sounding unhinged. "I just...have this sense that whatever the Ripper is, it was after me somehow, or maybe watching me. It tore the head off a bird I met and left the body for me to find, I think. Also, boys from the village attacked me one night. Marston, Erl, and one other.

"It may be a coincidence, but the Ripper killed Erl, and he wasn't a child like the rest. But as a counterpoint," Greydal cleared his throat, "I didn't know the children who were taken, so I'm not sure what the truth is."

Neither Roan nor Marcos offered any immediate explanation, so he continued his story. He told them about the Grime family going missing, his father's execution, the fire, Alom's death. When he got to the part about killing the sheriff, Roan interjected, "You see, King Marcos? A slayer of monsters *and* men."

Greydal didn't feel like a slayer. He had gotten lucky both times and still lost his leg. He shook his head and explained, "It was the axe. Whatever it is, it cuts like magick."

The king laughed and replied, "It does at that, lad. But yours was the hand what swung the thing. Please, finish your tale."

It took an hour, but Greydal told them the last bit. The only part he left out was his dream inside the house at the edge of the pit. Nevertheless, Roan was entranced. The firelight swam in her eyes as she murmured, "You escaped the Friars, not once, but twice. Impressive."

"Why Friars? Are they monks of some kind?"

King Marcos stroked his beard and said, "Of a sort. Let me fill some of the gaps in your story. You said you didn't know why your Calahurst would turn on the village. I think I do. It ties in with the things your da' was keeping and the mark on your axe."

"The mark. You both recognize it." It wasn't a question.

The king shook his head as if denying the claim. Then he said, "We do. It's a dangerous thing to be displaying in the open like you were."

Greydal paled. "I was a kid," he said. Roan raised an eyebrow. "It's just something I made up," he insisted.

The king twirled a finger in a lock of his beard. He glanced at Roan and appeared to reach a decision. His voice was grave as he said, "No, it is not. The fact you unknowingly had it on your weapon terrifies me."

Greydal sensed a great mouth, invisible but imminent, threatening to swallow him and the rest of the forest.

The feeling burst when King Marcos said, "Can you tell me one more, trivial thing? I want to hear what lore you keep about the Mansions."

The shift in topic took Greydal aback. After a moment, he said, "Well, I know of them. We call them the Mansions of the Dawn, where the Bishop went to live after he crafted the sky." Greydal saw both King Marcos and Roan waited for him to continue, so he added, "The Bishop was supposed to have left the Legate behind to guard access. That way, only the righteous dead can enter."

Marcos nodded. "Thank you, lad. And this Bishop and his Legate, would you call them gods?"

Greydal tilted his head. "If they're real, then they fit the concept as much as anything. I don't think I believe in them necessarily."

Roan murmured, "Oh, little warrior." She sounded amused.

Marcos picked up Greydal's axe and held it aloft. "This symbol represents something like a god, such as your Bishop, but it is much older than him. It predates our people, maybe all people, everywhere." Marcos got close to Greydal. The man dwarfed him. The forest was quiet as the giant spoke, "It is very, very dangerous to be associated with this thing."

Greydal connected the dots. He asked, "Is this god of yours called the Interloper?"

The old king replied, "When I was a lad, my da' called it Old Man Moonlight, for night's its time. Others may call it different. The Interloper is a name, same as any word. It tries to describe something in the world. Yet, the thing behind this symbol is not like a tree, or a person."

"What is it?" Greydal's voice was hollow. A new wind stalked through the trees, a school of invisible, whispering animals spilling their bizarre secrets into the night air. That odd thought blew through his mind as he noticed he could only just glimpse Roan's face now out of the corner of his vision. Her eyes bored into his head, and her pupils seemed too large. When had the forest gotten so dark?

King Marcos took a breath. His eyes were jewels in the light of the fire. He put a heavy hand on Greydal's good knee and said, "If you went an infinite distance in one direction, what would happen if you went one step further?"

Greydal blinked and shook his head, replying, "I-I don't know."

King Marcos nodded and said, "Alright. Instead, say you lived in something flat. Like a drawing. How would an *un-flat* thing, perhaps a child's ball, appear to you if it touched you?" Greydal made to reply, and the king interrupted him, "Take your time, think about it."

He paused and did as King Marcos asked. After a time, he answered, "I don't know, a dot... a point? I wouldn't be able to interact with the whole of it, only the part that touched me."

"Exactly. *That* is the Interloper."

"I don't understand."

"I know you don't, lad. Your brain isn't tuned for it. All of us fail in the exact same way when interacting with the things truly bigger than us."

"Okay. So, what's your point?"

"Lad, the *point* is we make symbols, like the one on your axe. They act as a kind of shorthand. In your case, it signifies you're part of something larger."

The wind kicked up embers from the fire, and Greydal's eyes bulged. "Toshi. Dammit!" King Marcos sat back and eyed him. He could see the king's curiosity, so he elaborated, "When my friend and I were younger, we'd pass each other notes written on parchment. I wanted to be secretive to add an air of intrigue, so I always signed my name with that symbol. Jon told the sheriff during my trial that Toshi and I were friends, and was clearly worried I'd rub off on him somehow." His thoughts raced.

King Marcos looked bemused. "Aye, that might do it, lad."

Greydal continued, "Someone broke the back window of their cottage, but they would have opened the front door for the sheriff. Jon loved him. If Calahurst found that symbol in the house, like on Toshi's papers, there's no telling what he would have done. Calahurst was smart, and I doubt he would have thought Jon was involved, but—" Greydal slowed, "the windchimes."

Roan piped up, "Windchimes?"

"The Friars—" Greydal's breath had deserted him, but his mind blazed. It was *his* fault. Toshi's father and the sheriff were both right. He *was* dangerous.

Marcos locked his fingers together and leaned back. "Greydal, my lad. Here's what I believe. Your father, for reasons unknown to us here," his eyes flicked to Roan before returning, "kept items. Items relating to things which the wise counsel your village considered *fearsome*. At least one of those objects was connected to my grand-da's Old Man Moonlight. That was enough for the Red Faith to burn your village and come after anyone associated."

That surprised Greydal. "What's the faith got to do with it?"

He heard Roan laugh. "Oh, little warrior, everything."

"Know this, lad, the one you call the Bishop has a grievance against that mark. Those terrors that attacked you, the Friars? They're the shock troops, if you like. They don't show up ever, unless there is something that needs dying." King Marcos stood. "You're lucky to be alive."

Roan leaned in and asked, "Have you ever heard tell of the House of Petals?" Greydal shook his head. She grinned. "The Friars are why."

NOCTURNE

They huddled together in the dark of the wagon like thieves. King Marcos had dismissed them, ordering Roan to help him back inside. She lit a candle, which did much to illuminate the shadowy interior. The fading smell of smoke filled Greydal's nose as they sat close together, Roan on the ground and him on the stretcher.

"Thanks for the shift, by the way."

She smirked at him. "I'm glad my clothes fit you."

He asked her to show him some of the objects littering the interior, including an old, handheld mirror, not mentioning the book he had spied earlier. Roan held up the mirror so Greydal could see and angled the candle to provide light. The glass showed a stranger. He reached a hand up to his face, and his copy did the same.

"I look haunted."

Roan giggled and replied, "What makes you think you aren't?"

His fingers traced the curvature of his jaw and chin. The blue of his eyes was stark against his hollowed-out face, and he muttered to himself, "How much weight did I lose?"

"Including the leg?" She placed a hand on his shoulder and added, "Look on the bright side, it brings out the stubble poking through that rosy skin of yours." Greydal smiled. His skin used to be something approaching pink, but now he was a flushed specter.

Greydal surprised himself when tears swelled at the corners of his eyes. He wiped them away as Roan gazed at him. She whispered, "I'm sorry about Tier." The girl looked as though she meant the words. Then she sat back. "You've conquered a lot, little warrior," she assured him. After a beat, she added, "Tell me about him. Not his death. Tell me who he was."

Greydal took a shaky breath. The mutterings of the wind as it rattled the great boughs filtered in through the closed door, and he closed his eyes saying, "He was tall and strong. He loved to tell stories, re-tell them, and his eyes were warm and brown. He always smelled like leaves, and his skin was the color of Alom's coffee when he put milk in it."

"He sounds human," Roan said, "not tulka."

Greydal nodded. "He was human, same as you," he confirmed.

For several breaths, she said nothing. Then she spoke, "How is it that Tier came to be your father, then?"

"The same way King Marcos came to be yours, I imagine."

That caused her to laugh. It reverberated in the cramped space of the wagon.

"You're clever. You try to pretend you're unassuming, but you're not." She didn't sound angry. He shrugged. He didn't feel very clever.

"You're a mystery to me. So, here is what I propose. I ask you a question, you answer it. In return, you can ask me one, and I will answer it. Is that fair?"

He sat up from his side position on the stretcher. "That's fair," he confirmed. In the dark, with only the candle to illuminate the two, Greydal felt as though they were the only people in the four corners of existence.

She asked him, "What are those ash-colored marks on your neck and chest?" This caused him to blanch as her impish grin return. She explained, "I've wanted to know since I first saw you sprawled on the riverbank. King Marcos knows, I think, but he won't tell me."

He lowered his head. "I'll be honest. I've never met anyone who didn't know what my marks were."

"Hmm, you're from some valley in the hills I've never heard of, though. Is it so surprising I wouldn't recognize them?"

He shrugged and dove into the telling before his emotions caught up. He told her about the wasted land to the east of his village, that forever stretch of moistureless badlands where the birds went to die. "By the time I was very young, the village had written off the whole place because of the lives lost to it. Explorers didn't always return, see? But when I was eight years old, a thief escaped the town barracks, our jail. Instead of fleeing to the forests, he climbed the east wall and ran into the dust. A month later, he returned, dying."

Greydal took a breath and wiped a tear from his cheek. He looked at Roan and continued, "No one knew how he had stayed alive for so long since there wasn't supposed to be any vegetation or wildlife in that direction. He was covered in gray scarring on his face and hands."

The wagon was quiet. He didn't want to talk about the Ague anymore and thought about ending his story. Yet, he saw how his tale had already transfixed Roan. He had to finish it. His hand flexed as he spoke, "The thief died. Two weeks later, people started getting sick. It spread like a fire amongst the young and the elderly." He glanced up and stared into the girl's dark eyes. "Of the one hundred and twelve people we know who got it," he continued, "one hundred and eleven died. The corpses didn't look like people anymore."

"Terrible." Her voice was heavy, but she didn't sound aghast.

After a moment, he added, "I'm surprised Marcos recognized it. I know there were some of the afflicted who fled the village and sought places like the monastery for divine help." A flash of his father fiercely gripping Greydal's hand broke into his mind's eye.

He cleared his throat again and tried to master his voice. "He— Tier tried everything when I was in the throes of the Ague: potions, herbs, religion. There were these vines that would reach across the road on moonlit nights. Tier made me swallow a concoction from their squeezings. It tasted like poison," he chuckled. "Maybe one of his methods worked. I recovered if you can call it that."

"How do you mean?"

"I was bedridden for months. Everything ached, and I almost couldn't move. It was as though I had to relearn how to use my body. When I woke up on your stretcher, it was like I was back there, a child again."

"And those marks, this illness put them on your skin?" she asked.

Greydal pointed to the ash-colored scarring, which crept up his neck towards his jaw. He answered, "The Ague's reminders. So people would know how I survived while their children and parents didn't." Greydal lowered his hand to smear a wet spot from his cheeks. "That boy Marston, from my story? His younger sister was one. It's part of why he hated me...but he was born a shit, so who knows?" He tried to smile.

Roan was silent for a moment, and then clapped softly. "Curious tale. Maybe our king ran across one of your sick. I doubt he visited your valley."

The Ague spared many of those who lived outside the village—at least those who rarely entered town, Greydal knew. He wondered how they fared now, with the valley scorched and monsters roaming the hills. "I hope he never does."

Roan uncrossed her legs. "Now, it's your turn. Ask me anything."

Greydal looked at her in the flickering dimness. He ignored the question that rose in his mind and instead said, "Alright, why does Marcos call himself a king?"

Roan raised an eyebrow at his question. "Because he is one, you doubter. His adoptive father is the late King Aloysius Relk the Second. By all rights, Marcos is the heir to the drift kingdom, Abyddion."

Greydal didn't know what any of her mouthful meant. "Drift kingdom? Is that like a transplant?"

She clarified, "Things carried over from elsewhere, you mean?" Greydal nodded, and she said, "Then yes, if transplants are what you call them, though King Marcos says almost everything you'll ever encounter here is a *transplant* of some sort." Greydal inclined his head. Tier had said something similar, long ago.

"If he's a king, does that make you a princess?"

Her eyes glinted in the dark. "Greydal, I love the way your mind works. The world is lucky I have no interest in being the female heir to an orphaned kingdom. Oh, how I would have my *way* with the handsome guards who were sworn to protect my life." She put a finger to her chin. Seeing Greydal's expression, she laughed and chimed, "Of course, I'm pulling your leg." She patted his remaining foot and added, "Guards are notoriously boring."

Then she held up the candle and blew it out. Darkness filled the air. Greydal waited for her to open the door of the wagon and leave, before he realized she wasn't going to.

*** *** ***

They continued along the westward track for another week. When asked where they were headed, Marcos and his daughter offered only vague answers. Under normal circumstances, Greydal would have put up more of a fuss, but these were anything but normal circumstances. It seemed the removal of his leg had removed his volition. He was tired, though glad to be alive and well-fed.

King Marcos had fashioned Greydal a crutch from a shaved branch, but promised to find him something better. Even with the branch, Greydal found it awkward to try and traverse any distance with only the one leg. When he was thirteen, he had broken his foot and used a crutch then, but that had been simpler, as each half of his body had weighed the same, and he had been able to use his broken foot to catch himself when he was close to falling. Now, he grappled poorly with his own lopsidedness.

For most of the ensuing journey, Greydal sat in the back of the wagon, doors open, as it was pulled by Agatha, a type of beast Roan called a she-bull. Roan walked behind the wagon to talk to Greydal, and sometimes rode inside with him as King Marcos invariably strode ahead, pulling at Agatha when the animal decided it was time to rest or graze. When they stopped to eat or gather water, Marcos and Roan forced him to exit the wagon and made him practice walking with the crutch or balancing on his left leg. He worked to not allow despair or self-pity keep him from earnestly trying at the exercises, though he felt foolish.

The girl pelted him with questions. Once, she asked him what his children's family name would be since his people reserved Alone for the first of a line. He told her, "They'd take my first name as their last. So, Marcos Greydal, if you like." That seemed to tickle her. He asked her where they were going yet again.

"You'll learn."

Each night, they sat around a makeshift fire of stone and dry wood. King Marcos would sing, his gruff baritone echoing from the surrounding trees. It was as though some spirit of the wood welcomed them to sit down and partake in the warmth of the campfire. Greydal didn't understand the words to any of the king's songs, but was nevertheless moved. Marcos sang with an abandon that made him like the giant tulka, in spite of the man's strangeness. In the firelight, the king's skin shone red, and he looked like he had been born from the flames, an elemental hero of old.

After one song, Greydal asked, "What did that lay mean, King?" Greydal was still unsure how he was to address the man. Marcos didn't appear to mind.

He belted, "It's a song my grand-da' taught me as a young lad. He was a king, too. I never knew what to call him," he said as if he had read Greydal's thoughts. The king continued, "Granda' or My Liege? You see the trouble? No one ever tells you things like that. One is expected simply to know." He looked at Greydal.

The tattoos around King Marcos' eyes shined, and Greydal heard Agatha low. They had tied the she-bull to a tree so large, he couldn't glimpse any part of the animal when she circled behind the trunk. They had used quite a bit of rope.

"The song was about the Loaming Ocean, a sea greater than any other body of water. The sailors of that time would test their mettle against the Loaming's towering waves and groping deni- zens. Many were lost, year over year, but the survivors were held up in their glory and given the command of wondrous vessels, made of glass and wood and gold."

A gust of wind made Greydal's skin prick against the cool air. "It sounds incredible. Where is the Loaming? I've never seen any- thing larger than the river you pulled me out of."

Marcos looked sad as he sighed, "Far from here, lad. It belongs to another time and place."

Roan stood and wandered towards Agatha, whom Greydal heard straining against her tether. He watched her go. Then he turned to the king and mustered his courage.

After several anxious moments, he spoke. "I know you're a Kludde. You've been to my village. Does Roan know?"

King Marcos eyed him. "I wondered when you would ask. Though that was more of a telling. But you're wrong, lad, I'm no Kludde."

"Don't lie. I remember you. You were the one who peeked into the village barracks that night, during the Kludde's assault. How did you get past the south gate?"

"I climbed down your cliff."

Roan petted Agatha and tried to soothe her as the she-bull strained against her restraints. The Pneuma, spirits risen from the soil of the Barrens, agitated the kindly beast with their mere presence. "Shhh, girl. They're only visiting." Agatha pushed her massive head against Roan's chest. "Be brave."

She ran a hand through Agatha's mane. Roan rebuffed a visitant, which bled from the bushes.

"Leave my lady alone, all of you," she whispered. Roan watched the specters retreat into the shadows.

She looked over her shoulder at the two tulka sitting at the flames. Greydal appeared as a child next to her father. Her eyes narrowed. The wind carried their voices away from her, but she could see Greydal was angry. She watched the boy stumble to a standing position and limp away from the fire, wandering into the surrounding obscurity the trees provided.

She sighed and told Agatha, "I'm sorry, girl, I've got to go save the day." Agatha nodded. When Roan reached the campfire, she raised an expectant eyebrow at her father. King Marcos smiled guiltily and shrugged. "You're full foul," she said and added, "What did you say to him?"

Her father replied, "We spoke of some of my covert activity for the kith. Nothing more."

She groaned and walked in the direction she had seen Greydal limp. At least he wouldn't get far on that leg of his.

She wove through the trees and spotted him. The boy stood where a line of firs terminated. She blinked. Was that...? No, there was no one with him. Roan approached. The sound of her feet crunching the grounded needles and twigs announced her.

"What are these?" Greydal looked over a vast drop off, where the ground vanished, a blackened void replacing it.

Roan put a hand on his shoulder and replied, "Chasms. There are spots where the ground isn't stable, and it all just...falls away."

Greydal turned and looked at her. For a moment, he fought with himself. Should he tell her what he knew of her father? He stifled the urge. Instead, he said, "What causes them?" She looked at him strangely, and he suspected she noted his guile.

She replied, "I'm not sure. The world is old. It's bound to come apart in places." He didn't reply, and she told him, "Come on, it's hazardous out here in the dark." She pulled at his elbow, but he shook his head.

He asked, "The Bishop. Who is he?"

She answered, "You want to know about him? Now?"

Greydal nodded.

"Well, my people, the Sophites, don't know him by that name. Sorcerer, Demiurge, Wyrm," she counted the names off her fingers. "Those are the titles we know."

There was that word again. "Worm? Like those wriggly bugs born in mud?"

"No, lovely. Wyrm, like serpent or dragon. He is the great jailor."

Greydal didn't know what that meant. He asked, "What about the Legate?"

She shrugged and said, "I doubt he's a separate person. King Marcos doesn't think the Wyrm would suffer a rival. Many cultures multiply or contract their gods if you give them long enough." Greydal considered that as the girl pulled his elbow again, and he allowed her to lead him to camp. As they returned, he looked at the spot where the chasm had yawned. *Do all these pits lead to the same place?* What a strange thought.

That night, as the fire waned, Greydal tried to piece the story together. According to the two with which he traveled, someone in charge of the Red Faith didn't want other ideas in the mix. That was believable. So had the sheriff's unidentified visitor been one of that ilk, someone Calahurst had known before he came to reside in the valley? Greydal thought that tracked.

He knew the sheriff and the tulka had spoken, based on what Alom said. Presumably together, they decided Calahurst needed to search for further corruption. The visitor must have left then, and the sheriff? That would have signified the start of his investigation. Jon Grime's son was a logical first stop in the search. The sheriff must have found some of the notes Greydal had written to Toshi. At least a few of them would have had his mark on them, the one supposed to be the Interloper's. *There* was the sheriff's proof. But why had he done away with the Grime family? That was a gap Greydal couldn't fill.

Regardless, Calahurst knew danger lurked in the hamlet and needed to be eradicated. Here, the sheriff would have encountered a problem. It was doubtful he could have convinced Maizy and Crawl to re-try Greydal, when the damning notes didn't have a name on them. Is that why the Red Faith sent those creatures, the Friars?

But how had the creatures arrived at the valley so quickly? Another mystery. There had been one of the creatures at Toshi's home when Greydal visited, the thing in wait like an alloy spring-trap patient for its mouse. The thought paled him. How close had he come, unknowingly? Had it been made to hide there (closet? side room?) for him? If so, why not his barracks instead? But then he recalled the jingling, sloshing corpse outside his barracks the night of the fire...

Something went wrong that night. Alom had said the attackers were going after tulka, not just Greydal. Had the Friars not understood who they were to kill? Or had they simply broken with the sheriff and begun to rampage? Somehow, he didn't think the creatures would have needed much prodding in that direction.

"He looks lost in thought, doesn't he, King Marcos?"

Greydal glanced up to see Roan's black eyes shining in the firelight as she smiled down at him. *No, they aren't black,* he told himself. Her eyes were dark brown.

EMPEROR

On the morning of the day they were to turn south, Greydal spotted the owls. He leaned against Agatha and petted her with the brush Roan loaned him. As he retrieved a tick from the animal's thick fur, he murmured, "Careful. These things carry sickness, and we wouldn't want to lose you. You pull the wagon." Agatha grunted.

He pocketed the brush and gracelessly hopped over the ropes, making to untie them from the trunk of the old fir to which they were attached. His heart missed a beat when he caught movement behind the trees to the north. Past the maze of trunks and filtered sunlight, a wall moved.

"Roan!"

They were huge. He couldn't tell from the distance if furry scales or some sort of feathers covered the beings. It was as if the herd had sprung directly from a giant's fancy, swaying in the breeze and resplendent in their lush coloring. Behind his right shoulder, Roan giggled.

She whispered, "I was wondering if we'd catch a glimpse before leaving the Barrens. Say hello to this land's namesake."

"Those? Where I'm from, owls are...birds."

"King Marcos. He gave them their title as a boy when he stayed amongst their kind for a season. Beautiful, aren't they?"

After hearing the goliaths named, Greydal could identify a vague similarity. They sported massive eyes and had shiny mouths shaped like beaks, but the resemblance faded beyond that. The creatures had long white beards as old men sometimes do, and stood on four powerful, digitigrade legs from which spines or feathers stuck like arrows. Even stranger, they were thin in frame like some small stream-inhabiting fish Greydal had occasionally seen. One turned its body in his direction, and the creature became a fraction of its previous width.

"He *lived* with them?"

"Only for a short time as he tells it. Earned their trust, and they taught him some very odd things indeed. Newborn secrets that aren't true...yet." She smirked, and then repeated, "As he tells it."

"Are they dangerous?"

Roan patted his shoulder. "Not usually. Scared, little warrior?"

Greydal cleared his throat and told her, "I've never— They're almost...graceful." As he watched, one reached its head towards the needles of a nearby tree. An iridescent neck uncoiled from the tuft of material near the owl's shoulders. "They *are* beautiful," he allowed after a breath.

"You should see them when they get riled. They can navigate the trunks better than dancers."

"I'd rather not, thanks. Maybe from a distance."

"Take a good look now. You're not likely to spot any more where we're headed," she told him.

Greydal shifted his crutch and turned to focus on her. "You haven't told me where that is," he said.

The girl nodded and stated plainly, "Wouldn't want to spoil the surprise."

She whirled and left him.

He watched her stride away, gloomy dress muted in the morning sun. Greydal thought again about the other night, the one in the wagon. After, he had asked her how old she was. She replied she didn't know. She had seen at least two hundred new moons so, at minimum, she would be seventeen years old.

Greydal had nodded and said, "We count our dead moons on staves of wood. I should be coming up on my seventeenth year soon." She had laughed at that, he remembered.

He turned to Agatha and finished untying her. "Don't worry, girl. If the owls come this way, I'm sure you're faster than me." She poked him with her thick nose. "C'mon, I need to get you hitched to the wagon."

He pulled her ropes and was thankful Agatha complied as he hobbled towards the camp's center. He tied Agatha to the wooden hooks the way King Marcos showed him and patted her head.

"Thanks for not taking advantage and dragging me through the pines." Thinking for a moment, he added, "Do they unnerve you? The pines, I mean, not the owls." She didn't answer, and he rubbed a hand on her nose before leaving to climb onto the wagon, setting himself with his good leg hanging from the back so he could watch the landscape change while they traveled for the day.

Soon, Marcos tugged on Agatha's reins, and they moved. Greydal peered to his left through the trees and gave the owls a final look. They didn't appear to consider him in the slightest.

*** *** ***

Hours later, they reached a fork in the trail as the Barrens began to recede. The trees near the fork were mere shades of their taller cousins, and the ground was darker with more prevalent low vegetation. At this fork, they stopped so King Marcos could kill a large hare his daughter had spotted. Marcos walked to the rear of the wagon and produced a leather sling from near where Greydal sat. The man placed a small rock in its pouch and flicked his wrist. Greydal heard a sharp cry. Roan left, and then shortly returned, carrying the animal in a bloody arm.

"Watch him for me, will you?" she huffed and laid the dead hare down beside Greydal before hopping in the wagon herself. Behind him, he heard a drawer open, and then the girl returned with a small parcel. She opened the item, which proved to be a tightly bundled collection of waxy parchment. Roan retrieved the dead hare from where she had set it and wrapped it tightly.

"Are we eating that?" Greydal asked.

"*We* aren't."

With that cryptic remark, she descended to the ground with her moist parcel, and from the ensuing sounds, stowed it somewhere on (or perhaps beneath) the wagon's exterior. Afterwards, they made to continue down the path. However, they hadn't gone twenty feet before Greydal uttered a sharp cry, almost like the hare's.

He had spotted a pinkish body, stripped nude and hanging from a nearby tree. Material that might have at one time been rope wove about the man's neck and arms, holding him below one sturdy-looking branch. For nothing, perhaps, as the body couldn't have weighed much at all. It was bisected, missing everything below the navel.

The wagon halted as Greydal's eyes roved the sweaty contours of the tree's inhabitant. He searched for signs of animal attack, but there were none to be found, only a twisting, black tattoo, covered in methodical lacerations which greatly spoiled its form. These wounds were replicated elsewhere with obvious care, maybe of a sort implying a post-mortem rite or ordained degradation. In spite of the display, Greydal was relieved as the wounds indicated a deranged, but sapient source. As he continued to gaze wide-eyed at the suspended torso, Roan and King Marcos appeared from around the wagon. Greydal pointed at the tree's inhabitant.

"Ah," King Marcos whispered, "you've met the hanged man."

"You know him?"

"We do," Roan confirmed. "He's been a fixture since before I came to these woods. He was present when King Marcos first explored this place before I was born. Isn't that right, father?"

"Aye, he's not always in the same spot, so one never knows when a reunion might occur." Marcos replied.

Greydal glanced up at the figure. The tulka's pink skin looked bright, surely as bright as the day the man had died. That was the most unique thing about his race, Greydal thought. *No rotting.* Tulka seemed to be alone in the world in that respect. "Who put him up there?" he asked, ignoring Marcos' comment. He eyed the sigils carved into the tree, which held the corpse.

"Who knows, lad? Even *I* don't recognize that language. Maybe he was a villain."

"And his face?" Greydal asked. The dead tulka's skull was flayed, exposing a hidden countenance of bleached bone.

"Unnerving, isn't it?"

"Shouldn't we take him down?"

Roan replied first, "You can't read the writing, and you would tamper still? Tsk, tsk, tsk."

King Marcos patted him on the shoulder and said, "Let's keep moving. Our man can stay amongst the pine needles."

As if on cue, a lone branch, barely more than a twig, fell to the ground. It landed in front of him and he looked at it. The needles stuck out at even angles, three on one side, two on the other— unless the broken one was meant to be one as well. It was just a piece of foliage, but Greydal thought it looked like a symbol of some kind. Or message. For whom, he couldn't say.

Agatha started moving, and he edged deeper into the wagon and stared at the cadaver until it disappeared a minute later. Despite the distance, Greydal could see the tulka's body in his mind, as if it now dwelt there instead of on the tree. Trying to evade the mental intrusion, Greydal used the next hour to half-heartedly meditate, and then replace the bandages and ointment on his leg, though he hated the odor of the mossy smear Roan had provided.

The previous day, he had pulled off the other bandage on his ear because he was sick of its scent wafting to his nose. The cut disgusted him, though Roan had helped him clean the thing.

"It's healing," she had assured him. "You may have a little notch there, though."

As he fixed the bandage below his knee, he tried to remember as many people from the village as he could. How many corpses had he seen that he could confidently identify? Not as many as he should have been able to, he realized to his shame. But the ones who mattered to him were all dead, weren't they? He had held Alom as the man bled out, the sheriff had shot down Ida, and Toshi had gone missing. And Tier...

Greydal thought about his father, about the weak look on the man's face when the spears entered him.

After a while, Greydal laid down and thought about not much at all.

*** *** ***

By evening, the track they traveled disappeared, and an indentation in the unsteady ground replaced it. Greydal couldn't guess what line they now followed as it looked almost like a natural part of the landscape, not something people made. Greydal watched the trees, and eventually the greenery itself, vanish over the course of the next several hours. By the end, the wagon moved along a rocky, windswept plain, and the last of the trees trailed falteringly behind. There were now low hills to the west and south, but Greydal couldn't identify any other distinguishing features of this new landscape.

He called out to Roan, "What is this place? We've left the Barrens, haven't we?"

Roan slowed so she could walk near the back of the wagon. She explained, "It's not the place we're ultimately headed, but right now, we're approaching the eastern edge of Abyddion."

That surprised him. "Huh. I had no idea it'd be so close. I got the sense it was far off somehow."

"In some ways it is. It's been a long, long time since King Marcos has been this way. Traditionally when we come south, we avoid this area and keep to the Barrens."

He eyed her. "Why not avoid it now?"

She smiled, but Greydal thought she looked gloomy. She sighed, "We can't go around it."

Hearing Tier's words caused his throat to close. He told her, "My father used to say something similar. It was like a song." Greydal recited it for her: "Can't go *around* it. Can't go *under* it. Can't go *over* it. Gotta go *through* it."

Roan nodded. "How sweet. Wise words, for most occasions."

"He'd hit me with that first line any time I tried to avoid chores or some other difficulty," Greydal said.

Roan gestured to the rocky expanse. "It's much the same here. There's somewhere we must go, and this is the best way."

He replied, "You avoid the west and the east. How do you get anywhere?"

"Think of me...and King Marcos' travels as a figure eight, going from north to south. The Owl Barrens are the center. Wherever you came from lies to the right of the Owl Barrens, and Abyddion lies to its left." She drew it in the air with her finger. "Also, we could always go around Abyddion on its northwest side if we needed to. Although, this time, we had to avoid the main southern road. Hence us finding you."

"What's west of Abyddion, then?"

"Maybe you'll find out." She leaned into the wagon and kissed him before disappearing around the side.

Greydal sat in silence for a time, a warmth spreading over his cheeks and between his legs. Then he resumed his watch of the landscape. To his surprise, they didn't stop to camp when twilight ended and the dark of the night suffused the expanse they roamed. The sky had become invisible behind the ponderous bodies wandering through the darkness far above the wagon. Under those clouds (and they *must* be clouds) the trio approached the hills. These were the ones he had initially spotted to the south, now rearing before them.

The wagon climbed the slow incline, and he was granted a view of far-off structures to the west. He stilled himself against the rumbling wagon and stared. Could that be Abyddion? It was massive. The outline of the distant buildings showed only barely against the charred sky. He tried to identify signs of life, but the whole of it was dark. If anyone lived there, they didn't light fires at night.

They succeeded in surmounting the hills. The new terrain Greydal and his companions traveled was more featureless than the rocky plain before. This space reminded him in some ways of the area around the Rings in the valley. Although, where that had been a dry deadness, here, the ground was succulent and alive, if that was possible. He imagined himself carted over the ebon skin of a colossus, like in the tale of Jack from the valley's theatre stage. The sensation was unnerving, but something about the plain was comforting to Greydal. It was cozy, and in some way he couldn't define, he sense he belonged to the black sand pulsing beneath the wagon.

Greydal smelled the rain before he saw it. He waited for several minutes, and then watched the ponderous bodies from before disgorging an incredible downpour. Roan and King Marcos were forced to stop and unlatch a folded tent from beneath the wagon. It expanded like magick, and a great tarp covered them both. Greydal looked around the side, where Roan sprinkled an unidentified material on the ground. "This will keep us dry as we sleep and prevent our wagon from sinking into the sand and dirt," she explained. "Here, let me put some on the bottom of your crutch."

Greydal slid out of the wagon and leaned on her as he handed it over. "Thank you. Now, take this." She passed him the jar she was holding and added. "Rub a small amount on the wheels of the wagon where you can. Don't worry if you can't get to all of it."

He took the jar from her and limped towards the far side of the wagon. To his astonishment, his crutch didn't sink into the soft ground. He took a pinch of the powdery material from the jar and rubbed it between his fingers, examining it. Both his index finger and thumb lost most of their feeling. He then did as Roan asked, and used about a fourth of the jar to lightly coat the wagon's four wheels in the substance.

"Want some for your hooves?" he asked Agatha when he neared her. She wouldn't lift her legs to let him apply the substance, and he didn't feel confident bending to try and lift them. "Suit yourself," he told the she-bull.

He heard Roan speaking to King Marcos. "I told you," she said.

"That you did, lass. I'm glad you brought the meal, or we'd be sunk." Greydal saw her pat the giant man's shoulder.

"You're lucky I'm here to cluck over you," she teased.

King Marcos let out a belly laugh and boomed, "Oh, I cannot deny it. You're a better daughter than I deserve. I hope I can return the favor soon."

She leaned on him in response and added, "I'm sure we'll find it. The catcher wasn't vague. Once we get closer, I'll check it again."

The king nodded and said, "Good, I'll want as much information as you can stand to give me before I head in." They saw Greydal watching them, and both smiled.

"Greydal, lad! Let me show you how to change the length of ole' Agatha's ropes so she can lie down."

*** *** ***

The rain continued through the night. It cooled the air, which Greydal thought had an almost salty taste. He didn't share this revelation with the others, and instead, spent the beginning of the downpour lying out under the sky. He had earlier removed the pants and short shift Roan had given him and now sprawled, nearly naked on the black ground. The icy wetness sprinkled him, texturing his exposed skin with creeping bumps, and he shivered. He relished the sensation of the sky washing him and felt time stutter, and then collapse as he drifted behind his closed eyes. When he heard the soft crunching of footsteps, he looked up with a start, but it was only Roan. She was nearly as naked as him and scrubbing her hair with a bar of brown soap.

"I suppose we were all becoming a tad musky," she snorted as she caught him watching her.

He nodded in agreement. "It feels good to wash away the road."

She crouched next to him, and he saw a dark shape beyond the camp behind her. "What's your father doing?" he asked. King Marcos was shirtless and sitting away from the camp on his knees. He was motionless.

Roan answered, "He's meditating. It's been a long time since he was this close to home."

"I know meditation. Tier taught it to me for times when I was overwhelmed. I think the last time I successfully used it was just before my trial." Greydal considered mentioning his poor attempt in the wagon but decided against it. He concluded, "I ought to get back into the habit."

Roan held out her hair for the rain. "Tier taught you a lot, from what you've shared. What about your mother?" she asked him.

Greydal allowed the sound of water hitting the sand to answer her. She persisted, "Did she die as well?"

He gave her a sidelong look and replied, "I never had a mother."

She laughed. "That's obviously impossible, my sweet."

"It's true, in a sense."

"King Marcos was right. You *are* coy."

Greydal sighed. "Tier forbade me from discussing it with the village. He came up with a story that he'd found a tulka family slaughtered beyond the valley. I was supposed to be the sole survivor. When I was older, he told me the truth."

That intrigued her. "Mysterious."

He shook his head. "I just had the terrible luck of being Tier's son. He was always complicated."

"We're all complicated in our own way," she answered.

Greydal didn't know how to respond to that. He inhaled and said, "Tier found me, but not in a razed farmstead beyond the valley. He just plain found me." He could tell she didn't understand. The sound of the rain changed his voice as he elaborated, "Tier came from beyond the valley, somewhere, but settled in our village when he had just become a man. Throughout his later life, he left the valley on isolated sojourns, though only a few knew about them."

Behind the girl, Greydal saw her father raise his arms to the sky.

"And on one, he found an infant tulka, is that it?" Roan asked.

Greydal nodded and said, "He wouldn't tell me where, but said that I looked just born. He had to nurse me on razorback's milk."

Roan had a strange expression. He could tell what she was thinking.

"He didn't kidnap me. He's a liar and a killer, but he rescued me," he told her. The girl nodded, though she clearly didn't agree.

When Greydal later recalled that night on the wet sand, he would wonder at two things. First, was Roan's reaction to his story due to her own hidden knowledge, or had she simply not believed him? Second, was it only the rain and darkness that caused them to miss the stranger's approach? It seemed like it, at least at the time.

"Greydal. As I live and breathe."

The voice was cheerful as it was awful. Roan and Greydal whirled towards the camp to find a man, lit as though by a lantern they couldn't see, standing beneath the tent near its edge. His dress was odd. He wore red gloves, which appeared to melt, and a golden suit of armor encased him to the neck, garish next to his unadorned, pink face. A tulka.

Two golden-clad Friars crouched at the man's feet, houndlike. The holes of their helmets dripped something viscous.

Roan was on her feet. "NO! If you hurt him—"

"Roan Hale, daughter of the late Jezebal Hale. Tell your Mabet hello for me, will you? It won't be long."

The man held his red gloves out from under the tent and let the rain wash the color away.

"Tell her, too, your Marcos paid the price for warring against the safety of the world," the man crooned with his horrible voice.

Though Roan was almost naked, terror clothed her, a sinister radiation of power. A wind Greydal didn't feel whipped her hair as she raised her twitching hands towards the tulka. But then the man disappeared. He didn't run or sink into the ground, Greydal just blinked, and the man was gone.

Next to his ear, a phantom voice whispered, *"Another time."*

A pale symbol, like a series of interlinked spirals, carved the air in front of Roan's face. A split second, then it was gone.

A wave, invisible but palpable, exploded from Roan, speeding towards the Friars. Red mucus spattered the area beneath the tent and rent, golden shards peppered the ground. The girl collapsed to her knees. For a breath, Greydal was frozen, shock turning him as cold as the rain. Above, the plummeting slickness lessened somewhat, becoming a tittering pitter-patter. Perhaps some unseen audience enjoyed the devastation, and the rain was its laughter. Greydal took hold of himself and crawled to Roan, making to touch her shoulder, but she pushed his hand away and howled. She then stood and ran towards the other side of the camp.

"Oh, Marcos."

He crawled over to his crutch and raised himself from the ground to hobble after her. He halted, almost slipping in the sand, and about-faced, moving with as much haste as he could muster towards the wagon. He retrieved bandages from his supply, and carried them to where Roan sat crouched over King Marcos' prone form.

"Is he breathing?"

"Oaf! Help me get him under the tent!"

Greydal bent and grabbed the man's shoulders. He tried to lift Marcos to an upright position but couldn't stay balanced with his crutch and fell.

"No, please," Roan pleaded. He got up and tried again, but the man was as substantial as Greydal imagined Agatha to be.

"Can we move the tent?"

Roan shook her head. Rain mingled with the tears pouring down her face. "Not quickly. Marcos, can you hear me? Father? Please!" She held the man's bearded face in her hands. Her hands looks small next to the king's visage. Greydal let his crutch fall and dropped to his knees. He ran his fingers over two oval wounds on Marcos' side. Greydal could tell they went deep.

"Roan, is there anything in that wagon we can use? These bandages aren't what we need."

"Stay here. Put your hands where he's bleeding." She rose, and Greydal followed her commands. She returned with a knife, a satchel, and the dead rabbit in its wax cocoon.

Greydal's hands were slick with the king's blood and the rain.

"What do you need me to do?"

She shook her head and dropped the items she held. "He's dead."

Greydal looked and saw the king's chest was motionless. Beneath them, the sludge of sand and dirt smelled like copper.

It happened again, his heart said. Above, the sky laughed or cried.

CHAPTER

12

VOLITION

They sat back-to-back for the rest of the night, unspeaking. Twice, Greydal nodded off, only for Roan to nudge him awake. Then she slept, and he sat watch over her. The deluge created small islands of moving sand and dirt, which shifted in the murk. The rain ceased before dawn. When Roan stirred, they used Agatha's strength to move the king's body onto a dry patch of ground. They then coated her father's body in a pitch-colored jelly, retrieved from a hidden drawer in the wagon, and covered him in a white shroud stored in the same compartment.

Roan whispered something in a language Greydal didn't understand. Then she asked, "Could you say something?"

He leaned on his crutch and stared at the king's body. Even in death, Marcos looked powerful and hale. "He was...big," Greydal began, "and warm. I don't know why he lost his kingdom or what tragedies he endured. I don't know what designs or plans he left unfinished, but the world is less colorful without him. May he find his kingdom in the far territories." Greydal placed a hand over his heart before letting it fall. That sounded better than he had hoped.

A tear rolled down Roan's cheek, confirming his thought. The girl nodded at him, and then continued to speak in the strange tongue he had heard before. He caught the word *Marcos*, but only that. Soon, she stopped and appeared to come to a decision.

He hadn't glimpsed her holding a fire starter, but after a gesture from Roan, the white shroud ignited, burning with a pale fire. Greydal watched the flame creep across the king's hidden form. After a time, he asked, "How is he burning from within already?" Roan didn't answer, and he let it drop.

They stood in silence as the smoke from the body swirled around them. It reminded him of the village, and he spat. As the morning hurdled towards midday, the king turned to ash, and Greydal and Roan intuited at the same time it was over. They left the diminishing pile of soot and as they strode away, Greydal glimpsing the wind blow the king's ashes north, the direction of the structures he suspected comprised the remnants of Abyddion.

"Come help me switch the ropes on the wagon," Roan told him in a tired voice. He followed her, and they set it up so the back, with its open door, now became the front. They then loaded the tent and the camping items, taking care to avoid patches of ground where chunks of the destroyed Friars had landed the previous night.

As they finished, Greydal approached one of the decaying monsters and looked at the mucus congealing below the thing's helmet. The worms or spines dwelling inside the crimson goop were still, their animating force now absent. "I think these are...corpses," he said after a moment. "I can see a body, old, inside this one's armor." Considering the creature further, he added, "Are the corpses the Friars, or are they this red gunk?"

Roan didn't know and said so. Leaning on his crutch, he stood. He hawked a ball of phlegm on the dead thing and followed her as she entered the wagon. They sat with their legs dangling, and Roan whistled to Agatha saying, "Come on, girl. It's time to leave." The she-bull complied, and they crept southwest.

Clouds covered the sky, but they weren't as dense as the previous night's, though the landscape looked no less alien in the hazy light. Greydal turned to his companion and said, "When Tier died, I blacked out. And then I hallucinated, I think." The wind snatched his voice, and he continued louder, "I just want you to know there's no response too peculiar or ugly. For this, I mean."

After minutes, she spoke, "He wasn't supposed to die."

Greydal nodded. When she didn't say anything else he answered, "That's how I... well I told you about Alom. It was like someone had made a mistake." Roan frowned and shook her head. She replied, "It's not that, not only. He was important."

He opened his mouth to reply but paused, waiting for her to continue. She said, "His people— my people. He was our heart." She put her head in her hands. "Telling them is going to be a trial."

As the gale shook them, Greydal imagined it tried to form words, warning him, maybe. He watched the horizon unfold in increments, all of it flat and dark, even at midday. His own words were a surprise: "I'll tell them with you when you go. I'm guessing they'll need to know how he died. I can speak to that. I'll explain how you saved me, and then after...Well, you're the daughter of a dead king now. I have to think things will become harder." He thought for a moment. "I'm yours."

She stared at him.

"What?"

"Idiot. You barely know me."

"In fairness, that's not really true."

She sighed. "Think deeply about what you're asking. Truly. There may come a day when you want to undo your promise but can't."

"I *want* to help. I owe you, Roan. And your father."

"It sounded nice without you saying you owe me. We didn't aid you to enslave you." She raised her hand to pick apart a knot in her hair, adding, "But my people maintain a...custom, which you might learn about. Your words just now were the first part of it."

"Oh?"

"As we come to understand, so do you. The beginning, a desire. You are ours, we are yours." She recited.

"Well, I don't know what that means. I only said what felt right."

"Or are you a spy? You even used some of the correct words." Despite her evident exhaustion, there was a glimmer in her eyes.

He smiled, but it soon receded. "Not a spy. Maybe more spied on, if anything." His eyes widened when he heard what he had let slip. Roan said nothing, though, only tilting her head. He stuttered, "What I mean is— I..." How to explain it?

Up until now, his musings had been only half-gathered, unassessed. At length, he exposed them in their unfinished state: "Since the fire in the village or maybe just after, I've been different. My thinking has been, at least."

"I imagine it ought to be. Mine would." She saw his look and corrected, "That's not what you mean."

He shook his head. "When Rulf and I got to the long grass west of my valley, I realized something. I was using the word *we*. In my thoughts."

"I don't think I follow."

"I'll give you an example: In the grass, I thought, *Alright, we need to get somewhere safe before Rulf brains us in our sleep.* Does that make sense? I thought it was just a fluke, but I kept doing it. I've stopped now, mostly, but only out of effort."

Greydal searched her face to see if she caught his meaning. She didn't look wary, only curious. He groped for a better explanation. "It's like someone grabbed an older boy and poured him into me, like I'm folded back on myself. That's how it feels. Or maybe I'm a cottage and someone added other rooms without my permission."

The girl patted his back. "You've gone through terrible troubles, and you're changing. Now, you're intertwined with me and my sorrows. Bad luck." She frowned, but her eyes didn't reflect it. "I have to tell you what we're doing. Now that my father is dead, I'll need your help." She pulled her legs into the wagon and turned towards him before putting on a brave face. "But first, we have to talk about the other thing."

"What other thing?"

"Greydal. You know."

He shook his head. "I don't. What are you talking about?"

"That's a lark. You can't tell me you didn't notice it. He had your face."

Greydal folded his arms and didn't reply. She pinched him, and he sighed, looking away as he sent a distant gaze to the pooling shadows which slunk along the landscape. Then he said, "We're both tulka, that's it. He was older, for one. There are plenty of rosy ones. They're not all red or plum-colored. Similar features."

She wasn't convinced. "You can pretend as much as you want, but that was *you*."

He glanced at her. "How is that possible?"

"I haven't the slightest. King Marcos would have known." Her face was grim. "If we complete our task, the one we're approaching, I'll have someone you can talk to. She's old and wise...whereas, I'm only wise."

Greydal smiled, but a disquiet settled on him. "Whether he looked like me or not, I know who that was."

Her eyebrows arched. "How?"

"I've seen it before, that armor. It's the same as what's depicted on every shrine in Harlow Valley. They're all dedicated to the Red Legate."

A gust of wind kicked sand into their faces. Roan digested the information and breathed through her nose. After a beat, she whispered, "So, that was the Wyrm himself."

"Maybe, if they're the same thing," he replied.

The wind almost obscured her next words, "Well, Wyrm or Bishop or Legate, he has to die."

*** *** ***

They stopped sleeping outside. At night, they fed Agatha from the reserves strapped to the top of the wagon and shut themselves within. It was stuffy and cramped, but they were able to fall asleep without waking every few minutes to look for an attacker in gold armor. He glanced at Roan out of the corner of his eye, only just able to perceive her in the dark. On the outside, she looked like any woman he could have met in Harlow Valley, except for her wild black hair. He had watched that hair writhe like snakes when she killed the Friars, though. Greydal recalled his first assumption the owners of the wagon were witches. It occurred to him that he may have been right.

Well, witch or not, he had promised to help her and would if he could. She had told him they approached a place just southwest of Abyddion, a kind of shrine or temple. She would go inside and recover an item—she called it the Allthame. The retrieval of the artifact was why she and King Marcos had initially traveled south from their home and how they happened to encounter Greydal. Accessing the shrine would probably be dangerous. In the faded light, his fingers traced the sign on his axe. He slept with it now, though he wasn't confident he could swing the weapon with the one leg. Could he protect Roan with it? Did she need his protection? Probably not.

Besides, a cripple with an axe was hardly a worthwhile guardian. Not just an axe, he corrected himself. An ancestor weapon, made by the Old Folk themselves, if King Marcos was to be believed. He had cornered the man a week ago and asked after the implement. According to Marcos, it worked via crafty design, technology its source.

"Magick is very real, lad. It's just not in your axe."

Reviewing the conversation with the giant in his mind, he found he missed the man. First Tier, then Alom, and now Marcos. Greydal couldn't escape the notion that, somehow, all three deaths were his fault. He was curious if the Legate would agree.

*** *** ***

Two days later they arrived at the shrine. On the way there, Greydal found time to open the book he had spotted before, *Killer of Witches - Combatting Agents of the Interloper*. He spent an hour poring over it while Roan directed Agatha across the black sands, which undulated under the wagon.

"You won't learn anything in there. Most of it's lies and half-truths," she called to him.

"Do you have any other books about it, the Interloper? Or tales from your father?"

"Sorry, darling."

"Then I'll read this. It might help us."

It was harder than he anticipated. Most of the book used terms that meant nothing to Greydal, like *the enclosure* and *liminal apertures*.

As he read, he told her, "I think this book is for the Legate's missionaries or some other wing of the Red Faith. Granted, I know next to nothing about it as an organization. Either way, it's obviously not for the Friars. I doubt they can read." The back of her head bobbed with the wagon as it bounced over a divot in the ground.

She said, "King Marcos told me that most of what's in there is designed to teach people how to make others afraid and want to turn in their neighbors."

Greydal nodded but didn't respond out loud as he continued to read the book. Through his browsing, he soon discovered the next section of the book was titled *At the Mouth of Trepidation,* and apparently dealt with the supposed nature of the Interloper itself:

> *The curse of the Interloper is that it does not respond to logic or reason. The tools of men turn on their masters, the plans of ages are confounded, the stars themselves change shape. The abyss moves, and we cannot escape it. The liminal apertures were seized and guarded against at great cost while the Bishop, Lord of the Mansions of the Dawn, sacrificed himself through transmigration to allow—*

Greydal stopped reading. The rest of the book's messaging was harder to parse. Eventually, he put it down and returned to the front of the wagon.

As it was, they almost passed the site before Roan spotted it and shouted, calling Agatha to a halt. In the middle of the sandy plain, there crouched a copse of trees a hundred paces to the south. It was incredible they hadn't noticed it on the horizon during their approach.

Greydal surveyed the inky landscape as he hopped from the wagon, clutching his axe and crutch. To the north, there were hills, low clouds pressing them into the ground. The landforms were similar to the ones they had climbed to initially access the plain days earlier.

Based on Greydal's reckoning, he and Roan would be just southwest of where he had glimpsed Abyddion. Directly to his south now, towards the circle of trees, there was nothing except a dark, shimmering horizon. To the west lay more endlessness, a flatland of pure shadow.

"I thought you said this was a shrine to the Interloper?"

Roan bounded from the wagon, holding a satchel. "I said it's a holy site, little warrior."

"And you knew this was here? How?"

"How indeed?"

He made a face, and Roan laughed. "King Marcos came here once, as a child," she told him.

Greydal was silent. The dread he had felt when she first told him where they were going resurfaced. She reached beneath the underside of the wagon and grabbed the rotting rabbit corpse.

She told him, "Hold this, please." It wasn't a request.

Greydal took it and grimaced as he asked, "Why do we need this?"

"You'll see," she replied.

I can see that it's half-maggot and half-rabbit he didn't say.

Staring into its faded red eyes. Greydal grappled with his rising nervousness. His companion had briefed him about their task, and he worried for them both. She was to enter the place that held the Allthame, this holy site. If by midday she didn't return, Greydal was to come after her. If he couldn't find her immediately, he was to leave with Agatha and travel west to the road, and then north until he arrived at a town with multicolored buildings and a bridge. He was then to (discreetly) ask the owner of that town's inn about how to get to the home of the Sophites. Once he determined how to get there, he was to travel to the Sophites and relay news of Roan and King Marcos' deaths.

"Why can't you just tell me how to get there now?"

"I'm forbidden," was all she would allow by way of an explanation.

He accepted this as something she was bound to and didn't press her on the subject. Greydal looked at the clouds, which had migrated from the low hills to rest directly over their heads. These forms were dense and freighted, but not with rain.

He asked her, "Why are the clouds like that?" She didn't answer. Greydal had come to suspect this was what she did when she knew something but didn't want to lie about it. As he thought this, Roan intruded on his contemplation, "Let's eat now. I don't know how much time we'll have after, unless I'm fast successful," she said.

Greydal nodded, though he didn't quite understand her, and opened the side of the wagon to retrieve a small box of salted meats and stale bread. Both were wrapped in material that reminded him of plastick. He had asked King Marcos about the stuff when he first found it and learned, "People more cunning than we found ways to tie together substance. They used it to forbid access to gnats and the rot."

That had sounded an awful lot like plastick to Greydal.

After she finished eating, Roan took something from within the wagon. It was the velvety spider web. Five paces from the wagon, she turned, facing south towards the copse. She sat on her knees like he had glimpsed King Marcos do the night he died, placing the spider web before her. She then withdrew two small knives from her boot and set them horizontally above the web.

Greydal put down his meal and hobbled closer to her so he could watch what she did.

She told him, "The hare. Grab it and set it down, please. Belly up." He retrieved the coagulating rabbit before lowering himself to the sand and setting the animal on its back.

"Stay close. I may need you in a moment."

Greydal didn't move from where he crouched haphazardly on the sand as Roan picked up one knife and opened the rabbit, starting from the neck. A foul substance oozed from the split, and Greydal fought not to gag. Then the girl raised her palm and cut a small incision in her forearm with the clean knife.

She asked, "Could you squeeze my arm so the blood drops onto the catcher? I need to remain as still as possible."

Greydal blinked. The catcher must be the spider web. He reached to her and massaged her pale arm. Cherry beads fell in dense droplets.

"Good boy, thank you. Now, whatever you see next, please, relax. And especially, *don't run.* Just stay still as you are."

"Do you think I'm capable of running? I mean that as it sounds."

"Shhh."

They waited.

CHAPTER

13

EXTREMITIES

It was midday, and Roan hadn't returned from the circle of trees. Greydal stood, his lower back aching. He glanced at what was left of the devoured rabbit and blanched. He had avoided looking at it since Roan left, keeping his head turned from the bony slush that had earlier been a small carcass.

Staring into the distant circle of trees, he ascertained it would be wise to examine his equipment and ensure he had all he needed before he set out. He leaned on his crutch and mentally went over his list. His axe was in his off hand. *Check.* There was his small satchel containing bandages and a tiny organge stone—covered in ridges—which Roan said would glow when struck against a hard surface. *Check.* He didn't look battle-ready in the girl's clothing, but it was all he had. At the least, he appeared stealthy in the black pants and shift. *Check?* He grunted to himself and left the perimeter of the wagon while avoiding the pile where he vomited earlier, near the end of the ritual. He had dwelled enough already on the sights to which he had been subjected. He would wait to digest those until he could speak to Roan.

Had he possessed both his legs, the trek to the thicket would have taken less than a minute. As it was, he found it difficult to hobble over any great distance while both carrying his axe and maintaining any semblance of balance. Recalling the exercises Roan and King Marcos had him do, Greydal decided he was glad of them.

Approaching the trees, he perceived they were as inky as the ground and likewise without adornment. Leafless, they had seemed quite short from a distance, but now reared skeletally above him. He didn't think the trees looked dead, though. In fact, they seemed as alive as the plain itself. If the ground was the giant's skin, was the thicket its crown?

He shook himself. The trees were wet and porous. Maybe that was why he thought they looked fleshy. But that was all. There was no need to imagine worse things. Feeling nervous despite successfully reprimanding himself, he moved beneath the groping boughs. They received him, ushering him deeper.

He was back in the old house. That was the first thought. It was the smell, salt coupled with rain and animal musk. He closed his eyes and re-opened them. The vision of the ancient home and door vanished, but the scent remained, tantalizing him with its familiarity. As he pushed onwards, he found the grove appeared to be much, much larger from within than it had looked on afar, perhaps swelling as a lung full of water to bloom outwards along an increasing but uncertain perimeter, just beyond sight. In addition to this seeming impossibility, Greydal noted the ground dipped towards the thicket's center, as if to coerce him deeper.

Was he going the right direction? On approach, he had assumed it would have been easy to find Roan. But as he stumblingly descended, he soon discovered he had a supremely difficult time navigating the new terrain. Ebon roots began, and then continued to trip him, never where he expected them to be. It made him wonder if the trees here were similar to the moving plants in his home valley. However, he never saw the roots actually shift and decided to blame his clumsiness.

As he walked, he kept an eye peeled for those...things, the ones that had appeared during Roan's ritual. But he hadn't spotted any of their translucent faces peeking from behind trunks or through the branches. Despite the apparitions' apparent absence, he shuddered. Recalling his promise to himself that he would wait until he could talk to Roan to think on such matters, he put the strange beings out of his mind.

Then came the crickets.

These didn't chirp, and Greydal's foot crushed the first one before he knew it was there, smearing it into the soft dirt. He looked down because he had felt the crunch, and started when he saw red blood. The tiny insect twitched as it lay mangled, crimson leaking from its skin-tinted body. *Like a little old man fallen from a height*, a thought murmured.

Others approached, though he didn't see from where, slowing as they neared their fallen brethren. Wrinkled and pale, these crickets. But beneath, a darkened pulp enlivened their carapaces. Greydal backed and annihilated another, this one far larger and fatter. He *heard* the squelch as bloody stuff shot from the corpse to coat the blackened ground. The little ones turned from their first deceased to look up at him, their creased faces unreadable. Several raised tiny, arthropod legs. Then they moved in unison, closer.

"No," he said to the thicket and turned to abandon the horde. Then he tripped, his crutch catching on a root. The thought of falling into the things, breaking their bodies en masse as the survivors climbed him, made him quick. He shot a hand to the nearest tree, grabbing hold and steadying himself. The bark, if that's what the substance was, was warm under his hands.

Repulsed, he used it to leverage himself over the nearby roots. One of the pale things he had begun to suspect were not crickets had climbed his crutch, an abductee taken from its family as Greydal continued to navigate the grove. He flung it against a nearby tree when it continued to seek his hand, climbing higher.

After several minutes absent of more molestations, he allowed himself to relax somewhat.

Then he reached the center of the copse, that relaxation disintegrating. "You're fucking winding me," he muttered.

A dark hole spread like a well at his feet, gaping across an open space. Only clouds ceilinged the pit. As he leaned against yet another fleshy tree for support, his heart raced. Feeling anchored and safe from immediately falling to his death, he shifted his stance and gazed into the depths. His eyes at first only told him a hole plunged into the shadows, a pitiless wound goring through bedrock.

Yet, his heart insisted this was the door from his dreams, or something akin to it. Then his vision swam and resolved to a new pattern: a spiral ramp curling into the void at his feet. He had missed it before, so shallow and thin, it mingled with the dark. If he were to descend (*please, no*) he would have to lean on the wall or maybe slide down on his rump. Was it some sort of cistern? Or well? Or merely a dungeon?

"Roan! Can you hear me?" His echo answered him, sounding like someone else's voice.

He looked at his surroundings, unsure of himself. The branches from the enveloping trees curved at an almost glacial pace in his direction, as if reacting to his outburst. A more poetic part of his mind made the comparison: they were parishioners, and he the interrupter of some inaudible gathering.

But they looked wrong, ready to burst or unfold, these worshippers. And below his perch, the void was no more. In its place the well and its ramp now coiled into a scintillating blackness of pulsing no-color, a thing his stomach felt, more than his lying eyes saw. He took a deep, shaking breath and glanced around once more, hoping for a sign of the black-haired girl, a return to normalcy. There was nothing. Only the well. And the ramp leading down.

This was why he was here, he told himself. He tried not to imagine the trees reaching for him as—

As Greydal's foot crossed the invisible threshold separating the well from the surrounding ground, a bolt of fire struck him in the chest. Air whistled past his head, and he fell. Panic erupted as he tumbled in the dark.

Faster and faster until... No, not falling. Was he underwater?

Impossible, eyeless shapes moved in an expansive deep. One twisted towards him, its vast wriggling the movement of eons. Then his vision darkened before exploding outwards. He hung upside down, arms pointed to the bloody dirt. The drops had stopped falling hours ago. Flies sipped at the blackened pool, their drying feast turning to smoke to billow around his head as he burned. Greydal strained away from this new reality, his inverted pyre. Phantasmagoric flames rose and leaped into him, attempting to make him whole. He screamed, but no sound came as, from beyond the wall of neon smoke, a horror emerged: a twitching effigy of hair and spit and hooves, crawling towards this reunion, his second birth.

Somewhere, a goat bleated and flute music befouled the night.

His essence *heaved*, and the effigy became a crow with broken wings. It took him in its beak and cracked him, an egg whose insides sought the outside, as truth devoured his mind. He became the many-in-one, mad spirit of Nature. The negative rainbow blaze burned on.

The Interloper, Voice of the Gods, He-She-We-It spoke:

The lattice became spoiled. Old Night saw to its rehabilitation.

He watched a crumbling sphere of meat, at first convex, and then concave, bloom in a raving eternity. It was one of countless others, confluences of madness or the domestications of some great utterness. All seemingly clung to a vast web that spanned a space more alluring, more rottenly grave than he could hope to grasp—it was beyond the scope of his still-blossoming conscious-ness. All stilled as a smoldering and holy *animal*-darkness poked through the background, then drifted towards the first of the de-cayed spheroids. The crackling beast suffused the sphere, making it more than whole. Not restoration. Furtherance.

Greydal watched the outer tissue of the orb shudder, begin-ning to expand as great wings of red unfolded, stretching towards its nearby, former twins.

Many would die.

Left here, we set ourselves to flesh. To partake.

A new knowledge bloomed, and Greydal feared it. The reve-lation would undo him. He pulled away and there was a wet *pop* within his skull, resounding across the emptiness behind his eyes. The sound of yelling woke him. Yet, only when he closed his mouth did he know it to be his own. Back in the world, sweat drenched him, and something like the Legate crouched over him before vanishing into a darkened doorway, its echoing footsteps becoming confused, and then not footsteps at all.

Greydal shook his head, and he was lying on cool ground be-neath inky trees. The sky was overcast, and the clouds twitched above him in their inebriation.

"Greydal?!" A blonde woman with pearly skin and the eyes of the possessed appeared behind a thorny hedge. She carried a glowing stone and a second, longer item covered in a dusty veil.

He didn't recognize her but felt he should. "I heard you yell. Are you alright?" she said.

Roan. Her name was Roan. He looked at his hands. Was this his body? It seemed as though he had been away from it for a long time. It ached, the spot where his leg ended, angry and bandaged below the knee. He felt the phantom limb there for a moment before the sensation evaporated.

"Roan," he croaked. He was dizzy. The day rushed back to him, and he remembered it all. "I-I came to find you. You were gone."

"You..." Roan looked concerned. "I told you to wait until at least midday. Why didn't you listen?" she asked. That confused him.

"But it's past then," he told her. "I waited until the sun was brightest, and then when you didn't show, I came for you." It hurt his throat to speak.

She shook her head. "I've only been gone fifteen minutes at most," she replied.

Greydal stopped listening. "Where's the well?" he asked. She appeared confused, and he tried to clarify, "The hole, the well. The one with the ramp? I stepped onto it to follow you, to come find you."

Roan looked around. "Greydal, I never saw any sort of... I've been in the maze, looking for this." She held up the covered staff. Seeing his expression, she explained, "It was dark, but it wasn't a well. Are you alright?"

Greydal sat up. He still held his crutch and his axe. Beyond Roan, there sat a stone wall, barely visible behind thorny vines. He could tell it extended into the rest of the thicket. Glancing around, he discerned they were now at the edge of the tree line, not the center of the copse like he had thought. He could spy

Agatha in the distance, idling near the wagon. He made to stand, and Roan helped him.

"Thanks. You found what you were seeking?" he asked her numbly.

She ignored his question. "You don't feel sick. You had some sort of episode, did you?"

He nodded.

She helped him limp out of the shadow of the thicket, and they walked towards the wagon. She peered at him out of the corner of her eye. "King Marcos said this place was dangerous. I wonder if he didn't just refer to the glamor of the maze."

"See, I don't know what you mean. That wall back there? You say you were inside a maze? What's something like that doing out here?"

She stopped and turned to him. He could see worry on her face. "Greydal, I told you about it, days ago. The walls were designed to confound me or anyone else who wanted to find this," She gestured with the veil-covered item. She saw by his expression he didn't remember and said, "Either you experienced a bout of hysteria, or something here reacted to you. King Marcos said that when he visited as a child, he never entered the trees, yet watched his father cross a stream. I spy no water here."

Greydal was dizzy. "Was it the ritual, maybe? I know I vomited when they started tearing into the hare."

She nodded. "It's possible, maybe... but it wouldn't be anything sorcerous. The wights are just animals, in a sense. They don't play with your mind." She patted his shoulder and said, "We can discuss this more while we're traveling. Let's get you back to the wagon." Greydal allowed her to lead him to the campsite.

Agatha snorted as they approached. Something was very wrong. What had happened to him? Despite what Roan had said, he *knew* they had never discussed any sort of maze.

He wanted to tell her the other thing, too, as he watched the weak sunlight glint off her wild, flaxen hair. *Your hair used to be black,* he didn't say. It would frighten her.

*** *** ***

She wouldn't let him look at the Allthame. "I'll keep it covered until we understand what happened to you. For all I know it was something to do with that place." Greydal was disappointed, but he let it go. He had other things he needed from Roan.

"Fine. I need you to tell me something, though. Two somethings. The wights, what are they?"

Roan finished packing away the Allthame in a long chest, carefully ensuring its veil kept it covered. "Nothing important. They were what allowed that magick to transpire. The smell of the rotting hare brought them. My blood activated the catcher and the wights, once satisfied, directed the ritual so I could penetrate the mysteries of the grove."

"Are they ghosts?"

She shook her head and chuckled. "No, sweet. Not ghosts. Think of them as animals or people, only from places not like this one." She gestured at the wagon. "Because the place they come from is different, they look different. Does that make sense?"

He supposed it made as much sense as anything that had happened to him recently. He nodded. "Okay, I accept that. Now, the Interloper. Old Man Moonlight."

"You heard King Marcos spin what he knew, same as me."

Greydal shook his head. "No, that was a vague string of metaphors. What *is* it? Why does the Legate want anyone associated with it dead?"

"You think I would know?"

"Don't lie to me."

"I do my best to never."

"Roan, give me something. The Legate came after me. *Himself.* That has to mean something."

She was silent a moment. Then she said, "I can tell you about Abyddion."

Greydal's face hardened. "I don't *care* about Abyddion."

She sighed and said, "You should. What happened to your village was replicated there." Wiping her brow, she added, "And, for the record, the Legate didn't come for you. There's a reason why King Marcos is dead, and you aren't."

"I doubt it."

"This is a fresh world to you, and you've already decided how it works? My father led the Sophites. More than that, he was from Abyddion. It's okay, I know you don't understand." She looped Agatha's reins to the side of the door. Roan took a sip from the nearby canteen.

She started, "I will tell it as it was told to me when I was a little girl." Then she began, almost in a singsong voice to recite, "A long, long time ago, there was a disaster. The disaster was so bad it affected everything, everywhere. In every world, in every time. It pulled the skies apart, it pulled the ages together. Men who should never have met, who should have been separated by centuries, found themselves neighbors. Beasts grew like plants, and plants hunted like beasts—"

"You're just describing the Red Faith's dawn tale," Greydal interrupted.

"Let me finish," she chided him. She cleared her throat before continuing, "But all was not terror. The world that formed from those melted realms was beautiful beyond words, despite its fierceness. And it went on forever.

"But there was a man who could not abide the changes, for he was vain and believed all he saw was his. This new eternity had *robbed* him of his past. So, he became the worst monster of all."

"Are you talking about—"

"*The Wrym*," Roan forged ahead, "made himself ageless and took from the world a piece for himself, to do as he wished. But the world kept changing—the forests he planted vanished, the cities he built walked away. And worse, other locales replaced them, townships over which he had no command appeared. Which," Roan arched her eyes, "brings us to Abyddion. By our reckoning, Abyddion came to this place at least five hundred years ago, if not double that. When the Wyrm later locked away the world, it trapped everyone, including my father's kingdom."

Greydal's eyebrows rose. "I was taught that we swam in a kind of soup. The Bishop saved an island in that chaos. He was supposed to have set the sky over it, which is why the heavens look so strange compared to the ground."

She shook her head. "Propaganda. The Wyrm, or Bishop if you like, is just tyrant phrased differently. Dreadfully imperial."

"Wait, so you were taught that there is an actual functioning existence out there, beyond the firmament?"

Roan nodded. "Just before Abyddion arrived, the *changes* had slowed dramatically. King Marcos says— *said* it was because things were settling, healing. There were already working tribes and nations that had sprung up since the catastrophe."

"What happened to Marcos' kingdom then?" Greydal asked.

"The Wyrm. He destroyed Abyddion when King Marcos was a child."

Greydal's eyes widened. After a beat, he spoke, "Is that why it was dark at night?

She nodded. "Nothing that lives there now needs torches to see."

Greydal frowned. He didn't like the sound of that. Then he thought of his own fire.

"Is it madness?"

She shook her head. "There's a different, but common thread, lovely, though the Wyrm may have few loose ends in his tapestry.

Old Man Moonlight, that's the through-line. King Marcos thought the Wyrm is afraid of it, of your Interloper, whatever the thing might be. *I presume* it's just another monster torn out of time."

"That doesn't explain why the Legate killed your father."

"But it does. My father's father, Aloysius Relk the Second, and his father, the first Aloysius, worshipped Old Man Moonlight."

"What do you mean *worshipped*? Like my people would the Legate?"

She nodded. "I believe 'venerated' may be a more accurate term. From the way King Marcos told it, Abyddion found themselves in a world they weren't familiar with and panicked—it's understandable—there was an enemy power in the form of the Wyrm and his legions bent on subjugating them. King Marcos said Old Man Moonlight somehow contacted the leader of Abyddion. I'm not sure whether that was my great-grandfather or his son. Either way, the entity gave whomever it was knowledge. In return, the people of Abyddion communed with it."

"In places like the grove?"

She inclined her head. "Instead of protecting Abyddion, *that* pact ensured their doom. The Wyrm's slaves found them out, and when the tyrant learned what Abyddion had been up to, he withdrew all his forces from neighboring regions to attack Abyddion. He supposedly abandoned two wars to do it. It was over in a night, and by the end of things, nearly all the kingdom's inhabitants had been murdered, or worse."

Incredible. Greydal couldn't imagine the type of power that would take. From what he had spied over the horizon, Abyddion must have been ten times the size of Harlow. He whispered, "That would have to have been nearly ten thousand people."

Roan shook her head and replied, "A fair estimate, but no, it was far more. I've never been there, but King Marcos said they built their structures tall and deep. Many could be housed."

"Did he mention anything about what wisdom the Interloper allegedly gave?"

"Dear, do you think all of these things are just chronicled someplace? You have to understand, King Marcos was the *adopted* son of Aloysius the Second, as you'll recall I once told you. He was tulka, not human, and only learned what his father and grandfather told him before he was forced to flee the kingdom during the Wyrm's attack. At the time, he was younger than you or me."

Greydal processed this information, and a new thought occurred to him. His skin prickled, and he lowered his head. "It's the same." Roan stared at him, and then stayed silent for a long while.

Outside, the wind picked up and sang. He smelled salt from somewhere.

*** *** ***

The next day, Greydal tried to read more of *Killer of Witches*. The book was almost in another language, so it was difficult to decipher. There were sections detailing the signs that indicated the Interloper had corrupted someone. The alleged signifiers included sleepwalking, something called 'sleep paralysis,' unexplained wounds, communion with beasts of the wild, hearing voices, promiscuity, and other drivel.

He skipped ahead to another section. This one was titled *Tenebrous Fauna*. It was a bestiary, he realized. Tier had maintained several in his collection of books. Greydal's eyes traveled the ludicrous depictions of fantastical beasts, which the manual assured him were birthed directly from the womb of the Interloper.

One animal, called the Seeping Howler, was said to live in small burrows and scream like women in distress. It used this tactic to lure the unwary before cracking them and drinking their bone marrow. He chuckled at the lurid description.

He was about to close the book and return to the front of the wagon when his eye caught the phrase *"...as the limbs of us, in the branches of trees."* Turning the page toward the light, a horrible drawing stared up at him. He ignored its gaping eyes and read:

The Vog (or "The Hungry Spirit")

Be warned, all who read. Some terrors are worse than others. Unlike any animal to walk the reaching wilds, it possesses much room in its stomach for the naive and unlucky. You will know the beast by these portents:

We will go missing when frolicking outdoors.

You will discover our blood and vital organs strewn about the sites wherein we were stolen.

Intrepid investigators shall discover our stored remains, such as the limbs of us, in the branches of trees or on the roofs of abandoned structures.

It is said to respect the sign of the Interloper and those possessed by it. Be not bewitched by this into using the tools of the Enemy to protect yourself or others against the hateful Vog. It is but another ploy to trick the weak-willed. The Fiend seeks always to turn you from the good and orderly path as it turned us into ghosts.

May the Holy Red Legate, hallowed be his name, protect you from the beast and its master. Go forth and watch your steps.

Greydal slowly closed the book, then placed it on the shelf. He was quiet for a time before a sigh escaped him. Why was it that everything always tied back to the Legate or the Interloper? That book had described the Calf-Ripper. There was no doubt. He shut his eyes. It wasn't fair. He must have eventually entered unconsciousness, because Roan's voice shook him from it.

"What?" he sputtered as he raised his head from his arms.

"We're almost here! Come look."

He scooted towards her and looked to where she pointed. "What is that?" he breathed.

"That, my lovely Greydal, is the sea."

CHAPTER

14

RESTORATION

Great bodies of water are magicked mirrors. We see them and sense the tides prehistoric. And, sometimes we, too, feel old. As we stare at the sightless deep, we become more ancient than our own memories. Is this a secret? If it is, it's part of a larger mystery. Greydal didn't reckon it, but he had long approached that strange wisdom. It was nearer now, swelling in time with the waves stealing his breath via their soulless majesty.

After a moment, he said, "I had no idea there was this much water in all the Four Corners."

Roan laughed, bells of black sunlight. "This is just an inlet. It goes much farther out to the south."

This must be the shimmering on the horizon he had spotted when near the grove of the Interloper, he thought. "It extends all the way from the thicket to here?" he asked.

"Farther. It's large, indeed."

"Is it the Loaming Ocean?"

Roan smiled and told him that vastness was lost to time. "The Loaming is from wherever Abyddion initially came. This is only a sea." She looked over the ground they traversed. "We have to stop the wagon soon. It's going to become more sand than dirt."

"We're getting out?"

She smiled. "But, of course, little warrior. This is what I wanted to show you. The moment we removed your leg, I knew we had to come here."

Greydal gave her an uncertain smile. "How do you mean?"

She only shook her head at him and called Agatha to a halt. She sprung from the wagon and disappeared around the side.

The smell of salt stung his nose as he grabbed his crutch and slithered from the wagon. His crutch sank into the sand, but he didn't call to Roan for any of the bone meal, the substance they had used the night of Marcos' death. He didn't want to be the reason something as useful as that was wasted.

As he limped behind the wagon, he inhaled the textured air, then rounded the wagon to see Roan's somber dress hanging from a wooden hook. Her pale form withdrew to the liquid shadow of the waves. Greydal fumblingly removed the clothing he wore and hobbled after her. The footing surprised him. Instead of growing more unstable, the sand hardened as he neared the water. The wind blew his short-cropped hair and chilled his body.

"Drop that crutch!" Roan rose from the water and padded towards him, bending to slip underneath his arm as he set his crutch on the dark sand. Her skin was cool.

She led him into the water. It was cold, and he inhaled when it got to his ribs. "Don't swallow any or you'll regret it," she whispered to him. The water was salty, she meant. Greydal could tell from its scent.

She took him deeper. It was up to his chin and to her neck.

They submerged, and she released him. For a beat, he panicked. The thought of being carried to the depths with only a leg to kick himself to shore jolted him. When his head broke the surface, he heard her say, "It's okay. Relax." The salt stung his eyes, and he held them shut.

"Now isn't the time to fight."

He stopped paddling his arms. He floated. "How—"

"It's the salt. There's something about it that helps you stay buoyant."

He didn't recognize the word, but he knew her meaning. He was weightless. Greydal relaxed his arms and legs, and instead of sinking, the water held him afloat, letting him bob with the waves.

Until that moment, he hadn't appreciated the stress to which his body had been subjected since the night Marston attacked him. As he drifted, his limbs outstretched, a terrible heaviness drained away, and the water comforted him, replacing pain with a clean, frigid kindness. His thoughts melted, and he was a rosy leaf, washed down the road by the rain.

He cried.

*** *** ***

The witch Roan submerged herself to her nose and watched the boy. He floated on the black water like a flower, naked and vulnerable. Around her, the Pneuma of the waves rose ghostlike from the spray to observe alongside. One reached a pale arm towards him, and Roan shook her head. The statuesque figure dissolved with the foam, respecting a sister's wish.

*** *** ***

They spent days on the beach, laughing and playing and screwing. Greydal showed her a tower he built from the wet sand. They watched the waves eat it bit by bit. At night, they glimpsed lights moving under the water far out at sea.

"What do you think they are?" But Roan didn't have any idea.

After the beach, they headed northwest, around the west end of Abyddion. To Greydal, the world was refreshed. He was stronger somehow, more in tune with his body. He stopped treating himself as an invalid and found ways to exercise in spite of his maiming. He discovered he could perform push-ups one-legged, and used the hooks on the exterior of the wagon to lift his body. It felt good to do something approaching climbing again.

On the day they achieved the road and turned directly north, Greydal looked at the southern horizon. Somewhere out there was the black sea. In it, he had sensed an offer, barely understood. As he floated, there had been a presence calling to him softly as if across some measureless gulf, with only an echo finding its target. The presence spoke not in words, but in the coldness of the waves and the baptismal darkness behind his eyes. When Greydal felt close to understanding the source of the thing, this mute offer, Roan's soft embrace had tugged him back into the world.

Had he failed? He hadn't sensed a return of the offer and whatever that thing behind it had been, if anything, didn't reveal itself. Even now, a small part of him wished to return to the beach and the endless shadow beyond. But despite these stirrings, Agatha pulled the wagon away from the unfathomable, and they soon neared the Kingdom of Abyddion.

He could spy it in the sunlight, incredible towers tipped with gold and other metals. All of them shined below with glass. Because a series of massive hills defeated his view of their base, he could only guess at the state of the city complex itself. Greydal expected horrors to pour from the hills after what Roan had told him of the place's fate. Yet, only a single creature pursued them, and that was when the city itself was no longer in sight.

They noted Agatha's agitation before they heard the thing bounding after them. Singing, it was, but of a kind that curdled the blood, darkly reaching their ears to tunnel deeper. Then Roan sprang into action and pulled the taxidermized, doglike animal from the corner of the wagon's interior.

Greydal stared. "What are you doing?" he asked. The empty eyes of the dog gazed back, its toothy grin offering no answers. Roan scooted closer to the open face of the wagon where the road hurried to greet them while Agatha reached something approximating a gallop.

"Keep me from falling."

Roan leaned from the wagon to look behind them, dog in hand. Greydal snatched her other arm and braced himself as her weight nearly made them both tumble from their seats.

"Roan!"

The singing seemed close as she whispered something to the dog, and its stupid grin widened. Roan then tossed it to the air, and he glimpsed it bouncing on the stone before he lost sight of it under the wheels. He pulled Roan into the wagon, and they fell on their backs.

Before he could ask what she had done, he heard the sound of a monstrous animal snarling and the din of a fight. The yelps and roars of the dog and panicked murmurings of the unknown creature faded as the wagon gained distance. Roan brushed a blonde strand of hair from her face, and Greydal opened his mouth but paused, thinking better of it.

Some truths were more comfortable as mysteries.

Two months they traveled north. They were on their way to the home of the Sophites, the prodigal daughter returning to report her father's murder and bring home the Allthame. Greydal wondered with trepidation how that interaction would play out. Despite his promise to help her, Roan had told him next to nothing about her clan. Would they be pleased to see him? He doubted it.

For the first few weeks of their journey, there was only the unending road stretching beyond the horizon. But the landscape slowly changed. Twisting wildflowers blanketed vast fields, and trees unfurled lively ambers and browns. There were huge hills crowned with ruins where Greydal glimpsed hints of movement at dusk. They passed signs of civilization: first farms, and then villages and towns. They visited few of these, stopping only to trade for food and supplies. The mysteries of the wagon never ceased to amaze. At the first settlement they struck, a tiny hamlet carved into a mound, Roan produced a chest of minted shavings with which they could purchase necessities.

"Where'd you get the shavings?" he asked her. He stared at one. The outline of a man was pressed into its metal.

"Is that what you call them?" she asked. They used the shavings to buy more food and a few apples as treats, though these looked different from the ones he knew.

"Ish shour," he said with a mouth full of the green fruit.

"Oh, are they bad?"

Greydal shook his head and swallowed. "No, delicious."

They continued north and passed a lake over which sprawled a colossal bridge, a multicolored town hanging beneath. Later the same day, they encountered what Roan called the Armargure, a great procession gleaming on the horizon and heading south along the wide road. Upon spotting them, Roan told Greydal to sequester himself in the back under blankets.

"Why? Is that trouble?"

"Yes, now hide! And stay quiet," she hissed. But she didn't turn from the road onto the grassy fields. Instead, she kept a steady pace as the sound of a hundred marching feet reached Greydal's ears. As he peered from beneath his blanket, he spied only what the rectangular doorway allowed. But, from it, he saw the figures were like the Friars—that was his first thought.

As they neared, he could tell they wore similar armor, only without the scaled coats and giant orb-helmets. Each man and woman's face were unadorned and exposed to the heady sun. As the cavalcade became close enough to touch the wagon, Greydal perceived none of the soldiers were dressed exactly the same. Each suit had minor differences, a pauldron here, a gauntlet carved with animals there. The procession parted wavelike around the wagon, and he locked eyes with a purple-faced tulka, this one covered in a shining weave of overlapping golden bands. Greydal held his breath, and the tulka glanced away before passing out of sight. The man hadn't spotted him.

He looked to Roan and saw only the back of her head, aimed straight and unmoving at the horizon. The stragglers at the end of the march finally passed from his view, and he listened to their footsteps recede for over a minute.

Then Roan turned and said, "You can come up now."

He clambered from his hiding spot and sat next to her, asking, "Who were those people? They looked almost like him."

"Natives of the western brink. They're the Wyrm's people."

"He has people?"

"The Armargure. Come from wherever he roosts. We haven't been able to find the specific location, but it's to the west, probably at the Edge, or maybe just beyond it."

"There's nothing beyond the Edges. Only the firmament."

"And how would you know? I thought you never left your little valley?"

"Tier told me once."

To that, Roan said nothing. They continued along the road in silence.

Later that day, Greydal snoozed in the back but woke to a sound he would never have expected: soft crying. He opened his eyes, but all he could spy was Roan's head, looking roadward and backlit by evening glow. About to ask after her wellbeing, his common sense thankfully took over, and he held his tongue just as a meager 'What's wrong' began to escape his lips. She deserved to mourn in peace.

Instead, he closed his eyes, and his thoughts drifted to Marcos, then Tier and Alom, before falling away altogether.

*** *** ***

The amount of visible wildlife increased as they traveled, forming a veritable menagerie—hooved and horned animals which bounded on lithe limbs, fat rabbits like small men who hunkered under the shadows of bushes, and other odd lifeforms. In the latter weeks, the terrain became difficult and rocky but no less vibrant. Peach and lemon-colored bushes hung from the sides of low cliffs, and hundreds of purple lizards spied from their stone homes. The cool air turned warm, and Greydal savored it. But then, they broke a wheel and had to wait a day for another traveler to stop and help them with repairs.

This caused a realization to form, that the absence of even slight movement under the blazing sun was enough to balloon the heat in one's own mind. They were lucky the eventual helper was someone familiar with woodworking.

"Now, be sure to go easy on the rough, y'understand? Don't be afraid to hop on out and clear the rocks when you can. I replaced that spoke and fortified the felloe, but it'll only hold for maybe another week of careful ridin', alright?" the man said.

Greydal nodded, but didn't think the wagon's wheel looked fixed. A type of glue and several screws held the wood together in places or pieces.

"Thank you," he told the man over his shoulder.

"Not a problem. Jes you and your wifey get where you're going, alright?"

Greydal turned to correct him only to find the man's hand outstretched. At first, he assumed the hand wanted payment until Roan stuck out her arm and grabbed the worker's, shaking it twice. The man seemed satisfied and left them.

As he disappeared in the distance, Roan whispered, "We were fortunate he was a craftsman. King Marcos handled this sort of triviality in the past."

"Let's just go easy on it if we can...wifey," Greydal said before avoiding a pinch.

As if defying the craftsman's advice, they turned off the relative smoothness of the road the next day as it curved west. Near late evening, the pair entered a patchy forest of spine-covered plants, which soon fell to a brilliant, dry wood. The trees were short and the ground stony, but the air buzzed with the activity of insects. Greydal even spotted a tiny mammal, which flew on stretches of skin, though it appeared to be the only non-bug life present. They then traveled through the brush and came, surprisingly, upon a tiny hamlet. Its quaint, blue roofs and colorful trim were pleasant and mysterious in the evening light, though out of place within the arid hollows in which the village nestled. To Greydal's great suspicion, neither he nor Roan spied any dwellers, whether in the square or through the windows of the small homes.

"I think we should keep going."

"Don't be silly. We need food."

"Have you been here before?" he asked.

"Look at it. Don't tell me you're scared?"

"I'm paranoid. Where are all the villagers?"

She shrugged and leaped from the wagon. Greydal grimaced and followed, but not before placing his axe in its sling and over his shoulder, now hopping after the girl. Roan approached a blue-roofed building that looked like it could be a kind of general store.

"Hello?" she began. "We're here to trade! We have minted chips and books if you prefer those!" All was silent.

Greydal eyed her and raised an eyebrow.

"Please! We would like to purchase some food!" she yelled.

A shutter to her left slid open, and a gloved hand patted the counter jutting from it. After a beat, Roan approached and emptied a small pouch of shavings on the counter. The gloved hand pulled them into the obscurity of the storefront before sliding the shutter closed. More silence. An awkward minute passed where Greydal strained his ears for any sounds not made by the she-bull behind him.

"Did we just get robbed?" he asked at length.

The shutter opened, and the hand returned to place a large, burlap sack on the counter. Greydal approached and picked it up with his off hand. His eyes widened, and then he turned to glance at Roan. She only shrugged. They retreated to the wagon, and he patted Agatha before he placed the sack in a side compartment and climbed up himself.

As they pulled away from the village, he turned to Roan and asked, "Was that a person-sized mouse, or am I hallucinating again?"

*** *** ***

Five days later, they arrived at the home of the Sophites. The only thing Greydal could think when they rounded the bend of the crevasse was that Tier had been right. Powerful mesas jutted from a horizon thick with fog.

"The Sect of the Mist," he whispered.

"What's that?"

"Nothing." Nothing at all.

CHAPTER

15

BASIN

Roan and Greydal exited the crags. Agatha pulled them along the path, thorny bushes guarding their sides as they descended into the mist. As the fog swallowed them, Greydal stared at the prism of the sky.

Tonight ought to be the brightest moon for a month, he thought as he watched the sun's light change like a slow, parting cloud to become the cool illumination of its other half. The moon was brilliant, even through the fog. The mist, refracting its light, caused the world around them to bloom fiercely with a pale glow as they inched towards the mesas.

In a younger Greydal's imagination, the mesas were jutting towers of rock with flat heads. However, the ones he and Roan now approached were more akin to a single, contiguous structure like the spine of some great colossus with the top sliced away, as though from a gargantuan sword strike.

"I never knew anything could be so tall," he said. "Do your people live near the mesas?"

Roan's face was eerie under the emboldened moon. "Very near," she said.

The landscape around the wagon was almost invisible through the opaque fog. Though at length, he believed he could spy strange shapes off to the sides, twisting like underwater plants.

"What are those?" he asked.

Roan looked to where he pointed, but said she saw nothing. His eyes narrowed as he noted the set of her mouth and realized she had just lied to him, perhaps for the first time since they met. But, if he was wrong and she truly couldn't see the strange figures now keeping pace with the wagon, she might begin to fear for his mind should he press the issue. He hadn't convinced her that he had recovered from his spell at the Interloper's shrine. That didn't mean he could stop from watching the beings, though. The shadowy figures still loped alongside the wagon, slowly, as if trapped in molasses. It occurred to him that if the shapes were something only he could see, they might be related to what he had experienced in the grove.

At once, one of the figures seemed to absorb the fog's density and take on a more person-like form. Greydal shook himself, turning his eyes on the approaching mesas, what must be the very spine of the Four Corners. The mesas were more massive on approach, a great wall of darkness that swallowed the horizon. It took the better part of the night, but he and Roan closed with the base of that landform, the followers in the mist departing as shadow banished the moonlight.

Because of the mist, Greydal hadn't appreciated they had entered the mesa itself until the glow of strange lights embedded in the stone replaced the dark. After several minutes of quiet travel through a tunnel of uncertain proportion, he asked, "How close?" as his voice echoed across the rock.

"Almost there." Roan's was strained. Even in the compressed murk of the tunnel, he could sense her eagerness. She held his hand tightly.

Agatha knew the path. At a point that looked no different than the rest of the tunnel, the she-bull halted. All was still before something let out a shrill yell.

"Haieeeeee!" Roan returned it, an animal's call.

The ground moved. They were ascending somehow. As the weak illumination of the tunnel disappeared, he was barely able to discern that the wagon sat on some sort of stone platform, which lifted vertically. The walls rumbled, and he tried to determine how the structure moved, but in the gloom, he could only decide it lifted slowly, like a piece of wood in a flooding well. After a long while, the sounds of grinding machinery slowed, and the darkness opened to bathe them in pale moonlight once more.

Singing. That was the first thing he noticed. It increased in pitch as their heads rose above the ground, the noise taking on the shape of a surrounding crowd. By the glazed light of the sky, and the sickly torches attached to great, spindly boughs, he saw the crowd was in the shape of a semicircle surrounding the rising wagon. These people wore robes, strange flat armor, and despite the lack of sunlight, many sported broad, pyramid-shaped hats. The singing itself was a kind of chant, frantic and harrowed. As far as he could tell, this chant originated from just a handful of the gathered people. They stood at seemingly random places within the crowd, with higher voices wailing alongside the guttural growls of several long-haired men.

"What do they say?"

Roan looked at him with tears in her eyes. "They mourn the loss."

He whispered to her, "How do they know?"

She shook her head and replied, "Later."

Was it only because the man was absent? No, the Sophites must have scouts, he figured. Perhaps *they* were the shapes he had spied in the mist. He peered at the crowd hedging them, noting how the group was a mixture young and old, tulka and human. Some surely could have matched the forms of the fog people, couldn't they?

Even as he thought this, he recognized it as wishful thinking. Then his eyes traveled behind the throng. The basin they all congregated in formed a kind of natural bowl, nestled in what must be the top of the mesas. Behind a curve in the rock at the end of the basin, he spotted the corner of a swooping structure.

Roan spoke, "I've returned, my hunt finished!" Her voice was high and firm. The singing stopped, and no one spoke. Then the crowd parted, and a woman approached. Skin wrinkled and hair white, an overlarge, dark robe engulfed her. The ancient woman stared up at Greydal, and then Roan.

She must be less than four feet tall, he thought. Then the woman spoke in a soft voice. The words were in a language he felt he should recognize, but couldn't place. Though he didn't understand her speech, her irritation was clear from her expression. Looking behind the woman, he found with unease nearly half of the crowd shared it. No, *they* looked furious. What agitated them so, his presence or Marcos' fall?

The subtle feeling of potential violence snaked lazily through the air and he grimaced as his stomach involuntarily turned at the realization. Then Roan stood, hanging from the wagon's entrance by one hand. She spoke in the same language as the old woman, and Greydal recognized it as what he had heard when they burned King Marcos' body. He supposed it to be the native tongue of the Sophites. Was he to divine the meaning of these people's words through expression alone, then? He looked to his companion, but her focus was on the crone. Though Roan radiated confidence, he couldn't decide who led these people in this moment, her or the old woman?

The crone answered. Her voice was faint, but in it, Greydal heard the strength of command. He caught the word *Marcos*, but whatever she said, it infuriated Roan. The blonde girl swept a hand through her mane and shouted a series of rhythmic phrases. If the old woman's voice held command, Roan's now held power.

The old woman nodded in response. But someone else spoke then, a man Greydal couldn't spy. His voice was low and reminded Greydal of Sheriff Calahurst in the worst way. Like the sound of broken teeth.

Roan shook her head at the unidentified speaker "This is he!" Roan shouted, now in the familiar tongue. She gestured at Greydal with an outraised palm. "This is my chosen! He will speak to you all! You will know why I have done what is *my right* to do."

His heart froze in his chest. She wanted him to do this *now?* He fumbled and stood. As he leaned from the wagon's interior, he heard a mix of laughter and outrage from the crowd. Then a large man with red hair pushed through the people and yelled something in the Sophite tongue. That was the one with the voice like the sheriff's, all gravel and quiet arrogance.

The man was probably around twenty years old but carried himself as though he were older. Tattoos covered his face and gave his countenance the illusion that vines crawled it. The man pointed at Greydal while staring at Roan as he spoke through a sneer, clearly denouncing the maimed stranger. Roan cut the red-haired man's speech short with an upraised finger. Greydal had expected the man to continue his tirade, but he went quiet at the girl's gesture.

"Silence, Yphrus. You'll have time to talk...later. Now, Greydal will speak." She looked at Greydal and nodded, smiling. He stared into her dark eyes and produced a weak grin. She really expected him to speak in front of every one of these people. How did she imagine that would go? Her eyes held no answers, only encouragement.

He sighed. Can't go around it.

Greydal leaned as far from the wagon as he could, and then straightened. He looked at the sea of faces staring at him, and his mounting panic nearly forced him to start speaking immediately, but he managed to hold his tongue. He knew if he gave in to that anxious impulse, he would only fumble at the mouth. Instead, he closed his eyes and shut out the crowd, taking a deep breath. In it, he noted how the warm night air tasted of spice, of cooling stone. He held it here a moment as the quiet shuffling of some of the crowd reached his ears, and beyond them, the sound of the wind courting the top of the basin, whistling its ancient longing. Then he released his breath to join that high, coursing air before he opened his eyes, his gaze immediately connecting with that of the old woman.

He spoke, "My name...is Greydal Alone. I come from a village far from here. Several months ago, I escaped my home after soldiers of the Legate assaulted it. You know him as the Wyrm, I think. Marcos— *King* Marcos told me the soldiers who attacked me are called the Friars. I killed two of them, but lost my leg, as you can see."

He smiled, but no one returned it.

Clearing his throat, he continued, "Roan and her father found me as I bled to death. Their quick attention and prolonged aid kept me from it. Death, I mean. Gratitude and dependence, that's why I went with them. On the way, we were attacked, this time by a man I believe to be the Legate, the Wyrm. He killed King Marcos before we knew what was happening, and if not for Roan, I would be dead with him. We burned the body..."

As he spoke, he scanned the faces of the crowd but couldn't tell if his speech was having the effect he wanted. Each visible member was unsmiling and dour, none more so than the old woman. Her face was inscrutable, nestling a darkly intense gaze.

"I don't know who you people are," he continued. "I'm not the face you wanted to see, that's clear. I only know you're Roan's family and the family of King Marcos, and your customs are likewise lost on me. In that, I hope you'll forgive my ignorance. More importantly, please, forgive Roan for any harm caused by bringing me here. In return, I pledge to help her, and by extension, you in any way I can." He nodded to himself. "In any way I can," he said more quietly. That was the best he could do.

Later, he would look back on that speech. He had spoken from his heart when he stated his intention to serve Roan, it was true. He owed her that after all, and more. Yet, even at the time, he knew he had lied to the crowd in pledging himself to the Sophite cause (whatever that was). His only desire had been to keep the throng from rushing the wagon. How could he have known the way his words would twist against him, snakelike?

The old woman spoke first, "Bythos, or is it Barbelo? You come as if unknowing. Do you think I cannot see?" Greydal turned to watch Roan's response only to find she gazed at him with wonder on her face. He turned to the old woman only to find she wasn't looking at Roan.

"I'm sorry. I don't understand." He watched the old woman's eyes scour him and saw the set of her small jaw.

After a protracted silence, she replied, "Have it your way, *Nara*. The others here know not of what I speak, and you may maintain your cladding." Her gaze shifted, and she nodded at Roan.

The girl started as if out of a daze and returned the gesture. Then she hopped from the wagon and helped Greydal do the same as the crowd stood in silence. After a breath, the one called Yphrus pushed his way through the throng, towards the rear of the basin. Greydal didn't understand what had just occurred, but he smiled at the old woman. He felt sure she was the reason he hadn't been attacked. She ignored him, however, and so he allowed Roan to lead him to a tall tulka who strode from the now-dispersing crowd. Birds covered the left half of the man's face.

Tattoos. Did all the males here have them? Greydal thought of Tier, who had been considered a rebel for his own marking.

Roan said, "Loken, take him to the meetinghouse. No one is allowed to see him, understand?"

The man nodded and placed a broad hand on Greydal's shoulder. "Come, friend. You can go put your legs up." Greydal looked to Roan.

She nodded in encouragement and said, "Go with him. I'll come find you later."

The remaining crowd parted, and the man led him through the gap. Over his shoulder, Greydal saw others climb the wagon and lead Agatha away. *His axe!* He had forgotten it. He'd have to ask Roan to make sure the Sophites returned it to him. Although, on the other hand, it relieved him to see the congregation appeared to have forgotten him altogether, all concentrated on Roan, the old woman, and the she-bull.

He eyed his guide. This man, Loken, was unique-looking, tall and well-muscled. Long hair reached the man's sculpted, ruddy shoulders. Because of his profound height, the man had to keep a slow pace to account for Greydal's hobble, and as they walked, Greydal decided who Loken reminded him of—the Harlow Valley minstrel. Frowning, he then wondered if that other man was alive. Had he seen his body during the fire? When was the last time he had thought of him?

"Come. This way. Past the yurts," Loken said in a soft tone, interrupting Greydal's musing. He blinked, and then headed the direction the man indicated. They walked through a colony of round, sturdy tents.

"Is this housing temporary?"

"It is. The mountain, many of the kith do not live here. They traveled here to welcome Marcos Relk. I feel sad for them."

"Them only?"

The man smiled. "I live in a real home. I had to travel nowhere."

"No, I meant about King Marcos. Everyone looked like they were ready to murder me."

"They would not have done so just then. But no, I made my peace with Relk's death. Long ago."

Greydal frowned. "How would you have known?"

The man smiled. "It is not my place to say, friend. But I am sure you could tell Relk didn't hide his shine, no." Greydal nodded, and Loken continued, "He was sure to run into something more dangerous than himself, would you not say?"

Greydal didn't know what he would say, and so remained silent. They traveled through the basin, which proved to be more expansive than he had initially suspected. Loken had called it the *mountain*, and Greydal assumed that to be these peoples' word for mesa. Then they exited a line of yurts and gained on the swooping structure beyond. Was that the meetinghouse? An exquisite, multi-tiered tower with many roofs, all like wings, the thing itself growing as if directly out of the rock.

Greydal breathed, "It's massive."

Loken chuckled and replied, "You should have seen our *starik*, our old woman. It was the meetinghouse before the mountain."

"How long have you all lived here?"

Loken calculated for a moment. The man replied, "I would say just around eighty years? Eighty-one, eh? Still debated what makes the mountain being settled. The earliest of us here lived under sky alone."

"You're the oldest man of our race I've met then, if you remember something before that."

"You knew Relk, no?"

"Marcos? He acted funny. But, sometimes, it's hard to tell with us. Was he older than you?"

Loken laughed, deep from within his belly. He replied, "My friend, Marcos Relk was from Abyddion. He knew at least three hundred years."

*** *** ***

They climbed five flights of stairs. Greydal had to sit on a carved landing to catch his breath. He ran his hands over the turquoise tile splashed across the floor. "This," he inhaled a gulp of air, "is beautiful."

Loken grinned and replied, "You have good taste, my friend. I helped place the murals on this floor."

"Is that why there are birds?"

The man chucked and replied, "Why, because of my *tatu*?" He helped Greydal stand.

Greydal nodded and said, "They look real."

"The mural or my tatu?"

"I think both."

"This way." Loken led them along a corridor flanked by the busts of peculiar-looking people, with wide, low eyes and parted lips.

"What are these?" Greydal asked.

"The Heads of Orostron. From a jungle far to the north. The Drop, do you know it?" Greydal said he didn't, and Loken replied, "I thought not. You have not have the bearing."

"What bearing do they have, northerners?"

"They are...how do I say it? Imposing, yes. Even the friends feel like enemies. Am I making sense?"

Greydal nodded, though he didn't think he understood. He didn't want to offend the cheerful tulka and said nothing.

They arrived at a chiseled doorway, which flared at the top, as though someone had carved a large mushroom from the wall, sans spines. The man gestured at the aperture, and Greydal entered, parting the silken fabric which acted as a barrier. He inhaled and turned to Loken, who gestured for him to continue inwards.

"You were not expecting this, I think?"

To say the room was lavish would have been an insult to those who created it. The dwelling was shaped almost like a vase, its walls rounded and curved, tapering at a hole in the ceiling. Greydal entered the room and looked up. The hole was dark, but he surmised it was supposed to be some type of chimney. Below it, images covered the walls, painted on the wood itself. In them, he spied landscapes and great proceedings through the actions of tiny, illustrated figures. Pieces of a terrible blade, shattered, hung from silver chains in the center of the room, suspended over a fire pit wrought from lustrous metal. Cushions ruled the space.

"Make yourself comfortable, my friend. I will return. With tea."

Greydal gave something like assent as his eyes roved the room. Loken left him, and he wandered further in and sat on a violet pillow as large as his body. He sunk into it and had to fight to right himself, then pulled his crutch over and leaned it within reach. A deep sigh escaped his belly as he shut his eyes. He must have fallen asleep, because when he opened his eyes, a steaming cup on a tray sat to his left. He struggled to lean up, and upon succeeding, sipped at the tea. The liquid burned his mouth, but tasted incredible and smelled better, soothing a headache he hadn't known he suffered.

The proceedings he had witnessed earlier, his thoughts flitted to them. It seemed like he and Roan had stirred trouble. He hoped the retrieval of the Allthame would mitigate some of the people's ire, though he didn't know *what* the artifact was. Roan never let him see it, keeping it hidden in a drawer for the entire journey.

He assumed the thing must be valuable, though, if the Sophites had sent their leader and his adopted daughter after it.

A stirring of the silken fabric at the entrance made him turn. Loken entered, carrying a carved box and a leather satchel with a handle. "Roan will be longer than she hoped and asked me to see to you, Greydal Alone. That is your name, yes?"

"Greydal is fine, thanks."

Loken approached him and pulled up a cushion. "The fire, would you like me to show you how to light it? It will be cold tonight."

"Not just yet. What is that?" Greydal indicated the satchel and the wooden box.

"This," Loken replied, "is a gift from Roan." He set the bag aside and opened the container.

Greydal raised his eyebrows. "Ferrous wood?" he asked.

The man pulled a block of the wood out and replied, "We know it as Iron's Bark. It is harder than steel and light as cypress." He set the block down and opened the satchel, pulling out a string and a piece of sharpened coal. "All right." Loken smiled. He looked Greydal over and said, "Now, I must take your measurements."

*** *** ***

Roan climbed the stairs and ran her hand along the bone banister. It was late, almost six hours since she had left the wagon to go with Mabet. She was wearier than she had been in days, and blessedly, she would soon be able to sleep. There was only a final duty ahead, a thing long dreaded. Admitting her deception to Greydal would be...complicated. What was it the boy had said? 'Can't go around it?'

Stupid phrase.

CHAPTER

16

ENDINGS

Surely the boy could handle what was coming. Now, had Roan tricked him? Yes, she couldn't deny it, yet she had saved his life and taken a burden upon herself for her choice. He had said he owed her, and she supposed that to be true, but Roan didn't envy his path any more than she loved her own.

And there was that *other thing*. The thing she couldn't tell him. Mabet had smelled it on Roan immediately. Unsurprising— nothing slipped past the old woman.

Greydal's laughter preceded him, voice high and breathy. She parted the curtain to her father's room and saw him dancing and jumping for Loken. The boy looked up at her and beamed as her heart melted.

"Roan! It's almost good as new!" He shook his wooden leg at her.

"Easy," Loken urged, "still, I have to adjust the socket, *Mercure.*"

Greydal walked around the firepit with a slight hobble and hugged Roan. "I can't— Did you know it springs ever so slightly?" He showed her by leaping over a hassock.

"Careful, I don't want you out the window."

Greydal glanced at the small aperture at the east wall. He laughed and replied, "How short do you think I am?"

"All you tulka look the same to me." She rolled her eyes and shrugged before Loken lightly tossed a pillow in her direction.

"I think we could take her, Loken, just say the word," Greydal commented in between his erratic dancing.

Roan shook her head. "Maybe another time. Could you please give Greydal and I the room?"

The older man's face hardened, and he bowed and left. As he exited, he spoke over his shoulder, "Find me later on the second floor, yes? I will make the fitting more to your shape."

Greydal said he would and watched the tall man disappear behind the wall of fabric.

"You have bad news. Do I have to leave?"

The girl shook her head. "Sit down. I have to talk to you." She sat and patted a cushion next to her.

Greydal remained where he was and replied, "Thanks, but I have too much energy to sit. I think I might be able to run with this, can you imagine?"

She smiled, but it didn't reach her eyes. "Greydal," she began, "you know next to nothing about us. With time, you'll learn. But the first thing you should know is there are only ever five hundred of us, never more than that."

"It's to stay small, right? For the Legate. You're here hiding from him."

Roan's eyebrows raised, and then she smiled sadly. "That's one of the reasons, to escape the Red Faith's eyes. But the important thing is, when someone new comes, someone else must go."

He considered that. "So, I fill King Marcos' spot. Is that it?"

She sighed and replied, "No. Outsiders never assume a vacancy if you would think of it that way. We keep space for any future children who are born within the kith, the tribe. If an outsider wants to join, they need four things. First, a true desire to aid the kith. You've got that, and wouldn't be here otherwise. Second, you require a sponsor. In this case, you have me. I named you as my chosen, my beloved, sufficient to allow you asylum here."

"Beloved—"

She cut in, "Third, you must *publicly* state your desire to join us, before the kith. You did that atop the wagon..."

Greydal still reeled from the title she had bestowed on him. He never thought of what they did together in *exactly* that way. Not that he didn't necessarily think of her as—

"Lastly, you must participate in the *Nayuda*, the Duel."

He almost didn't hear her. She remained silent as he mentally went over what she had just told him. "I'm sorry, like a fight?" He stopped leaning on his new leg and lowered himself to a cushion.

She nodded and replied, "Yes, lovely. It's a rite that's sacred to our people and is how King Marcos and several others joined our ranks."

He stared at her and said, "I won't— I'm not a fighter, Roan."

"You killed your Calahurst and *two* Friars, a thing nearly un-heard of... for one such as you."

"You know that was an accident. Both times. It was the axe, not me."

"King Marcos thought differently."

"He was wrong. Also, I have no interest in earning another enemy," Greydal said, thinking of Marston.

"You won't."

He saw the meaning in her eyes, and he said, "No. *No.* It's not happening. I won't kill just to stay here." He made to stand, and she placed a hand on his wrist.

She told him, "You have to. You can't avoid it."

He pulled away. "I can run. I'll leave."

A tear streamed down her cheek. "Greydal, little warrior. You've been inside our home. You have a *relic* on your leg. You're one of us. They won't let you."

A slow horror dawned on him then, as he realized what she meant.

He asked, "*When?* When was the point of no return? The mists?" She didn't answer immediately and he shouted, his voice filling the room, "When should I have turned back?!"

She lowered her head and sighed, replying in a tired voice, "The tunnel. That was the last chance. Your speech is what prevented Yphrus and the others taking you from atop the wagon. Now, you have a chance to save yourself."

Fury bubbled in his chest, shaking him. "Y-you knew! When you first found me, you knew what you were going to do." It wasn't a question. She nodded. "Why...?" It was all he could ask.

Her dark eyes brimmed as she looked up at him. She replied, "You have to understand, at first, we were going to leave you. The kith aren't allowed to jeopardize our hunts for *anything*. That includes joining with outsiders unless sanctioned beforehand."

"I don't—"

"The quest for the Allthame was supposed to be a secret. King Marcos and I broke oaths just to resuscitate you, much less keep you alive for those first few weeks. By the time you awoke in the wagon, the Nayuda was already destined."

He was stunned. "And you didn't—" He put his head in his hands and tried again, "You didn't think to warn me, Roan?"

Tears streamed, but her face was hard. "You might have fled."

"Why would that have mattered?"

She opened her mouth, and in the moment before she spoke, Greydal saw her change her mind about what her next words were going to be. What those words might have been, he wouldn't be able to guess at for a long, long while.

"I would have had to return without my father..." she said after a breath before adding, "and two oaths broken."

"Two?"

She bobbed her head. "First, we revived and took you with us. Then we exposed the Sophites' secrets to you in at least a hundred small ways. I told you of Abyddion."

"I don't understand, Loken just mentioned Abyddion a few hours ago."

"That man is a special case. I'm supposed to lead these people. I have to be an example." She wiped her tears and added, "For what it's worth, I tried to tell you without spelling it out. I asked you to consider what you desired, and you said you wanted to come and help me."

He shook with fury. "This is my life!"

"I *saved* your life! You have no idea what that cost me."

"How could I?! What do I know about you? That you're witches who steal artifacts? Is that why the Legate hates you all?"

She remained silent for several breaths. "You're right. I shouldn't be defending myself." She sighed and wiped her nose. "I've seen you, poring over the books in the wagon. *Riddles, Eibon,* others. It's knowledge you want. Well, this is its home."

What Greydal wanted was to leave. He wanted to escape. How had he been so blind? His gut had told him from the *beginning* he couldn't trust them, that they were dangerous. He never thought he would have admitted it to himself, but he missed Tier. His father would have known what to do. What would he have said had Greydal come to him for help?

Can't go around it.

In spite of himself, a grim smile crept across his face, and he chuckled.

"You're laughing?"

He looked up at the girl. "I almost hated my father at the end. But you know what? He was always right."

*** *** ***

"These are the rules of engagement. Yphrus is giving you the choice of weapons." Roan held the vacant, red envelope in her off hand. Her left held the parchment, which she handed to Greydal.

He took it and said, "I can't read this."

"I'm sorry I forgot. Most of it's drivel, just Yphrus boasting he volunteered to fight the outsider, blah-blah-blah, and as a sign of his honor, he is letting you choose the weapons with which you two will battle."

"Why does it have to be Agatha's brother?"

Roan laughed and said, "Yphrus wishes he were part bull. He's big, but stupid. In truth, this may work in your favor. I was afraid someone else would have volunteered who had more flowers in the upstairs garden."

Greydal looked over the nonsensical sheet, and then asked her what would have happened if no one volunteered, would he have been allowed to leave? She told him no, the eligible, single combatants the tribe would have had to draw straws to fight the outsider.

"Figures," he muttered. Then he asked, "Does this say if there are any rules against fighting cripples?"

"You're not a cripple, you have a new leg. And no, every man here has to be able to pull their weight in battle. For one to join us, they must fight. Even the incapacitated."

"What about women?"

"We have to test our wits and mysteries against Mabet. Much more brutal, I assure you."

He shook his head and replied, "Fine. Well, I choose my axe. Do you people have another one of those just lying around for Yphrus?"

"I presumed you would. And I'm not sure, but we'll find some- thing similar." She took the paper from him and wrote on the bottom in red ink. Then she folded the sheet and placed it in the envelope before retrieving a vial of wax from above the firepit. Greydal watched her pour a circle. "Your thumb, please." He let her take his hand, and she pressed it into the hot wax.

"Ow! Why?!"

"It would have been more painful if you had anticipated it, dear." She rose and kissed him on the head before leaving the room. He watched her exit before returning his gaze to the crack- ling fire.

It had been two days since they arrived in the basin, and he hadn't been allowed to leave the meetinghouse or explore it. His world consisted of Loken's quarters and here, the room in which he now apparently lived. He hadn't forgiven Roan, but they had arrived at a kind of truce the day before. He didn't need more enemies, and if he was honest with himself, he didn't have the energy to panic about his upcoming fight *and* stay angry with her. He was sure he would find the time to reignite his fury if he survived.

It was an hour before Roan returned. She carried a blue en- velope. "What's that?" he asked. She told him it was Yphrus' response. It contained the man's parameters.

"He's the defender, so he can name almost any condition he wants. Knowing him, he'll probably ask that it be at dawn so the red of the sun shines off that silly mop of his."

Greydal tapped his prosthetic on the side twice to remove it. The wood relaxed around his stump, and he set the artificial leg aside. He had asked Loken how he made the wood behave that way, but the tall man had only replied that the technique was a *family secret*, whatever that meant. Greydal later asked Roan, too, but her response had been only slightly more enlightening. According to her, Loken was a master craftsman. His was the hand behind the wagon and other Sophite tools. Greydal rubbed his stump and stretched, wondering if he could ask the wonder-worker to make it so the ferrous wood leg would allow for climbing, perhaps a hooked foot?

Roan's stillness to his left interrupted his musing. He looked over to see she had a hand covering her mouth, eyes wide. His heart thumped as he asked, "What is it?" She only shook her head, so he repeated himself.

She whispered, "Yphrus...he demands the Nayuda be conducted in the flesh alone. Unclad."

"Well," Greydal replied, "it's not like armor would help against the axe."

"You don't understand. An unclad fight means nothing is allowed, nothing except covered loins. You can't use your new leg. *Or* your crutch."

He nearly laughed. A gagged silence held between them, and he turned away from her to stare at the window, which faced the eastern edge of the basin. The sky glinted, looking almost within reach.

"Greydal," she said to his back.

"Don't. Just... When is the fight?"

"Tomorrow at midday."

"Come find me when it's time. Actually, a bit before. Until then, I think I want to be alone."

She got up and left. He knew she paused at the curtain because he still smelled her hair, strangely enough.

"I'll fix this. I'll beg him to reconsider."

"Would that work?" he asked.

She didn't answer.

"Then don't bother. Maybe I'll get lucky again." He didn't know why he tried to reassure her, now of all times. He was going to die tomorrow, and her feelings towards him would be without meaning or purpose.

*** *** ***

The morning sun reflecting off the rocky walls of the basin caused blurry shadows to leap from Greydal as he sat at the edge of the fight pit. Were the shades trying to escape their tether? He didn't blame them. Instead, he gazed at the plates of the sky, the now-orange sun swimming behind their translucent faces, reaching from horizon to horizon. The underside of an incandescent monster.

No ants to distract him this time, only himself. He looked at the assembled Sophites. Only a handful had shown so far, most wearing the odd, pyramidal hats he had seen before. In the valley, no one but farmers wore hats, and then mostly on rainy days. No one aside from the sheriff, Greydal corrected himself. He imagined there would be more strangely dressed onlookers by midday, come to watch the one-legged intruder die. The Sophites present spoke amongst themselves and largely ignored him, except for one, a younger kithsman.

The Sophite was a human boy of what looked to be around fifteen, who now hissed at him from across the pit, "Hey, *brut*, outsider!"

Greydal offered no response. Maybe if he didn't look at him the boy would get tired and leave.

The boy tried again, "Warrior!"

Greydal rubbed his eyes, and upon opening them, registered he was now accidentally staring into the speaker's eyes. "If you slice Yphrus before going down, I'll make sure you get a sky burial," the boy said. He wagged his eyebrows at Greydal, who didn't answer and resumed his watch of the heavens.

He had decided not to eat that morning and now regretted it. His stomach gurgled and seemed to ensure a hungry death. But, like everything else, it was now a trivial thing. Putting the

| 213 |

sensation of out of his mind, he thought about Yphrus. What kind of man was he? Greydal supposed he had a clue. If it was accurate, he had a chance, but only that. He would have to rely on his lame appearance and a copious amount of good fortune. Decided, he tried to meditate to calm himself. It would be the only edge he could create at this late stage.

It took half an hour to quiet his mind, but he arrived at a place almost like serenity. The world fell away, and he drifted in darkness.

A hand on his shoulder woke him. It was Loken.

"Where's Roan?" Midday light streamed over the courtyard and the massive crowd encircling him and the pit.

"She is with Mabet," Loken replied. "Cannot be seen with you until this is over. In case you fail."

Greydal didn't understand, but found he didn't care enough to determine what the tulka meant. Loken carried a knife and a small vial. "What's that for?" Greydal asked.

"I must shave your head. It is the *Tiga*, the renunciation."

Greydal nodded and allowed the tall man to coat his hair in the oil from the vial. Loken's knife felt like a foretelling as Greydal listened to it scrape across his skin. The onlookers watched the slippery work. When he finished, Loken wiped Greydal's now-gleaming scalp with a soft fabric he pulled from his satchel.

"You are ready, eh? Do you have something of worth to leave behind? I will take those from you. The words."

Greydal thought about that. He didn't and said so. What did he have to give the Four Corners besides an incoherent death? Then Loken raised his arm to the right half of the crowd. No, he alerted a small group of people on the meetinghouse's balcony. Among them, there was Roan and a small figure that must be the old woman. Was that Mabet? The crone raised her arm in return and seemed to summon a stealthy chorus, the women of the surrounding crowd beginning a low muttering. Then the whispers became a hum, and the hum turned to wailing. Greydal's skin prickled at the sound. Behind the muttering, slow and guttural chanting emerged, the growls of animals. This went on for minutes. When it reached an unbearable pitch, it ceased, the echoes of the chant dancing along the basin's cliffs.

Yphrus stood before him across the pit. His vine tattoos shined in the sunlight, and his red hair hung in braids over his shoulders. The man was nude except for a thick, white cloth tied around his waist, the same as Greydal's dusky one. Yphrus turned to a squat man beside him. They conferred, and the squat man nodded before raising his arm to the meetinghouse, then disappeared into the crowd to leave Yphrus standing monolithic under the hot sun. All was silent.

"Brut," Yphrus' voice was rocks and daggers, "your ash markings! Are you trying to take your place amongst us with tatu before it is earned?"

Greydal heard a few laughs from the men in the crowd. He ran a hand over his axe laid across his lap and examined its sheen. *The men who made this made the sky,* he thought. That meant the Legate, or others like him.

Then Yphrus' voice cut in. "Nothing to say? Typical outsider cowardice!"

Greydal looked up. Someone had handed Yphrus a weapon, a handled saw of the same make as the axe. It would be just as deadly.

"Yphrus," he called. His voice sounded like another man's. "I'm glad you can speak my language. I want you to know what's going to happen." He let his echo hang in the air. Yphrus' eyes narrowed. Now came the words he knew would have angered Marston, "That shitty orange rag on your head? I'm going to take it after I kill you. Do you understand? I'll scalp you and use it to wipe my crippled ass."

There was silence. Then the boy from earlier cackled from somewhere in the crowd, and Greydal heard muffled laughter from the watchers. Yphrus' pale skin reddened. Before the man could reply, Greydal slid from his seated position into the pit, its walls coming to his shoulders. He leaned against them so he didn't fall in front of his opponent.

"Come on!" he shouted. "Don't be afraid, I'll end it quickly." Yphrus' face twisted into a sneer and the man leaped into the pit.

Greydal's heart pounded like a drum, but he was detached from it, like it was someone else's death he was about to experience. He fought to stay upright on his single leg, but the task was difficult without his crutch. Trying to keep his balance, he held his axe loosely in his right hand and hopped towards the center of the ring.

"You're going to die, brut," Yphrus looked furious as he spoke.

Good, Greydal thought. He would be more likely to try to end things with a single, crushing strike. Now, all that was left was to fight for balance and wait for the call.

It came. A single shriek like a bird—Roan.

Immediately, Yphrus charged him from the other side of the pit. Fifteen feet. Ten feet. Five feet. The metal saw flashed in the sunlight as the red-haired man brought it down. Time slowed, and Greydal glimpsed the weapon descend towards his shoulder. When it connected, it would bisect him. But he was already falling.

At the five-foot mark, he had let his body collapse as he pulled his leg out from underneath himself, heel to glute. Still, a sharp pain bloomed across the meat of his upper back, the same instant his stomach slammed into the dirt. Greydal arced his axe away from him, a farewell, perpendicular to the ground. Its hum was a moan.

He sensed Yphrus fall to his right, and he rolled as fresh blood on his axe spattered his face. He heard the man howl and shifted to look at his opponent, a beautiful sight greeting his bleary eyes: Yphrus holding a pale foot in one hand and destroyed ankle in the other.

He had done it. Greydal yelled and used his axe to hook the handle of Yphrus' saw and pull it away from the bleeding man. Someone, maybe Loken, called out, "Do not leave him in agony. Finish the Nayuda." Greydal nodded to no one and dragged himself towards his enemy. He must have looked terrifying because he saw horror in the man's eyes.

A bloody, pink doll crawling across the dirt, a snake come to take your life.

He lifted himself like he did when performing push-ups and swiped at Yphrus with the axe, causing the man's head to roll away and a geyser of blood to shower them both. Greydal thought of the beast he and Rulf had hunted in the long grass and smiled.

***   ***   ***

They had to help him out of the pit. Whether from adrenaline or hunger, Greydal shook like a rattle. He could barely hear beyond the sound of blood rushing in his ears. Loken pulled him up and patted him on the back.

"*Intach!* Fantastic! They will never stop telling this one."

He struggled to speak through his shaking jaw. "L-Loken, I th-think—" he swallowed and pointed to his back.

"Ah, he barely caught you! Do not worry, my friend. We will stitch you."

Greydal nodded and let Loken fasten the wooden leg to his knee. He panted for a moment, leaning against the older man.

Then the world resolved: the noise which deafened him wasn't the rushing of blood.

It was cheering.

PART

TWO

FOR SOME NEW DELIGHT

"As a child I felt myself to be alone, and I am still, because I know things and must hint at things which others apparently know nothing of, and for the most part do not want to know."

-*Memories, Dreams, Reflections,* by Carl Jung

CURSE

Greydal went to Mabet for the first time two months after Yphrus' death. It was the eve of Greydal's tatu ceremony, and he was in a hurry. The boy, Higg, dogged his steps as he left the basin, seeking an isolated corner of the carved mountain range. It took Greydal the better part of an hour to make his way through the artificial corridors hewn into the rock. The night sky materialized over their heads as they escaped the tunnel, and he whirled on the boy who had tried and failed to follow without being noticed.

"Stop."

"Stop what? You'll have to be more specific, *sckapod.*"

"Mabet is liable to turn us both into trees."

"You know she can't do that."

"I have no idea *what* she can do." After a moment, Greydal added, "Just tell Zela how you feel. You don't have to avoid her."

"You're already half a tree anyway, what do you care?" Higg dodged a smack from Greydal and said, "As for Zela, you're crazy. Have you seen her?"

"I have, and you're her match. Don't be intimidated."

"Oh, like you and Roan?" The boy made a sound like a clucking bird.

"That's different," Greydal replied and continued walking along the ridge towards the summit. The night was clear, and the vast framework behind it loomed just over his head, almost as if it were close enough to touch as he climbed to the sheer surface of the mountain's scalp. The air here was thinner than in the basin and caused his breath to shorten as he spoke over his shoulder, "I know you're following me."

"I'm not going away."

"Fine, then juggle rocks or throw them off the side. Just don't come any closer or I'll beat you." He didn't wait for Higg to respond and strode across the stone.

In the distance, he spied a twisted metal structure sprouting from a rocky outcropping. Roan had told him to look for something called *the aircraft*, and he supposed the burned, silver wreck to be it.

The thing glowed from within, and when he drew close, he called out, "Mabet! It's Greydal." But the night remained still, and he heard no reply, only the cackling of a fire from a circular portal to his left. Glass rimmed the opening like teeth, and he wondered at their thickness, at least two inches in width.

He wandered around the ruin and encountered a second aperture. It was a door of some kind. The silver oval rose diagonally from the shale, which half-consumed it, and an unidentifiable leather glued to the metal acted as a barrier. He placed his hand on the spotted hide and pulled back the opening—a darkened hallway materialized. Assuming this to be a sort of test, Greydal entered. A sense of familiarity descended on him as he noticed what the metal hall reminded him of: the barracks. Did the Old Folk make this building? The Legate himself, or only others like him? Greydal didn't know.

The interior was sparse, the footing uneven, and even with his new leg, he had to take care. As he turned a corner, a blaze greeted him, illuminating a small room. Then he smiled to himself, relaxing. Not a blaze, a dying fire. Smoke rose from the flames and curled through a jagged hole in the sloped ceiling.

He entered the lit space and looked for Mabet, but the old woman wasn't present. Had he come at the wrong time? Roan told him that the *veya-bruya*, the old witch, would wait for him at a fire. He stood in the empty room, unsure of what to do. Noticing the broken window from earlier, he walked towards it and peered outside, but there was only the darkened scalp of the mountain, spreading into the night. He watched the inky shadows of clouds inch across the rock. He blinked. Had he seen clouds on his approach?

Mabet spoke behind him. "Your name, do you know it?"

He whirled. The old woman sat on the other side of the flames. Her dark habit made her form hard to distinguish, and in the uncertain light, Mabet's eyes were like Roan's. Behind her, the woman's shadow spread across the metal, quivering with the erratic palpitations of the flame. But the crone's eyes weren't fixed on his. They appeared to stare at something just behind him.

He tried to maintain his composure, though his heart raced. "Dame Mabet? Is that how I'm supposed to address you?" He added lamely, "It's how we did it in my home."

Mabet didn't respond. She continued looking over his shoulder at the window. Did she even see him? He opened his mouth to speak, but the woman interrupted, "I see. You need help. I will give it." She made a strange gesture with her hand. Her shadow on the wall copied her.

Of course, it did.

Then a fierce image flashed in his mind, a circular portal of stone. He saw the way to open it, how to climb down. Greydal squeezed his eyes and dispelled the intrusive thoughts. Mabet had just done something to him.

"What—" He shook his head, opening his eyes. The image of the circular stone pressed its way back into his awareness. He leaned against the metal wall. The old woman stayed where she sat, somehow now in front of the exit.

"Do you see?" she asked as the image of the stone faded somewhat.

"What... did you do to me?"

"You are—how does Loken put it? Wedged between a hard place and stone."

"I don't understand." She looked at him expectantly, and he tried again, "The hole, why am I here?" Still, she said nothing.

Greydal decided she wouldn't answer, and he stepped away from the wall to make his exit around her when she replied, "Do you wish your friend to hear this as well?"

"My...friend?" Who did she mean was with him? Mabet raised her eyebrows.

Oh. Greydal turned and yelled at the shattered window, "Higg! I swear to the Dawn, I will throw you off this mountain!" He heard light feet scamper away before he turned back, now waiting for Mabet to explain why she had summoned him to this blasted heap. He fought to ignore the still-swirling illusions which peeked from the edges of his vision. The old woman's wrinkled face peeled upwards in a smile, something Greydal had not seen her do before.

"He is a good boy. Your influence on him will benefit the kith, I think." Greydal thanked her to not appear rude and returned to the task of steadying himself on the dull wall.

Mabet continued, "I will explain. I am sure you have questions. First, know you are stuck, like a baby deer in the mud. And like a baby deer, you fumble. You have no hope of leaving the mud. So, I gave you a push."

"A push," Greydal repeated.

She nodded. "You will one day come upon a place, a series of warrens, seemingly on accident. It will be no accident. Old and hollowed is this realm, filled with pits, tunnels. Within just such a catacomb is that which will force you to either die or accept the truth."

"What is the truth?"

She smiled. "Would you believe it were I to tell you? I think not."

"Try anyway."

"Oh? You have command of me now?" Her grin widened further, raising the hairs on the nape of Greydal's neck. "Roan, she says you had trouble in the grove," she whispered.

Greydal shook his head. "Trouble's a word for it."

"And? Have you not once dwelt upon your experience there? The grove is a sacred place."

Greydal frowned. Of course, he had. But the events in the thicket meant nothing to him, despite his attempts at worrying free some sort of understanding. He had seen...

What *had* he seen?

"You saw the beginning of the death of the realms, and their rejuvenation at the hands of Bythos. Or perhaps its parent."

Bythos. There was that word again. "A name? You said that earlier. When Roan and I arrived," Greydal stated.

"Interloper. Old Man Moonlight. You may call it what you wish. It, *or* that from which it issued, is the sole reason the realms, such as they were, are not now decaying piles of rot."

"The Interloper? What do you know about it?" Greydal's pulse stuttered.

She raised an eyebrow. "Not as much as you, I suspect."

"I don't—" He grew flustered.

"You want to know the link?" Her expression was playful. "Perhaps you simply are unready to hear the truth. You should know by now. I suspect the *incident* in the grove was not the first in which you had...trouble?"

His thoughts flashed to Alom's study. To the night in the old house. "I think I'm haunted." The words left his mouth before he knew what he was saying.

The old woman cackled. "The only thing you are haunted by is yourself."

He folded his arms. The witch seemed incapable of speaking in anything other than riddles. He was more confused than when he had entered the old woman's ruined home. Not for the first time since his and Roan's fight, he wished he was with her. He and the girl had barely talked since the Nayuda.

"Tonight, I will send Roan away." The witch's words broke his reverie.

He was quiet for a moment. The sound of the flames could have spoken for him, but he replied, "Does she know yet?"

"The last dark moon. That is when I told the girl."

"It's because of me, isn't it?" Greydal asked at length. "Because of her oaths?"

Mabet nodded but said, "You represent her here, Greydal the man. Yet, it is not her oaths alone that send her far from us."

"Oh."

"I have something I must show you."

"Like you did when I entered?"

She smiled a second time. "Look to the fire," she stated. He stared at her, wary of another trick. The intensity of her gaze forced him to glance away.

Fine. Fire it is.

Greydal looked at the flames and was shocked to see images dancing in the piercing light. He watched them flutter and toil. After several entranced minutes, he broke his gaze and whispered, "These...they're Sophites, aren't they?"

"Look again."

He obeyed and yelped when he saw what had become of the fiery figures

No.

No, no, no.

It was either the flames themselves or the images of strewn bodies, which now summoned sweat and fear, the same he had experienced on the night his village blazed. He fought to breathe as the old woman watched him. He withered under the light and Mabet's black stare, and he forced himself to look at the images the fire produced. In between the dancing tongues, Greydal recognized his name.

'Greydal, Come To Us.'

His hand was over his mouth, and he spoke through it, "Some of these...the Friars did them. You can tell by the way the stomachs are opened, the necks and mouths, too. But the others..." The dead Sophites' heads were twisted around like owls.

Mabet spoke, "Valbadaoth, the Wyrm. Roan tells me you call him Legate."

"He wrote my name."

"In the blood of our people, yes."

Greydal shook his head, speechless. The man still sought him? This went beyond the Interloper's mark, surely. The laughing of the flames filled the cabin for a time, and when he looked again, the dead Sophites had vanished. Only embers were there now.

At last, he spoke, "What does he want?"

"For you to go to him."

"But why?"

"I hope Roan will find answers for the both of us. Though, I maintain suspicions."

Greydal examined the old woman and calculated the odds of her lying to him. He decided confrontation was his best approach. It was unlikely she didn't know already, after all. He started slowly, "My second night here, I found something. A book. It was in the spot Loken placed me, King Marcos' old room." He waited to see if she would ask him. She didn't. But *she knew*, he could see it in her eyes.

He continued, "The book. I've seen it before, its type, all wrapped in plastick. It came from my village. From Harlow." Again, Mabet said nothing. She waited for him to finish. He furrowed his brow as he said, "You *sent* him to us, didn't you? Disguised as a Kludde. Was it just for that book?"

Her face remained serene, and Greydal gritted his teeth. Why wouldn't she answer? His voice was harsh as he said, "If you sent Marcos for *that* book in particular, you know more about the Legate than you're letting on, so don't lie to me."

This time, he forced himself to wait for Mabet's reply. He would sit in the chamber with her all night if that's what it took. He needed to hear her acknowledge it.

He didn't have to wait long. Mabet spoke, "Those books, they are not from your village. Tier did not have the right to take them. Our Marcos tried to recover them all, and failed, though he managed to slip away with the one you speak of."

Greydal blinked. He stared at the crone and felt the air leave the room. Slowly, he lowered his head into his hands as the wind picked up outside, creating a howl to mirror his thoughts. He had been so fucking blind. How had he not seen it? For a time, he let the silence hang between him and the old woman.

Eventually he sighed. There was no point in arguing with her about his father. He knew it was true. Instead, he said, "Alright, so my point stands. That book, Number 03 It tells us about the Legate, though not directly."

"I have not read it, though I am familiar with its contents." She was smiling again. She continued, "I know what you are going to say. It is a mystery. How can tulka be a crafted race as the sky was crafted?"

Greydal nodded. He said, "The Old Folk made the book. Rather, books, since there were several. They made my axe. They made the Rings from my home. They did the sky and the walls beyond the Edges of the world. But that book, it said they made my kind, too, the tulka."

"You doubt it? The first of you were theirs."

Greydal shook his head. "See, that doesn't make sense, though. The Legate is tulka, like me. So, how can he be one of the Old Folk who *made* us?"

"Ah..." Her wrinkled grin widened, becoming close to her misshapen ears. Greydal spotted three teeth in haphazard arrangement. The woman whispered, "It seems I am more familiar with the plastick book than you are, Greydal the man."

"What do you mean?"

"I will let you discover that for yourself. The second part of the tome tells of your peoples' creation in the old world. Why not read further?"

Though her suggestion sounded innocent, the gleam in her eyes made Greydal afraid to find out what else Number 03 could tell him.

*** *** ***

He returned to Mabet's home several years later, the day before he left the Sophites for good. This time, when he exited the mountain tunnels, dawnlight saluted him, spraying the ridge with a vivid crimson. He sidled along the outcropping and surmounted the sheared plateau. Mabet's downed craft was the same as it had been the night he received his tatu. What had he and the old woman spoken of then, aside from the plastick book? That fiery murk shuffled, a warm dance in his memory. He shook his head and approached the crashed flyer. No smoke billowed out of its top this time—Mabet stood in front of her home, waiting for him.

She was much smaller in the light. Prior to this moment, he had only encountered her a handful of times, seeing her perched atop ridges overlooking the basin to greet or perhaps inspect returning crews. Other times, he caught her speaking to the kith's children, giving them toys, and spinning them odd tales. Yet at her friendliest, she unsettled, as she did now.

Greydal swallowed as a pale curve emerged from the woman's habit. It was a hand, holding out a red envelope. He approached, and his throat tightened. "Do we have an outsider?"

He hoped not—he had no desire to fight a third Nayuda. And besides, he had given his axe to Faros, Yphrus' brother, two years back.

Mabet applied her usual tactic of failing to reply, so he took the envelope as her withered limb retreated to darkness. He discovered the envelope already opened and slid out the letter before recognizing Roan's handwriting. It was hard to parse and appeared written in such a way an outsider wouldn't gain much from the text. It read:

M, I know you're reading this. Please, pass this to him.

Lovely, I found it. Go to the spot where that nice craftsman helped us, you remember? Then go left for a long while until you see a white tree, hollowed out in the center by a tiny home (quite small, you'll see it if you look). At the tree, go right and stay right until you see a fallen, golden roof. Take the left fork. You will encounter a pond. Go the direction we went when we saw the owls (I forgot to mention, pack heavy). Don't leave your path. You will look for an animal, the same one on L's face. Find the place where we floated.

Kisses, R

A cool breeze ruffled his short topknot. He gazed over the top of letter at Mabet, who watched him. "What does she mean?" he asked.

"I imagine she means what she says, as is her way."

Greydal folded the letter and placed it in his satchel. He stroked his stubble. "You know I have to go, don't you?" he asked.

"They are loading Agatha as we speak, I think. You will leave the red wagon here."

Greydal shook his head and said, "No, the kith needs her. I'll take a hinny." In response, Mabet smiled and said, "The she-bull trusts you. She may stand you in good stead. You are going into danger, though you do not yet know it."

"What are you saying?"

"Only that you seem to have forgotten our last meeting in this place."

He admitted he mostly had.

She replied, "Do not rely on your kris alone. You are soon to treat with the otherworld...once again, I fear."

Greydal tilted his head. "I... otherworld?"

She nodded.

"You talk like I know what that is."

She waved a hand. "Just what is always around the next bend."

"I don't understand."

"Have you not seen it in dreams? Wise children fear what lies under their cots... wise men avoid the woods at night. Mankind later chose to look past the sky in wonder. Collective unconscious, Milky Way, Arcadia—these all mean the same. This place is within your own heart. Remember that."

He didn't know what she was talking about so he nodded and asked, "Is that it, then?"

The crone paused for a moment and then smiled to herself. She replied, "Ensure Higg does not follow you. He will try. If you return, we will welcome you."

Greydal frowned and nodded, the bright morning sun blinding him momentarily as he glanced up. Always, the past seemed to reach for him.

"I'll leave tonight, with the mists."

As he moved away, beginning to stride towards the edge of the mountaintop, she asked softly, "What I asked of you. Did you do it?"

He paused and turned. "I'm— what?"

"Do not play the imbecile. You read it all, did you not?"

Falling quiet, Greydal thought about what she said. Of course, he had read the rest of the plastick book. Number 03, with its damning secrets. He had read it more times than he could count, but what emerged from his mouth was, "No."

***   ***   ***

"*Intach*," Greydal told Faros. "It's delicious."

The blonde man nodded. "The last of our batch. How are you always so lucky?"

Greydal smiled and said, "I'm all bad luck, I promise."

Faros smiled and replied, "Is that so? And you brought it to my door?"

"It's the ancestor axe. I need to borrow it."

The man raised ink marks where his eyebrows would have been. The curved room in which they sat in became pregnant with the ensuing silence. After a time, Faros stated, "You're leaving." It was not a question.

Greydal confirmed it and told the man it wasn't for a long time, or so he hoped.

Faros replied, "I cannot return it to you, I'm sorry. It has my brother's blood on its edge, and I won't part with it. What if you don't return?"

Greydal nodded. He expected the response. "I understand. It was worth it to ask."

He made to stand, but Faros cut in. "Why? You've left on hunts in the past and simply taken a kris or long blade. Where are you going?"

Greydal smiled and replied, "I can't tell." It was the truth. He had the name of a location and a series of directions. Though he had no idea if that would be where he ended up.

He stood, and Faros said, "Wait. I will not let you leave empty handed." The man rose from his seat and left the room, soon returning with a velvet bag before handing it over. Greydal opened it and pulled out the contraption within. He stared as he held it under the skylight. The blades were hidden now, but he recognized the weapon, nonetheless.

"It's called a *dai-strelok*."

"I-I've seen one before. I don't think I ever told you about my ear."

Faros laughed deep from within his belly. He exclaimed, "Someone shot you with a dai-strelok?! You *are* lucky. They should have made your tatu a hare's foot and not those tangles."

Greydal smiled and replied, "Roots were considered more ironic at the time. Also, I think they might have been the only things that could properly cover my markings without looking silly."

"Well, the weapon is yours now. Do you know how to use one?"

Greydal said he didn't, and Faros showed him how to activate it. "You can draw and shoot without priming. But if you know you will be battling, place your finger here to alert the blades within. They will emerge."

"Thank you, Faros. Hopefully, I won't have to use it."

Faros put his arm on Greydal's shoulder. He said, "Wherever you are headed, I wish you well, my friend. Don't flinch." Greydal said he wouldn't and hugged the man.

"See you."

"You as well."

Greydal put the dai-strelok in its bag and hung it from his belt, then left Faros' quarters. As he strode through the meeting-house's golden corridors, he thought about the task ahead. He would need supplies, though Mabet indicated Agatha might already be packed with them.

He set his mind instead to how he would prevent Higg from following.

***   ***   ***

An evening escape, just after the sun gave way to the staring moon. He didn't ride Agatha through the mists but led her by her harness. "Come on, girl. It's going to be a long journey," he whispered. The fog stole his words.

As they neared the rising crags, he thought of his first time in the mists and shivered. Once he arrived at the crevasse, which led away from the mountains, he breathed a sigh of relief and helped Agatha find her footing over the loose rocks. They walked through the night, passing the surreptitious thorned forest where the animal people went about their bizarre lives. Near dawn, he reached a road. South for a while, then west all the way.

It was a month before the Legate found him.

OCCULTATION

There was a face just beyond sight. A tongue, clamoring at the edges. It sought the special thing hiding behind blood and bone. Greydal shook himself, tried to send it anywhere else. But the air buzzed. The thoughts which swarmed him had emerged from the surrounding road several hours before like the impossible memory of someone else's dream, and they *clung*. Weeks of trudging wildernesses and half-seen places coming to fruition: the truth long after him now near, or rabid.

There, they came again. Not whispers and not thoughts, but something in the middle, crashing against his psyche to help him understand what he refused to know:

Interpret all things and change them. Count all the gods, the demons. Know that there is one more. There is one more. There is one more. There is one more. There *is—*

Mercifully, Higg spoke when Greydal's wayward strides brought them close to collision.

"Too close!"

Greydal's eyes opened, and he returned from...where? The winding farm road had hypnotized him, he had lost himself amidst confused mysteries of dirt and wind. But yes, he was back, himself. He was travelling west along a farm road with Higg and Agatha. The boy juggled three apples he had swiped from an orchard that morning. Greydal nudged him with his foot, causing Higg to drop one.

Now, one month later, the boy juggled three apples he had swiped from an orchard that morning. Greydal nudged him with his foot, causing him to drop one.

"Ass! I was doing so well."

"Look," Greydal said with a confused tongue, gestured at the oncoming barn. The building rose monumental, a castle of wood and iron. He said, "That has to be bigger than the meetinghouse."

Higg stared in shock. "I'm more interested in those," the boy said and pointed beyond the barn. "I didn't know they made equines that large."

Greydal searched where his companion indicated and found he agreed. The hooved creatures striding the field beyond the building were the largest animals he had ever seen. One turned its head towards them, slow as melting ice.

"Gah!" Higg exclaimed. "Its eyes!" he laughed. Though the thing was misty from distance, Greydal saw the protruding white orbs on the equine's massive skull. They stared at the travelers with dimwitted intelligence.

"I hate it."

"I do, too," the boy agreed.

"What about you, Agatha?" Greydal asked.

The she-bull resolutely avoided looking at the behemoths in the distance. "Probably a good tactic," he told her. He turned to

Higg and inhaled deeply, somewhat clearing the cobwebs suffocating his tired thoughts. Then he said, "I don't think they're dangerous, but let's hurry to the tree line."

Higg nodded, placing his apples into his pack. They jogged the rest of the way to the woodland, a wall of fat, colored trees crouching low a mile ahead. As they closed the distance, the two perceived buildings within the forest itself, their tops peeking over mangy, convoluted crowns.

Greydal huffed as he ran, "I wish I had Agatha's stamina."

Higg looked over his shoulder at the she-bull cheerfully trotting behind them. The boy replied, "Hey, stop complaining. One less leg to get tired."

Greydal tried to swipe at him, but Higg evaded it, as always.

After several minutes, they reached the forest, only to find it wasn't one. What they had imagined as trees now appeared closer to stone, porous and growing labyrinthine into one another, save for the space the road carved.

As they approached the intricate growths, Higg whispered, "It looks like sponges."

"What's that?"

"Sponges."

"You said that. What are sponges?"

"Oh, type of animal. Saw them in one of Shezarhi's books once."

"Hm." Greydal nodded sagely.

Green polyps, tinged with red, shaded them as they approached. Thick, yellow orbs hung like fruit beneath the puffing boughs. "Candy," Higg said. Further in, the pale buildings the two had spotted before jutted from deep within the confusion of not-stone. A metal cross with a long bottom crowned each of the visible structures.

"Those are temples."

"How do you figure?" Higg asked.

"Look at them." When Higg tilted his head, Greydal explained, "They're overbearing and humble at the same time. Built to be seen."

As Higg stared at the half-hidden ruins, Greydal turned and gave one last look behind him at the creatures near the towering barn. All five of the distant equines were looking in his direction. He hurried into the shelter of the polyps, and Higg laughed.

Greydal replied in irritation, "Be quiet, both of you," causing Agatha to produce a confused, cowy expression.

That night, they made plans to camp at the side of the road. Greydal unloaded the utensils from one of Agatha's satchels and asked Higg, "Will you start the fire?"

The boy nodded but complained as he trudged into the honeycombs to search for something burnable. Greydal ignored him and turned to Agatha.

He patted the she-bull's large head, telling her, "Thanks for protecting us from those things in the field, brave woman." She blinked in response.

He set down the utensils and pulled the brush from her saddle, running it along her flank as Agatha swished her tail. He slowly moved back to her head, then sweeping her neck and front.

"In a minute I'll get that pack off you, and we can brush underneath it."

As he worked, he saw light gleam in her wet eyes. "Thanks, that was record time," he told Higg.

The Legate replied, *"I try, but we dance at your pace."*

*** *** ***

Higg grumbled as he pushed through the thick undergrowth. Why did Legless always make him search for kindling? Every time he asked Greydal, the older boy would rub his stump and complain while looking out the side of his eye at Higg. Higg supposed he had asked for it. He was the one who followed the man out of the mountains, after all.

The towering sponges and their fruits were all soft to the touch, though parts looked like rock. But on the bed (he couldn't think of it as the ground), small tubes poked in their dryness, bones of something that had once grown verdant before perpetual shade deprived them of vitality. He broke, and then carried this bundle of pale twigs as he wove between the elaborate maze of porous structures, returning to camp. Light in the distance greeted his eyes, and he paused. Had Legless already started a fire somehow? The bastard. Higg dropped his twig-bones and made his way towards the glow but halted when he heard voices.

Who was Greydal talking to? Not Agatha. Higg crouched and crept across the soft bedding. When he nearly reached the road, he encountered a bizarre sight. Greydal stood with his back to Agatha, dai-strelok in hand. He spoke to someone hidden from view. In front of the man, the wildland disappeared. A golden, marbled floor replaced it, flickering in and out of sight. Where had *that* come from? Light spilled from it across the hardened path.

Higg strained his ears, but couldn't make out what his friend said. Creeping closer, he tried to ignore the swelling fear gnawing at his heart. Greydal looked like he did that day, the time he killed the bully Yphrus. The sharp potential of violence tightened the air. In it, Higg thought he caught a whiff of something pleasant. Perfume? As he drew almost flush with the road he heard a horrible voice, dispelling these thoughts.

"If you fire that daggergun, I'll take it from you. Then I'll break your arm. The witches aren't here to protect you."

Greydal replied, "Not if I shoot you in your fucking head."

"Quaint. You're welcome to try. Or you can put it away, and we can speak like adults."

Higg poked his head from behind a damp polyp and evaluated the speaker. It was another Greydal, encased in a kind of shining suit, almost up to his chin. No, not armor, something else. It looked like ancestor tech. Higg's eyes widened further. It *was* Greydal's face, no doubt. Yet, a different intelligence animated it, one practiced at a great, superior disinterest.

The second Greydal spoke, *"Answer me this. There is a house one enters blind but exits seeing. What is it?"*

Higg's Greydal said, "What—" and a golden blur blinked across the space. The other Greydal now held Higg's by the throat. A hiss, like a serpent reached his ears, and Higg saw steam escape the attacker's golden suit. Higg's hands closed into fists. He had to do something.

*** *** ***

Greydal fought against the Legate's grip. He tried to bring his weapon to bear but a second vise closed on his wrist as screeching 'cada bugs muttered in his ear, *"You and I are going to put—"* the hand forced his arm towards his satchel, *"the daggergun back into your bag. How does that sound?"*

The hand squeezed Greydal's wrist until his bones bent. He dropped the dai-strelok, and the pressure on his arm vanished. The Legate now held the tool.

"Impressive make. I won't take it from you." The man flipped open the satchel with the tip of the weapon and dropped it inside before latching the flap. Greydal continued to try and free himself to no avail.

"I can see you're in no mood to talk. That's fine. Either way, you're coming with—"

A loud yell interrupted the tulka. There was a smacking noise and Agatha lowed, almost trampling Greydal as she barreled into the Legate. Greydal fell to the ground and fought for his breath, almost immediately feeling hands dragging him up.

"Come on! We have to run," Higg hissed.

He let his friend pull him to his feet, and looked over his shoulder at what had become of the Legate. The tulka laid on his back, near where the road ended at some sort of shining room or hallway. Agatha was attempting to gore the man and dragged him across the ground with her rudimentary horns. Higg pulled at Greydal, but he shrugged the boy off.

"Agatha!" Greydal's shaking hand tried to unlatch his satchel, but he couldn't feel his fingers. As he fumbled, he saw the Legate punch the she-bull from his prone position, causing her head to whip back. She stumbled towards the shining room.

"Greydal," Higg pleaded. The golden man rose and approached the stunned she-bull.

Greydal got the latch open, only to watch in abject horror as the Legate grabbed a dazed Agatha's head and broke off one of her horns, then plunging the short spike through the she-bull's skull.

"NO!" He withdrew his weapon.

The air shifted.

The Legate and Greydal froze. Both, in their own way, felt the sky descend, though the Legate was the first to look up. He made a sound like a startled cat and vanished, along with the after-images of the magick room. Darkness returned to the road as every hair on Greydal's body stood at attention. A lump crawled towards his throat.

Higg let go of his friend and gazed around in bewilderment. Where had the golden tulka gone? Even the curious, marbled room had disappeared.

He sensed movement overhead and looked to the sky. A cloud, huge and dark, eclipsed the furtive light of the moon. The under-side of the cloud roiled as though filled with eels, and seemed to hover only feet above the indistinct heights of the tallest of the polyp conglomerations. Lights like windows opened and closed along its circumference.

Greydal was in the thicket. In the old house. They were one and the same, conjoined in the twilight of the road. Black water poured into his body from a direction he didn't know existed as he falteringly looked up at the mask of the Interloper, the thing covering the night sky.

Then that *changed*, becoming a nest of lengthy hair, all blackened blood and bursting skin beneath. It clogged the sky, and a smell unlike anything he'd ever experienced wafted down, burning his nostrils; a cloying thing that infiltrated his skull and flashed his mind with images of pale figures, emaciated and hunched over someone on a metallic table. Then the vision burst as the coiling ropes above him shuddered and a keening rose, almost like the sound a flute makes, splitting the night. But even this horror wasn't the real thing, he somehow sensed. If he would only wait, it would reveal its true shape, if anything could be considered true in this place. Yes, even now, the scalp beneath the writhing hair parted to reveal it wasn't.

Each of the filaments rose now into an infinity, fishing lines from the heart of creation. Yet this, too, was a lie, he somehow knew; a mask rearranging to form a face both familiar and horrible. But the grotesquerie from before was already enough. His mind fled the sight.

"Hail! Hail! Hail!" the polyps screamed.

*** *** ***

Minutes passed. The eyes that stared down at Higg made him an insect. Drool leaked from the boy's gaping mouth as he ogled without thought at what the cloud had become. A tiny voice, a mouse in his brain, told him to run, to seek the safety of the spongy labyrinth. Yet, he couldn't move. He dimly registered Greydal had fled, that he stood alone.

No, not alone. There was dancing in the woods. Lights flashed and drums beat.

He whimpered as the face above quivered, and then sloughed away, peeling back into a fearless, seismic night, one far vaster than any he had witnessed in his short life.

*** *** ***

Gloom. Pain. Greydal shook his head. Where was he?

He curled on a soft floor amidst clotting shadows and a cold wetness invaded in his cassock, under his arms. Fear sweat. He blinked and became aware of a column of cold moonlight, which illuminated him in a perfect circle. A round hole in the ceiling. He was inside...something. Greydal fumbled for his satchel and found it unlatched and almost empty. He pulled out what he sought, a glowstone. It was the same one Roan had used in the thicket's maze years ago. The thicket. Greydal blinked again and struck the stone against the metal latch of his satchel. The world expanded around him.

By the artifact's light, he could tell that oddly-shaped tunnel openings surrounded him like the legs of a spider spreading outwards. That seemed to mean he was in the center room, or *a* center room of whatever complex he inhabited. Greydal peered up at the circular opening from which he had presumably fallen. Near it, greenish roots of a strange, porous make plunged from the stone via cracks and holes. So, he was underground, then. He must have fallen and hit his head. Greydal rubbed his temples and tried to remember:

An image of a fire, and that of an old woman sitting across it were the only things he could recall. He falteringly stood then, and spun in a slow circle. The corridors would have been lightless, but with the stone, he could tell they hoarded objects in haphazard arrangement on uneven shelves. Some of these shelves were bolted to walls, while others were crafted like bookcases or door-less cabinets, likewise bolted or leaning. As he peered, gleaming dust rose from the carpeted floor, filling the space before him and bouncing along the stifled air. As it joyfully crept up his nostrils, he halted a sneeze. His fall must have disturbed the dust, that was why the stuff was so active. He ignored the glinting particles and turned to the nearest tunnel opening. He couldn't say why, but he was anxious to be out from under the hole in the ceiling. Walking forward, he left behind the untroubled particles which still sought his nose and mouth.

As he trudged, he kept his head straight, and his eyes un-focused. Where was Roan? He was supposed to meet her. Of that, he was positive. *Her letter!* He remembered now. Her letter was so sparse it was almost an insult. But what else wasn't he remem-bering?

A series of unclear images emerged and made him drowsy with effort, so he released them.

It seemed he had been running at the very least. Within its wooden housing, the bone and flesh of his stump flared with heat and a sweaty ache. That didn't bode well, but he contin-ued walking in the near lightlessness of the tunnel, holding the stone before him. As he did, an unhappy, but unrelated, follow-up thought reared. Why wouldn't he look at the contents of the shelves which crowded on both sides?

He kept his eyes fixed to retreating gloom ahead, for a time, trying to remember what he was doing here.

*** *** ***

The festival continued as a sweltering twilight overtook the day. The tavern owner told him the event would last three days and three nights, but failed to mention that the revelers didn't seem to require sleep. Greydal was unsure what significance such a remote location held to the yellow-eyed visitors, but admitted to himself that they were likely harmless. Or rather, uninterested in causing harm. The strangers appeared content to chat and sing and carouse through the tavern grounds and the impending woods. *Woods.* Greydal shook himself and continued to climb the stairs to the third floor of the tavern. The shouting and cheering below grew indistinct but no less deafening.

Why couldn't Roan have chosen a better meeting place? It didn't matter now, he mused. He was here and he'd paid for the room for the week. All he had to do was wait. He made himself continue to climb, eventually mounting the third-floor landing. The gleaming light of the sconces and the smothering heat of the evening made the space appear to shrink. His clothes were damp as he marched down the furthest hallway. Greydal passed closed and empty rooms, arriving at the amber door the innkeeper had referenced. The key slid in with no effort, and soon after, he was inside the lodging.

At first, he couldn't tell what was wrong with the room. He laid his pack by the entrance and paused to let his eyes adjust to the sudden lack of glare. The space was dark, but moonlight or something like it streamed through the disc-shaped window at the far end of the chamber. There was a bed, a chair, and a table. A dresser gaped in surprise at the empty space. A faint smell of fungus lingered.

The raucous sounds from below were louder here, probably streaming in through the thin glass pane. Yes, his eyes told him that he was the sole occupant of the lodging. But the hairs on his arms and neck stood as he sensed a surreptitious activity, an attention all around him. It was just beyond his ability to identify, and he stood there frozen for a moment, trying to understand what he was experiencing.

As fast as the feeling had come upon him, it left. He was alone.

*** *** ***

By the second night of the yellow-eyed strangers' festival, Greydal had almost had enough. If the previous evening was hot, tonight threatened to turn his bed to a mire. His room smelled like toadstools and mold and the cacophony below sounded like the cries of a town drowning in a mudslide, set to string music.

Greydal lay on his side, facing a wall which writhed in the dark and the heat. He had long since removed his clothes, and though he had abandoned the sheets as well, he was smothered. It was like he shared his small bed with an overly affectionate but invisible companion. Greydal wished he could push it off him, but there was nothing there. After several minutes or hours of gazing at the wall, he surrendered, rising to stand in the dark of the room, the light from the woods streaming across the floor. Troubled, he left the lodging.

As he made his way down the hall, he paused outside one of the empty rooms next to his. He thought there was movement on the other side of the door, sending shadows to pool at the bottom of the entryway. He held his breath as he stared at the squirming patterns. Was he imagining it? He could have sworn the tavern owner had said this floor was empty.

No, he wasn't mistaking the movement because he could hear someone on the other side. A faint rustling, like the leaves of some old tree chuckled beyond the painted door. He stood there, sweating. This had happened to him before, hadn't it? He shook his head, he couldn't remember. Though he had left his sodden room, the odor of fungus seemed to have followed and accumulated around him, causing Greydal to wrinkle his nose. The smell must be from whoever was hiding in the empty room. He was sure of it.

As he made to reach for the handle and fling open the door to expose the dweller, a sound to his right made him stop. More than a sound he realized, turning to discover one of the yellow-eyed strangers peering at him, less than three strides away. It stared the way a dead animal's eyes stare, without comprehension. Something about the stranger bothered Greydal to his core, but the intensifying fungal stench made it hard to think. He let his hand fall from the door handle and turned to face the visitor. It made no move towards him, but appeared to stretch closer.

Greydal backed. Or tried to. A strange sensation overcame him then, the same one he had only recently experienced in his bed. It was as if he had walked into a forest of spiderwebs or a lover's hair. The rustling from beyond the door intensified as the invisible presence continued to caress and smother him. He struggled to breathe.

He hadn't noticed the yellow-eyed visitor move, but it was now within arm's reach. Greydal registered with great dismay what bothered him about the stranger. Faces shouldn't have seams.

He came to with a muffled gasp as he wrenched himself from the dream of the tavern and its occupants. The glowstone now lay on the ground to his left, and was no more than an ember while the thing which reached out of its stone bowl on the shelf enveloped his face and neck. Its dry leaves or auricles shined with golden dust as they tickled him. He fell backwards, and the tuberous appendage of the inhabitant on the shelf retracted in a lazy fashion from deep within Greydal's throat.

He coughed and shielded his eyes from the blazing aura the dweller emitted. The whole tunnel was hot as an oven, and the material under his hands didn't feel like a carpet. Averting his gaze from the shining plant caused him to discover, though the thing was bright, it illuminated none of the tunnel. With a lurch, he understood that the light shimmered in his head, not in the world around him. He could see it still, wherever he looked.

The plant-thing, twisting sluglike in the stone bowl, sighed. Greydal turned from the shelves to look at what the dweller seemed to indicate: the yellow-eyed visitor from his dream. It crouched only steps away in the hulking darkness of the tunnel. He recoiled as though struck, crawling backwards as fast as he was able. His wooden leg slid on the wet floor as, in his panic, his hand somehow found the dying glowstone. He swung it in front of him to ward off the watcher as he stumbled upright. The plant to his left withdrew into its housing.

The yellow-eyed visitor bleated and gazed at him vacantly. Greydal moaned as the thing *unfurled*, growing almost large enough to fill the tunnel. Some part of his mind howled that to wait was to die, but he stood rooted in panic, as if ice seized him. Feeling numb, he watched the thing's eyes bulge, and then distend, curling low to the living floor.

Tiny, translucent filaments followed. These filaments flicked towards him, but Greydal felt nothing as the now-red tubes pulled away and partially retracted into the creature's widening cavities. The revulsion rising like bile in his stomach allowed him to move. He made to flee, but not before he glimpsed the thing ripple and bend low to the ground, its eyes splitting apart like worms as it made a second, muffled bleat.

He rushed without thought, wishing that whatever was in the tunnel with him wasn't agile on its flexing protrusions. Wouldn't it injure its eyes, using them like that to propel itself?

His ruined leg ached, and sent a bolt of nausea up his body, but he reached a full sprint, and his stomach turned as he found he had no idea if he was going towards the entrance to the catacombs. Was he delving deeper into the subterranean complex? It didn't matter; he wouldn't turn around, not towards that shape which now fumbled after him.

As he fled, he glanced at the contents of the shelves by which he raced. How it was he had passed these things and not realized something was wrong? Why was he in this lightless space to begin with? The last thing he remembered was traveling to meet Roan.

No, there was something wrong with the sky. A face or presence arching down towards him from beyond the prism of night, bigger than the world. He recalled with dismay he had crawled into the honeycombed undergrowth to escape the presence. But why had he entered this place? How had he found it? He skidded to a halt, almost falling on the wet, furry floor. A column of soiled moonlight streamed through the ceiling.

A quick look the way he had come. There was no sign of yellow eyes or not-plants at his heel. Only rows and rows of terrible objects lining rotting shelves which squatted in the gloom. Greydal glanced at his only exit. Though the smell of fungus choked him, he could feel a cool breeze sinking down into the room. He watched as golden dust, which floated of its own accord through the tunnels, wafted towards the night sky.

He had to get out.

The thought was all encompassing as he spun in a circle. The dust obscured his vision, though it couldn't be on purpose. On a whim, he limped to the furthest tunnel from the one which he had just fled.

He almost cheered when he spotted a rope on a bookcase-like shelf to his left. Reaching for it without thinking he exclaimed in disgust upon realizing it was just something long and covered in hair. The item twitched as his hand almost brushed it. He backed involuntarily, his head pressing against something wet which hung from another shelf. He yelled and turned, batting the seeping thing away.

Snarling then, he grabbed the molden shelf, which housed the rope-like worm and other travesties. With a might fear granted him, he pleaded to the dark that the thing wouldn't come apart in his hands and heaved. Its moorings popped and the shelf tilted, its contents falling to the floor in a crash. Some of the items mewled and whined as he dragged the shelving with him, to the room with the hole in the ceiling.

The yellow eyes had multiplied since he had last seen them. They now filled the darkness of the first tunnel as the visitor emitted a child's scream and appeared on the cusp of spilling into the circular center room. Greydal's vision blurred.

Sometimes, in moments of extreme stress or terror, the mind finds ways to operate with all its faculties by adopting a form of madness. His panic deserted him as he switched to a better grip on the shelf. He dragged it the last few feet to the spot where tired moonlight activated the column of swirling pollen. The flowing, yellow-eyed horror was almost forgotten as he mounted the shelving, not knowing if the rotting timber would break under his weight. He climbed as though it would not. Rising until he stood, he balanced on the second to last plank and reached for one of the thick, polypal roots which plunged into the room. He grabbed at it with both hands, knowing that if he missed, he would fall.

It was enough, and Greydal kicked from his perch. The shelving tipped and fell across the sodden floor as he hauled himself higher towards the exit, flinging an arm out into the night air. He overshot and grasped soft bedding as his legs swam in the void. Then his hand found a stone rim, which surrounded the opening, and he leveraged himself up and out of the pit.

As he did, his flailing foot connected with what felt like one of the spongy roots. One savage kick, and he sprawled under moonlight across the bedding, then pulling his legs from the hole to lay on his back. The bloated forest shielded him as he wept and gasped.

Coming to his senses, he crawled from the mouth of the pit, certain that the silence from below did not mean he was safe from whatever had been groping after his foot as he dangled. Greydal crept on all fours and passed a disturbed, circular stone— the cork to the nightmare catacomb below.

He rose and trudged once his body allowed it. It wasn't clear at what point in the catacombs he had dropped his glowstone, but he was thankful that the treacherous moonlight was enough to navigate the underbrush. It had to be the moonlight that was so bright, he told himself. It wasn't the shining rays which still filled his mind finally spilling into the night.

He shuddered and spit, the taste of decay and mold pungent in his throat. The world was a puzzle of shadows and curved shapes as he stumbled through the weeds and groping branches. No, not those. He was in the sea of polyps, that strange un-woodland which pretended at foresthood. Nearby, the dilapidated corpse of one of the stone buildings menaced, the metal cross at its crown glimmering.

Soon, he came to the road. In the pulsing light of the night sky, he looked at himself, wiping the remaining pollen from his clothes and face, though his spit shined with it.

He stifled a yell.

CHAPTER

19

MEMBRANE

To Greydal's great displeasure, he remembered everything as he limped along the road. Agatha. Higg. The Legate. Even the face in the sky. Time had rewound to that night after the fire in Harlow Valley as the rules to which he had been accustomed crumbled, the world thrusting him into horror.

He located Agatha's body after a short time on the path. He cried and hugged her. She was too heavy to move. As he had tried pulling her, he flashed to Marcos' death. The two bodies were nearly the same: condensed and powerful, but now irrevocably still. He hoped someone would take the time to bury the she-bull if they came across the scene. Or cremate her like the king.

Higg wasn't on the road. However, Greydal managed to accidentally kick the fallen dai-strelok in the semi-darkness, and he picked it up, placing it in his satchel before pulling a bag off Agatha's torn saddle, filling it with salted meats, shavings, and other sundries. He called out for Higg but there was no answer. Sighing, he began a protracted search for his friend. An hour later, he passed out on the side of the road as he came trundling up from the fattened brush. There was no end in sight to the waste-land of polyps, and he couldn't make himself walk any more.

He slept.

Sunlight woke him. He opened and then closed his eyes, but the brightness didn't go away, so he rolled and rose to his feet. He blinked and turned, bewildered. Morning had yet to arrive, but a shining radiance pierced his vision. A tickling rose in his throat then, and he coughed, golden pollen floating away along the night air. His eyes widened, and he gagged. Greydal could *taste* the light inside of him, weighing down his skull. He staggered as it slowly turned to heat, to great pain. Greydal pawed at his satchel for water and found the canteen, quickly pouring it on his head, in his mouth. But the water did nothing. If anything, the shining only increased in power, as did the nauseous pain.

He yelled, and the night fled at the brightness in his skull. Spin. Stumble. Was he dying? The incandescence mushroomed and became truly, unbearably spiraling. He needed to find help. Walk. Fall. The ground was liquid fire. He tried to find the edge of the old stonework, thinking to dig, to hide in the softness, away from the awful radiance. Nothing but an unending, white field filled his vision as pain arced up his spine and across his body. He could feel it in his missing leg, and he panted like a dog.

There! An unlit rectangle in the distance. He stumbled upright, and then ran towards the sole point of darkness in this blazing world he inhabited. As he drew nearer, the light in his mind dimmed, but his suffering increased, and he howled his torment. Yet, he skidded to a halt when he recognized the space. No. No, it couldn't be. It wasn't *fair*.

The walls of the old house flexed around him, and obsidian, fleshy trees pushed in through the cracks. The well. The door to nothing. He backed from it and the light returned, stronger than ever as Greydal tasted blood. Despite the impossible glare, he could see who waited for him in the blackness. It was the face in the sky, the dweller who now stuck out a hand. A hand that gestured for him.

A small part of his mind knew this wasn't happening, not really. That plant in the catacombs had infected him with something. A poison, maybe. But it was more, wasn't it? In a split second, Greydal knew that, even if he *was* hallucinating, there was still someone standing there in the dark. It might not have been a shadowy copy of himself like his fevered brain insisted, but *something* reached for him from that lightless abode.

It was all one thing. The knowledge struck him like a blow. Ever since the Calf-ripper had come to Harlow Valley, his world had changed. The footsteps in Alom's hallway. The nightmares in the old house. The vision of an ancient apocalypse in the thicket. The well, the trees, the hand; they were all abstractions, like the golden lock at the northern gate of his home village. Gears beneath.

He gasped as a second wave of fire coursed through his bones, and in that moment, he surrendered. If the thing wanted him so bad, it could have him. Anything to stop this putrescent light, this torture. He dove towards the maw and its waiting inhabitant, and as he did, the black water from before drenched him, inside and out. A moan sounded in his mind as the plant's glowing presence died, incredible darkness replacing it. Then Greydal stood alone.

The only sound he now heard was his own ragged breathing. The pain had vanished, too. But where was he? He spun, seeing nothing, so he waved his hands in front of his face but perceived only far-flung dark, a newborn void rolling into the flat distance.

To the animals, nature is not wild nor is it mysterious. It is a duotone backdrop whose shades are life and death. Yet, there are some animals who, in the course of their winding lives, occasionally brush against things which stand out from the stage. Things which set whiskers a-quiver and make the animal mind think thoughts which are much too large.

Greydal bent to touch what he thought of as ground, but there was no sensation, as if cool, empty air pressed firm against his palm. *How was that possible?* A tiny thought whispered, the voice of a hare.

The coolness uncurled, draping over his skin like a second layer of clammy flesh. Though his breath was now shallow and quick, he fought to stay silent. Somehow, he could tell he wasn't alone. Something (or many somethings) perceived him, even if he couldn't see them. Their awareness was a small thing, like a drop of rain before a heavy downpour. But a strange, almost ancestral knowledge seemed to say these drops of rain hid mountains and would have the weight of mountains if he drew too much scrutiny.

Backing, he tried to clear his thoughts. The coolness which enveloped him congealed, dripping down his forehead, and he raised a hand to bat the feeling away. But then, seemingly without cause, an odd idea emerged from the sprawling hollowness he inhabited, squirming into his conscious awareness. His hand shook as he continued to raise it towards his face.

What face? What hand?

The answer, the *knowledge* was the key to his personhood's unravelling. The enveloping darkness rocketed away from him as Greydal escaped its confines, emerging into a *new* wilderness.

He became not himself. A crow with broken wings transformed into a twisted creature of hair and bile. They merged and bulged, and then burst like a bubble. Everything replaced them, a kaleidoscopic infinity. Greydal saw it all, *was* it all. And he was more. A shrieking chorus of life filled his guts as he tasted the black hysteria of the ever-expanding limits of his endlessness.

But his awareness shifted. Something greater loomed. He was as a mote next to this new thing which now regarded him.

Greydal had been here before, this place of impossible, lunatic beauty. And as he pondered this, a hand like the one he had recently owned reached from behind his shoulder, hatching from the place he had just escaped. It found and seized him as its owner whispered, "Sorry, it's not time for us yet."

All thought disappeared as the hand pulled him into the small, two-dimensional dream of his life.

Someone else opened their eyes and gasped.

*** *** ***

Strong hands carried Greydal like a baby. He struggled to open his eyes but couldn't manage it. Time stretched, and the even steps of the traveler lulled him to sleep.

He came to as the hands gently laid him on a bed of something soft, perhaps ferns. "Roan?" Greydal asked. A voice replied, "Easy, just sleep now. She's nearby." Greydal complied and let the darkness swallow him a second time. It felt like home.

He woke to real sunlight, though he flinched from it. The terror of the bright plant lingered in his memory like a threat, reminiscent of the Harlow fire in all the worst ways. As he carefully surveyed his situation, Greydal found himself sprawled (along with his bags) on a bed of pale flowers. The morning sky was calm, cloudless. He stood and numbly collected his things.

He wasn't crazy, was he? His thoughts fizzled. It would be easier to digest what had happened to him if he were insane, if he could accept that the trials of the previous evening were a break from reality. But he couldn't fool himself. They had always been real—or real enough—his...hauntings. Though starved and thirsty, he forced himself to sit back down. Trying to ignore his otherworldly experiences had clearly not worked. He needed to understand.

His thoughts bent towards creating a narrative.

"*One day* a Sophite man named Tier left his clan to settle in a faraway valley," he muttered. Maybe hearing it out loud would help. "There, he concealed items and artifacts, at least one related to the Interloper. On one of his solitary sojourns, that man came across a baby tulka, abandoned. He raised the child. Years later, a monster associated with the Interloper wandered..."

No, *was drawn*, Greydal's gut told him.

"—to the valley where the ex-Sophite and his son lived. Then things spiraled. While the local Sheriff began an investigation into the previously hidden objects, the now-grown child experienced—

What, exactly?

And what was meant to happen now? He frowned. He needed to find Higg. Maybe his friend could fill in the pieces of what happened after the sky had descended.

He stood and scanned his surroundings, determining he was at the other edge of the colored polyps which he and Higg had approached the day before. Real trees seemed to have supplanted this side of the woodland. These were the same color as the polyps but had true branches and bark, even leaves. He looked for the road and found it easily, as it spun away only twenty paces to his left. The track curved towards a series of oddly colored hills in the distance and something beyond. Perhaps there *were* clouds roaming about. He spied a dark wall where the horizon met the sky. Hunger gnawed his belly, and he forgot the shape in the distance.

He thought about eating his supply of salted meat, but something about the idea made him queasy. Then he considered taking one of the thick, yellow fruits which hung from the nearby branches, but thought better of it. For one, he didn't fancy ingesting anything grown from the soil where that yellow-eyed monster and the bright plant apparently dwelt. Second, he didn't like how the fruits had somehow found a way to migrate from their honey-combed parents to drink the life from these barked saplings.

As he left the tree line, he discovered he was already close to real habitation, not just farms. He noted the telltale signs of multiple wagon tracks in dirt offshoots from the stony road. Footprints littered one, all fresh. The villagers at the previous hamlet had told Greydal and Higg that the town of Heron hid in the hills. The mounds in the distance must be they, he reasoned. He walked for a time and soon discovered the short grass covering the hills waved iridescent in the light breeze. *That* was new. As he climbed, he thought he glimpsed something pale-amber and shifting. Gaining the top of the nearest mound, he found his vision hadn't misled him. Tents covered the shimmering, grassy hillocks.

The sound of voices and clanking pans quickened his pulse. Could this be it? He had been told the town of Heron was large enough to easily house thousands. Even if that was an exaggeration, the twenty or so odd lodgings wouldn't account for such a number. Shifting his pack on his shoulder and making sure his satchel was unlatched, he continued. Greydal passed the first few tents and saw no one, though he heard movement and conversation inside some. It would be early morning still, an old thought said. Then a small, muddy dog burst from between two yellow flaps and barked at him before fleeing at his approach, tail between its legs.

Greydal called out, "Ho! Greetings!"

All was silent. Then someone he couldn't see responded, "Hey! Name yourself!" It came from the tent to his right. Greydal waited and heard stumbling from within, followed by the sound of someone dropping a pole, or maybe spear or pike. He answered, "I'm a traveler! Seeking water if you have it!" Then the tip of a bronze spear parted the amber flap of the tent and a short-haired woman followed it. She wore a blue, armored jacket. As she righted herself, she said, "Ah, a traveler. That's not a problem, then. Where are you from?"

Ida almost snagged him with her spear as he flung himself onto her. "Hey—" she protested as he swept her up in a hug. He laughed like a maniac and sang, "Ida!" as she protested, "Ster, please— Wait, Greydal?!" Ida's eyes bugged from her head, and she joined his laughter. "You're alive!"

"*You're* alive!" he yelled. "I thought you all died!"

"We thought *you* died, you shit! What's with that hair?!"

He let her go, grinning from ear to ear. "What— I mean, why are you here?"

"We live here," she replied and matched his smile. "At least for the time being," she added.

Someone else called out, "Who is it?"

Ida replied, "Come see!"

A villager Greydal faintly recognized poked his head out of a separate tent. He exited it and approached, saying, "Tier's boy? It is! I'd recognize you anywhere." It embarrassed Greydal to not know the man's name so he forced a laugh to cover it. Others left their tents. He knew few by name.

But then a ringing voice said, "Greydal? Greydal Duinn?" Maizy Hawker pushed through the approaching onlookers.

"Maizy!" He went to her and hugged the woman. She looked old.

He whispered, "I thought for sure Calahurst got you..." *like he did Alom.* She waved off his comment and held him at arm's length. "Hold on, let me get a look at you. My eyes weren't good to begin with." Cataracts made her gaze milky, but she apparently saw enough to say, "Oh, Dawn, you're all chewed up."

He blinked and asked, "Oh! My ear?"

"Legate, your leg! And are those...tattoos?"

He looked down and saw the neck of his cassock had fallen to reveal his collarbone. Ida intervened and said, "Alright, come on Maizy. Let's get him some water and food, and we can catch up."

Greydal thanked her and said food wasn't needed, but he would be grateful to fill his canteen. "We'll give you more than that," Ida said, and smiled at him.

She led him deeper into the nest of tents away from the milling crowd of Harlow villagers as Maizy called out, "I'll meet you both at the totem!"

Greydal paused and looked at Ida. This wasn't a dream. "Rulf said Calahurst shot you, that you died," he muttered. She led him further through the camp and replied, "Well, remind me to show you my scar. It's fair killer...and ladies don't mind it either." She bounced her eyebrows. Greydal laughed.

After a silence, the woman added, "Rulf said you died, too. That those golden bastards got you."

"They did— Wait! Rulf's alive?"

Ida smirked and said, "He's the reason we're here. He negotiated with Heron to let us stay until we can build some blasted homes."

"*Rulf* negotiated something?"

"He did. He's a regular diplomat."

"It can't be. I know his brand of diplomacy."

"Yeah?"

"Yeah."

Ida chuckled. They arrived at the center of the tents, and the hill dipped towards a shallow valley. Towering structures filled it.

"That's Heron?" he asked.

His old friend confirmed it, "A more off-kilter town you'll never meet, I wager."

They sat down on hewn logs which sprawled beneath a pale, carven obelisk, broken at the ten-foot mark. Maizy called this thing a totem, but Greydal recognized it. The spire was a lodestone. The Old Folk used them to keep the ground stabilized when they first stole the world. At least, that was how Loken told the story.

"Funny thing, isn't it?" Ida saw him gazing at the lodestone. "It seemed as good a place as any to place our town square." She smiled to herself and added, "Too bad there's no stage, huh?"

Greydal copied her smile and paused. "Did you have any other visitors this morning or last night? Maybe a young kid with a cropped mohawk?"

"Oh, the yeller? Yes, Ster! He woke us all up middle-of-the-night-like, whooping as though the world was ending. That was three days back, though."

Greydal stared. *Three days?* "But...did he have a tatu of a dagger along his skull?"

"I thought it was more like a snake... you okay, Grey? You look a bit peaky."

He nodded and said he was fine, just thirsty. He didn't mention how his stomach grumbled. "Oh! I'm sorry, one sec," Ida exclaimed. She rose and left him sitting beneath the lodestone to weave between the nearby tents. He waited for her to disappear and then exhaled. Three days.

The Sophites' library, despite hoarding a staggering number of scrolls, books, and tomes, had almost nothing to say about Old Man Moonlight. The best Greydal had ever been able to exhume was a journal, surprisingly fresh (when compared with some of the items sourced from *before* the Four Corners). Written by an explorer dubbed Ivin the Eye, the journal was a chronicle of exploits and wonders.

From what he had been able to tell, Ivin was one of the earliest Sophites, and had made it his mission to scour the Four Corners for treasures and insight, long before that doctrine became stamped upon the essence of every member of the kith. In one erratic section of Ivin's writings, there was a detailing of what the man called, "the Progeny of First Dark," or interchangeably, "the Hidden Face of Nature."

The writing's meaning was elusive. But Greydal had pieced together this: Mabet's Bythos, the Interloper, Old Man Moonlight, and probably several other monikers represented the same thing, some sort of mystic aberration, at once everywhere and nowhere. This had uncomfortably recalled what Rulf once mentioned in the Whisper Veld—something about how one mustn't examine certain aspects of life too closely.

Strangely, and in his own peculiar way, Ivin tried to explain that the Progeny operated on a similar ruleset. As the explorer interpreted it, the thing both *wasn't real* and was *more* than real. To Ivin, the Interloper and "its horrid parentage, lightless genealogies of inhospitable super-reality" (whatever *that* meant) were to waking life what that life was to a dream. Awareness was the trouble, a costly thing, for it opened oneself up to the "un-ness of higher spaces," as Ivin put it. Greydal hadn't understood that part, and yet Ivin indicated that contact with those higher unknowns could sometimes take the form of strange occurrences and altered states of consciousness.

Synchronicities also obsessed Ivin, near the end of his life, consuming his every waking thought. Unrelated occurrences frequently proved to be strangely linked, the discovery of such connections timed in such a way to suggest life might be playing tricks on him. Ivin had been convinced that this was a result of contact with "the ones who sit above and also below." Synchronicities became synonymous with hauntings, and Ivin went mad. He thought coincidences and certain, unnerving phenomena were the aftereffects of something otherworldly interacting with the material realm.

The Sophites erased nearly all mention of him, except for certain scraps and the journal. When he discovered all this, Greydal idly wondered what Ivin would've made of Roan, of Mabet. Those two were clearly "otherworldly," though maybe in a manner different to the phenomena Ivin described. Greydal had witnessed much that was odd, frightening—but didn't sound like what Ivin meant. The singing presence from Abyddion, the village of animals, the violence of the Calf-Ripper. The sigil Greydal saw when Roan obliterated the Friar... incredible, yes. But those things weren't driving anyone insane, at least not in the way that Ivin experienced.

The world swallowed Ivin—he was ostracized, and fearful of the night to his very last day as a Sophite when he disappeared, or was maybe secretly exiled.

Greydal's takeaway was this: Ivin though he bumped into something so big, that the world couldn't hold it all. And it changed him forever.

Is that what had happened to himself? Greydal could only recall leaping into the hungry blackness and a mouth closing shut around him. A story his mind likely told him to make sense of things, or so he hoped. There had been more though, hadn't there?

He looked himself over. He didn't feel different. Tired, maybe. There was no terrible brightness lurking in his mind, nor did he sense the doubleness, which had troubled him since that first night out of Harlow. The extra rooms he had once described to Roan seemed somehow gone. Was he free? Almost immediately, a small inner voice told him *no*.

A shiver leaped up his shoulders, and he reflexively ran his hand over the log on which he sat, focusing on its texture. Not for the first time, he wished he somehow possessed the rest of the books Tier had given Alom. He had the hang of the Old Folk's language now, and figured the texts could have told him much.

Out of the corner of his eye, he finally noticed the blurry faces poking from nearby tents. How long had they been staring at him? Lengthy hair obscured their features, but he could tell they stared in his direction. One caressed its neck with a slender hand. Not villagers. Not wights, either. He sighed and ignored the specters. A rational part of his mind dimly recognized them as the slow lopers in the mists, the ones Roan had said she couldn't see. What did it matter that they looked almost solid now? Corporeal or not, his best bet was probably to pretend they didn't exist. He didn't require any more sorcery for the time being, thank you very much.

Despite this resolution, oncoming footsteps from Greydal's right startled him as he looked up into Ida's face. She carried a leather waterskin. "Here, slug this." He thanked her and took it, glancing at the tents. The faces were gone. Ida sat in silence as he chugged from the skin, emptying it. When he finished, he wiped his mouth, and his friend said, "I have to ask, how'd you find us? We only set up shop here a few months back."

"You've been here for *months* and haven't set down housing?"

Ida frowned and replied, "Well, we had a spot of trouble. Heron isn't as accommodating as their folk would lead you to believe, funnily enough."

"Glad you have headbasher-in-chief, then. Where is he?"

"He's around. We—"

Maizy's voice chimed, "Greydal, dear! Marro just got back as well! I told him you were here before I went and grabbed your things. He wouldn't believe it."

Greydal turned to see the old woman hurrying towards them from across the circle of logs. She carried a tattered bag. He watched her almost trip and said, "Easy! Let me help you." He rose to take the surprisingly-heavy woven container.

"Tent's inside," Maizy whispered to him. "Careful, though. They open like nobody's business, let me tell you."

He smiled. "Thank you. But I'm—"

"I thought it couldn't be you, boy. I see I was wrong." Greydal fumbled with the bag and turned to see a large man approaching. Marro's pocked face wore an expression of amiability, but his eyes were dull.

"Ster Finch. Your hair's gone gray."

The man laughed. "A side effect of old age and wisdom, I'm afraid." Greydal held his gaze until Marro glanced down. Maizy interrupted, "Come, let's get your tent set and I'll see about getting you breakfast." Greydal replied, "Thanks, Maizy. I mean it. But do—"

"Oh, it's not a problem," she cut in. "Marro, help him and Ida, and I will go see about Rulf. I have no idea what could be taking him so—"

"Maizy. I'm sorry, but do any of you know where the boy with the mohawk went?"

"Oh, the yeller?" the man asked, and Maizy added, "With the snake tattoo?"

"It's a dagger," Ida informed.

Greydal took a breath and said, "His name's Higg. You said he ran through here a few days ago?" Ida nodded and replied, "Think he went to where Rulf is at the moment."

"With that damn woman," Marro said.

"Right," Ida said.

Greydal looked at each of them and asked, "This woman. Is she near a beach by any chance?"

"A beach?"

"A sandy place, with water."

"Well, Rulf's at The Sands..." Seeing Greydal's look, Ida elaborated, "That's the local tavern, on the southern edge of Heron."

"Alright, thanks. I'll head there."

Marro blocked his path. "Easy. You don't want to be trafficking with her kind. Stay here and let Rulf handle it."

Greydal set down the tent and his bags, aside from his satchel with the dai-strelok. "Are you listening?" the man asked.

Greydal slipped a hand into one bag and transferred several sticks of meat to his satchel. He looked to Ida and asked, "Watch these for me, will you? They have all my shavings and the rest of my food."

Maizy spluttered. "Now, just hold on! You've been missing for years and the first thing you do when we find you is run off again?"

"We just want to know what happened to you," Marro added. "You disappeared during the attack, after all." The man let the silence linger.

"What are you saying?" Greydal asked. Ida stepped in, "He isn't saying *anything*. Are you, Marro?" She raised her eyebrows. The large man didn't reply.

"C'mon, Grey, I'll walk you to The Sands. No one will touch your stuff." Greydal nodded and followed Ida as she slipped him around Marro.

He ignored Maizy's entreating, pale glance as they left the two standing there.

When they were both away Ida whispered, "Don't listen to Marro. We know what happened. Rulf told us. You probably saved our lives."

"Hardly. We just barely managed to escape ourselves."

"I mean Calahurst, you dunce. Yorn saw it."

"It was self-defense."

"It was heroic. When the sheriff went down, those golden things froze for a sec, and then came after you two."

"Ruined their day, huh? They sure showed it."

"Don't be hard on yourself. The leg's striking."

They walked in silence for a time and eventually neared the end of the tents. As they ambled, Greydal retrieved and gnawed at a stick of meat to quiet his gurgling stomach. They passed the last of the tents and the iridescent hill curved downwards towards a town, which was stranger than he had ever witnessed.

Darkened stone edifices rose in uncertain, ovoid uniform, stretching to the north. Each of the buildings were multiple stories high, and their bases and edges gleamed with shining metal. Gold. In that aspect, the town reminded him slightly of Abyddion, but it was clear that the hands behind Heron had minds as alien as any he had encountered, a fact represented in the oddly shaped structures and ever-present shadows, which appeared glued to every available surface. In the early light, he could spy sad gleams flickering at the towers' crowns, the only features aside from the gold plating that broke the illusion of a single, solid object, stretching dolefully away from sight. If he squinted, he could perceive hooded figures, hurrying into that vague lightlessness. Each became lost, nooks and crannies invisible to his eye swallowing them. Yet somehow, he sensed, maybe with a sort of dream-logic, that paths and methods unknown to him crisscrossed, or *ought* to crisscross, that spanning cityscape.

As he and Ida descended the hill and neared the first of the smaller, edge buildings, Greydal ascertained the shining metal was more than simple gold. Incredible bas-reliefs lay inset with the foil. He approached the nearest building and laid a hand on the aureate carvings. "Wow."

"Wait till you see some of the ones further in. They're something else."

"How did they—"

"I don't think these people sleep. At least that's what Rulf says. I bet they spend all their time on these. You should clock the rest of the town. I mean it."

He had eyes only for the carvings. They depicted moths, flies, and beetles. Other bugs, too, he couldn't identify. Some played instruments while others seemed to lead groups in dance or combat. "They're all like this? They look real." He wasn't exaggerating. The creatures were more lifelike than even Loken's handiwork, ready to leap off the wall itself.

Ida replied, "As far as I've seen, all of them. Wonkier ones are further in."

"The rock beneath is strange, too. Did you notice? It has some give," he said. It was faintly sticky as well.

"The whole town is made up of that and the gold. We tried chipping some when we thought the locals weren't watching, but it's solid. Couldn't mark it."

"The gold?"

"Both."

Something occurred to him. "Where are the windows? The doors?"

"Further up, only at the top."

Greydal gazed skywards. Though the immediate structure sat shorter than the others, he had to crane his neck to see the single, faintly-luminescent hole, which pierced the center of the wall, five feet below the flat roof. He circled the building towards its left side, head craned back, and his feet found a hard surface. This caused him to discover the stone of the towers also coated the ground.

His gaze followed the matte material that led between the two nearest buildings towards an open street, which the first building had obscured. Something stood in the middle of the avenue: a masked and hooded stranger in a colorless robe. The person faced him, but Greydal was unsure if they could see at all, as the mask had no visible eyeholes. Then the hooded figure jolted and turned, shuffling along the stone walk. As he watched the person shamble away, Ida's footsteps sounded from behind.

He turned and asked, "Where to?"

"Follow that fella. This road circles the whole place."

Greydal did as she said and stepped onto the street. The hair on his arms rose, and he coughed. The air tasted strange, like smoke. He looked at his companion, and she said, "I know. No clue why." He nodded, but wondered.

They proceeded along the thoroughfare. After a time, they came upon a golden ladder sprouting from the side of an approaching building, running to its roof. A sign next to the ladder winked to life as they neared. Greydal watched the nonsensical figures resolve into his language: *Traveler. Buy Packaged Goods.* A phosphorescent arrow squirmed along the sign and pointed at the ladder. He eyed the building with suspicion as he passed. As he did, three smaller townspersons, masked and hooded, left a nearby alleyway so thin, they had to exit single file. They remained silent in passing.

He would have paused to examine the crew, but his gaze happened to glance across yet another oddity; a bas-relief more disturbing than the ones before, this one on the side of the laddered building. It looked to be a mass of leaves with the head of an earless and eyeless dog. The carving was so realistic, it made Greydal's stomach tighten.

He stopped walking entirely and stared in silence at the creature. The relief seemed to indicate the leaf-dog was in the process of shuffling into a headless body of flowing, yet boxy proportions.

After a beat, he whispered, "What happened to you all, after the fire? Why are you here?"

Ida spoke behind him, "Why else? Aside from the people Calahurst locked in the town barracks, almost everyone inside the walls died."

"The south barracks. Is that where Maizy was? We couldn't find her before Tier's execution."

"Others as well. Crawl, the Grimes."

Greydal broke his gaze with the leaf creature. He turned to Ida and asked, "Toshi...is he?"

"Dead. I'm so sorry, Grey. We left the valley with a few dozen others from outside the walls. We couldn't stay after everything...the fire and Calahurst's betrayal. We made a spot near a lake to the valley's west for a time. Something lived in it. We didn't know."

"It attacked?"

"It ran us out, but killed a few. Crawl, Toshi, Jon, Provik, and Yorn."

"His mother?"

"She's with us."

Greydal nodded and sighed. "Come on," he said. They left the carved beast and let the hushed street draw them along the city's circumfrence.

EDIFICE

As they walked, the shadows of the looming towers cooled their path, while the narrow road wove inward so that more buildings obscured the hills beyond the city. Greydal could tell he and Ida walked near the edge, because the densest and tallest of the edifices remained always to his right.

Despite Heron's vastness, they encountered few townspeople. He asked Ida why there were so many buildings for so few dwellers, and she told him that the inhabitants were different from other folk, adding that, "Most live inside. That's their world. They only come out for going between the spires or dealing with outsiders."

Greydal eyed the ebon towers overhead. What went on within those mysterious premises? The silent town made him uncomfortable, and he didn't understand why the people here didn't just put doors at ground level. They continued to trudge in silence until they exited to daylight. Beyond the last line of buildings, a structure unlike the rest squatted amid two, glittering hills. The nebulous polygon took shape in sections as the two approached, then rounding to its front. A featureless, slate roof slanted from a seemingly random point above the building, and two windows of darkened glass smiled equidistant from a nondescript door. Above it, a sign turned on. Again, the strange language wriggled before Greydal's eyes and became his own: *Tavern. Sands.*

"Uh-huh..." he said. Ida grinned and pushed him towards the door. "C'mon, let's reunite you with your buddy." Did she mean Higg or Rulf? He pushed on the handle-less door, and it blistered away, becoming a well-lit space. Scarlet wood curled in intricate patterns on the floor. In places, the wood extended upwards to become columns, each helping to hold a misshapen balcony, which itself hunched above the open dining space. The tables strewn about looked stolen.

Roan stood behind a long bar. She wore a grimy, pastoral headband which only just kept her blonde locks from her eyes as she poured the second of two drinks sitting on the counter. "Ah, lovely, just in time. You've got to try this fermented tea."

Ida stared at Greydal, and he smiled in guilt. He entered and set his satchel on a nearby table while at another, Rulf was locked in an arm-wrestling match with one of the Heronese, a massive and hooded figure. A spiral, pink mask ogled from beneath that one's hood while veins bulged on Rulf's shaved head. "Ida—" Rulf huffed, "Keep him from—" he grunted and continued, "distracting me."

"No need," Greydal told her. He ignored Rulf and walked unsteadily to the bar. Despite his long journey, he hadn't planned in the slightest what he would say upon their reunion. Now, staring into Roan's dark eyes his stomach quivered, as it had on other occasions when faced with the strange woman. He opened his mouth, but she broke the stalemate first, leaning over to kiss him. Greydal returned it, and then said, "You're a little flirtatious for a barmaid, don't you think?"

"Keeps them coming back. Here." Roan raised the two glasses, and Greydal took one. They clinked them and both drank. The liquid tasted bitter and sour, and Greydal coughed. "First thing you do is try and poison me?"

"If you'll recall, I kissed you first."

Ida cut in, "Sorry, what language is that?"

"Oh," Greydal reverted to the Four Corners' common tongue. "I didn't realize. Didn't mean to exclude you."

A *bang* made him whirl. The big Heronese had Rulf's arm pinned against the splintery wood. The ex-watchman cursed and said, "Bastard! Fine." The Heronese made a gurgling sound, which Greydal took for laughter. It, and it *was* an it, he realized, stood.

"Greydal, tell your scary wife to pour me a shot," Rulf shouted.

Roan replied, "You've had plenty, I think. How about some hydration? Looks as though you've sweated everything out."

"*Wife?*" Ida inquired.

"Here," Roan said. She pulled a glass jar of a clear liquid from beneath the bar. With her teeth, she yanked the cork from the top, and then reached into her shirt to remove a small vial. She opened it, and sprinkled a finger pinch of its silvery contents into the jar. "This will help the churl recover."

Greydal took it and Ida said, "I'm sorry, but hold on. Rulf! What's going on? You're supposed to be negotiating."

"What does it look like I'm doing?" Rulf said as he tried to stand, and then wobbled. Ida replied, "*This* is what you meant when you said you wrestled them for our spot? I thought you were being, you know, metaphorical?"

"It's Ida, right?" Roan asked. Ida looked at her and nodded cautiously. "Perfect, can you help me bring some liquor up from the... I suppose we shall call it a basement?" Roan ushered her into a darkened back room, Greydal watching them disappear behind a silver curtain. The tall Heronese behind him coughed something like a word and blundered out the front door. Rulf called after it,

"Yeah, you too." And with that, Greydal stood alone in the room with his old acquaintance. He took a deep breath and grabbed the jar of clear liquid.

Greydal slowly approached the table, carrying the jar. The ex-watchman turned to look at him.

"So, what is it? You a ghost?"

Greydal sat down opposite the man. Rulf looked larger than he remembered, shoulders bulging and forearms veritable roots of sinew beneath rough skin.

"Here," Greydal said, "this is water, I think."

"A pink ghost." The man chuckled to himself.

"I'm no ghost. Ida isn't either. You said she died." Greydal set the jar closer to Rulf's side of the table.

The ex-watchman considered and then replied, "I said I saw her go down. I saw *you* dead though, on the riverbank. Tried to pry your axe away, but your corpse wouldn't let it go."

Greydal didn't know what to say to that, and so asked, "What happened?"

"You mean my hand?" He waved his left arm, showcasing the three remaining fingers. "The last golden came after me when you croaked."

"That's impressive," Greydal told him. "I found out most don't survive their encounters with the Fri— Er, the golden men."

"It's not. It wasn't me."

"Sorry?"

Rulf sighed and removed the cork from the jar and chugged. He emptied half the container before wiping his lips. "Like I said, I tried to take your axe but you wouldn't let me. I was about to give up when one of the bastards jumped from the water. I was ready, though. I had the sheriff's knife thrower and—"

"That's what you dropped! That night in the house!" Greydal exclaimed. Rulf must have grabbed Calahurst's dai-strelok after the sheriff went down.

"Are you gonna listen or not?"

Greydal sighed and let the inebriated man continue. Rulf muttered, "Like I said, I shot it. Shot it, shot it, shot it. Nearly emptied the thrower. Knocked the thing down for a second, but didn't do shit else.

"It leaped up like nothing and came at me. I rolled but it snagged my hand with that red shit. Tore fingers off, but I ran." Rulf drank more of the clear liquid. He remained silent.

Greydal said, "So? You escaped?"

Rulf shook his head. "The Ripper."

"What?"

"The Calf-Ripper," Rulf said.

"It *followed* us?"

The man rubbed his neck with his hand. "Golden was almost on top of me, and then this... wolf. It dove from the trees like a falling barn. Didn't seem to see me, just went right for the golden. Wrapped it all up in its arms." Rulf glared at the table. After a moment, he continued, "I thought the red shit was bad, Greydal. That thing... it's...it's evil. Carried the dead golden up the tree and just ripped it to pieces."

Greydal was silent as he watched Rulf. A dark brooding had overtaken the man. But he couldn't resist. "It *was* a wolf, though?" he asked.

Rulf glanced up. "Like a tree's a leaf, I guess," he replied. "Huge and twisting. Had too many arms, like those bugs beneath the statue of the First Maer. And it's face... covered in these black fibers that were a third as long as the body. Fur maybe, but it looked like a woman's hair."

Greydal sat in silence for a moment, thinking. "I've seen a drawing of it."

"Well. I'm just lucky it didn't come after me next."

"It wouldn't have, probably. You attacked the Friar."

Rulf looked up at him and stared. After an awkward moment, Greydal asked, "What?"

"How would *you* know what it'd do?"

At that instant, giggling interrupted them. Ida and Roan returned, carrying a tray of luminescent bottles. "Help us, will you?" Ida asked. "Ro' says we're about to get some visitors."

Greydal suppressed a smirk. He stood, and Roan winked at him from over the other woman's shoulder.

*** *** ***

They spent the entire day in the tavern. The Ichablists, the proper name of the Heronese, arrived minutes after Rulf, Greydal, Roan, and Ida finished setting up the tables and pouring glasses of the glowing liquid, which Roan said was *technically* non-alcoholic. "Thanks, but I think I'll abstain, if it's the same to you," Greydal told her as they both stood at the bar. Ida and Rulf sat at the other end of the room, conversing in low tones.

"Sourpuss." Roan said, and mimed pouting with an extended lower lip.

Greydal smiled and replied, "Save it for Ida."

"Is that jealousy I detect? My, my."

"Never. Ida's funnier than me anyhow."

She rolled her eyes. "You know I'm dedicated to you, you rotten man."

"Your loss."

I know, by the way. That's what Greydal wanted to tell her. That he knew about Tier. After a beat, he said, "You told Rulf you're my wife?"

"That's not what you were about to ask me, is it?"

He quickly picked up a shining glass, taking a sip of what revealed itself to be a vile beverage. He made a face. Then he said over the rim of the glass, "Higg. Is he alright?"

Roan observed him and slowly replied, "Higg's upstairs, re-covering." Greydal nodded. "Did he say anything about what happened to him?"

"He tried."

"Alright."

"We need to sit down. Not now, but soon. I—"

The door to the outside opened, and a procession of masked figures entered. Greydal turned towards them, defensive. The visitors didn't wear the colorless robes he saw before. These strangers stood dressed in jet-tinted metal, which draped from their shoulders like weighty blankets, turning them to soft rectangles. He didn't know what kind of metal flowed like that, but guessed it must be a terrible burden to wear. The strangers' collars ran high, and he could only spy the top halves of their masks poking from the onyx garments.

As his eyes darted to his companions, he found that only Ida seemed alarmed, and so he momentarily allowed himself to relax. Nevertheless, he sidled towards the table where his bag and dai-strelok sat, just in case. As he did, the lead stranger stepped forward. This one's mask was a white diamond with a silvery arc across the middle. Like the others, it lacked visible eyeholes. The thing spoke as though underwater, and Greydal had to concentrate to understand.

"En-chant-tress. Head-man. It-is-al-most-time."

As the other masked individuals fanned out into the tavern, Roan spoke. "How many?" Greydal grabbed his satchel.

"I-speak. For-Twen-ty-and-one-hun-dred."

The witch sighed and said, "It'll have to do. Thank you." The white diamond bobbed above the black garb. Roan added, "Ravo-bisob, this is Ida," and gestured to the woman, who paled. "She's one of Rulf's." Ravobisob nodded again.

He murmured, "And-the-woun-ded-one?"

"Greydal. He's mine."

Ravobisob turned from them, and Greydal saw that the man's mask held nothing—that there sat no skull behind it, only empty air. A chord dove from the middle of the mask's backside into the pit of the thing's collar. Ravobisob was not a human or tulka, then. What were these people? Ravobisob spoke to his companions in a wet dialect. They all nodded in unison, and each moved towards a table. Ida visibly shied away from the red-masked thing that sat next to her. Rulf didn't seem to mind, though. The man kept his head down and rubbed his temples.

Then the leader glided over. "Grey-dal. Greet-ings."

"Ravobisob? Did I say that right? I—" he cleared his throat.

"Do-not-be-ner-vous," Ravobisob interrupted. "We-diff-er-on-ly-in-meat."

Greydal saw Roan smirk out of the corner of his eye. He tried to smile and said, "I'm not. I just... haven't seen anyone like you before."

"I-am-Ik-a-blist. You-are-Tulku. Zhuga. As-strange-to-me-as-I-am-to-you."

Tulku? Not Tulka? Had this thing read the Old Folks' books? That was the name given to Greydal's race, before his language changed it. Roan spoke, "Kindly Ravobisob here is going to help us."

"Oh? It— I mean he is?"

"I-am. Did-you-know? Long-a-go-some-pri-sons-let-you-leave. They-called-it-Pah-Rowl."

"I don't understand."

"Upstairs," Roan whispered. "Ravobisob, if you would?" The tower of onyx nodded and rounded the bar towards the misshapen stairs. "Wait," Greydal said. "Why are they gathered here? Something's happening, and it's not anything to do with the Harlows."

"After him," Roan said and turned away.

After him? Just like that? Greydal clenched his jaw. He couldn't fathom why he thought she would have become more forthcoming years on. He followed the witch and Ravobisob up the stairs. Behind him, Ida's voice echoed. "What do you mean they're *troops*?" she asked.

The hallway on the second story split into alcoves, which each housed crooked doors. Behind one, Greydal heard snoring. He made to reach for the handle, but Roan stopped him with a hand on his chest.

"Why can't I see him?" Greydal asked.

She leveled a gaze at him and replied, "Frankly, love? I'm worried what it would do to him to see you." Greydal frowned at her. She turned, and he would have stopped her to demand an explanation, but the white-masked Ichablist loomed over them both.

"Where then?" he asked to her back.

"Here." Roan pointed to a slanting door of burgundy wood down the hall. They approached, and she twisted the knob. The door shuddered and peeled away, revealing a room identical to the ground floor, only a third its size and lacking the downstairs bar. The two misplaced tables were copies of the ones below.

To the side, Greydal recognized Roan's belongings, including a rollout cot and a long, shrouded object. The Allthame. *She still had it.* He could *feel* the thing beneath its covering. Roan and the Ichablist moved into the room, and he followed them as they sat at the table furthest from the door.

Greydal spoke first, as he scooted the chair towards the table. "Okay. What is this?" His voice sounded harsher than he meant it to.

"It-is-plan-ning-time. We-will-break-the-I-ron-seal."

"Obviously," he replied in irritation.

"Greydal, please."

"What?"

"Just take a deep breath."

"Why do you think I would need to?"

"Does-this-one-not-know-of-his-in-tern-ment?"

"My what?"

"Little warrior, just…just listen, alright?"

He held his tongue and waited for her to continue. She sighed and said, "I dragged you into danger, with Yphrus. I'm about to do it again." His heart skipped a beat. She continued, "I found it. The Wyrm's compound."

In the ensuing silence, Greydal thought he could perceive a keening, just beyond his range of hearing from the direction of the hidden Allthame. "Well?" Roan asked.

"Well, what?"

"Do you wish to come with us? I'm giving you a choice this time."

He shook his head and replied, "I'm sorry, to do what? And with who? You and these Heronese?"

"Ik-a-blist," Ravobisob gurgled.

"They're called the Ichablists, Greydal. And no, not just them. There's someone else who hates the Wyrm."

"Do you mean me?"

"Do you hate him? I'm referring to Rulf."

"Wait, *Rulf*?"

"I told you, remember? The Wyrm has to die." She leaned forward. "Rulf wants revenge, same as me."

"Roan, that's a terrible idea. You know the forces he can field. How many Armargure do you think he keeps nearby?"

"That's why we're not storming the compound as a great army. He's been watching the north and the east. If the kith left in any large number, he'd prepare."

"How do you know he *needs* to prepare?" She didn't answer. He asked, "I assume this compound of his is close?"

"A-few-days-aw-ay."

Greydal turned to Ravobisob. "You support this?" he asked. "Your people will die."

"I-think-not. We-have-an-al-ly-on-the-in-side-al-read-y. We—"

"You mean one of the Legate's people?" Greydal interjected.

Ravobisob didn't answer the question. Instead, the Ichablist continued, "We-wait-ed-on-ly-on-the-in-stru-ment."

The Allthame, surely. Greydal turned to the witch and asked, "That. Why is it here?"

She replied, "We need it."

He shook his head at her. "What is it? You never told me." Instead of waiting for her reply he added, "Mabet sent you after it at the cost of Marcos' life, but when she expelled you, she *gave you* the thing."

"She didn't give it to me. It was mine from the moment I touched it."

"Okay, fine. What is it then, a weapon? I read a hundred tomes and found nothing."

"It's new, my darling. It didn't truly exist until I took it from the grove."

"That doesn't make sense."

"Not to you. Mabet understood."

Ravobisob cut in, "Woun-ded-one, a-great-cat-a-cly-sm-app-roa-ches-the-past. The-in-stru-ment-is-its-end. It-will-stem-the-cos-mos."

Greydal sat still for a moment, taking great care to master his irritation. "Do you have any idea how little that clears things up for me?" he asked. "What are you trying to get me to do?"

*** *** ***

That night, he strode along the stone road under a blanket of smoking shadows. The responsive signs lit his path in spurts as he fished a slice of meat from his satchel and chewed it, ruminating.

Marston. Who would want to avenge that bastard? Rulf was crazier than he had already assumed. And who did Ravobisob think he had as an ally in the west?

Greydal shook his head and turned his thoughts away from the events in the tavern. It had all felt like scenes in a play, a world of which he was no longer a part. Soon, he would have to reckon with what had happened to him in the forest. It had changed him, a quiet voice reminded. Although maybe he had been changing already.

As if in response to his thoughts, a cold wind whistled down the street. Its sound continued after the breeze died, and suddenly Greydal was ill at ease. He was the sole traveler on the street, and yet he thought he could perceive whispers, just at the edge of hearing. He looked, but there was only the low, cloudy sky and hedging, windowless towers. He quickened his step. Once he retrieved his belongings from the Harlow camp, he could return to the bright rooms of The Sands and their relative comfort. He walked in silence for a time, aware of his loud breathing and clacking tread. He was careful not to imagine other, more furtive steps behind him, and eventually, he arrived at the end of the slow, spiral road. The clouds opened beyond the town, revealing vertical columns of fleecy moonlight, and Greydal halted. This was the east exit.

He must have accidentally passed his turn for the tented hill. He stepped off the stone road and onto the iridescent grass which now glimmered in the night. As he did, the burning smell he had somehow forgotten vanished, bringing it to the front of his mind. Leaving the town had the effect of quenching a thirst.

As he blinked in disorientation, he turned and saw that the hills far to his right just barely obscured the glow of campfires. A last look behind him told that there was no one, but he shivered, nonetheless. Turning towards the warm light of the distant encampment, Greydal began walking.

As he trudged through the phosphorescent meadow, faint strums of music reached his ears, descending spirits from the glowing hillocks. Several minutes later, he reached and climbed the first mound. Beyond it, amber tents radiated warmth, and he made his way towards them as the heartfelt music increased in volume. Multiple someones sang along with the thrumming of a guitar. The lines were ones he hadn't heard since boyhood:

> *"A pall has lain o'er this stale, tired land*
> *Chop! Pull! Chop-pull!*
> *Heave! Ho! Heave-ho!*
> *Dig! Plant! Dig-plant!"*

Greydal murmured the next line, "Up, root, up-root...." The chant continued, and he hummed along for a bit, a dusty melancholy curling in his chest. He passed the first of the tents and determined the merrymaking originated from the direction of the lodestone. The whole clan must be there. He grinned. If he were a thief, he could have rifled through half of the Harlows' tents before they became wise.

The sight of movement to his right slowed him, his smile faltering.

A nude figure, a woman, stood between two tents. Her long, ginger hair draped over her face. The apparition raised a pale arm and pointed to Greydal's left, but he only stared at her. This was one of the watchers he'd glimpsed that morning. The lopers in the mist. But this one looked as real as any person he had ever met.

He tried to peer through the evening murk to see her face, but hair obscured it too much to let him identify more than a small, chiseled chin and bloody-red lips. Her muscled arm continued to point at something to the left, and he turned. He saw what she indicated, a partially open tent, twenty paces away.

He watched Marro's fat hand further part that tent's drapery to allow a young boy to exit. Tears streamed down the child's face, and he shuffled away, towards the sounds of singing. The tent flap closed, and Greydal clenched his jaw. He glanced at the apparition, but she moved as if underwater, stepping behind a nearby tent to vanish altogether.

Greydal turned towards Marro's tent. His hands shook as he marched towards it, the sound of rushing blood replacing the din of distant revelry. The other makeshift dwellings to his right and left blurred as he approached, and soon, he stood outside the amber pyramid. Tears rose at the corners of his eyes as he unlatched his satchel.

Greydal parted the flap and stepped inside.

CHAPTER

21

LABYRINTH

The next evening, Roan sat across from Higg on the ground floor of The Sands. Rulf stood with his arms crossed, leaning against a wooden pillar. "Tell it to me again," the witch commanded.

She watched the boy swallow the rest of the water she had given him. He then wiped his nose. "You— Why *Wirza*? Ma'am?" Higg struggled to speak in Rulf's native tongue. "I told you already," he added.

"Tell it again, for *Rulf's* benefit," she replied, exhausted. She grew weary of the boy. How had Greydal put up with him for so long?

"Alright, okay." He raised a hand upon seeing her expression. "It was that *izha*, perfume."

"What perfume, please?"

"The one I smelled on that...the other Greydal. Or maybe not him but that gold...ah, *lusio*— Er, room he brought."

"Nah," Rulf interjected. "Greydal ran. He shot Marro in the heart with a knife thrower and split. I have the same one and I know what the blades look like. Not sure where he got—"

"No," Higg said. "Well, I mean yes. He may have. *Virt*— Run, I mean. But he tried to come to us."

She let Rulf reply. The man asked, "Why? Just because you smelled something pretty you think this other tulka snagged him?" Higg made a face and turned to Roan. He searched her eyes and said, "He tried to get Greydal the last time, with me. He would have done it but that—" Higg paused, and then placed a hand on the table. He took a substantial breath and continued, "That third one, the one in the sky—"

"Oh, for the love of the Dawn, there's *three* now? Roan, no disrespect to you and yours but you are *both* out of your damn minds. I don't need fairy stories."

"Higg, please tell Rulf about the third Greydal."

The boy looked between her and the brawny man. Higg ran his hand across the table and muttered, "It wasn't him, not really. It was a cloud at first, then his face, Greydal's. But then it...it did something and wasn't either, after. Before that, it had scared the second Greydal off. He and the *lusio*- ugh sorry, fake *room* just vanished. And then the cloud..." He took another deep breath. "But that's why I think the golden one got ours this time. I smelled the perfume again. Outside." He pointed at the exit to The Sands. "It's the same. Greydal didn't take his things, no? Only bag that's missing is his satchel?"

Rulf and Roan both nodded. "See? He, what's the word, *filleted* your Marro and tried to come to us after, but the other one got him first."

Rulf grunted and said, "Him leaving his heavy bags doesn't mean shit."

Roan sighed and looked up at the ex-watchman. She told him, "You may be right. Either way, we're advancing our departure. We leave at midnight."

***   ***   ***

Greydal stared through his reflection. The warm water ran over his wrists as he soaked the blade. The Legate had surprised him, allowing a razor for shaving. He reached his hand up and continued the sopping work. Greydal didn't know when or if he would get his chance to fight, but he didn't want his topknot to give the Legate or anyone else an easy hold. He had learned his lesson. He would go bald, until he freed himself. *If* he freed himself, he corrected.

The dark, red locks fell into the sink, a clone of the appliance Greydal and Tier had used in the barracks. He gazed at the scars on his hands as the water cascaded over them, trophies from climbs as a child and Sophite artifact hunts. These hands now itched to hold his axe. It could have breached the door to his cell, he was sure. He decided grimly he should have never given the tool away, marvel that it was. But, at the time, he had held no desire to ever see it again, the thing being a reminder of dark thoughts and darker deeds. And yet, those thoughts, those violent acts had followed him, hadn't they? He had carried them close across the short years while pretending they were left behind in the dust of the fight pit. A sharp nick on the back of his head brought his awareness home. He cursed and finished his bladework. Then he washed under the sink, afterwards reaching for the nearby towel, a heavy shape of dark cotton. He dried himself and pocketed the razor as he stepped from the restroom into his temporary lodging as the cool air stung his exposed cut. His eyes traveled as he rubbed his head, smearing the blood.

Whomever decorated the place had an eye for luxury. It reminded him of Alom's home in some ways. A thick carpet lay across the floor and bulky sheets transformed the spartan foldout-bed into something luxurious. There was a bookshelf, half-filled. The paintings were what surprised him, though. Their likeness to the one Alom had owned was suspicious, though Alom *had* said the painting was sourced from the Mansions. Perhaps Greydal should have simply believed him.

He looked down at his torso. The gray marks of the Ague had long since been changed to black roots, giving his body the appearance of inhabited, rosy soil. Did his tatu differentiate him? He couldn't avoid the knowledge any longer. Roan had been right. The Legate wore his face. What would it mean if the man shared his body's markings?

Thoughts decaying into soup, he ambled to the bed and sat, so as to remove his leg. That done, he rubbed his stump. When they arrived the night before, the Legate had handed him off to a soldier—one of the Armargure. That woman looked similar to the warriors Greydal had seen on the road with Roan years ago. He had tried to talk to the armored human, but she only gazed at him with severe distaste. Another guard, a tulka, joined them, and the two dragged him through twisting, metal halls towards his current lodging.

A red-robed senior, likely a monk, hobbled into his cell shortly after and prayed over him. Greydal recognized the litany from his time under the Ague and spit on the floor. The robed monk didn't react. At the time, he briefly considered attacking the senior. Yet he hadn't been confident the Legate would have considered the old man valuable enough to negotiate a ransom. Greydal decided his best chance was to wait. So he did, refastening his leg and brooding in his plush prison. As it turned out, his choice regarding nonaction quickly bore fruit.

A different guard, this one in golden robes, unlocked and opened the opulent door.

"Greydal Alone?"

"That's me. You the executioner?"

"No. My name is Sebastian. Our Most Holy One, may his sleeps be restful, charged me with ensuring your needs are met."

Greydal eyed the space beyond the guard. The metal hallway sported incredible decoration, armored statues looming beside beautiful banners and tapestries. When the earlier guards had dragged him through the hall, he received the impression that someone must have worked hard to enliven the desolate corridor.

"My needs?" he now asked the golden guard.

Sebastian nodded and replied, "Yes. I see you did not touch the food prepared for you." Greydal glanced over at the silver tray which a woman, who had earlier led the monk away, had left for him. He assumed they had meant to drug him.

"I'm not hungry."

The man interlaced his fingers and placed them over his stomach. "A walk, then? This room has kept you for a time. Would you care to stretch your legs?"

Was that a joke?

*** *** ***

The next day, a sleepless procession gained towards the western boundary of the world. Though the company approached at speed, the firmament grew only marginally as they rode, the wall remaining misty with distance. Yet, the group was near enough to see where the sky itself connected with the firmament, high above and *beyond* the Edge. Two riders, ahead of the rest, paused to allow the remainder of the company to close the distance.

As they waited, one spoke. "I never thought I'd see it." Roan turned to look at her companion. Ida's eyes squinted against the glare of the fierce sun.

"Daunting, isn't it?" Roan turned and surveyed the land leading to the dull, gray wall. Somewhere out there hid what Greydal called the Mansions. Roan idly wondered how the two other Harlow natives would handle coming face-to-face with their legends. Truth be told, it didn't matter much to her.

The landscape between them and the hidden compound was so pale, it was nearly gray and smelled vaguely foul. The ground itself was cracked and dry, and the whitish grass which sprouted from it withered in the dirt. Behind her, Rulf pulled up on the gangly equine he had chosen before the group set out. "This is ugly, as far as places go."

Ida snorted and said, "It could use a watering."

The man sighed and said, "I also don't see any *forever city*, and I don't see any tracks, which—"

"Tracks-shmacks," Ida interrupted.

Rulf continued, "*Which* should be everywhere if armies left from here."

"Is he always this faithless?" Roan asked. Ida replied, "Oh, he's normally worse. He's on his best behavior for you."

"Ida. Don't make me regret letting you come," he grumbled.

"Oh, let me, did you?" Ida scoffed.

"You two, please," Roan said. "Our friends are waiting on us." The two ex-watchmen turned to see the silent Ichablists sitting on their equines only a few feet behind. A warm wind drew a large cloud of dust along their path, coating Roan's eyes. Ida and Rulf coughed simultaneously. From somewhere in the middle of the group, Higg sneezed, and then coughed.

"Sorry," the boy muttered.

Ravobisob approached the three and said, "Friends. Are-we-not-con-cerned?"

Roan looked at him and asked, "Of?" The Ichablist gestured towards the Edge, and she replied, "It's down, remember? Past the Edge."

"I-real-ize-the-jai-lor's-home-is-sub-ter-ran-e-an. I-re-fer-to-the-butch-erd-wild-life."

Roan, Rulf, and Ida shifted to peer at where the Ichablist pointed. A headless, white rabbit spilled from the dead grass. Ravobisob spoke, "An-om-en-of-ter-ror."

Higg called from behind, "Hey! Who is that?"

Past the dead hare, far on the horizon, a hazy figure material-ized. Then a second cloud of dust washed over the group and two coughed. The Allthame twitched on Roan's back and she replied, "I don't know, but prepare yourselves."

Ravobisob tightened his hands on the reins of his mount and gurgled, "We-are-but-days-from-the-ex-trem-it-y. The-Edge. It-may-be-an-a-gent-of-the-jai-lor."

Higg (and the Ichablist he shared a mount with) approached the forward group. "Who is it?" he hissed.

"I-can-not-see-ve-ry-far. Please-de-scribe-them."

Rulf replied, "It's a tulka. That's all I can tell at this distance. Anyone else?"

Higg and Ida shook their heads. Roan remained still until the Allthame squirmed in its sling. "Wait here," she commanded and kicked her mount into a gallop.

*** *** ***

The complex was beyond belief. On the second day of Greydal's imprisonment, Sebastian took him to the outskirts of the Legate's home, to a balcony, which stretched for hundreds of yards in either direction, and gave him a daunting view of the termination of the world.

Canyon of canyons, an abyss without end. The whole struc-ture suspended above it, the Legate's colossal compound bridging between Edge and firmament. The chasm yawned away from Greydal and receded into the far distance. *That must be north*, he thought. Behind him, he knew the vast trench would stretch at least equally far in the opposite direction, now filled with the stone and mortar of the Mansions of the Dawn.

The audacity to build such a home between the Edge and the very walls of the world staggered him. His shaking hand found the railing as he peered over the banister. The darkness below leaped to meet him. He surged forward, but Sebastian's long-fingered hand gripped him by his shoulder and pulled him away from the railing.

"Careful, you would fall for a long time."

Greydal barely heard him. What would his father have thought, his son now standing here beyond it all, in the land of fables? Greydal shrugged off the guard's hand and crept towards the railing a second time. He gripped the translucent banister with both hands and inhaled as he gazed over. The Legate's compound dove to his right and left, past the massive balcony. Greydal looked several hundred yards to the east. A wall of gray clay and rock extended halfway to the sky. That was the Edge. The light of the sun streamed down its face, creating the illusion of frozen figures. Greydal turned away and looked the opposite direction, to the west. His eyes roved the incomprehensible blankness that was the firmament wall. It extended to the heavens and formed a crease with the framework of the sky.

He fought the urge to look straight down and failed. The light of the sun streamed directly into the chasm, but didn't illuminate the bottom, if such a thing existed. The world was said to have four sides and four corners, and since youth, Greydal had imagined a semi-flat plate below the cradling sky. But he had not anticipated how deep the bedrock truly plunged. There was more world beneath the ground than there was air above it.

"How?"

"Did Our Most Holy One, infinite is his wisdom, create this shrine?"

Greydal had meant the world itself, but he said, "Your complex must be miles long. To stretch between the gap."

"Long, yes. And wide. It extends south along the void for days. We are on the northern side. Most have to take a train to go between sectors."

Greydal didn't know what kind of animal a train was and said nothing. A second look at the Edge and the stone wall, which cascaded from it into the dark. His eyes traced the illusory shapes which the sun cast, and he started, blinking to make sure he wasn't deceived. No, he could *sense* it there. How hadn't he noticed before?

He took a deep breath and forced his eyes away from the crawling shadow. It must be large indeed, to be visible from Greydal's vantage. He glanced to his left at Sebastian, who smiled at him. The man hadn't spotted it, surely. Greydal tried to make his voice normal as he said, "Well, I've been to your Oraculum and the Edge so far. What about the Grand Library you mentioned?"

"The *Hallowed* Grand Library is half a day away, though there are several smaller repositories scattered in this area. You, however, have the enviable honor to dine with Our Most Holy, may his plate be ever full, tonight."

"Maybe next time, then." He had wondered when the Legate would make an appearance. He hadn't seen the man since the ruler had kidnapped him from outside The Sands.

"I can take you to your quarters now if you would care to rest before dinner. You have several hours yet." Greydal nodded but frowned. The walk to the balcony had taken a long time, and he didn't envy the journey to his cell. His leg ached fiercely as it was.

Sebastian turned and strode towards the nearest hall entrance. Greydal followed him, but not before glancing over his shoulder at the distant Edge. The moving shadow had vanished, yet a leaden feeling in his sternum told him the shape was out there, getting closer. He shivered, then hurried after the guardsman. The two left the balcony and made their slow way back.

When they arrived at Greydal's room, he discovered someone had set out a clean set of clothes for him, including a single, left-footed boot. He nodded at Sebastian, who closed and locked his door. Greydal turned to the clothes and picked up a blue jacket. If not for the waist-high cut of the jacket's skirt and rippled texture, it could have passed for a watchman's. That made him think of Ida, which made him think of Marro. That had been the first time he'd killed someone in cold blood. Though there was no guilt, he knew the act had been different from the slayings of Calahurst, Yphrus, and a later Nayuda casualty, Irgurd. He gazed at his hand, the one that had held the dai-strelok, and recalled the surprise on Marro's face when he had entered the man's tent. That surprise had quickly turned to a look of cunning.

Marro had spoken first. "I knew it was you, boy. I bet you thought no one would see, but I did. I was out that morning, before you arrived in camp I saw you, walking along th—"

The hiss of the dai-strelok interrupted whatever the man meant to say. Greydal left Marro there, with the look of surprise back on his pocked face.

***   ***   ***

Later in the evening of Greydal's second day at the Legate's compound, Sebastian arrived to retrieve him. They exited the portions of the complex he was familiar with and walked half an hour southwest. The man, who he was coming to suspect was no mere guard, lead him through a series of metal corridors which gave way to a long and curving wooden one. As they stepped into it, Greydal found he could smell the sap still clinging to the rough planks. It was a welcome reprieve from the subtle, ever-present perfume of the twisting compound.

Triangular doorways, wooden, branched from the hallway at regular intervals. As they walked along, Greydal noted each entrance opened on peculiar scenes. He stared at a wall of green, which pressed against the opening of one. Almost of its own accord, his hand reached forward until Sebastian stopped him.

"I'm sorry. It is dangerous without proper safeguards. The technology can hurt you. Look but do not touch."

Greydal nodded, but his eyes lingered on the dense jungle beyond the opening. A man covered in hair peered at him from deep within the foliage. Greydal blinked, and he was gone, but the image of the man's sad gaze lingered in his mind.

They passed other openings, all as strange as the first. Through one, Greydal could spy fields, half-submerged in water. Distant figures tended crops the size of razorbacks. Or perhaps the figures were not so distant, but only small, and the crops were regular-sized. The shimmering veil between himself and the field made it hard to tell. The harvest looked delicious, though, orange fruit swelling and gleaming under the fading light of the sun as the farmers worried over them. The two passed another opening, and Greydal froze. He recognized the wall, though it had been years since he had seen it from that angle. The south perimeter was a dark ochre in the afternoon sun, and the tops of homes poked from beyond the wall's crown. The wall was gray with old ash at its bottom. The village looked quiet, if such a thing was possible. No smoke from hearths lingered in the air. No birds flew in circles around the market. The hamlet was a painting, rendered in somber, ashy hues.

Sebastian urged him onwards, and Greydal followed the man after a moment of stunned silence. The other doorways were equally strange, and some opened on scenes almost as familiar. Minutes later, he and Sebastian reached the entrance to what the golden-robed man indicated was the dining hall. Doors that climbed several stories high loomed half-ajar and the space before and behind them was dark, lit only by flickering torches which hung in molden contrast to the bright oto-lanterns from the earlier sections of the complex.

Greydal was wrenched from his brooding as several Friars stepped from the dimness, the tinkling of their scaled coats announcing them. He fished the razor from his pocket, teeth bared. As he backed, he bumped into Sebastian.

"Easy," he said. "They will not hurt you, though I would put away the blade, else they become...agitated."

More windchimes sounded, surrounding him. His breathing was ragged as he forced his hand into the pocket of the blue coat. He kept it there, fist curled around the handle of the opened razor. Sebastian laid a palm on his shoulder and led him towards the massive doors, which shot into the darkness over their heads.

Greydal kept his gaze forward, but couldn't help to glimpse the Friars' helmets moving to track his path. He shivered, and fought the curious urge to vomit. As they passed through the entrance, he found himself wishing Sebastian or someone else would close the doors behind them to block the Friars. Having the terrors at his back made his legs weak, and he struggled against the urge to flee into the dark.

As he moved forward, the aroma of cooked meats reached his nose, and his mouth watered at the smell, despite his mounting terror. The intense gloom confused his gaze, except for a lone light several hundred yards away, while the two's footsteps both followed and greeted them as they strode towards the flickering. If the echoes told anything, it was that the hall was expansive.

As they neared, he recognized the light as the glow of a table full of candles and candelabras. A rich, red tablecloth spanned its length, and became dark as blood in the places where the light was feeble. Food of a kind Greydal had never seen filled the table, and at the wooden span's end, sat the Legate. The man swirled a golden goblet and inhaled, eyes closed.

"Theodore, isn't it? Wait, no. It's Sebastian. I'm still learning names as you can see. You may leave us."

Sebastian bowed at the waist and retreated into the shadows, leaving Greydal alone with the king of the world.

CHAPTER

22

ENTREATY

Strangely, the Legate's golden suit didn't reflect much of the candles' glow, causing his shaven, pink face to appear as a floating oval in the murk. It was a bizarre sight for Greydal, seeing his own countenance changed so.

Watching the man, he became aware of just what differentiated them. It was the eyes. The Legate's were cold and vain, lacking a sort of fundamental softness Greydal had occasionally spied in his own through clear glass and dingy water. And yet, the other man's crooked smile and carved jawline were identical.

Was it the fear clenching his guts, which caused him to recall that morning, years ago? His hands could almost feel the moist bark of the roadside tree. There had been something else, then, hadn't there, before he awoke? A dream of the hunt.

You reach the limit. The way out is through.

The Legate's candlelit face betrayed no sign of having heard the speaker. Greydal felt a part of himself slip away, and he became momentarily calm as he approached the table and sat. The heavy chair scraped as he inched it closer to the table. "Was that how you got around? Those doors?" Greydal asked.

The Legate swirled his goblet and replied, "*The gates? Sometimes. Others use them more often as I-I generally have no need.*" The Legate gestured at the stacks of food before him. "*Please, have some. I know you didn't eat your previous meals. You must be close to witless from hunger.*"

Greydal didn't waste time asking if the food was drugged. He reached out a hand and grabbed the nearest delicacy, a slab of cooked meat between two slices of wheat, vegetables, and cheese. He took a bite. It was delicious.

"*Good choice. I've made sure the staff here maintained the ingredients to make those for the past thousand-odd years. Much good it does me.*"

He looked up at the Legate and replied between bites, "You don't talk like you're that old. If I had to stay alive that long, I think I'd go crazy. Act like a maniac, maybe."

The Legate didn't rise to the remark and replied, "*The perks of my station. I get to rest for the majority of my rule.*" He pointed a finger to his right and a distant light bloomed, illuminating a device Greydal had seen before. It was one of the strange beds with the snakes' nest of tubes. He recognized it from the Old Folks' book he had opened in Alom's study. Then the light disappeared, and the Legate added, "*Almost everything is automated now. Bureaucratic process set in stone, you know.*" The man took a sip from his goblet. "*Speaking of, let me apologize. It wasn't my intention to sic the Good Friars on you and yours.*"

Greydal's jaw involuntarily clenched. He swallowed the mouthful of food and growled, "Your intention? You butchered us." The Legate paused and stared at him. After a beat, the man slowly set down the goblet and wiped his mouth, but Greydal paused as he registered how close he had just come to riling the man. He had to be more careful. Whoever the Legate was, he wasn't like Yphrus or Marston. Greydal needed him calm, not irrationally angry.

"Sorry," he said. "It's a sore spot."

The Legate nodded. *"If it's any consolation, the man who authorized the deployment of the Good Friars is now dead. I have a mechanism in place for signs of...disturbances. There was a report of a tulka boy with dangerous associations to the east. By the time I exited my sarcophagus, your village lay burned, and you were in the hands of Sophites."* Seeing Greydal's look he added, *"Of course, I know what you call yourselves. Don't be defensive. They're not why you're here."*

"Yeah? Why then?"

"Because I want to tell you a story."

Greydal risked a glance over his shoulder. No sign of the Friars. He felt watched, though. A presence, subtly making itself known by excitedly prickling the hairs of his awareness. Not the Legate, sitting diagonally across from him. He thought of that morning on the balcony, and almost choked on his food when he deduced who it was that now crouched in the dining room with them, hidden. Had it followed?

He glanced across the table, but the Legate only stared at him in bemusement. Greydal hurried and took a sip from the glass before him. Wine. He tried to sound relaxed as he said, "Story..."

The Legate replied, *"Yes. I expect you'll find what I have to say enlightening, if you give me time."*

"If I give you time," Greydal repeated.

The man leaned forward in his high-backed seat. *"You've been with the Sophites for several years now, over there in your mountain range."* Greydal froze as he made to scan the dark once more. A sick knot twisted his stomach, but the Legate continued talking, seemingly unaware, "*You call those who dwelt in the olden days the* Old Folk *or sometimes the* ancestors, *is that right?*"

Greydal said nothing, his thoughts racing. Mabet, Loken, Faros. Was it too late already?

"*I'm sure you've put this together yourself, but I'm one of them. I'm from a time before there was…*" The Legate waved a hand around, "*all this.*"

Collecting himself, Greydal cleared his throat and replied, "I grew up in the faith. I know the story."

"*Not like this. When I was young, I was a teacher, did you know that?*"

The Legate didn't wait for his response, continuing, "*We had others, only much smarter. One day, they determined a way to reach out to other worlds. Now, I'm not referring to planets—you may know those as the spheres mentioned here and there in old texts—I'm referring to other realms of existence entirely. Do you understand?*"

What the fuck was he talking about? Did he not realize they weren't alone? Or hadn't been? The silence dragged and Greydal mustered a response. "I don't— You mean like those gates back in the hall?"

"*No. I mean we found ways to contact spaces* outside *of our reality. These sat directly on top of us, only in such a way that normally you wouldn't be able to see, hear, feel, or otherwise interact with them. Do you follow so far?*"

Greydal blinked. "My father called them transplants, if you're referring to all the orphaned lands strewn about the Four Corners. Except, you can interact with those." Greydal's awareness flicked to the heavy patch of audient darkness to his right where he had sensed the presence. It was no longer there. A bead of sweat slid down his temple, and he fought the urge to wipe at it.

"*That's similar, a side-effect that came later. Originally, it was controlled. We had gates, almost like the ones you passed. Except these went to other dimensions, our admittedly colorful word for these new places. As I said, they existed on top of or outside our reality, and once we figured out the trick to accessing them, it opened a whole new chapter of our history. We blossomed. People became wiser, more well-traveled."*

Greydal gripped his goblet and tried to appear calm as he listened to the Legate's tale. Where had the presence gone?

"The problem was, we hit a snag," the Legate continued. *"We thought we had the method of travel down, under control. But there was a place, a desert, where none of the interstices functioned correctly. It was a bit like if you opened the door to your bathroom, only to accidentally fall off some distant mountain. But there were graver consequences. Things which weren't supposed to be in our home started appearing. Well, our very smart leaders sent a clutch of scholars to investigate the epicenter of these malfunctions, a cave at the dead center of the desert. It wasn't on any map, and the running theory marked it as a place that had somehow slipped through the cracks. This cave, as we thought of it at the time, was what had caused the trouble with the nearby access points.*

"That was when the real problems started. Scholars went in." The Legate paused and took another sip. Greydal noticed the man hadn't touched any of the food sprawling between them. The Legate continued, *"Scholars went in and were never heard from again. At the time, our people thought it was something the team themselves had done* inside *the cave."*

Greydal risked a glance to the dark at his left. Then above him. Had the thing left the room? "What?" he asked when he noticed the Legate waited for him.

"It. The nightmare. After that day, everything fell to pieces. The cave vanished, jumping half a billion miles from us. I mean that literally. After, all *the gates on every one of our spheres started misbehaving. Whole countries disappeared. Sometimes, other things*

replaced them. You have no frame of reference for something like that, but it was chaos. Though that wasn't quite the real dilemma."

Greydal tried to concentrate. For a moment, he thought he had heard something. The sound of a fight, though it passed before he could be sure he hadn't imagined the noise. "What then?" he asked after a beat.

"The real problem was that we started encountering other places that weren't all that dissimilar from ours. At first, we believed we had discovered time travel. Do you know what that is?"

His eyes found the Legate's. "I think so... Tier—I mean my father—used to tell me a story about a man who tried to go back in history and fix a poisoned well. He succeeded and healed the well, but he couldn't return to his own time."

"Quaint. What we found at first wasn't time travel, but it was close. We started getting bleed-over from other planes, one which were almost identical to our own. I'll call these types of planes Type Twos, as opposed to the first kind which I mentioned—dimensions that were more often simply strange and held little in common with our reality. But these Type Twos were unique—they seemed only a little further in the future or very rarely, further in the past from us.

"As we discovered, these spaces were a different kind of alternate reality, spots similar to our own except for minor changes. A different leader here, a new technology there, you understand the concept. Now, aside from the cataclysmic issue of people thinking they could predict our future by observing these Type Two realities, we encountered a greater trouble."

The Legate paused and stared. *"People began having what they thought were memory issues. They would return home to find their partners gone from their lives, or strangers inhabiting their houses. Children would hug parents who didn't recognize them. All of us had something stolen, whether we recalled it or not. But very quickly, we realized that memory itself wasn't the dilemma. The truth was, the*

Type Twos had followed the behavior of the Type Ones. They were collapsing too."

"In effect, every reality—ours, the alien dimensions, and *the alternate histories—they tumbled into one another. A single, fermented universe where there had once been millions or more. As if it couldn't get worse, no one could predict the changes. What caused one reality to partially overwrite the other? At the time, no one understood."*

Greydal didn't know how the Legate expected him to respond. At length, he croaked through a mouthful of wine, "It sounds like a mess."

The Legate chuckled. *"An understatement. You recall I said I was a teacher? How do you teach about the history of the Roman Empire, holy or otherwise, when it turns out no one in the world remembers the thing? I was selling a fantasy, one I had spent my college years mastering. And then one morning I woke..."* The man grew silent, his buzzing voice dwindling. Then his face became animated again. *"Well, we all had things stolen, as I said. For one, a new knowledge had infected me. World leaders I had never heard of were calling me, insisting I was a great mind. My teaching days were done."*

"Why are you telling me this? I assume you're not fishing for a new student."

The Legate tilted his head and laughed, the sound of a thousand hornets, and Greydal saw for the first time that the Legate's golden armor didn't just have a high collar. It penetrated the man's skin, below the jaw. What in the Four Corners had happened to him? Greydal tried to stay composed. Whatever the man was, they were on the right track, the Legate was talking and engaged. There would come a moment soon when the man would lower his guard. That would be the time to strike, or flee from what had seemingly entered the compound.

Greydal returned his focus. The Legate was speaking, "—*ightful, as I remember. No, I'm afraid those days are long finished. What I want is your cooperation. It's something I should have sought in the first place.*"

"What—"

"*I'm talking about the cave, or like I said, what we* thought of *as a cave. After my people spotted Armageddon on the horizon, they decided they had to go to the source. A second expedition.*"

Greydal didn't understand. "Didn't you just say your cave moved a billion miles away? What does that have to do with me?"

"*Half a billion. And it has everything to do with you.*"

The Legate paused and eyed him from across the table. "*Your dreams have been strange ever since you were young, haven't they? Sometimes, involving things that haven't happened yet?*"

"I don't know what you're talking about."

"*I think you do. The reason I stayed alive all these years, became a deity to these people? It's so I could meet you. Do you understand what that means?*"

Greydal shook his head. "That's... No, that's insane." His skin prickled.

"*Hmm. Maybe you're right. How about this? I'll tell you the end of my story, that may help. Then I'll ask something of you.*" The Legate raised his goblet and guzzled the last of its contents. He slammed it onto the table. "*So, the cataclysm we feared came to pass. The fluids were mixed. On the positive side, the end of the world caused things to stabilize somewhat. There wasn't much left to collapse, after all. Just a handful of Type One tears remained. Likewise, we could only find a single Type Two after everything was said and done with.*

"*I believe the other reason the pond became still, so to speak, was that I— we finally isolated the source anomaly, built a barrier around it, using lessons learned from previous encounters. Much harder for it to cause trouble, after we did that...*"

There was a look then, that the Legate gave him. Greydal missed its significance, but he caught a momentary shift in the man's voice. That unnerved him, though he couldn't tell why. The Legate continued, "*But our history... Well, everything was mutilated, all past saving.*" The man leaned back and quieted. Greydal realized he waited for a response.

"Uh— the end?"

"*The end. Families lost their loved ones. Mankind lost its history. Behemoths roamed the heavens and physical delusions— No, horrors replaced wide swaths of existence. And it will stay that way unless I can fix it.*"

Greydal sat in silence. The man across from him was out of his mind, yet that didn't mean his story was wholly a lie. The "collapses" were probably real. Greydal had experienced one himself, hadn't he? Roan used to have black hair.

So, had there been a "collapse" when he entered the thicket, years back? Some strange history falling over and covering the familiar one?

There was much the tale corroborated. "How would you fix it?"

The man replied, "*Hijack a perfect, last collapse. Undo the previous ones.*"

"How, though?" he said, trying to keep the man speaking.

"*Those Type Two alternate realities weren't* really *gateways to the past, you understand? They just followed very similar paths to our own and generally had alike physical rules. But we* could *change our own history by forcing the collapse of a Type Two we liked, though it was dangerous and rarely worked the way we planned.*"

Greydal wiped the sweat from his brow and rubbed it on his pants. His hand entered his pocket and found the razor again.

"*The problem with this idea is that Type Two dimensions were never exactly how we wanted them. Therefore, it wouldn't do to have their history bleed over ours, do you understand? It would be* no use to, say, undo a holocaust if it also made it so that none of us were ever born.

In the beginning, there were only two interstices we could find that went to places configured like the time before the original anomaly was discovered, the time before it moved, meaning there were only two known options which could be collapsed to return history to a familiar state. But even these were not exact—not how we needed them to be. For one, neither had experienced the Holocene extinction, so even though they bore similarities to our world, both Type Two realities were alien histories, as far as we were concerned.

"We ascertained what we had to do was send someone across, to change things first. Make a Type Two compliant to our history before collapsing it."

He ran his finger over the razor's blade, and he said, "You mean me? You have one of these tears here in the Mansions?"

The Legate shook his head. "There's one left now, but it isn't here, though it's close. Very close. But it's also not the one I need. My aim is to prevent everything, even the Type One collapses from the beginning, before we began to discover Type Two dimensions.

"I don't want to just fix history, I want to fix biology, physics as well. All of it."

"Oh, so... how?" Greydal tried to keep his voice steady.

The Legate's eyes reflected the tiny fires of the candles. "When Type Two dimensions fell into our reality, with some of our people on the other side, where do you think those people went? Not back to us directly."

"I don't—"

The Legate interrupted him, "Think of a river. The water is us, and the muddy banks are nearby Type Twos. If you leave the water and access the bank, the river you left keeps moving. When you return, tracking all that mud with you, you are no longer in the same patch of water. Nor is the river itself unchanged."

Greydal tried to wrap his mind around what the Legate told him. He could be wrong, but the analogy didn't seem... correct. His pounding heart made it difficult to follow the madman's words.

"Alternatively, you can think of it like this: there are two ways to change the past. The first way, you overwrite your history with that of a Type Two. Did the Type Two version of yourself die in infancy? Did he not exist in the first place? Then once the collapse happens, you disappear, seven times out of ten. Do you see how dangerous that is?

"But there's a second way, and it involves a follow-up action to the first. You displace someone, one of your own, by making sure they're present inside a Type Two during its destruction. That person will re-enter your world on the collapse. Of course, at that point, it's not entirely your history any longer, but you get my meaning, don't you?"

"I'm lost," Greydal truthfully told the Legate. He betrayed no emotion as he tightened his grip on the handle of the razor in his pocket. Only a little longer.

"Try to understand, really think about it. Time travel is real, but only for the person who goes into a Type Two and gets displaced during its dissolution. That person re-enters the prime narrative, only at the point in the river that matches where they were inside the Type Two. That person could change history, real history, however they liked. They wouldn't have to rely on the collapse netting positive results."

The Legate looked relaxed as he spoke, and Greydal tensed his legs, taking a deep breath. He said, "How would you ensure the—" What had the man been calling it? "—the Type Two, the one where you sent someone, would come apart? Would collapse?"

"Back then? A colossal amount of wealth and time, or luck. Now, though, you wouldn't need to do much at all. I'm almost certain there's but a single prime existence, one last narrative, after so

many years. Any remaining Type Two is almost guaranteed to fall into ours, one day, a splash in the ocean at this point.

"And you want me to help you, what, enter and change the last realm before it collapses? So, you like the results? Or find an older one and prevent your cave from being investigated in the first place?"

"Neither. I need your help creating a new Type Tw—"

Candelabras tumbled as Greydal leaped over the table, razor extended. He angled it towards the Legate's eye, hoping to drive it into the man's brain. A hiss of steam obscured his vision, and the Legate's iron grip closed over his wrist. As the steam cleared, he saw blood dripping from a cut on the Legate's cheek.

"Ah. That was a poor decision." A golden fist connected with Greydal's temple, and his vision went white. He sprawled across the floor next to the table. The Legate stood and circled the long table. *"Greydal, Greydal, Greydal..."*

He blacked out. When he came to, the man stood over him, and then bent to pick him up by the collar, one-handed. *"I didn't bring you to my home to kill you, don't you realize? I need your help."* The Legate backhanded him, and there was a horrible crunching in his nose. Blood poured down his face as his vision blurred.

"Greydal? Can you hear me? Look to your right, if you please."

He coughed and lolled his head to the right. Glowing figures hung suspended in the far darkness. *"You see?"* the Legate hissed. *"I'll be honest, I don't know your relations to some of them. Are they your friends? I know the tow-headed girl is... Jezebal Hale's orphan."*

"N-no," he spoke through a mouthful of blood.

"Yes. You will help me. You will—" The Legate paused, and Greydal turned his head towards his attacker. The man wasn't looking at him.

A polite voice spoke from somewhere to the left, "I'm sorry, Most Holy, but there's been a complication."

"*Can't you see I'm busy with our guest?*"

"It appears one of the insurrectionists may have evaded the initial sweep. This sector's Friars, they're..."

"*They're what?*"

Greydal started laughing. "You—" he wheezed, "I'd say look in the trees but—" He coughed, and the Legate dropped him. He grunted from the impact.

"*Handle it. I don't have time for—*"

"SHELL BREACH. SECTOR ZERO," a new voice radiated from somewhere far above. Greydal looked for the speaker but saw no one.

"SHELL BREACH. SECTOR ZERO," the voice repeated. The Legate staggered as if from a blow. "*No.*"

Greydal peered at the golden-armored tulka from his prone position. Absolute terror contorted the Legate's face.

"SHELL BREACH. SECTOR ZERO."

"*Watch him!*"

As Greydal stared, the Legate and a tumbled candle at the man's feet both evaporated into the dark. For a moment, he could see... Who was that, waiting in the shadows where the Legate had vanished? The image dissolved as the Legate's portal faded away.

"SHELL BREACH. SECTOR ZERO."

Soft hands helped him sit, and then stand. Sebastian said, "Come with me. We don't have much time."

CHAPTER

23

SECRETS

Sebastian ushered the reeling Greydal towards the backlit, suspended figures. His bleary eyes made out Roan, Ida, Higg, and Ravobisob. "Come, I know you are hurting, but we must move," Sebastian said in his ear. Greydal nodded and increased his pace, leaning on the man for fear of tumbling to the ground.

"SHELL BREACH. SECTOR ZERO."

It took them thirty seconds to reach the edge of the room. Sebastian released him and approached a rectangular pillar, waist high. Above it, the four figures floated as if by magick. "Are they alive?" Greydal asked in a stuffy voice. Each of the figures' eyes were closed, aside from Ravobisob, who had none he could identify. "Watch," the golden-robed man replied.

"SHELL BREACH. SECTOR ZERO."

Sebastian placed his hand on the pillar, which ignited. After a low buzzing sound, the figures descended to the floor. Roan opened her eyes first.

"You're bleeding." They embraced as Ravobisob and Ida stirred, and then stood. Ida rotated her shoulder and moaned as Greydal whispered, "I'm... When I saw you, I thought—"

The next interruption muffled Roan's response. "SHELL BREACH. SECTOR ZERO."

"I'm okay. Where did he go?" she repeated.

Greydal made to respond, but turned and vomited at the last moment, sparing her a shower of pureed meats and bread. Ida's voice echoed, "Oh, Dawn! Grey, you sick?" Someone put their hand on his shoulder, and he waved them off as dizziness made the world spin.

"I'm—" he wiped his mouth, "I'm alright."

Sebastian whispered, "He received a rather severe blow to his skull, from what I viewed."

"It's happened—" Greydal paused and took a deep breath. "It's happened before. I'll be fine." He looked up to see Roan's worry.

"SHELL BREACH. SECTOR ZERO."

"Ugh! What *is* that?" Roan asked, glancing upwards. Her eyes scanned the gloom as though reading it. Then Higg snorted from his prone position, moving his head back and forth before his eyes fluttered open. "Looks like the rabbit's up," Ida said, and turned to Greydal. "You should have seen him when they caught us. He leaped fair to the ceiling!"

Greydal tried to summon a smile as Sebastian turned to approach Ravobisob. "My friend, are you alright?" the seneschal asked.

Ravobisob replied, "Do-not-fear-for-me. I-went-un-scathed-dur-ing-the-am-bush."

Sebastian nodded and looked relieved. "Your people are being held two floors below. Some are wounded. We must go soon."

"Where's Rulf?" Greydal asked. Higg responded first, rubbing his head, "Good to see you too, *sckapod.* Your man... what's the word? *Conveniently* slipped off while the *blytan* Armargure hit us."

Ida said with a frown, "Rulf was smart. I just hope he didn't run into any trouble."

Greydal shook his head. He didn't have time to worry for the ex-watchman. "Roan. The holdout. The Legate knows where it is. I think—"

"I know," she interrupted, "I heard him."

"Wait, heard who?" Ida asked her. "Just before?"

Roan nodded slowly and Higg replied, "Hmm. I was *droze*—asleep—up there, or something like it."

"Same for me," Ida added. "Once they shut us in, I was snoozing."

"SHELL BREACH. SECTOR ZERO."

"Please. We must leave this place," Sebastian spoke through the voice.

"I-sus-pect-I-know-what-that-a-larm-means. He-suc-ceed-ed."

"Who?" Ida and Higg asked simultaneously.

"It doesn't matter right now," Roan hurriedly replied. "We need to find out what's happened, though I wonder if Mabet isn't already aware."

"Wait," Ida interjected, "What about your mission? Didn't we come here to off the Red Legate?"

"We did, but..."

"To-op-en-the-way. That-is-why. It-seems-all-we-had-to-do-was-bring-the-in-stru-ment."

"SHELL BREACH. SECTOR ZERO."

Greydal looked the crew over and rubbed his head. He felt terrible, but it wasn't just his head and stomach that bothered him. "Roan," he asked slowly, trying to enunciate through his blood-smothered nose, "Where's the Allthame?"

She shook her head and replied, "Later. It's safe."

"What's an al-dame?" Ida asked Higg, who shrugged.

Sebastian nearly danced in place as he said, "My friends, we *must leave* now. Please."

The witch replied, "We're leaving. Can you find us somewhere safe?"

"Hold on," Greydal said, and turned to the golden-robed man. "What about the gates?"

*** *** ***

They left the oppressive hall and crossed beneath the towering entry doors. As they exited, the group had to step over piles of spiny, crimson goo. "In-ter-es-ting," the Ichablist spoke.

"What in the Four Corners is this gunk?" Ida asked. "It looks like..." she began with a quiver in her voice.

"Dead Friars, from the looks of it," Roan responded. "How?" Higg asked, eyes wide. Only Greydal remained silent as Sebastian said, "I heard the fight, but caught no one. When I approached, I found only what you see. Could your Rulf have done this?"

"He wishes," Higg replied.

Greydal looked to the winding gloom above. Though he couldn't tell how high the ceiling was, he had an impression of extreme depth. Regardless, he didn't sense the presence there, even if a coldness in his spine and along his neck told him it wasn't far. As he glanced back, he found the group continued forward, towards the wooden hallway, and he hurried along to join them as his irregular footsteps echoed to sound the dark. Shortly after, Roan slowed to walk beside him, placing a hand on his shoulder.

They walked in silence.

"We shouldn't have let it go on for so long," Greydal whispered after a minute. "I ought to have written sooner," Roan agreed and added, "But you were where you needed to be."

"Sure. Somewhere Mabet could keep an eye on me."

"It's not always about you, love."

"Tell that to *him*. You heard, didn't you? Everything." As he said this, the voice which Ravobisob had called an *alarm* continued to blare its unceasing message from the direction of the dining hall.

"SHELL BREACH. SECTOR ZERO."

Sebastian looked towards them, "Dame Roan? Is that your name?"

She turned from Greydal and replied, "It's Roan."

"Roan, I will give you something to take before you access the gate," the man said. He added, "That goes for any who wish to accompany her."

Ida replied, "Wait, this *something* won't make me feel funny, will it? I think I've had enough heady stuff as of today."

"Se-bas-ti-an-would-not-do-that. He-is-en-light-end."

"It's nothing of the sort, dame," Sebastian told Ida. "The tablets I will retrieve only protect from the effects of the gates."

In response Higg asked, "Why would they need that?"

"The tablets?"

"Protecting," Higg explained.

Greydal interrupted, "It'll make you sick, won't it, Sebastian? Going through one of those? Contagious, too."

"Ah, yes. I'm surprised you're familiar after I had to prevent you putting your hands through one," the man replied testily. At the uncertain glances from the rest of the party, he elucidated, "The technology involved came from a rather unsavory land. The gates work wonders, but to pass through them unaided could cause...complications."

Ida turned from the man and asked, "That sounds bad, but how'd you know that, Grey? Been learning since you got stolen from the camp? Speaking of which, I just want you to know, I think I found out why you—"

"Enough," Roan said. "Greydal. Dear. Are these gates safe to pass through?" She didn't look at Sebastian.

"With his *tablet*?" Greydal pointed at the seneschal. "I have no idea," he admitted. "But I wonder if it would hurt me either way."

Roan looked confused, but then blinked, her eyes traveling to a spot on his chest where the blue jacket hid his root tatu. Greydal nodded and whispered, "I think so. Remember the thief?"

The witch nodded and completed the thought, murmuring, "You said there was nothing out there in the wastes..."

He smiled grimly and nodded. "Almost nothing. Turns out Harlow's escapee probably went a lot farther than we thought."

Roan looked up. "Sebastian, is there *any* other way I can contact my people?"

"Ah, yes, but none nearby. The gates will let you travel to most places within the demense, though you must memorize the way back, else you might not find the entrance. Each remains hidden at all times." Sebastian cleared his throat and added, "Aside from accidentally finding it, of course. However, the chance of doing so is quite slim, I assure you." The alarm, now more distant and muffled, sounded again as the crew convened.

"Alright, you know this place, so I'll have to trust you," Roan said. "Plus, who wouldn't believe a man that well-dressed?"

Sebastian blushed and replied, "Er, well, thank you. This way, please." Roan looked at Greydal and winked.

The group trailed Sebastian, and after several minutes of walking, he registered they weren't heading towards the wooden hallway. For one, the oto-lanterns had returned, lighting the current corridor in regular increments, blooming as the utilities sensed the group's approach.

"Where are you taking us?"

"Apologies. I have to retrieve the tablets first," Sebastian replied. Greydal grunted in response. After this, the group continued walking for another minute before turning a sharp corner, now arriving at a branching section of hallway. The procession went on, but Greydal halted and let the group pass. A pale figure had taken shape in the western-facing passageway, wavering. Roan was the last to stride by, but at the last moment, she paused, looking at him before following his gaze.

"You can see them, can't you?" he asked softly.

Slowly, she nodded.

"It wants us to follow," he told her as he eyed the stranger. The distant, nude figure swayed the way a lake plant might, all slow movements and uncertain currents.

Then Ida yelled, "Hey, what's with the dawdling? Seb here says we're close!"

Roan ignored her and whispered, "*It* is a she, a Pneuma. And she doesn't want *us* to follow." Greydal broke his gaze from the figure and glanced at the witch, who nodded. "It's okay," she soothed. "We'll see each other soon."

He leaned in and kissed her. They held each other for a silent moment before he broke contact and gazed into her eyes. They were black, despite the oto-lanterns' light. "Friends-I-think-we-must-con-tin-ue," Ravobisob interrupted as he closed from the group ahead.

Roan replied for Greydal, "Greydal's going to part with us for a time. He has something to which he must attend."

Sebastian turned and replied, "Please, it is not safe here. Let me help you return to your home."

"It's not *my* home," Ida replied. "I came here to help, and that's what I'll do. Grey, where are you going? I'll come."

"Same here," Higg added. "Not letting you alone, you know that, right?" Greydal glanced at his friends while, down the western hallway, the figure continued to sway, now standing farther than before. He shook his head and said, "You all go. She'll— Roan will need your help."

In response, the witch snorted, and Higg protested, but Greydal cut in, "Higg. Think of your mother. The kith are in danger."

"He's right," Roan allowed. "Our warrior-prince will return to us, don't worry."

Greydal didn't wait to see the boy's response. Squeezing Roan's arm, he left the group there, standing at the juncture of hallways.

***   ***   ***

It was a while before he closed with the visitant. Each time he gained on her, she would dissolve around a corner, always leading him deeper into the complex. As he chased the bleached figure through the twisting metal and marble corridors, all elaborately ornamented, he thought about what Roan had said.

She had called the figure a Pneuma, and he recognized the term. Once, during his explorations of the Sophites' library, he came across several books, which told something of the beings. *Between Cats and Snakes* described the Pneuma as akin to nature ghosts, a court of otherworldly denizens that might be encountered only in places of profound wilderness. Despite implying the entities were specters of a sort, the tome went into great detail to explain they were *not* immaterial. The Pneuma simply existed in spaces often unobserved, living beyond the unaided eye. Another book, *Dancing at Dusk*, stated that several ancient cultures of some far-off sphere called them the Neighbors.

The Neighbors would steal human children for vague purposes and replace the missing babies with their own. This forced the unassuming parents of the stolen children to raise look-alike Pneuma adolescents. Based on what he had read, Greydal presumed the beings were likely transplants, owing to their references in pre-Four Corners writings. And yet, he had assumed they were simple folktales. But Roan had seen the figure, recognized it, in fact. What's more, Greydal was now positive she had always been able to perceive the beings, perhaps even before that night in the mists.

Thinking this, he turned a corner and gasped in spite of himself. The Pneuma stood within inches, easily close enough to touch. Her nude body glistened in the light of the oto-lanterns, and tufts of hair or fur poked from her armpits and groin. Unlike her red-maned counterpart, this one's short-cropped hair allowed him to see her face, the first time he had been able to do so with any of the beings. Greydal's eyes traced the curvature of her lips and nose. Then his eyes locked with hers.

"Oh...of course," he whispered to himself. Black eyes stared into his.

"Greydal! Legless!"

He turned to see Higg jogging towards him from a separate hallway. The boy panted as he hollered in the Sophite tongue, "I thought I'd never find you! I—" He paused, placing his hands on his knees. "I've been running for the past five minutes."

Greydal glanced at the Pneuma, but she had gone. Behind where she had stood, there was now a shortened corridor leading to a wide, well-lit room. Higg joined him at the junction. "Legless, before you get mad, I—"

"It's fine. I knew you would follow anyway. I'm glad you're here."

Higg grinned at that. "I think that's the first time you've ever told me that. So, what is it? Are you here to kill the Wyrm?"

Greydal shook his head and pointed at the well-lit room. "I think I'm meant to go there."

"You meant to what?"

"No, I— she wanted me to...Never mind." Greydal sighed. "Let's just go." He walked the hall towards the room and the boy followed. "Where's that air coming from? Are we close to an exit?" Higg asked.

Greydal didn't respond, and examined the corridor as he walked. This one lay unadorned and could have passed for the interior of the barracks, if not for its width. That was it, then. The material had to be a kind of substicrete. It looked oddly shaded, and less rough, which meant it was of a much more refinded type than the substicrete found within the barracks. Greydal nodded to himself. That was how the Mansions maintained their form, suspended over the void.

In short order, the two reached the well-lit room, a place where the marble of earlier halls resumed, plastering the substicrete. Though the room was empty, it seemed somehow more luxurious than any other place Greydal had seen within the Mansions. Lofty columns of pink held the corners of the domed ceiling, over which a fantastical mural swam.

It depicted a man holding a shining jewel, which later transformed into a rectangular pyramid with a convex bottom. Another side of the mural showed the man, now visibly older, gazing longingly at the pyramid. Beneath each image were words.

The stench of wet dog marred the beauty of the room. Higg whistled. "What do you think happened here?" he asked.

Greydal's gaze shifted to one of the other parts of the mural, near the opposite end of the room. He thought it had depicted something like a sacrifice. The man lay down on a colorful mat, apparently dead.

As Greydal examined the rest of the room, he noted broken pieces of the floor lay strewn about the space, and separate impact points the size of large fists dotted the ground near the center, revealing the substicrete beneath.

The hints of a struggle weren't what held his attention, though. To the room's left, a massive black archway gaped. From it, a cold wind pried its way. "That's it," Greydal told Higg. "It's where she wanted me to go."

"Who? Roan?"

Greydal walked through the empty room and soon stood before the colossal aperture. The wind tickled his shaved head as he squinted against the draft. At first, he thought the tunnel was nearly dark as pitch, but he quickly perceived a light less than a hundred yards in. An opening or exit, ready for him. A sudden foreboding scuttled into focus. Why did this moment feel so familiar?

"Looks ominous, doesn't it?" Higg said from behind.

Greydal took a deep breath and backed from the archway, but his friend put out a hand. "Come on. I don't pretend to understand what you're doing or why. But it's obvious Roan thought this was where you needed to be, or she wouldn't have let you leave. Let's go."

The boy stepped past him into the darkened cavity, and after a moment, Greydal unclenched his jaw and followed. The wind increased as they walked, taking on a low humming as it coursed. Though the hall was nearly empty of light, he could tell the floor's make was different from the substicrete from before. It made a heavier sound when his wooden leg connected with the stuff, and seemed to have an altogether rougher texture. He didn't have long to contemplate it, as they soon neared the source of the light.

Higg reached it first. An exit, a furrowed hole in what Greydal now realized was a metal wall. No, a metal door, visibly thick, and obviously meant to be shut. Yet, something had *skewered* its way through the material, leaving a grooved path. Though the hole was nearly a perfect circle, it didn't appear to be the result of any tool he was familiar with. The wound looked almost organic, and as he came abreast with it, where Higg now stood examining the opening, he paused. His friend's eyes were wide with total incomprehension. Then the boy whispered, "What is... this?"

Greydal followed his gaze. Beyond the opening, a vast and wide plain stretched far below them, running featureless into the distance. At its end, where the horizon spread outwards, there reared a rumpled tower, a thing taller than any structure he had ever seen aside from possibly the firmament itself. The tower's exterior was waxy in the odd light of the plain, and was of some horrendous design, blank and pale. For a moment, he was reminded of the Ichablists of Heron, even if this spire was much less orderly than theirs.

"Greydal. *What is this?*" Higg repeated.

His eyes traveled from the gargantuan, white obelisk to dance along the plain below, and he saw now the landscape was indeed flat, but not totally featureless. A dark brown splotch the size of a large lake or town lay in the direct center of the gray waste.

"It's not real," Higg's voice was thin. "It *can't* be real."

Greydal blinked, and at once, the landscape resolved itself. His eyes darted to the tower, that impossible steeple reaching higher than the Sophites' mountains. It was a candle. The gray waste it sat on was a table. Greydal fell to his knees.

*** *** ***

Roan stared at the shimmering wall between her and the crooked tree. Around it, the cliffside path snaked farther down the mountainside, away from the kith's secret elevator. No sound penetrated the strange barrier, and if she unfocused her eyes, the space beyond almost seemed a painting. They would have to backtrack when they arrived at ground level, she mused, but it wouldn't take long to reach Mabet. Hopefully, the old woman had seen this coming. Hopefully, she would forgive Roan bringing an outsider into their midst, fighter or not. How many broken oaths would that make? After the first few, they had blurred.

"Do you know where to go?" Ida asked.

Roan blinked and turned to the woman. "It's my home we're looking at," she replied.

"It's...nice," Ida responded and offered a weak smile.

Roan sighed and said, "You don't have to worry. I know this spot. Though, I'll admit, I'm surprised this is here, this...gate. My people were lucky."

"How do you mean?"

"Just that it doesn't look out onto any place with foot traffic. That might have alerted the Wyrm to our location, though I suppose he found it, regardless."

Ida nodded, though she looked like she didn't quite understand.

Roan shook her head, eyeing the space before them. "I *can't believe* this was here," she said, mostly to herself.

"Well, Seb mentioned you have to take a running start. And it looks to me this one's on the edge of a cliff, so..."

"You'd be shocked. As a young woman, I had recurring dreams where I would fly. It might have been just like me to try it out."

Ida smiled at her, but didn't reply. They stood in silence for another moment before the short-haired woman asked, "How much longer, do you think?"

"He said fifteen minutes. Then it should be safe to pass through."

"Do you think it is? I mean, he locked us in here, though I'll admit, he *does* seem a bit sweet for something so nefarious."

Roan thought about Sebastian. The man had gone off to help the Ichablist chief recover his stolen comrades, shutting Ida and Roan within the cultivated wooden hallway. The act had been for their protection, Sebastian had said. Roan smirked. *Protection.* As if anything could be safe in this place, this fabricated Heaven.

"I heard you both, by the by."

Ida's voice broke Roan's reverie, "I'm sure I don't know what you mean."

"I'm not stupid. This thing gave him the Ague, didn't it? His chest and collarbone, that's where the gray marks were."

"Oh, that."

"Don't you think that's odd, though?"

"What is?"

"The Ague. Greydal. Out of every single person who got it, he was the only one to survive. Isn't that a bit miraculous?"

"Perhaps he got lucky."

"I saw the Ague. Took my mom. I wouldn't call him lucky. What I don't understand is how a magicky portal could make someone sick."

Roan was quiet for a moment as she stared at the gate. Then she said, "My mentor taught me about these a long time ago. There used to be more, and I hadn't imagined they were real until we entered this room. From what I was told, a person who goes through the gate enters a form of *midrymi*. A middle space. I suspect..." Roan thought for a moment and opened her palm by her side, feeling the invisible current spilling from the opening. "I suspect they go somewhere rather nasty, if only for a few heart-beats. These tablets the seneschal gave us? You can bet their purpose is inoculation."

Ida shuddered in her peripheral vision. "Don't fear," she told the Harlow woman. "We're likely going into less danger. Something foul stalks this compound, and I would soon be rid of it."

"Oh, it's not these doorways shivering me. I'm still thinking about Grey. I'm older than him, yeah? I remember what the Ague did to people. His father, Tier, tried everything in the Four Corners to keep that kid alive."

After a silence, Roan asked, "Yes...and?"

"Well, I guess he found something that worked."

At that, Roan looked away from the woman and stared ahead at the shimmering wall, keeping whatever knowledge she might have had to herself.

*** *** ***

Once, during his time with the Sophites, Greydal found a book—a common occurrence. In many ways, the book was similar to other tomes he had perused at one point or another within the Sophites' library or in King Marcos' old room. The cover was old and worn, yet the text was lurid. Tales of kings and queens, slayings and slavery, and magick filled its pages. Though he hadn't done much more than leaf through the book's contents (the tome was decidedly not to his taste), he found a line written in the Old Folks' tongue that struck him, only because of its sheer drama: *Bind him hand and foot, and cast him into the outer darkness, where there shall be weeping and the gnashing of teeth.*

That line rose unbidden in his mind as he sat slumped next to Higg in the impossible tunnel through the firmament. His mind glanced away from the knowledge for the umpteenth time, like a fish hitting a net. As he sat, the distant sound of marching feet reached his ears. To his right, the boy whimpered, and Greydal looked over at him.

How long had the two sat there in the dark, the wind whistling over their heads? He wasn't positive. Less than half an hour, surely. Had the Armargure come at last? Was that the leaden procession he heard? Perhaps they would be too afraid to enter the tunnel. The world beyond the gaping mouth was a horrible mystery. Its mere existence made his stomach lurch. So, why not the Legate's foot soldiers?

And yet, he had to fight the urge to stand up and look again. Something called to him beyond the skewered hole, pulled at an invisible cord between his guts and throat. His essence strummed as again the voice spoke.

You reach the limit. The way out is through.

He stood as if yanked upright, and his legs creaked at the joints like an old man's. The air from the world beyond the firmament smelled ancient as it blew through, tingling his scalp and neck.

His stump ached. He would have to take a look at it, if he ever found the time to care.

"Are you leaving me?"

Greydal looked down at the boy and responded, "Do you hear that? There's Legate soldiers in the marbled room. We—" he briefly closed his eyes, "we have to go out."

Higg didn't immediately reply, and so he added, "I won't force you to come with me. But if we head that direction," he thumbed east, "I'm afraid it'll mean our deaths, unless we're fortunate. Do you feel fortunate right now?"

Higg shook his head. "Alright, then," Greydal said and turned from the boy.

A hand shot out and grabbed the sleeve of Greydal's jacket. Higg whispered, "No! Please don't make me go out—"

"Shhh," Greydal breathed. "It's alright. I'm not going to make you do anything. I just said that."

"Then stay with me."

"I can't," Greydal told him. He didn't explain that it wasn't the threat of violence pushing him onwards. Fear or exhilaration made his eyes water, and a tear, black in the darkness, rolled down his cheek.

Higg spoke again, mostly to himself. "This can't be real."

"I think it is. I'm sorry. We knew it already though, didn't we? The Bishop and his sky?"

"It's not real." Higg's whisper turned to a whimper at the last syllable. In the distance, the marching of feet stopped. Tiny shadows from the direction Greydal and the boy had come now blocked the light of the tunnel entrance.

"Higg. I'm going to climb through, now. If you need some time to decide, I'll leave you with this. It's something my father used to tell me when I felt stuck:

"Can't go around it," Greydal began in a weak, singsong voice. "Can't go under it. Can't go over it. Gotta go *through* it." His voice cracked on the last syllable of the lyric. When Higg said nothing, he added awkwardly, "Do you understand?" The boy nodded, but remained silent. He put a hand on Higg's head and said, "This is one of those times, I think."

With that, he placed his arms in the rippled hole and lifted himself up and over. The wind cheered as he surrendered himself to what came next.

SOJOURN

A laughably simple ladder led down to the distant table. After a period of fierce vertigo the extreme height conjured, Greydal descended with his eyes held shut. In the distance, a series of low, resonant booms sounded periodically, and he ignored them, concentrating as he was on maintaining his footing to lower himself, rung by metal rung.

What was it he had once discovered? It was one thing to climb, but something altogether different to descend. Despite this traitorous thought, he stayed glued to the ladder. He descended. Each time he thought he must be close to the bottom, he opened his eyes and discovered to his dismay it didn't seem like he was any closer. His forearms and triceps burned and the wind playing at his back surged, as if to toss him to his death. It was grueling. After a period of outside time, could have been hours, could have been more, he reached the bottom. He let go of the handles, or tried to. He had to coax his hand away from the brass-tinted rungs. His legs shook as he turned, taking two steps forward. Beneath his feet, the ground shifted, and he forced himself to open his eyes, to look upon the world beyond the world. Endscape—if the Mansions of the Dawn were where good people of the faith allegedly dwelt after death, what was this nightmare meant to be?

The first thing he noticed was that there was no sky, which made a kind of awful sense as he appeared to be in some sort of room. Yet, the ceiling of the room menaced so high above him, and the table or vastness on which he stood, it seemed an impossible span. The distance between the Four Corners' sky and its ground, multiplied by ten, would only just cover the gap between Greydal's head and that oppressive, stone heaven.

The second thing he noticed was that the candle was smaller, almost imperceptibly so. Though it reared colossal on the horizon, it no longer reached the beyond-mountainous height from before. He turned around to look at the place he just exited, and his eyes widened. The ladder he had just descended was little more than a textured line leading up the wall.

The wall of the edifice itself stretched to his right and left as far as he could see, while above his head the dark firmament material transformed into a golden and silver array that leaned away towards some hidden center point. Greydal stepped back without thinking, to get a better look, and the gray wall quivered, then *shrank*. The previously mite-sized ladder was now too small to see.

He swayed with nausea and fought against his stomach's violent urge to rise to his throat, then holding his head between his shaking palms to fix his gaze at the ground. As he did, he noticed the curious material of the table pulsed red and rippled, just around the soles of his boot. Greydal turned and peered at the candle behind him. Taking a deep breath, he took a step towards it before the reality of his predicament set in. The candle and the room became noticeably smaller.

Again, his stomach churned. "Oh, Legate—" he complained, and then caught himself. The Legate didn't deserve his oaths, an angry thought told him. Fine. He would make like Loken and use that man's word, *hell*. It was supposed to mean a place of pain and terror, which appeared to be where he currently resided.

"Oh, hell," he tasted the word in his mouth. That sounded better, and hearing his own voice again served to ground him in the moment. The angry thoughts, now somewhat calmed, whispered to him. *Can't go around it*, they said. He began to walk.

As he made his way towards the dried, brownish-red lake at the center of the vastness, his surroundings continued to shrink. Now, the candle was only the size of a tower, like those in Heron. In the distance, the heavy rumbles from earlier sounded again. Though he couldn't identify the nature of the resonate booms, they discomforted him.

Was this how ants felt when a herd of razorbacks stampeded by their dirt homes? Listening to the diminishing rumblings for several breaths told him nothing, and Greydal gave up his half-hearted attempts to guess at their source. Instead, he tried to discern on what kind of surface he traveled. Whatever craft or magick produced the table caused it to act like firm sand where he strode, but appear rocklike everywhere else. It pulsed and shifted red beneath him as sparks flew from his boot.

After a time of uncertain traveling, he gained the center where the now firepit-sized brown splotch decayed under his feet. It was blood, he reckoned—very old, dried blood. Greydal turned in a circle to view his surroundings with the clarity of proportion. If he had to guess, he was now roughly six or seven inches tall. The candle from before stood just over his height, and the floor of grayish-green moss below the table looked to be a steep (though possibly non-fatal) drop. As his eyes scoured the room, he decided it was likely empty aside from himself, the table, and the place he had left, a sort of monolithic pedestal holding that structure aloft.

Greydal stared at his home. His world, the Four Corners, was a rectangular box with a pyramid-shaped roof or top. The pyramid was crafted from golden and silver glass, interwoven into tiny scales. Within the pyramid's depths, the orange light of the evening sun burned, brighter than he remembered. He watched it in silence for a long time as slowly, it morphed into the glazed, silver shine of the moon. Night.

The entire structure of the Four Corners was vaguely curved at the bottom. As a child, he had been taught everything beyond the firmament walls was total and utter chaos. They called it a soup. That had been a lie, he saw, though perhaps an unknowing one. Someone *had* made this thing, just like in the old tales. The Bishop, then, or someone like him? As he gazed at the Four Corners, its design struck him, and he decided whoever had made it likely was the same hand behind the Mansions of the Dawn and other Old Folk craftwork.

Something about the sight of his small home stilled him, and the remnants of his confusion and fear drained away. The unseen hand who strummed the chord within him paused.

With slowly renewing faculties, he scanned the room again, seeing the ceiling wasn't quite stone. It was closer to that of a chiseled cavern of mineral. He could discern the chip marks made from an unknown implement. Was this a cave, then? If so, how was it he could see its details? The candle at the end of the table was unlit, and the dirty light of his moon nestled within its pyramid should not have been able to illuminate the whole space. Mysteries piled on mysteries.

Not thinking, he took a step out of the splotch of dried blood, and the candle and room violently grew. Greydal steadied himself and paused as dizziness struck him. Breathing for a moment through his nose, he straightened, shuddering. So, the center of the table was the focal point. He was presumably at his largest there.

He gritted his teeth and stepped back into its center as the world became a more manageable version of itself. Looking at the circle of rot at his feet, he pondered its purpose. Why would there be blood here? He glanced around, and then an idea struck him. Not pausing to give himself time to reconsider, he raised his arm to his mouth and bit into it, wincing.

As the drops fell, the table in its entirety quivered, and then glowed.

All the blood left his body. His consciousness swelled, and he lost the sensation of himself, a great sea of hot liquid pushing from his pores. His vision blackened, and he fell as though from a high drop. Then as quickly as the feeling came upon him, it vanished. He stood on his own feet, flesh and wooden. His clothes were intact, not ripped to shreds by his own internals seeking the outside air.

Even more miraculous, he stood right-sized before the table, looking over it as one would a small gameboard. And the world to his left, it was now the proportion of a moderately sized chest or crate, the pyramid at its top a bauble, an artifact, not some great megastructure. Greydal smelled copper, and he looked down. At his feet, fresh blood covered the mossy ground, and a little at the center of the table.

*** *** ***

An indeterminate time passed. Or seemed to. He hadn't been able to make himself touch the exterior of the Four Corners. No one should have the kind of power he felt standing over that meager world. Had he a mind, he could have crushed it, bashed in the sky with his fists. Maybe that was why he kept from reaching out, concern he might kill it all in a fit of momentary madness.

He pulled away and walked from the cavern holding the home he knew.

It wasn't long before the rumblings from earlier sounded again, much closer this time. They announced him as trumpets were meant to precede royalty as he stepped into a further semi-darkness. Oto-lanterns lined the walls of a tunnel, built into the cavern rock, but all the lights were dead, refusing to brighten as he neared. He wandered for a time, and soon the tunnel deposited him into a great hall, unlit.

From his first glance he could tell the interior was similar to the Legate's complex, though perhaps in the way a corpse resembled a man. Here and there, he spied broken tables, tattered drapery, and chipped stone. Other strange implements were present as well. As he stepped fully into the hall, the ground rumbled, and without warning, the world went white. He crouched and blinked, fearing an attack.

Though the flash disappeared as soon as it had arrived, it took his sight with it. Now, he stood in total darkness. Another flash came, less intense than before. This one showed Greydal from where the attack originated: the heavens beyond the ceiling. The sky burned in its metamorphosis. Flashes of light from leering eyes or holes in the cosmos illuminated him in bursts. The air crackled, and the hairs on his arms rose as all noise died in preparation for the roars behind the glass. Then another *crack* split the air, his skull echoing it as light subsumed the world.

He could only navigate via afterimages. But they didn't make sense—the hall was a kaleidoscope of black and white. He tasted blood and waited for the next confused revelation, hobbling. Greydal sensed he wove through looming figures, statues or still giants reaching to the haunted night above him. Then the next flash came, stronger than the ones before, and he stumbled over what he assured himself was a cushion as the floor shifted. A new reverberation rent his ears, and the sky shattered the glass to invade the hall, issuing a deadly rain. He didn't shield himself as another sight had taken precedence. The shards of broken window pierced the ground, and the ground alone, for Greydal was no longer there.

A young man with rectangular spectacles sat forward on a chair with hinges. He closed a leatherbound book and looked up, smiling.

"Ah, you're right on time," he said. "Please, take a mom—" The man stopped talking and stared. "As I live and breathe." Greydal blinked at the harsh light and spun. The flashing hall had gone, while a small, well-lit room with white floors, walls, and doors supplanted it. He turned to the man on the chair, only to realize there was a pane of glass separating them. Greydal found himself at a loss for words.

The man raised a hand to point at him through the glass. "You... But where is— You're not supposed to be here." His voice sounded strange, almost like the Legate's in the way the inflection was off kilter. Greydal's mind spun. The Old Folks' tongue? The words were the *same,* but produced with an archaic flair. Likewise, the placement and cadence were staggered in such a way it sounded like a different tongue altogether. Another thing —the man's words buzzed, though to a lesser extent than the Legate's.

The man shook himself and cleared his throat. "My name...it's Doctor Michael. Can you understand me?" Greydal blinked again, and it clicked in his mind that the voice originated from a small, mesh square at the center of the ceiling.

Above the man's glasses, shaggy hair hung over a pale forehead. Below, umber eyes dwelt in hunger, and a young man's stubble covered the stranger's chin and upper lip. His manner of dress was odd as well, lined with buttons, while over it he wore a white cloak which was visibly wrinkled.

"Hello. *Can you hear me?* My name is Doctor Michael. Mike, if that's easier. Do you understand? Nod if you're able."

Greydal ignored him and turned around. Where was he? The room *smelled* bizarre, like nothing he had encountered before, though he couldn't identify exactly how it was different. But something was wrong. Was it his weight? Was he slightly heavier? The white room in which he was trapped (if the doorway out was as solid as it appeared) was roughly fifteen feet wide in both directions. It had an abnormally tall ceiling, but otherwise, there was nothing peculiar about it. He looked at the man in the white coat in time to see him speaking into a square, handheld box. Greydal couldn't quite read those lips, but he thought he made out the word *interpreter*.

"Where am I?" he asked in his best approximation of the Old Folks' tongue. Was that right? Hearing it out loud sounded...incorrect. The man called Michael raised his eyebrows. "You're on... No. You're not supposed to be here. Do you have any inkling how wrong this is?" Those hungry eyes searched his own for a moment before the man's lips quivered in anticipation. "I have to say, I never imagined I'd see that face popping into my interstice. I mean, I heard about the humanoid who showed up at Alice Rock, obviously. But *you*?"

Greydal shook his head. He didn't understand. How had he gotten here?

"Hm." Michael ran a hand through his hair, laughing at himself nervously before continuing, "I'm sure you weren't expecting this. Neither was I. I'm going to call—"

"A Type Two..." Greydal interrupted, the Legate's comment coming back to him. *The Type Two was very close?* Isn't that what the Legate had said?

Greydal sunk, falling to a seated position.

"You know? You *know*!" Michael's voice was ecstatic. "Do you recognize what this *means*? Your home, tell me about it! Did your people target our frequency to send you? You're the first—" The opening of a door behind the man stopped him cold. Michael turned, appearing annoyed, or maybe unnerved.

Greydal didn't need to read his mouth to see he complained at the intruders. They were three humans, dressed all in black.

Dark spectacles covered their eyes, and they held strange implements, vaguely reminiscent of dai-streloks. One said something to Michael, and the doctor turned to peer at Greydal, eyes wide. *Are you sure?* he mouthed. One of the three in the dark spectacles spoke again. Michael nodded, and reached a now-shaking hand towards a red circle nestled within a hanging box. At once, something yellow filled Greydal's side of the room, and he thought no more.

For a time, there was nothing. And then he dreamed an old dream, from a season of pain. He sat next to a dying campfire, surrounded by the decaying, tenanted firs of the Owl Barrens. Across from him the Sophite Tier and the Harlow-man Alom sat as one, their features intermingling.

Greydal spoke to his father, saying, "What's happening to me?"

"What's always been."

I don't understand, Greydal wanted to say. But his father would recognize the lie. He saw the campfire moving through the air, hurtling towards a sinister orb drowning in the void.

"There's a wolf behind you," his father warned.

"It's okay," Greydal replied. "It's mine."

In response, something large laid down behind him. He felt its bristled hair, thick lines of fishing twine, then the vibrations from its skin. The tremors told him not to be afraid. In the air, the sound of flutes drifted from far off. Above, the Harlow elders sat on their bench. "That's the bit, then, eh? You will go first. We will follow," Crawl Quymora's corpse whispered. Greydal knew what would come next. The fire. The blood. "Not yet," he told the dead. "Wait till I'm done."

Above the elders, the black marble reared.

Greydal glanced at his father and asked, "Where's the hand covered in steam? It was here, wasn't it?"

Around him, the forest whispered, "Can't go around it."

*** *** ***

"We've got to go through it, I imagine," a voice said.

Greydal blinked, and winced at the brilliant light piercing his vision. It recalled things he had no wish to remember, and he attempted to burrow deeper into sleep, only for his desiccated throat to drag him into awareness.

"For once, you're right," another voice said and sighed before adding, "Otherwise, this thing'll never end." Then Greydal heard a light tap, and he turned his head towards the noise.

"Look, he's awake," the first voice said.

The second voice replied, "God, it looks chewed to bits. Hadn't noticed the ear."

Greydal tried to sit up, but was almost too weak to lift his head. What was that smell? He groaned and turned to his side, now finding the white bedsheet on which he laid was soft and damp with his own sweat. He blinked, but had trouble seeing where he was. At the least, he could tell the room he sprawled in was extremely bright, enough to cause his eyes real pain. He fought to keep them open as he scanned his uncertain surroundings.

Before him, two indistinct figures resolved. These figures, also in white, stood facing him. He saw what looked like features: eyes, a nose, frowning mouth. "Where—" he tried to say, but his mouth was so dry, it only came out as a hiss.

"Get him some water," the first man said.

"Are you sure? We're supposed to wait for—"

"Fine, I'll do it."

Running water sounded, and then purposeful, rhythmic steps towards his bed. The figure in white crouched before him, proffering a cup of clear liquid. Greydal blinked twice to dispel the illusion. The man's pink face was warm and cheerful.

"Here," the Legate said. "This will help."

CHAPTER

25

BARBARIAN

Across from him, the Legate watched as he guzzled the contents of the water cup. Greydal coughed, and droplets spilled over his short beard. After he handed the cup back, he reached a numb hand towards his face and felt the growth. It was several days' worth.

"The white room," Greydal whispered. "Where's— What was that yellow muck? How long have I been asleep?" His still-bleary gaze told little about his surroundings, only that he was on a bed connected to a metal wall, and on the other end of the room, a glass barrier stretched from corner to corner. The only thing interrupting the glass was a rectangular archway, where a shimmering material winked in and out of sight. No, there was something else he could perceive—beneath him...a faint vibration. As he searched for its source, he was distracted by the thin, greenish bodysuit he discovered covering his body, wrists to ankles.

"What am I wearing?" Greydal asked. It hurt to talk.

"What's he saying?" the Legate asked.

"I have no idea. None of it's registering with my aid," the other one replied in a nasally voice.

"We need to get Mike in here."

Greydal cleared his throat, and tried his most pressing question again in the Old Folks' tongue. "How long have I slept?"

"He speaks!"

The man behind the Legate said, "Elis, we're not supposed to talk to it."

"Hey. Asshole," the Legate looked over his shoulder as he spoke. As Greydal's eyes adjusted to the glare, he saw the other man was a tulka as well. Three pink men in a white room. For some reason, the thought seemed funny. The Legate continued, "Why don't you give us some space, huh?" When the other tulka didn't immediately move, the Legate rose and turned towards him. As Greydal watched, the Legate grabbed the second man by his arm and shoved him from the glass room. An implement much like a dai-strelok hung from a sling over the Legate's shoulder.

The Legate turned and smiled apologetically. "Sorry, he's a bit dense sometimes."

Greydal wiped his mouth and managed to sit up on the bed. "I'll—" he cleared his throat. "I'll be honest. I'm feeling... the same."

The Legate laughed, a cheerful sound. "I'll bet. One sec." The man walked over to the side of the room and dragged what appeared to be a magicked chair towards the bed, some sort of floating pedestal. Greydal eyed the Legate's white uniform as the man did so. It looked to be a form of bodysuit, with a single seam running from the man's throat to his groin. Yellow, studded boots and gloves were the only things that interrupted the blankness of the clothes.

"That's impressive," Greydal told him.

"The chair? They're comfy, no doubt."

"I mean, it floats. Where are its legs?"

"Don't need 'em," the Legate said and winked. "Speaking of," he continued, "I think someone's bringing yours."

Greydal glanced down to see his leg ended at the knee. His wooden support was gone. He turned and looked the Legate in the eyes. Both he and the man were silent for a breath. Then Greydal said, "So..."

"So," the Legate replied.

Another silence. "Where am I?"

"Well, I'm not at liberty to tell you much, and I'm afraid that topic's one of the no-noes"

"No-noes," Greydal repeated slowly.

"Sure. Though I did kick ole' Petey out so I can alleviate your concerns without him badgering. You're not in any immediate danger, and we're not gonna hurt you. So, you can relax on that count."

"I didn't think you were. You didn't have to kick out..." Greydal tried to form the name, "Pieetey."

The Legate grinned. "No. It's Petey. Peter. Don't enunciate the first syllable as much."

Greydal tried and failed to prevent his anger and disorientation from seeping into his voice. "Sorry, it's the accent. Where I come from most tulka have normal names."

The Legate took it in stride. "Peter? He's no tulku, if you're talking about the same thing. He's just some rich gaúcho thinkin' he found a way to live forever."

That interrupted Greydal's irritation. "Gow-cho?"

"Yup. He would bust a vein if he heard me tell anyone, but he's on his second cadaver."

Oh, *gaúcho.* Shit. Greydal's heartbeat sped. "I don't— Do you mean he wasn't born one of us? I read about that once."

"*Read* about it? They told me you're from a Secondary. I figured if you had us, you'd have them."

I think we did, Greydal didn't say. How far back *was* this? If it was anything like his own world's past, then the possibility of gaúchos indicated at least a thousand-year difference. Greydal paled at the implication. At length he spoke. "Maybe," he said. "You're talking about humans who were supposed to have used us like one would clothes, right?"

"Uh-huh, but not past tense, bud. Peter didn't even bother to get old first. He just leaned on his daddy's money to hop bodies. Could be he just likes the dress-up."

That was it then, though his mind tried to rebuff the notion. It had been corroborated already, hadn't it? The plastick book, Number 03... Though he had never admitted it to Mabet, he had plumbed the depths of the tome's secrets. Secrets that told of the ancient arrival of the tulka, and the reason for their existence.

The Legate spoke again, "Do you *really* not have gaúchos on your side?"

Greydal thought about that. In the far-forgotten time of the Old Folk (according to Number 03), tulka were not born from coupling. Instead, the ancestors used technological magick to design the tulka race from nothing, making them fit to be worn like armor for the purpose of human pleasure or carnage.

The tulka bodies did not rot nor age past adulthood, and they were beautiful to look upon, making mankind's use of them prevalent. Yet, one day, some tulka rose without aid, without the piloting minds of men. Whether this meant that consciousness itself was an emergent system, or if some invisible travelers had set up shop, the Old Folk didn't know. Some ancestors of a more philosophical bent postulated a separation between consciousness and essence, to explain the self-possessed, ruddy figures now defying their riders' mental commands.

Regardless, most of these tulka were alleged to have escaped and made babies of their own, so alike was their physiology to that of their human operators. Greydal had assumed the miracle of tulka children had ended the practice, if such a thing had ever been real. For who could stand to commandeer the lifeless form of a previously thinking being? Yet, this Peter was one who apparently had made just such a choice.

Realizing he hadn't answered the man's question, Greydal cleared his throat and replied. "There might be one."

"Hopefully, he's of better stock than our Peter."

"I don't think he is."

The Legate cackled again, and Greydal found it was curiously muffled, though only slightly. This caused him to discover there was a sound associated with the vibrations beneath his body, an ever-present humming he had previously mistaken for simple disorientation.

When the Legate contained his mirth, he replied through a smile, "The kid's an ass, no doubt about it. Name's Elis, by the way. Can't remember if I told you yet."

"Greydal," Greydal replied.

"Like ladle?"

"Like cradle," he confirmed.

"Well, Greydal. I guess you're me from the Secondary."

He smiled in response, but Elis was wrong. Greydal knew it in his bones. The air around him was altered, shifting. What he had earlier interpreted as a smell was probably closer a coloring or texture in his mind. It painted the room in hot, jagged hues every time he breathed. Couldn't the man across from him sense how unstable everything was?

He searched Elis' gaze, but something altogether different occupied the tulka's mind. He watched as curiosity played across the man's face before words exposed it. "Are things different there?" Elis asked.

Greydal thought about what to tell him. After a moment, he settled on something safe. "Your spoken language is only slightly different from mine. It's mostly a shift in emphasis, word choice."

"No shit. I wondered how you learned to talk so good," Elis replied. "They said you likely wouldn't speak how we do."

"Well, for me, it was much harder to read your way of writing than to speak like you."

"Ah well. There are so many languages nowadays. Even reading's hard without an aid."

"There are?"

"What, aids?"

"Languages. I only know of three. Actually, four."

"Oh, boy, that's just a drop in the bucket, *amigo*."

"Ah-mee-go?"

"Means friend."

"I didn't know we were."

"Come on. You've got my face and most of my body. I figure that's as much common ground as exists."

"Fair," Greydal allowed at length.

"I should have said earlier, someone else is on their way to see you. He's my friend, too, so be nice. If he asks questions, answer them."

"I'll do my best."

"That's all I can ask."

A silence. "Can I get more water?"

*** *** ***

It was thirty minutes later, and Greydal was more uncomfortable than ever. The disturbances in the air itched his eyes and the back of his throat. Elis either didn't notice or didn't care.

"And you're saying they only had one flushing toilet?

"Two. One was in mine and my father's home."

"That's bunk!"

"I'm from a Type Two, remember?" Greydal lied. "Things are different there."

"Makes sense, I suppose. The doctor, this is my buddy I mentioned. He'll probably have a lot of questions about that. But he told me you were one of the first verified successes of a Secondary—a Type Two—handover, so you're something of a landmark."

"Hmm," Greydal grunted.

After a few seconds of silence, Elis said, "Your father, was he...?"

"One of us?" Greydal asked.

The man nodded.

"No, not one of us."

"Adopted, huh? There's a difference. Mine were purple as a plum."

"Your parents?"

"Yup. Funny that my kid's so red. We got the whole spectrum."

Greydal coughed as he sipped at his third cup of water. "Your—You have a child?"

"And a second on the way with my ex-wife. What about you? Got any little Greydals running loose in your dimension?"

A fluttered beep interrupted any response. Elis cleared his throat and straightened. Beyond the glass pane, a tall man in an identical suit to that of the friendly tulka's strode towards the flickering doorway. As the man stepped within the rectangular archway, the almost invisible material shined for a moment. Greydal's eyes widened. Before him stood a human male alike in appearance to the doctor from earlier, yet this one was older and wore no spectacles. What had the first one said his name was? Mikael? Mike? This new one had grayish hair at the temples and thick stubble. The doctor's father?"

Elis looked chagrined and not a little guilty. "I was just making sure he got oriented," he said.

"Yes, I see. Peter told me as much," the human replied. "No harm done. I was about to brief our friend here anyway."

"His name's Greydal. Like cradle," Elis offered.

An awkward silence descended on the room, making the ever-present humming more noisome. "He said the words are the same in both languages," Elis added more quietly.

"I see. Well, Greydal like cradle," the man said and smiled. "I think you and I have some things to discuss. Why don't you follow Officer Alberich and I on a...little stroll. That should allow you to stretch your legs."

Greydal tilted his head. "Alright," he replied. "I think I'll need one first."

"Oh, I didn't forget," the man replied, and reached a yellow-gloved hand into his suit. The sight confused the eyes, for it appeared the man fished around in some pocket sewn into the garment, yet Greydal couldn't see any seams. The man's hand simply disappeared at the hip. The human withdrew his fist and raised it out, palm upwards. Greydal leaned forward to better see what the man proffered, and watched as the yellow fingers uncurled. Flat across the human's palm lay the wooden leg, small as a bug.

"What did you do to it?"

The man blinked twice in rapid succession. At once the leg swelled, red sparks glancing from the ferrous wood. "My apologies. I didn't want anyone here thinking I had need of a cane."

"Or was looking to beat someone again," Elis corrected.

Greydal reached out a slow hand to take his leg. The man and Elis waited in silence as he fitted it to his knee. He tapped the wood to fasten it, then stood, groaning.

"Easy," Elis said. "You've been mostly horizontal for a long time."

"Elis," the human admonished.

"What does he mean?" Greydal asked as he steadied himself on the nearest wall. It buzzed under his fingers.

"Come on, we'll take a walk to my office, and I'll explain there. Officer Alberich?"

Elis nodded and made a gesture with his hand. Behind the bearded man, the flickering doorway slowed and vanished, leaving open air between the room's interior and the hallway beyond. Without waiting for either of them, the human turned and exited the room. Elis and Greydal followed. The hallway itself ended at a green door, which slid noiselessly apart to allow the three passage. Beyond it, the one called Peter stood at attention, a strange weapon at the ready.

"There's no need for that."

"Begging your pardon, Doc. But I feel safer as is, if that thing's going to be out and about."

"Hey, why don't you—" Elis began.

"Elis. Peter, follow us if you would? You can keep your weapon trained on Greydal here, if it makes you feel safer."

"He can?" Greydal asked.

"He won't hurt you," the man replied.

Again, not waiting for confirmation, the human turned and continued along the hallway. Greydal limped after, followed by Elis and Peter. Greydal forced himself to not look behind to see if the fake tulka aimed for him. He didn't know what the weapon did, but if it was anything like a dai-strelok, it was probably deadly.

Along the white floor was a green stripe, which began under their feet and ran down the hall. They walked it for a time, following its course, ducking under low arches and weaving past people busy about other errands. Every person wore the same white and yellow ensemble. "I feel like I stick out," Greydal said.

"Green's slimming," Elis replied from behind him, and his ears barely caught Peter whisper, "Idiot," in reply. The human leading them spoke over his shoulder as he strode onwards, "You'll be in one soon, I imagine."

As they hurried through the metal corridors, Greydal struggling to keep pace, he realized something that made his stomach turn: he recognized the passageways. It wasn't precise, but the likeness was there. Perhaps a different vessel? Either way, it was close in appearance to Mabet's dilapidated home, though now much restored and far, far larger.

Greydal slowed and said, "Is this an aircraft?"

Behind him Peter whispered, "Is it retarded?"

"Fuck you," Elis replied.

"It is," the human at the head of the group replied, either to Greydal or Peter.

"An aircraft?" Greydal clarified. "Yes, of a sort. At least it can be," the man explained. The group turned a corner, and he added, "Do you know what a starslipper is?"

The sight of a muscled woman with orange skin and metal hair stole Greydal's response. She walked past without glancing at the group, and he had the time to see that her hair moved on its own as if in a faint breeze. Greydal's head swiveled to follow her as she disappeared around the corner. As a consequence, he almost bumped into another white-suited woman.

"Move!" she said, and hurried past before Greydal could match her apology.

Elis laughed. "Don't worry, bud. Damsel gets me, too."

"Gentlemen, can we continue?"

"Sorry," Elis and Greydal replied together.

It took another several minutes of scurrying to make it to the group's destination, an office tucked away in the busiest part of the craft. On the way, Greydal witnessed a colorful parade of individuals, few alike. Men with glass spheres for eyes sipped from plastick bottles next to tulka women whose forearms *opened* to allow the retrieval of what he assumed were measuring equipment or tools.

Elsewhere, a man with stripes on his suit's arm and a crystal jaw yelled to no one Greydal could see, "Deck foray needs see eye! If an interloper turns the shitter into a—"

Greydal grabbed at the man's sleeve. "What did you just say?" The word hadn't been exact (the pronunciation had been strange), but he knew it.

Peter yelled as the man with the crystal jaw turned in surprise. "What? Leggo' of me!"

Greydal felt someone's hand on his shoulder. "Interloper! You said interloper," he told the man, trying to mimic crystal jaw's intonation.

Crystal jaw looked confused. "So?" he asked. "Doc, is this guy with you?"

Peter replied first, "That's not a guy. It's the specimen."

Revulsion played across the top half of the man's face. "Gah!" He shook his sleeve free from Greydal's grasp.

Then the doctor whispered, "Not here. Please, come with us."

"C'mon, bud. It's just a little bit further," Elis added. Greydal relented and allowed the group to herd him away from the panicked man.

Greydal followed the crew and took several breaths, deep into his belly, to try and calm himself. He examined the walls as they traveled and halted when he saw a yellow poster of a black silhouette being struck by arcing, black zig-zags. A warning?

"Here we are," the doctor told them. Greydal turned to see they stood before a metal archway with a silver door. Next to it a sign read: *Michael Bishop, MD, SPETNA.*

"Hell," Greydal whispered to himself.

*** *** ***

The doctor—the Bishop—made the soldiers wait outside. "Can I get you something to drink? You shouldn't be hungry quite yet, but revivification can make you thirst, believe me."

"Revivi—" Greydal began to ask.

"Nevermind." The man turned and moved behind a metallic desk stacked with slate-like tablets. He touched his collar, and his white suit vanished, revealing a two-piece undergarment made of what looked to be similar material. Above the Bishop's chest, a small, golden icon gleamed as it hung from a thin chain around the man's neck. Greydal's eyes traced its simple design. He had seen that symbol before. It didn't feel long ago, that eve of eclipsed moonlight and spongy growths.

"You're him," Greydal informed the man.

"Hmm?"

Eyeing the person across from him with new eyes, Greydal wondered what his father would have thought. It couldn't be a coincidence, could it? This was a legend sprung to life. "The boy from the white room," he clarified after a moment, having decided to reveal only his second revelation.

"Ah, yes. I am." The man sat on a seat presumably behind the desk.

"How long was I asleep? You've got gray hair."

The Bishop cleared his throat. He seemed to struggle with what to say. At last, the man spoke, "Sit, please," and gestured at a hovering disk, which slid from the desk to orbit Greydal's hips.

"I, uh—"

"It's simple, just as you would on your bed."

He lowered himself, and the disk rose to meet his glutes, steadying him. He leaned and allowed the seat to take his full weight.

"You see? That's why I wanted to speak to you before all this. The fact you didn't recognize a simple piece of furniture tells me that we've made basic errors of assumption about the place you come from."

Behind the man, four glass tanks blinked to life, revealing tiny worlds. In one, chips of wood made a jagged bed for an obese lizard with spotted skin to lay upon. Above it, in the same tank, fronds from a plant with a wide, brown stem shaded the lizard from the harsh light. Greydal was about to glance at the man, to demand an answer as to how long he had been unconscious, when a familiar sight arrested his attention. In another tank, this one with a silky cushion for its base, a barbed and crimson slug stretched upwards towards the glass. It swayed as if waving. He watched the slug split in two, revealing the deeper red muck within.

"As I hinted at earlier," the Bishop continued, "I'm here to do a bit of an unscheduled brief for you, as I think it'll aid us in the long run. I— Eh? Oh, looking at the clinger? Nasty thing, isn't it?"

Greydal swallowed. "You were going to *breef* me?"

"Yes. Well, I'll do my best. We don't have much time before we enter low orbit, and I want you cooperative. For the life of me, I don't know why the Directorate kept you potted for so long. I would have woken you up sooner if it had been safe."

"I'm sorry?"

"Yes, we're working out the kinks in the tech. I hope one day soon we can put people in the pods like you would a child to bed. In and out, see?"

Greydal answered honestly he did not see. He asked, "How long? How long has it been since I saw you?"

"Right now, it's the year 1985—our time. We think, at least. Disruptions to our own history renders the Gregorian calendar arbitrary. But that means thirty-eight years since you and I last encountered one another."

"I was unconscious for—"

"I know it's a shock," the man barreled ahead. "But, please, put it out of your mind for the time being. I'm afraid you have graver things with which to contend." Greydal stopped listening and lowered his head in his hands. A dull panic that had lain dormant since he came to now shuddered awake. It was as though he inhabited a vast nightmare he had previously expected to emerge from, only for it to come viscerally alive and suck him deeper inside, into a black lucidity. "What did you all do to me?" he asked.

"*Us?* Greydal, I've tried to find and help you since the day you appeared. There's been some dramatic shifts in my people's government since then, and I risked my freedom to get you awake and on this ship."

"Ship? I—" he took a breath, attempting to take control of his wayward emotions. "I thought you said this was an aircraft."

"We're in space, Greydal."

"You say that like I should know what it means."

The man eyed him from across the table. He rubbed the bridge of his nose and said, "Okay, I think we're getting off on the wrong foot. I apologize. I'm sure this is all a shock to you, so let me lay it out for you properly. I will assume you have no frame of reference for anything I say. Is that alright?"

Behind the Bishop, the red paste in the tank flared its spines. Greydal said nothing.

"First, do you have disturbances or fissures where you come from? A yes or no is sufficient."

Rubbing his temples, Greydal allowed at length, "You could say that." His eyes met the Bishop's. "Or we did, a long time ago," he added, thinking of Abyddion and Heron.

"Well. Here things are bad. We found the source of our woes, an interloper. That's our word for any unverified or uncontrolled intrusion from other dimensions. This one was a cave which appeared on my planet. When the precursors to the Directorate, my government, sent in a response team to investigate, the team vanished, and the cave went with them."

Greydal nodded but said nothing. How much could he safely reveal? The Bishop continued, "*We found it.* The cave. It's on an entirely *new* dwarf planet orbiting one of our former colonies."

Greydal nodded again, pretending at understanding. He had to find a way out. Presuming the Legate hadn't lied to him, wouldn't this Type Two eventually spill its way into his own world, the one with the Four Corners?

He closed his eyes. There it was—existence painted in shivering hues of negative space, like a white-hot, shattered pane of glass. The desk and the room were gone, but he could perceive some kind of activity extending forever in all directions. It wasn't the minute vibrations of the floor that caused this distress. Something about the world was poorly structured, like someone had shortened the leg of some cosmic table.

Michael was speaking, "I don't know how to ask this, so I'll just say it. How did you become what you are?"

Greydal opened his eyes. "A tulka?"

"Tulku. And no, you're no tulku, so be honest, please. We only have a short time."

He furrowed his brow. "I am tulka. I was born tulka. I'm not like your...what's his name, Peter?"

"You're a gaúcho, though. For what, I don't fully understand yet."

Greydal looked over his shoulder. Would Elis intervene if he could get the man's attention?

"Are you listening?"

He looked at the Bishop. "I don't know what you're talking about."

"The cave. It's alive and aware. It's *doing* this to us. So, I would like to understand how and when you started producing the same interstitial distortions." The sound of the sliding door made them both turn.

Elis poked his head through. "Mike, update from the bridge. We've got three hours till descent."

The Bishop smiled and replied, "Excellent. Time enough for drinks. That should loosen us up. Greydal, what'll you have?"

*** *** ***

It was like being in the wagon. Greydal was at the mercy of strangers, and he didn't know what to do other than follow along. But this time, it wasn't a physical wound that robbed him of volition. It was an exhaustion of the mind. As he sipped the drink the Bishop had provided, he ruminated and numbly answered the man's further questions.

CHAPTER

26

YESTERYEAR

The marble loomed, omnipotent and omnipresent, across Greydal's field of view. It was a god in the darkness. Behind it, sharp pinpoints of light flickered, tiny nothings next to an entity of dire shadow.

Upon sight of the marble, something loosed in his mind.

"Greydal. Is this the black orb from your dreams?" the Bishop—the doctor—asked.

Peter snickered behind them, "It told you about its dreams?"

Michael nodded, replying, "He. And yes. I think it has something to do with Greydal's disturbance of whichever tears he happens to be near. That, or he's already experienced this, which doesn't bode well for any of us."

They stood in the center of a vast, semicircular room, with a translucent, curved wall at its front. Over three hundred white-suited individuals worked at terminals, or hurried to and from the space. Shouting from a man with a high-collared ruby coat overlaying his white uniform told the room that descent would commence in five minutes.

"Peter," Michael said over the din, "we're getting reports of terrain shifts down there. There's a forest now where we planned to put Habitat 01, so make sure the party has the right tools."

"When did Tehom get an atmosphere?" Peter asked.

Elis replied, "Shoulda been at the last brief, Petey."

"Don't call me that."

Another man, from his seat in front of a glowing square, asked Michael, "Doc, is the habitat going to be safe? If there's such a large amount of interloper activity, wouldn't it be better to just drop you guys at the zero site immediately?"

"We need the habitat as a fallback in case something goes wrong. The cold iron should insulate it from the worst of the disruptions."

"Speaking of disruptions, is it coming down with us immediately?" Peter asked, sending a pointed glance in Greydal's direction.

Greydal's mind was elsewhere. The doctor had drugged his drink with something during the latter half of their talk, leaving him woozy and off-balance. But that wasn't why he was now enthralled. Nothing *existed* except the bruised orb in the far dark. It unfolded his mind like a flower, exposing him. The doctor had called it a planet. Tehom. That was a lie. It was a gate, an eye, a maw. The little finger of an unknown, negative god. It was the sea. Starless and eternal. Waves crashed, and Greydal felt a deep rumbling in his sternum, as if a giant from some far off land called his name. The rumbling grew louder, until—"

"Earth to Greydal. You in there, bud?"

He blinked as Elis waved a yellow glove in front of his eyes. "There you are. We gotta get ready. You keen?"

Greydal turned. The doctor and Peter were gone.

In fact, the orb was as well, replaced by a solid wall of shadowed, blurred forest, stretching to the horizon past the glasslike material. The speed at which their vessel soared over the treetops was startling. He reached hand to his cheek but found it dry. Then a confused grin began at the corners of his mouth. Was this...

Yes. The disturbance in his mind was gone. So, too, was the sense of a vast instability, the itching in his eyes and throat. The Type Two had collapsed. He knew it suddenly and utterly, though he wasn't positive how.

If the Legate was right, that meant he was now back where he ought to be, in the "prime narrative," as the man had called it.

Glancing over at Elis, he smiled fully. Ellis gazed at him, worry plain on his face.

*** *** ***

They descended, and made short work of erecting a series of domiciles. Prefabricated buildings, one of which Greydal recognized immediately. The interior was spotless, missing the dried mud, which had been near-chemically bonded to parts of the entrance and hall, in Greydal's memory. Now inside, he gazed at a spot on the floor where he thought a small hatch should've been. He was strangely calm, and it wasn't the drugs.

Eating and talking filled the newborn substicrete structure, echoing from the kitchen.

"Hey, creepy! Chow time!"

Greydal blinked. How long had he been standing there? He took a deep breath and slunk from the currently-empty storage area to enter the barracks hallway, passing the stacks of metal cases, which he gathered, held some of the team's contingency tools. Peter poked his head from beyond the corner. "You hear me? Doc wants you nourished. You can have my scraps."

From beyond the corner within the kitchen, Elis shouted, "Don't listen! I've got a plate for you.

Greydal continued to the kitchen, passing the other rooms, which he was sure were supposed to contain only rubble.

Peter turned to Elis and said, "Man, the thing's like three-fifths of a person. How much food could it need?" Greydal approached just in time to hear Elis whisper, "Are you fucking kidding me?"

"What? No! I meant his leg."

Greydal accepted the tray of food from a wide-faced man who sat at the table. As the man's fingers brushed his, he noticed they were hard and clear like glass, emerging from rounded sheaths at the man's knuckles. Next to him, another member of the crew sneered, this one a blonde kid who didn't look older than seventeen. Greydal ignored the glare and stared at his tray.

The gruel itself was an ugly square of brownish material next to what appeared to be furry, orange puree, or perhaps simply germinated mold. He inhaled, but couldn't smell the stuff. "Elis," he asked, "when did you all prepare this? I didn't hear anything when I was back there looking around."

A woman, this one with tall, hard-looking hair swept up in a wave, laughed. "What's that they say, in space, no one can hear you cook?" she asked. The wide-faced man beside her covered his eyes with his peculiar hands, maybe from embarrassment.

"It's 'hear you scream,' Diane," Peter corrected from his perch near the wall.

"I was tryin' to make a joke, Petey."

"He hates it when you call him that," Elis informed her through a mouthful of food. "Greydal," he added, "This stuff's premade, so you just open up and dig—"

An earsplitting roar cut off the tulka. The oto-lanterns above them flickered as the roar increased in volume and the floor shifted. "What on—" the woman called Diane began before something crushed the upper-right side of the structure. A crackling noise in the air savaged Greydal's eardrums, temporarily outcompeting the ongoing roar.

"Jeezus!" someone yelled—at least Greydal thought that's what they said. He crouched on the ground, fearing he was about to enter a second Type Two. At once, the roar ceased, dull rumbling from outside following it.

"Is that thunder?" Diane asked.

"Suits on, everyone!" Elis yelled and jumped across the table to Greydal. "Hey, bud. Just like I showed you alright?"

Greydal nodded and activated his suit. It slid up his arms and legs from the yellow boot and gloves before tightening at his neck. On his bad side, the material stopped and tightened around his wooden leg with an audible rubbery sound.

"Rebreather, too," Elis advised. Greydal tapped his collar and the shimmering material from before rose like a hooded snake from behind his head to envelop him. At once, the air tasted cleaner, less damp.

"Outside!" The crew of four men and three women hurried out the front door to devastation. On their right, the wide armament they had earlier used to laterally cauterize trees was split in two. The woman from before with the orange skin and shining alloy hair lay on her side, an ancestor axe clutched in her fist.

"Damsel!" the wide-faced soldier yelled and rushed to her. Beyond the rudimentary tree line was a new vision, a climbing wall of white and pink in the distance. More than ever, the western wall appeared a slab of raw meat.

"Where are the rest of the depots?" Diane asked. To their left where the roar had originated, there was now only a wide and empty field, shining with puddles of water. When Greydal had first entered the substicrete structure thirty minutes before, there had been other small buildings, nested in between the stumps of sickly trees. Easy come, easy go, he supposed.

That morning, he had emerged from the Old Folks' vessel, the ship revealed as a squat, colossal brick with a facade of glasslike material for its front window. He didn't know much about aircraft, but it surprised him the machine could get off the ground at all. Regardless, by what seemed to be a poor approximation of midday, the three-dee printers (as Elis had called them) had already been deployed and completed work on seven of the buildings. Now, all but two were gone, assuming the southern one, which had been placed far off as a "medical precaution," wasn't destroyed.

"Was anyone inside the others?" Greydal found himself asking. Then he grimaced. Why did he care? These weren't his people, and he was effectively their prisoner.

Peter spoke, "Can anyone get the bridge or the Doc on the comms? We've got a marsh where there used to be our supplies."

Wide-face returned with Damsel. He put an arm on her shoulder.

She spit and said, "Lay off. I'm fine." When he gave her an exasperated look, she complained, "You know that cutter's hard as hell to operate. I was just testing out the felling axe."

"Shoulda' been inside with the rest of us. You don't know what's out here. And you'd never outpace a beam-cutter."

"Wanna bet?"

Wide-face rubbed his face with his hand. "Leave it for now. I think Pete's— He's tryin' the comms. Guessin' El is gonna have us fall back to the ship"

Greydal stared past them at the ancestor axe lying in the dirt. He pushed by and walked to it. His shadow leaned away from him, covering the weapon. That would take some getting used to. In the Four Corners, outdoor shadows nearly always sat right underneath one's feet. But even in the poor light, this shadow was a semi-crisp copy of his own body, foretelling his next movements. Bending to retrieve the implement, his shadow gripped its spine, and his hand followed.

"Uh...should we let it hold that?" Peter asked from where he had been inspecting a waist-high pile of smoking metal. Greydal ignored the fake tulka and gazed upwards. When he had first left the ship that morning, he had found something preposterous;

the sky was gone. In its place, a vast darkness circled. Within, pale lights flickered and sometimes went out, wide and unknown shapes momentarily eclipsing them.

One light was different than the others, slightly larger. It hovered in place before streaking across the nether, disappearing from view.

In the far night, a larger glow bathed the land in cold hues and as he stared into the void again, Greydal felt as he had that morning. He sensed he was on the cusp of immensity, that he was about to fall upwards and never stop. Seeing the sky changed so dramatically brought to mind his father's Tale of the Wizard— the Excondalt. He was in it, complete with tiny fires filling the night and distant islands trapped in the yawning deep. Of course, he knew by heart how that story ended. Recalling it now, his stomach dropped.

"Hey," Elis said from close behind. "Why don't you let me hold that, alright?" Greydal blinked and looked away from the higher dark. A frightening thought had flashed in his mind, and he made to hand over the weapon before he acted on it.

But a sudden scream made them both whirl to the north. Beyond the ruined buildings, in the wet field, the blonde kid who had sat next to Wide-face now crawled across the ground. A broken, wine-colored snail's trail pooled behind him.

Where were his legs?

Greydal's blood started pumping, and time slowed as his hand involuntarily tightened on the axe. Collectively, the group ran towards the man. As they did, Greydal understood what had at first confused his sight: a piece of the marshy field *risen* like a flatfish.

It crawled onto slime-thralled banks, enveloping the bleeding kid's lower extremities. Then the flat thing rose, and its underside rippled, elongated eyes the thickness of tongues distending from the thing's belly. Four penetrated the boy, who didn't seem to notice.

"Oh, Christ! Rob!" Diane yelled.

A new eye emerged and turned to fix her with its dull, yellow stare. "CHRISTROB!" the thing bleated. The monster's sprawling back rippled, and for a moment, it no longer looked like a patch of marshy grass. Then the blonde kid screamed.

Elis, Peter, and Damsel unholstered their weapons, and six loud reports split the night as four apple-sized craters appeared in the flat monster's underbelly.

"CHRISTROB!" it yelled again. Something thick and dark slid from the prone victim's body up one of the penetrating eyestalks like a piece of rice in a reed straw.

The kid yelled again, his voice taking on a confused, childlike tone. As he tried to thrash away from his attacker, the creature enveloped him, but not before Greydal saw more of the kid's internals slide up the inside of the eyestalks. A muffled "Mom—" leaked from the gaps in the creature's flabby fins.

Greydal wanted to move. He did. His sweaty hands held the axe's spine so hard his knuckles had turned white. He should be running, attacking. But the sight of those yellow eyes...

More reports followed, and the creature fell sideways, becoming grass, then a brilliant shade of red, and then gray. It lay still. Someone hollered, "Get him out of there!" but Greydal had seen what they hadn't.

He found enough of his voice to shout, "There's another!" A patch of ground next to the woman with tall hair—Diane—was connected to her leg and buttocks via thin filaments. In the dim light, they slowly turned a dark red. Greydal's shout appeared to confuse Diane until she glanced down and yelped. That turned to screams. This beast was longer and sported rudimentary limbs. It rose and revealed itself, its weedy disguise abandoned. Diane backed away, and the thin filaments exited her, withdrawing into the horror's sides.

"Move! I can't get an angle!" Damsel barked.

Then the billowing creature reared and made a kind of plaintive, whimpering call. It echoed across the infant swamplands, adding its wetness to theirs. To say that noise filled Greydal with disgust wouldn't approach the sheer hatred it evoked in him. The heat of his revulsion melted the ice rooting him to his spot, blasting his temporary stupor. Without thinking, he sprinted towards the creature, axe at the ready. His ferrous wood leg bounced on the hard ground until it hit the fresh mire, and he almost fell. Righting himself at the last moment, Greydal swung downwards. The yellow eyes just extending from the creature's pale underside fell and flopped while the thing screamed. That scream sounded too much like Diane.

He switched his grip on the axe as the monster curled towards him. New, womanly arms extended from the thing's body, groping for his face, and a lightning bolt of anger coursed through him. As the arms neared, he yelled and swiped left, and the creature fell in half. Mucus sprayed, reflecting the encasing void.

He turned and pushed the woman called Diane further away before whirling on his enemy. He approached its prone form and watched as the thing's head stretched to form a crude facsimile of Diane's horrified expression. Yellow eyes above a beautiful nose stared at him. Greydal swung once more, and the face caved inwards and turned gray. He kept smashing, until an oily divot several feet deep scored the ground before him.

Buckling under a sudden dizziness, he leaned on his axe to wipe the sputum from his arms onto his white suit, staining it with warm shadows.

"Diane!" Damsel yelled from close by. "Can you hear me?"

Behind, Peter said to no one, "Maybe we should let it keep the axe?"

*** *** ***

They couldn't contact the members of the expedition like they wished. That was what he interpreted from Peter and Elis' bickering—that somehow they had expected to remotely reach out to the people on the ship. As a result, the crew decided that five walkers would head to the great vehicle, while two individuals would stay to tend to Rob's corpse. They left the scene in silence: Greydal, Elis, Peter, Damsel, and Diane. Each, aside from him, activated small lights on their lapels to carve blazing paths ahead.

After several minutes of tired silence, Peter whistled. The tune was reminiscent of a lay Greydal had heard once but forgotten, and he was about to ask the man its name, but Elis interrupted. "Pete. Shut up." The man's whistle died with a rising breeze, picking it up and carrying it ahead. They continued in that direction, the one Greydal thought of as north. That was where the habitat supposedly waited. Yet, he suspected he knew the site by a different name.

The reality of where and when he was *finally* settled on him. Though the crew of five walked on wine-colored dirt among a spattering of runt trees and a curdled marshland, his inner eye showed him something else: a stone road running past the cone fields. 'Cada bugs screeching in the tree line. The warm pattering of rain. He had made this walk, confusion and trepidation crushing him as a younger man. He looked up at the empty dark spinning over his head. When would they erect the sky? Would they carve out a chunk of this black night to squat over it all, mimicking the fate of the doctor's spotted lizard in its glass cage?

On the horizon, another orb peaked above the tree line. It was a brilliant shade of orange and brown. "Oh," Damsel murmured to his left. "I've never seen Indra this close before." No one else replied, and so Greydal said nothing.

They continued in the direction of the habitat. After several minutes, a mountainous, ruddy edifice emerged. The Old Folks' vessel. Blinding lights radiated from the craft to paint the landscape around it in white-gold hues. The craft was lopsided.

"Oh my god," Damsel said.

"Well, shit," Elis muttered. Greydal tried to understand what was wrong, and then recognized the vessel was two-thirds its previous mass. The swamps to their left spanned north, cutting into the ship and leaving the west side of the vessel missing. Even from the distance, he could spot the inner guts of the structure, exposed to the damp air.

"Well," Peter said, "I hope Tehom *keeps* its atmosphere."

As they drew nearer, what he initially took to be low, pale shrubs, became a crowd of at least a thousand or more. Almost all wore the white and yellow ensemble of the expedition. "There were that many people on board with us?" he asked to no one, and no one replied.

As they continued to approach, he wondered why the crowd was so silent. Then he saw the doctor (at least he thought the white speck positioned above the crowd was him). Michael stood on a jutting piece of the ruined ship, lights scorching him. He spoke to the mass of bodies His voice was amplified, though Greydal saw no horn or apparatus which would project the man's words.

"The first priority is safety!" the doctor called.

"*That's* a load of shit," Peter muttered.

Above the throng, the doctor continued, "We're moving everyone into the first section of the habitat while the machines clear out the rest of the pit." Someone must have yelled something in response because the doctor replied, "No. We won't be joining you, at least not immediately. The response party and I are going to the zero site."

The subsequent clamor from the crowd was frightening, but the doctor yelled over them, "This is why we're all here! You know it. I know it!" The crowd didn't quiet.

Greydal made to continue towards the distant congregation, but Elis put a hand on his shoulder. "Let's wait here, handsome."

*** *** ***

An hour later, the group of five conferred with the doctor near the stretch of ground which would one day be the mushroom-haunted crossroads of Harlow. "What happened to you?" the doctor asked as he approached, noting the bile which fused with Greydal's uniform.

Elis cut in, "Mike. Doc. That interloper that got the ship hit us hard. Depots are gone—"

"We need the magic touch," Peter interjected.

"Right," Elis added.

The doctor looked between them, and after a moment, turned to Damsel. "Madera, what's wrong with Foster?" he asked.

Damsel looked down at Diane, who leaned against her. "She lost some blood, sir. Also, she may be under some kind of soporific. That's not who we need you for." Michael raised an eyebrow. In the surreal glow of the black marble's constant twilight, amidst the violet dirt and puddles, the man looked supremely out of place, like a traveling dandy trawling village slums.

"Johns?" the doctor asked.

"No," Elis replied. "Campbell. He was attacked by these—"

"A lifeform?"

Elis nodded. "At least two."

"Did you get samples?"

"I—no. The biopsy javelins were in the depots."

"Ah, and you said the depots, they are...?"

"Not, er, depots anymore."

Damsel cut in, "Do you have it with you?"

"That's disappointing," Michael replied. "Yes, I have all we'll need to set out."

"Wait," Peter replied. "So, we're just abandoning them?" He gestured towards the glow of the downed ship in the distance. "We're the only ones with any combat time."

At first, no one replied. Then the doctor made eye contact with Elis, who sighed and said, "Not abandoning. They're *our* relief."

The doctor nodded and confirmed, "They'll make do in our absence and pick up our work if we don't come back." Greydal stared at Michael, a curious expression on his face. The man turned to walk towards the site of the destroyed barracks, the crew following in his wake. After a moment of silence, so did Greydal, axe in hand.

The trek was eerie. Small, flying bugs emerged from the puddles to produce muttering whispers, their form of insectoid music. Yet, every time Greydal tried to fix one in his sight, it blurred and vanished. The sounds of boots on wet ground—*plip, plop, plip*—marked the groups' passage, almost in time with the phantom insects' strains. Behind them, the whispering parts of the collective song intensified as the party neared the site of the destroyed barracks. Approaching it, Greydal's skin crawled, and he kept an eye out for any more of the yellow-eyed monstrosities from before. He was the first to realize there was no one outside the building.

"Where'd they go? Rob and the other two?" he asked.

At first, no one said anything. Then Elis replied, "He's right. Ready yourselves."

Greydal tightened his grip on the axe. Out of the corner of his eye, he saw the doctor reach a hand into an unseen pocket.

A wide, pale face emerged from the door of the barracks, and Greydal's heart skipped a beat.

"Get in here!" the soldier hissed.

"Johns, what—" the doctor began.

"Hurry!" the face interjected.

The crew jogged towards the barracks. Elis allowed each to enter before stepping in behind them as he scanned the horizon, weapon at the ready. Inside, Wide-face stood next to the flat stretch of metal functioning as the barrack's kitchen table. On its face splayed the dead Rob. The young man's body bore signs of significant disfigurement.

The boy's stomach collapsed in on itself, as if there wasn't enough present to support the tent of skin. The flesh itself was as pale as new clouds, drained of blood.

"Where's Alberts?" Michael asked.

Wide-face, which Greydal took to be Johns, replied in an unsteady voice, "I-I don't know."

Peter replied first, "What do you *mean* you don't know? We left both of you together."

"I don't know," Johns repeated. Beads of sweat flowed down the man's thick brow. "Dragged Rob in here and set him on the table when Liz said she heard something outside."

"More of those things?" Damsel asked as she set a near-comatose Diane on a nearby seat.

"I don't think so," Johns replied. "I thought I saw some in the dark out there, but it could've just been my brain playin' tricks. But we both heard voices. Not those things' voices, neither."

Michael replied, "What do you—"

"Was it whispering?" Greydal interrupted. The room turned to him.

Then Johns nodded. "It was, yeah. Close, and then real far away like."

"How'd you know that?" Elis asked.

"We all heard the bugs whispering on the way here, and I wondered if..." Greydal's voice trailed off. He could see the incomprehension on the groups' faces.

"Oh, great," Peter said.

"Bud, what bugs?"

"Didn't you all see them?" Greydal asked.

"*See* them? I can barely clock anything out there. I almost shot Parker just a minute ago," Damsel said.

Greydal turned to look through the open barrack door. As his eyes adjusted, he found he could easily see straight to the horizon. He made out what he took to be more of the yellow-eyed things crawling south, though it could have been a mirage caused by the marriage of anxiety and twilight.

"Greydal," the doctor said, his voice quiet. "Can you see out there? I mean, more than maybe ten feet away?"

He turned towards Michael. "You can't?" he asked the doctor. The group looked at one another, worry on their faces. Peter spit.

The doctor appeared as though he was about to say something, but Elis cut in, "Doesn't matter. Parker, you haven't said where Liz went."

Johns looked up. "Said I didn't know."

Elis shook his head. "That's not good enough. Explain the whispering." His voice had turned sour.

"*Hey*," Damsel cautioned. "Be nice."

The man called Johns closed his eyes and sighed. Greydal heard a light tapping. It was the glassy fingers, clinking against one another. After a moment, the man replied, "I heard muttering or something, and so did she. Liz poked her head outside, and then just..." the man made an expanding motion with his hand, "flew apart. Evaporated maybe."

"What the shit do you mean evaporated?" Peter asked, his voice low.

"That's what I saw," the man mumbled, and then added, "She was talking to me during. Something about her pup back home."

Peter moaned. "You're telling me we've got five people to hit the zero site with?"

To no one, Johns continued his mumbling, "I could hear her. After she went away. The pup's name is Sparky."

"Eight," Michael replied. "Diane, Rob, and Greydal."

Peter rubbed his forehead and said, "*It's* not a soldier, Doc. And Diane's half-asleep from blood loss."

The doctor looked like he was about to speak, but Greydal cleared his throat and interjected, "I'm sorry, hold on." The group turned to look at him. Under their collective scrutiny, he paused. Why was he trying to help them? Maybe he just wanted to understand. "It's obvious what you're planning to do," he said. "But you've got at *least* a thousand people just north of here. Your friend," he gestured at Diane, "is half-dead. Why—"

"You know so much, don't you?" Peter asked, his eyes hard.

"I don't—"

"How do you expect us to ask them to risk more than they have already? You saw what happened to Rob. None of this is fucking sanctioned."

Greydal held the man's gaze. To the right, Damsel's metal hair twitched, reminding him of Roan. "But why bring them in the first place, then?" A silence lingered.

Elis was the first to speak. "They're not roughnecks like us, bud. They're engineers, cooks, pilots, and the like. Still takes a lot to get a bucket like ours across the stars."

Greydal was quiet for a breath, and then replied, "Soldiers aren't what you need. Weapons won't help." *Yes,* a loud thought, almost a voice, whispered. It startled him, had almost sounded like not a thought at all.

"You might be right," Michael said. "But what other option do we have? Our people, the ones back home? They think of the cataclysm as a natural phenomenon, a consequence of tampering with the rougher dimensions. They'll never understand it's anything but."

"It hates us," a sleepy Diane murmured.

Michael nodded and continued, "Our mere presence on this planet is causing reactions. Antagonistic responses. Whatever the anomaly is, it's aware. The marsh, the attack you all suffered, whatever befell Liz Alberts, they're designed to keep us away. If we don't stop it here, I'm afraid the changes elsewhere will continue until there's not much left that's recognizable. Anywhere."

Greydal held his reply. The knowledge came on its own: the 'antagonistic responses' *were* natural. Like innate ripples echoing off the undulations of a great fish or worm, one too large to see. The doctor was partially right, though: the so-called anomaly was aware. But this group concerned it not at all.

"So, are we doing this or not?" Peter said, his nasally voice tight.

The doctor broke his gaze and nodded. "Give me some light and stay back." The man reached into his white suit and produced a small vial with something red inside. Michael set the vial on the kitchen table and blinked twice, causing the container to expand to the size of a brick. Within, a thorned slime writhed. Greydal backed, bumping into Elis. As the doctor reached a hand towards the canister, Peter spit again and shoved his way outside. No one stopped him.

"Is it time already?" Diane whispered in a breezy voice.

Greydal swallowed and tried to take hold of his fear. He told Michael with as much authority as he could muster, "Don't... You can't."

Elis replied in a soothing voice, "It's okay, bud. Doc here knows what he's doing." The doctor, his attention on manipulating the canister's lid, muttered, "Saint Paul, look at me now."

"Pall..." Diane mumbled.

Greydal ignored the woman, watching as the lid to the canister popped open. The slime within unfurled, and sent a probing finger towards the opening. With frightening alacrity, it swam out of the canister to balance on its mouth. Its spines twisted, simulating a wave. The thing had no eyes, but Greydal sensed he held the creature's scrutiny.

Then the doctor whistled, and the slime froze for a moment before darting towards the corpse. Greydal clenched his teeth involuntarily as the slug forced its way into Rob's still mouth. After two heartbeats, it had vanished entirely.

Rob gasped.

The tent of skin covering that naked belly swelled, new life nestled within.

No, the kid was only breathing. That was all. He sat up, and Damsel turned away.

"Campbell, can you hear me?" Michael asked in a loud voice, his eyes searching the boy's face. Something croaked a reply. Greydal turned as well and made to leave the barracks.

Elis said, "Wait." But he was ignored.

Outside the darkness swarmed, seeking Greydal's eyes. After his vision adjusted to the change, he stared into twilight. The fact he could see clearly while others couldn't made him ill from the implication. Or maybe the nausea creeping up his throat was only due to the scene the group had just thrust upon him. He mentally put the question aside for later and turned the corner of the barracks.

A tiny ember fallen from the void floated in the gloom. At its other end was Peter, exhaling smoke. "You know you're not leaving, right?" the man asked, then added, "What do you think's going to happen to you if we don't nip this thing?"

Greydal didn't reply. He didn't have an answer.

DOORWAYS

From what Greydal understood, this first jaunt was meant to be a simple sightseeing venture—go to the source of the anomaly, gather data, and later regroup at the habitat to discuss findings. Why he himself needed to be there, he didn't know, not for certain. But he could guess. They believed him to be a central pillar to some vague conspiracy against humankind, against reality. He was a prisoner of war.

Michael Bishop—*the* Bishop—thought to use him, perhaps to learn, or to stir things up. Though, Greydal was less concerned about the results of the Bishop's research than his *own* plight. How the hell would he ever get home? But then, what *was* home? Not Harlow. Not the tent city it had spawned, either. The Sophites were close to family, but he had left them knowing he might never return. No matter where he was or what he was doing, he was constantly, fundamentally, adrift. Even now, he sat listless in the rover, the wagon-like machine which Michael had produced from thin air to transport them. It carried him without his say, and just like with the wagon and Roan's quest, Greydal was now embroiled in a plot he didn't quite understand, nor sure he cared to be a part of.

The vehicle was an oblong, bleached cylinder, made of cabins connected like the joints of an ant or spider. Faint stirrings of dust floated through, lit by the oto-lanterns placed regularly along the vehicle's backbone. The rover flew over the featureless wastes, unseeing horizons which melted from sight. Greydal didn't waste energy asking Elis or the others about their heading. He already knew.

Rubbing the sleep from his eyes, he tried to reclaim the tatters of the dream he had only just escaped. Most of it dissolved on his awakening, leaving only a shallow pit in the bottom of his stomach. Across from him, Johns held up a hand as the man's glassy fingers slowly morphed into a series of utensils shaped like pincers and sharpened picks. Then Johns pressed that apparatus against Damsel's head, into her alloy hair. After a moment, small, metal shavings tumbled like hardened sparks to rest at the woman's booted feet. It took Greydal's sleep-addled brain a moment to realize he was trimming her hair.

To the right, Elis slept in something like a hammock, though it shifted against the movements of the vehicle, keeping the man steady, despite the sporadic oscillations. The tulka's body twitched in time with the noise produced by what Damsel had earlier called the engine, a small oval which glowed a tranquil blue at the rear of the vehicle.

Damsel leaned forward from her seat near Johns to examine a blade under the oto-lanterns' illumination. The weapon's metal was identical to Greydal's axe, the one they had unfortunately made him leave at the barracks. His fingers now itched for the grip. "How much longer do you think until we camp?" he asked.

She glanced at him from the corner of her eye. "Camp? We're not out here for fun."

A sleepy voice from Elis' direction muttered, "We're going all the way there, bud. Not leavin' these comfortable accommodations until we got to." Greydal nodded, though Elis couldn't see him. He wondered for a moment how long he would have to wait until he could exit the swaying vehicle. Its ceaseless movements had begun to wear thin.

The sound of water rushing made Greydal look to the front of the rover. Peter emerged from a side room, fumbling with his suit. "Is that a toilet in there?" Greydal asked.

Peter turned his nose up and said, "Go in a corner. The restroom's for people." The whine of the engine increased as the inside of the rover lurched to the side.

Greydal gritted his teeth and said over the sound of the engine, "Stop dancing around whatever problem you think you have. If you want to kill me, then come and do it. That's what you want, right?"

Peter paused as he made to retrieve a bottle of colorless liquid from a miniature white box which oozed cold. "Whatever problem..." he laughed and shook his head before straightening. "*The* problem is that the monster up front with the Doc isn't the most unnatural thing on this rover."

"Pete," Elis warned from his hammock. Damsel replied, "El, let him vent. We're all uncomfortable." Greydal glanced from her to Peter. Behind them, Johns stopped tinkering with Damsel's hair to shut his eyes and bury his head in his arms.

At length Greydal asked, "Just because I fell out of something you thought was an alternate reality? I don't know if you noticed but that doesn't apply anymore." Did they really not understand how this all worked? *They* were the intruders. Their world had collapsed, releasing them like shipwrecked fishermen to founder on the rocks of Greydal's existence.

"What's he talking about?" Damsel asked Peter.

Peter ignored her. "Half the shit in here is from someplace else," the man said. "You honestly think that's what bothers us?" Behind Peter, the horizontal window facing out of the rover showed a blurry landscape. Greydal noticed familiar-looking hills. In the distance, one moved on its own. Or seemed to.

"Hey!" Peter snapped. "You asked, so pay attention. I had a brother. His name was Harry. The Doc had a daughter and Johns was about to get married—"

"I looked normal," Damsel added.

Diane spoke up from her hammock, "Not everyone remembers. Most don't, actually. I had a baby, though. A little boy." Greydal was silent. The only sound was the changing whine of the engine filling the cabin.

At length he asked, "What about Elis?"

From the hammock, Elis replied by mumbling, "I'm just a god-damn hero, bud."

"Right," Damsel muttered. Another squeal from the engine coincided with a swerve from the vehicle.

Greydal looked into Peter's eyes as the man steadied himself against the wall. "You want me to be sorry? I am," Greydal said. "But it's got nothing to do with me."

"You really think you're clear of all this, don't you?" Peter asked. When Greydal didn't reply, the fake tulka added, "Well, maybe *you* are. But what you are isn't."

Another swerve caused Peter to nearly sprawl across the wall. Greydal steadied himself against the swirled, silver floor of the vehicle. Diane raised a head from her hammock and said, "Don't worry. I'm sure we're all going to die anyway, so it won't matter so much in the long run."

"Diane," Peter fixed her with a glare. "Shut up."

Johns raised his head from his arms and said to the cabin, "We're slowing."

Greydal glanced at the window. Sure enough, the closer portions of the unvaulted landscape were no longer blurry with speed. He eyed the familiar stretches of dark sand, and there was a stirring in his chest. A memory of a pale figure, swaying in the inky surf, swam across his mind's eye. Did tears perch at the corners of his vision? He wiped his face and convinced himself it was only the dust.

*** *** ***

Michael stood at the exit to the rover. The doctor held a golden, metal pack with straps, showing it to the group. Greydal's eyes widened upon seeing it. The shape of the device was different—but the golden backpack was of similar make to the Legate's golden suit. Eerily so. Even the way the dingy metal half-swallowed the light instead of reflecting it was the same.

"Before we exit," Michael began, bringing Greydal away from that curious line of thought. "We're going over this once more, just in case," the doctor stated.

"Doc, we've got it. You told us," Peter complained. The milky gloom of the clouded sky bled through the rover's windows to bathe the man's face.

Michael wasn't dissuaded. "We're going to make it so that everyone knows in their bones how this works. This knob here," the doctor indicated a metal dial on the golden pack, "should *never* be touched. The kefatz is keyed to the command bridge of the ship, which *is* still intact. I'll jump us out of the zero site if we need to retreat or if we get stuck. If for some reason I'm unable to, whether I'm dead or unresponsive, make sure everyone is touching or within reach and push this plunger," Michael pointed at a corrugated knob with a flat head sticking straight from the top of the pack.

"Again, do not touch the dial," Michael looked at each of the assembled team members. "It may take you somewhere else, and will very likely kill you. We haven't worked out half of the kinks yet. Do you understand?" Greydal, Diane, and Elis nodded.

Peter quipped, "What, is it going to throw us in the middle of Rushmore or something?"

The doctor fixed him with a glare. "It might." Behind the doctor, the thing that was no longer the kid blinked for the first time that day.

"And this is the important bit," Michael continued. "Make sure you have everyone."

"You think we'd leave someone behind?" Damsel asked and glanced at Greydal.

"Would you? The technology behind the kefatz pack doesn't do well with repeated—or rather, *back-to-back*—use. It takes hours to be suitable for safe operation again. Do you understand, Madera?"

"Yeah, yeah. Make sure we have everyone on the first go," she said.

"Don't sweat it," Elis cut in. "We're not going to have to use it. This is gonna work."

Accompanied by a popping sound, a metal weapon, identical to the ones the team members used, fell out of nothing from a point in space between the doctor and Greydal. It clattered on the ground and spun towards the wall as the rocking of the waves beneath the vehicle tilted the floor. For a moment, no one said anything.

Then Johns drawled, "...why'd a gun just fall out of thin air?"

Elis looked at the doctor. "Mike, I thought you said the cold iron would shield us." The doctor stared at the weapon. "Clearly, it's time for us to move," he said stiffly. Then he turned to the group and collected himself, saying, "First run is going to be fact-finding. I don't expect Tehom will grant us a second chance, so once we know what we're dealing with, return to the rover and grab whatever equipment I deem appropriate." Elis and Damsel grunted affirmatives.

"But...I thought we were going to study findings at the habitat, not out here. Wasn't that the plan?" Diane asked with a worried expression. The doctor ignored her.

"Diane, we're *obviously* without a plan," Peter said after a silence. The Rob-thing wheezed, and the doctor reached a yellow glove towards a red icon on the wall. With a *bleep*, the back section of the vehicle dissolved. Behind it, a broad expanse of damp rock stretched outwards. Michael nodded to his monster who leaped in silence from the vehicle. Dark waves washed over yellow boots, up to the thing's shins. Then, shouldering the golden pack, the doctor followed. He led the Rob-thing up the rocky bank to drier land. The world was brighter there than it had been outside of the barracks.

"Ah, some light," Damsel cheered when she pushed to the front of the group.

The crew copied Michael, and soon they each stood on the embankment. Once his eyes recovered from the sudden glare, Greydal turned in a circle. The onyx sea spread in all directions, falling from a knuckle of mineral which jutted from the waves. Far behind the capsule-like rover beached on the rocks, Greydal spied the shore. Was that the spot where he and Roan would swim? He couldn't tell.

Under his feet, the stone seethed livid like heated coal, curling with patterns that tickled a point on his forehead above his eyes. He blinked and the sensation vanished along with the illusion. The rocks were still. "Is that it?" Damsel asked.

Greydal turned to look where she pointed. A white triangle hunkered at the far end of the plain of rock. It burned Greydal's eyes, and he glanced at the heavens to relieve them. Pale clouds drifted there across the dark expanse. They, too, smoldered with a bleary glow.

"Let's get on with it," Michael commanded and strode forward, followed by the silent Rob. Greydal and the rest of the group did the same.

As they walked, he made sure to place his steps carefully, as he found the rocks unbearably slippery against the wood of his right leg. As such, he quickly fell behind the party. As he trudged after them, the stirring in his chest resumed. An invisible player strummed the chord of his being as the searing triangle in the distance drew him like a bee to nectar. Within its depths, an impossibility blinked awake. The clacking of his false foot and the soft waves were a rhythm which rose with the wind. It grew stronger the longer he walked. From the corner of his eye, Greydal glimpsed aquatic lights drift under the blanket of the far deep. Phosphorescence of some watery life? For some reason, he didn't think so. He ignored the lights and hurried after the team.

As he closed with them, there was a moment where he was undecided what the center of the island was meant to be. The bleak triangle was there, true. But, before it, there seemed to be an indistinct absence or oily slick. *A pit.* His stomach sank as he thought he recognized the well.

The image shivered, and the patterns he had imagined before returned, playing on the back of his eyelids when he blinked.

But then he arrived.

And there was nothing, no pit at all, just solid rock and the white triangle which proved to be a sort of austere home. A hermit's hut? The pale driftwood forming its exterior reflected the harsh sorrow of the roiling clouds. The group was eyeing the structure.

"Where's the cave?" Elis asked. "This is just a hovel."

"It's a shrine," a new voice said. At once, five members of the group produced their weapons and pointed them at the stranger who now stood in the doorway to the white hut.

"Identify yourself!" Michael yelled as the corpse of Rob stepped between the doctor and the stranger.

"You know me, Doc," the hermit said.

Behind Greydal, Peter moaned.

"That's not possible," Michael said.

The Rob-corpse gurgled.

"Possible?" asked the second Peter, standing before the hut.

Greydal blinked. At first, he hadn't recognized the fake tulka, so long was the man's hair and shaggy beard. But beneath the mountainous scruff peeked the same face, now fevered and gleeful.

"Will somebody please explain to me what the hell is happening?" Elis remarked.

The bearded Peter stepped forward and raised his hands, palms out. "May I?" he asked.

The real Peter took a step back, his gun lowering. A strained silence rose as Michael Bishop fought for a response. Beads of sweat grew at the man's temple. At length, he nodded. The other Peter smiled.

"You all are standing in the epicenter of where God entered the world," he said in a high voice. "And *you*, Doc, are a fool. You thought it would be a good idea to bring *him* here?" The mangy Peter tilted a finger towards Greydal. "*Oh, I know*," he went on. "Use him to cause reactions here, to *study them*. That's how you work: put everything under a microscope so you can feel *powerful*. So, you can pretend to be bigger than this. But some things are too big for us."

"Look, I need you to—" the Bishop began.

"Can't you feel it?" the new Peter interjected, raising his voice. "It's a done deal. You're questing after a dead end, Doc. We were never going to stop it—the calamity isn't ongoing. It happened a long time ago."

The others exchanged glances, keeping their weapons trained on the hermit.

"He knows. Don't you?" Peter's eyes found Greydal's. Some of the group turned to peer at him.

"What the fuck's he talking about?" Damsel asked.

Greydal swallowed. The hermit was right. He *could* feel it. The center of the island was like a broken bone, half-healed. Everywhere there were cracks and fissures, invisible to the eye but not to his gut.

"Greydal?" Michael asked slowly.

"There are..." he began, his eyes wandering the air. Time slowed, and Greydal's consciousness shuddered, leaking from his skull. Vertigo surged.

It was as though he was looked down at himself from an extreme height.

Little ants, frozen before a pale dwelling. Among the insects there were two Peter ants, a Bishop ant, a Diane ant, a Damsel ant, an Elis ant, a Johns ant, a dead ant pretending to be alive, and an ant that wasn't an ant at all.

Frightful energies emanated from this un-ant's core, sending unseen fingers towards hundreds of surrounding tears, little rifts in space and time. Slowly, those fingers unraveled the stitching, and the rifts gaped. Other, stale realities seeped in, changing much of what they touched.

The first ant to feel the effects of the opening slices in the world was Elis. A wind from a universe without numbers blew through, and the Elis ant budded like a branch in spring. From Greydal's current perspective, the Elis ant simply became many, a fountain of clones erupting outwards—first two, then four, then six, becoming piles. Two of the tumbling doppelgangers looked identical to Elis, but the rest were much younger. Elis recoiled from these child-selves whose shaking bodies spilled over the rocks. Nearly every one of the clones were mindless, dead, or dying, each lacking something essential to anthood.

At this sight, one of the Peter ants laughed, raising his hands towards the sky or Greydal. The other Peter lifted his gun and fired, turning his copy's head to mist. Then he too fell to his knees, dropping his weapon. The gun clattered across the stones before slipping through an open rift as a wholly separate tear swallowed the Peter ant, leaving only a crushed box of cigarettes to mark his passing.

As if excited to copy its friends, a playful rift opened under one of the only conscious Elis clones, a child-ant whose naked cries pierced the air. Then the rosy infant was gone, deposited in front of some gravesite outside a plain of tall grass, a gravesite which shined green from a fresh coat of paint.

Meanwhile, the Bishop ant fumbled with the straps to his golden backpack. Next to him, the dead ant pretending to be alive stared at the ground, a brown fluid leaking from its ears.

Now, the Damsel ant struggled with an unseen aggressor, a specter escaped from some fever-world of predatory fire. The specter was chewing at Damsel's mouth, then her ears and eyes. Her legs spasmed, and she squirmed on the ground.

The Diane ant was running, fleeing towards the group's little vehicle. As she hurried away, the Bishop ant finally succeeded in removing the backpack and gestured for the original Elis and Johns ants to come forward, to join hands. Elis stumbled from his clone piles, but Johns was unresponsive, now pressing his fists to his ears as he crouched. Perhaps this was to block out the pained barks and whines of the Damsel ant.

The Bishop ant waited for the Elis ant. He fished around in his pocket before raising an arm, now holding a darkened brick of glass. He aimed it.

Not at Elis.

At the nearby un-ant, who stood stock still, staring into the far distance. The Greydal ant. But then Elis, seeing the Bishop ant's intentions, stepped forward.

"Mike, don't!" the Elis ant yelled. But it was already too late. The Bishop ant's finger tapped a red icon on the brick's face and space *subtracted*. Instead of its intended target, the inverse beam struck Elis, who now stood in the way, leaving nothing between Elis' torso and the bottom of his neck. The Elis ant's head fell, and rolled at the Bishop's feet.

With a pained expression, the Bishop threw his spent weapon away and pursed his lips, signaling the dead ant. The creature twitched and whirled towards the still-unresponsive Greydal ant. Then the Bishop pushed the plunger on the golden backpack and disappeared, along with the Elis ant's head which had been sucked along.

Greydal had had enough. With a thought he urged the rifts to close, to relax. They followed his command.

But there was a problem. Though the rifts were now beginning to shutter after their outburst, the dead ant was still lurching towards—

Towards the un-ant, the Greydal ant. That was bad. The dead thing would commandeer the Greydal ant if it could—the red muck within preferred living flesh, he somehow knew. A spined slug poked excitedly from beneath the dead ant's eyelid, groping outwards.

From his vantage in the sky, Greydal scanned the remaining tears for something, anything he could use. One caught his eye. A tear directly inside the white hut.

It was like peering through a window, this rift looking out on some future event—a labor. There was a woman. She was hunched within a unlit barn, and she was beautiful. Blonde hair lay plastered to her forehead. Her jaw was set in agony. Above, sheets of sunlight separated the shadows and the motes of dust which inhabited them. There were no animals in this barn, just her. She screamed as her legs parted further. The baby was coming. A hand breached first, thin and long-fingered. Then another. Then two more. The arms parted her, and the child's head peeked through.

Greydal wanted to spill through as well, and comfort the woman. After a moment's hesitation, he instead took the child, vanishing it from that time and place. *I'm sorry*, he wanted to say. But she couldn't hear him.

Back on the island, he nestled the baby on the rocky ground between the Greydal ant and the approaching...the approaching Friar. Yes. That was its name. Time began to speed.

From the sky, he leaned down and whispered into the newborn child's mind. He indicated the stumbling Friar, now less than five feet away from the un-ant. The infant only looked up, not at the sky, but at Greydal. A wolfish grin spread across the baby's elongated face.

*** *** ***

Greydal woke in a daze to the scent of wet hound and salt. Blinking his foggy eyes, he rose to a seated position. He had been sprawled on the moist stone of the island. A fierce wind whipped his hair. He sat amidst mounds of himself, some his age but most of them younger. One near his hand was so small it could barely be considered a person at all. Each that he could see were dead.

He rose to his feet. At first, nothing coherent registered. His memory was blurry and offered only scattered images. It reminded him of watching a play on the Vermillion Stage, only from so far away all the actors were little more than blotches. As soon as he reached for the meaning behind the images, a violent pain arced behind his eyes.

Fine, he thought...maybe...maybe he would remember later.

Several yards away, behind the partial corpse of the original Elis, he spotted it—the body of Rob. The Friar's limbs had been torn away, leaving tattered stumps, and a small hole had been bored through the face, exiting near the ears. Red slime spattered the thing's mouth and the surrounding rocks. Greydal looked around at the blasted arena for the Friar's assailant, and his eyes caught the hut. It lay smoldering and demolished, a temporary altar to...

Greydal clenched his eyes shut, hard enough to hurt. When he opened them, he couldn't remember where his train of thought had been going. He then patted himself for signs of damage, and in frustration, ripped off his gloves. He let them fall to the briny rocks. The wet air breathed life to his choked fingers. He discovered that the rebreather Elis had taught him to use was disabled, must have deactivated some time ago. Had it turned off before they stepped foot on the island? He hadn't noticed at the time.

An uncomfortable feeling made him pause. He looked back, towards the rover. It was gone. Only the black sea remained, its waves chuckling as they danced into the distance. Perhaps one of the soldiers had taken the craft, leaving him to his fate, maybe the tides had simply swallowed the vehicle. He supposed it didn't matter much and closed his eyes again, this time for a while.

CHAPTER

28

YEARNING

A day later, he contemplated trying to eat the Elis copies. His hunger was compelling, enough to make him sniff the doppelgangers. But when he imagined cutting into them and becoming some bizarre auto-cannibal, he blanched.

Next, he thought about trying the others. Damsel and Johns. But where the Elis cadavers had at least appeared like meat, the others' corpses didn't pretend, now turned into abstract sculptures that bore more in common with foliage. He wasn't sure what had happened to them. Damsel looked half-eaten—her eyes and lips and much of her face was missing—and her body was opened near the sternum, like a jungle flower, while her legs curled inwards as though she were a dead spider.

Johns' corpse was stranger.

The man was hunched into a near perfect ball, all his edges and irregularities shaved away. It was like the man were a statue someone had taken a diamond-tipped saw to, or maybe one of the tools the soldiers had used to slice away trees near the barracks. In the sheared spots, thin bouquets of pale veins or something else swayed in the wind like weeds. As Greydal's stomach gurgled, a teasing part of his mind reminded him of the buck he had killed in the tall grass as a boy. He hadn't been picky about raw meat then.

Dejected, he walked the length of the island, thinking on his current circumstances. He was stranded, there was no doubt. And as sure as he was stranded, it was almost as certain he would never make the swim to shore, far as it was. Yet, the longer he waited, the lower his chances grew. Oddly, the thing that came to mind then was his childhood friend. He hadn't thought of Toshi since walking with Ida along the streets of Heron. Despite the absurdity of his current situation, Greydal lived while the boy was dead. Would be dead. What had Toshi's friendship with him gotten the boy, other than a few short years of make-believe, and then undiluted terror and ultimately death, after being driven from the valley?

How was it fair that Toshi should *die*, killed by some lake beast, while Greydal was—What? Not thriving, surely. But...

The fact he hadn't bit the dirt after so much horror wasn't comforting. It was frightening.

Before him, the waves bristled and churned in a manner unfitting of saltwater or even liquid. Greydal eyed them and felt his throat catch as a quiet ball of something ice-cold and undiluted melted behind his sternum. Terror. That *was* its name, wasn't it? A constant companion.

How was it fair that terror loved him, but no one else?

Before he could make himself move, the fear mastered him, and he briefly pondered whether he could fashion the destroyed shrine into a raft. One glance at the rickety detritus told him it would be more trouble than it was worth, and likely only further exhaust him.

And so, without much thought he stepped into blackness, the grasping tides. A part of him already knew what he would find. It had always been there, waiting for him, the knowledge pressing against him his entire life.

It lived just out of sight.

It could be remembered if he would only...

Let...

Go.

*** *** ***

He was in the thicket. The fleshy trees pulsed in his mind's eye, followed by the startling void of the well, and then both fell away, revealing a deeper darkness. It was that place he had entered on the road outside of the town of Heron, where the nothingness stretched in all directions and the great, invisible awarenesses lived. But this time, they were gone, those unseen mountains he recalled. Something in his cooling brain told him that the reason for their absence was the reason for the tenderbird's: *A greater animal had decided to roost.* It was why he stood here in solitude, understanding more than feeling that inky water filled him to the brim. Was he drowning?

"What is this?" he asked the nothingness, or rather the thing behind it. A familiar voice echoed him:

What is this?

"Who are you?" he asked the voice.

Who are you?

The question was a key to the lock of his memory. The revelation! Like before, the shadows rocketed away as Greydal became not himself. An egg pretending to be a planet bled over a body hanging from a tree. They merged and bulged, and then popped like a bubble. The truth came then as a flash of thunder, and he devoured it, unraveling the secrets screaming behind the wall of night. He was the knower and the knowing, the lover and the loved.

Interloper, Voice of the Gods, He-She-We-It spoke:

"Oh."

Elsewhere, a pink corpse floated among the sightless waves.

*** *** ***

A different dream then, unlike the others. Years and years hence.

A man walked alongside a large boar, known to him as a razor-back. The boar pulled a small cart, which contained pots and pans, an old axe, and among other things, a sleeping boy. The boy moaned in his disturbed slumber and the man looked down.

"Shhh," he said. "We're almost there." His smile was strained. His child lay close to death. Beneath the wool blanket, the gray marks of illness marred that flushed chest. Was it his imagination or did the ashy fingers grow closer to the boy's throat before his own eyes? He shook his head and stirred his boar onwards. He had to hurry.

Precisely one hour later, the boy, boar, and man arrived at their destination. The copse of trees rose like a crown from the shadowed ground in the distance. The man suppressed a shiver and urged his beast onwards, but the boar resisted. After minutes of struggling, he left the animal behind. The man carried his now still child, finally sleeping deeply in his arms. The shrine of something his former people had called Old Man Moonlight waited ahead.

He paused outside of the tree line. Marcos had told him he must never, ever enter the thicket. Only speak to it. He hitched his boy higher into the crook of his arm. For a moment, he considered turning back. But he couldn't. No more than he could leave his son to die.

The man cleared his throat and began his entreaty, "Old Man Moonlight! Hear me! My name is Tier." Silence. He continued, "I arrive as a supplicant. This is my son. My only son. Show yourself, if you're present!" The man waited for a reply. If one came aside from the creaking of the skeletal boughs, he didn't hear it. "If you're listening, I— The boy needs your help. He's dying. An illness brought him low months ago, and his condition only deteriorates. Medicine, the Red Faith, superstition, nothing services." He held his breath and peered into the grove.

For a moment, he thought he spotted something—movement. But no, it was only the clouds above, causing shadows to shift. Then the man felt a cold breeze, somehow blowing directly *from* the thicket of trees. He shivered.

"I know I've never...followed you or given credence to your name..." He cleared his throat. "I love my boy more than anything. I would do *anything* for him. Do you understand?" Name your price, he didn't say. But he thought it. The man paused and exhaled. "Please, help," he finished.

The rising wind rattled the trees. Within the thicket, something stirred.

A nightmare presence carved from antecedent awareness, now fragmented and half-stranded within the cavernous grove. This was all things, and none of them. A fantasy of black waves and cold skies, of rainbow eyes behind the walls. It was uninhabited palaces and woods that revolt against the lying light of day. It was a symptom of that Secret Truth which squirms at the heart of existence, that quiet knowledge inherent to all life, which whispers to us there is something strange, just out of sight. Something dark and wonderful that leans against the membrane of the world, its slipping mask.

This thing reached out a questing finger towards the man and the boy. Interesting. The man had said *sick*, not dead. The presence observed the child and confirmed no life dwelt within that small frame. Yet, the body was warm, so recently had the boy expired. The presence considered for a timeless moment. It would *not* tell the father the child had given up the ghost to wander the wider haunts, to slide between those great, damp muscles cocooning the universe. No, the presence could do better than paltry fact—though, by this act, it would sacrifice much.

Let it not be said the gods are unsympathetic to the plights of small creatures.

Later, after much of the man's weeping and cheering, the presence, channeled by the thicket, watched its smaller half get carried towards the waiting swine.

This could be a good thing, the presence reasoned. After all, an age had passed since it experienced childhood.

*** *** ***

More than two decades later, something in the shape of a man emerged from nothing. It woke from what felt like a long sleep. Strange images played at the corners of the man-thing's awareness, phantom memories of a greater life. In its arms, a different, more fitful self dozed. Greydal, the sleeper was named.

Something inside the man-thing shuddered.

Incomprehensible geometries folded inward, becoming a mammalian—or almost mammalian—mind. Screaming colors and shards of intelligence like ice became simple thoughts, and the broad memories of a different sort of lifeform translated into flat, understandable allegories. The great god Pan is dead. Long live Pan.

Guilt. Why did that have to be the first emotion? The one who carried Greydal stared down at its other half. Things had not gone the way it intended. What had initially been a lark to ease the suffering of a troubled father had ballooned into a serious problem. Mortality was a stickier substance than initially anticipated. At least, this was the story its now too-mortal mind told itself.

The thing men knew as Interloper had tried, it *had*. But the other half—the Greydal half—refused to assimilate, even though the Interloper had had the decency to wait. Once the father was arrested and partially entombed, only *then* had the being come to the boy's side. *It had waited for adulthood.* After all, adulthood is the time for acknowledging difficult truths, for assuming responsibility. But the boy had resisted.

So, the Interloper had tried again when the young tulka was atop a cottage, watching a crowd gather around a village stage. But that attempt failed. Another attempt followed. But the result was the same. *So, another, and another, and another.* Each time the Interloper got closer to cracking the boy. But Greydal was stubborn. Like a child, he refused his responsibility.

At least, this was the story the man-thing's mind told itself now, the images flowing like a river.

And if this story was true, or could be pretended to be... maybe some of the boy's childishness had rubbed off. Maybe, when the being and Greydal conjoined on the road to Heron, something unexpected occurred. Instead of becoming one, the Interloper decided to remain two.

There was, the being had discerned in those intimate moments where it and Greydal became intertwined, a way that the fruits of life could be enjoyed, and yet the great duty still fulfilled.

That great duty: *mend the rifts caused by the Lattice's restructuring.*

The method by which this could be fulfilled: *complicated.*

The Interloper looked down, and then took a step. It could walk. That was good. This new, experimental course required a body capable of locomotion, among other functions.

It walked for a time, eyeing the overgrown road as it traveled. Eventually, it reached the terminus and set its younger self down upon a cozy bed of pale flowers at the edge of a sweeping tree line. In the far distance, an amber-tented hill rose bucolic. The tents' inhabitants would soon stir, going about their morning tasks. The Interloper inhaled and grinned. The air smelled of pollen.

Below, the other Greydal muttered, "Roan?"

"Easy, just sleep now. She's nearby," the new one told itself. It watched the younger one fall asleep. The face was scarred but handsome. The notch carved from his ear, rather than making him ugly, gave Greydal an adventurous, rough-and-tumble look. It would keep that, the Interloper decided. So, too, would it keep the tattoo of aphotic roots, so reminiscent of its own, ancient symbol.

The missing leg, though: *bothersome.*

It would forgo the missing leg. Settled, The Interloper made the changes on its own body, and something within its breast shifted.

The Interloper's head bent, eyeing Greydal, then leaning closer. If someone had been watching, they might have been reminded of a snake cornering a mouse, or of an evil twin about to work some mischief on his better half.

"There we are," it—*he*—said in a new voice and smiled as he eyed his younger doppelganger. "But what to *do* with you?"

The sleeping tulka didn't respond. "That's okay," the new Greydal whispered. "We already know, don't we?" The new Greydal reached out a hand and, with a single motion, siphoned something dark and shimmering from the sleeping tulka's body. Not all of it. But enough.

"Now, you can go on being you, I can go on being you, and *you*," he gazed at the wriggling essence in his grip. "Be still. Be matter."

The ephemerality hardened, becoming a crystal rod for just a moment, before reverting to its angry essence. The shining thing squealed and the surrounding trees shuddered. "Shhh," he told the essence and frowned. The staff didn't want to be a staff.

"We're going to have to let you get your wiggles out, I think," he muttered. "That's okay."

With his other hand, the new Greydal tore open a rift to a world much like his own as the last of something deep within his chest dissolved and seemingly vanished. "Off you go," he told the wriggling inhumanity and tossed it through the gap. With both hands, he gripped the rift and closed it.

Hah! *That* should settle the thing, give it time to relax before its work came due. Unless he was stupendously unlucky, the adjacent realm to which he had just transferred the essence would eventually collapse, sending the essence tumbling into this world. And, of course, he knew where—*when*—the essence would land, where it would be going. The Interloper smiled in satisfaction.

Then his eyes rolled up, and he fell to his knees.

When he came to, he sat in place for several minutes, his thoughts white static as ragged sobs bounded from deep within his chest. He had lost something dear by that last act, that much was evident.

But he could barely remember what.

*** *** ***

Elsewhere, a horror slumped through the murk. Vog. Calf-Ripper. Rimwolf. The hound had bedeviled mankind and other, less easily definable life from Harlow Valley to the northern Drop for almost a thousand years. Ever since the leader of the red filth snared the hound and the rest of the world within the great box, the beast had stayed on the move. The cur was a rover at heart, yet it knew its master, and came when called.

The hound dripped through the branches of the ripening trees and their nearby, polypal overlords. Silent as death, not a one heard its passing. Yet, the animals of this place quivered and knew great terror.

The same could not be said for the traveling merchant who had decided to take a side path through the wilderness. The man transported goods the bizarre denizens of Heron forged to the wider country, and thought himself wise, as there were many who would pay top shavings for the Ichablists' craftwork. But when a shadow, too large to be a cookaroo bird or one of the hybrid forest's carnivorous deer draped over his cart, the merchant's pulse quickened. The scent of wet canine permeated the overgrown track. But when he searched above in the whispering boughs, the merchant saw nothing, and so made the sign of the Legate.

The hound left behind the shivering man who scoured the trees for something that wasn't there. It poured through the undergrowth on its hands and knees, crawling like a child. The only sign of the grizzled old wolf's course was a shadow, too large to be a tree, gliding through the foliage-induced dusk. At last, it came upon the boundary. Fat fruits hung in their disgusting magnificence above the hound, tiny next to its massive frame. The beast inhaled. The scent's source was near. The hound crept along the tree line, following the spoors of its maker. At last, it spied him, the boy, now a man. The tulka was a vision out of the hounds' first memory, a place of black rock and blacker water. Only this one wore no white and yellow suit. He walked naked, a flushed ghost wandering under the shade of parasites and freighted branches. The tulka paused and sniffed the air, unknowingly mimicking the hound.

After a protracted silence, the man spoke, "You're close, aren't you?" Somewhere in the underbrush, a hare screamed and ran.

The Interloper-turned-Greydal spun to see a horror inches behind him. Though he knew the beast now, his heart hammered in his chest. The Red Faith had it wrong. The Vog looked almost nothing like its drawing. But its eyes, round and forward facing, its eyes were the same. It appeared much as it had on the island, only far, far larger.

If someone had asked him to describe the beast, Greydal would say the now-grown wolf was closer to a man in shape than anything else. The creature's body was furless, and much of its skin the color of dry shadows. The thing crouched on its hands and knees, looking like an old man searching for something lost in the grass.

Only there were too many limbs.

The Vog sported six—four, semi-translucent arms ending in wide hands and two, thick legs tipped with grasping hooves. All were as free of fur as the hound's pitch-colored torso. The head was what shocked him, though. A long, canine snout extended from a powerful neck and was covered in what at first Greydal considered hair. The black filaments infested every inch of the Vog's face and skull, draping low to the dirt and obscuring its features. Yet, its eyes shone through, deep disks of wavering light. They reflected Greydal's pained expression.

Infantile shuffles brought the hound closer, the creature's onyx tresses dragging across the leafy ground. If not for the thing's odor, he could have almost believed it to be illusory. The Vog was utterly silent. Its horrendous skull was nearly the size of Greydal's torso and moved lazily, a leaf in the wind. Despite his disquiet, or because of it, Greydal smiled. He reached a hand towards the wolf of his dreams.

"Do you know me? Only as master, or as..." He didn't finish the sentence.

The cords falling from the thing's face were heavier than fur or hair, yet they were thin like both. Beneath his fingertips, the wolf's skin vibrated, like the purring of a cat. The beast's eyes bored into his, and a fearful intelligence sought his own. Images of hunts old and recent filled him.

His mind was invaded. With the Vog, he tore into the flesh of men and animals, blood spurting like candied juice into his waiting bellies. A flash of a stag in long grass, slain by an axe. The Greydal-Vog consciousness tore into it, too, finding it savory and tough. Another flash, this one of the red filth. A series of images emerged, golden helmets broken open to reveal the painful mire within. The Greydal-Vog hated the parasites, their awful, maiming touch. Yet, it was a sacred duty to exterminate pests, and a thousand years was no time at all. The Greydal-Vog would spend as many ages as it took to remove the red filth from the waking world.

Greydal gasped and pulled himself from the hound's consciousness. He jerked his hand away from the vibrating skin beneath the long, dark filaments. "Ah," he breathed, and backed from the hound. "We have to be careful with that, don't we?"

The Vog said nothing. But a deep awareness dwelt there. It was *your* hand, it seemed to whisper.

"Alright. Come on." Greydal turned and continued west, not looking back. The only sign the Vog followed were the occasional squeals from small animals in the underbrush and the persistent scent of wet canine.

*** *** ***

Roan, Ravobisob, Ida, Rulf, and Higg—plus the Ichablist sharing his equine, sat on their mounts gazing at the distant wall of the firmament. Behind them, the rest of the Ichablist host waited. Higg pointed out movement on the far horizon. He asked who it was. Roan looked at where he indicated and caught sight of a hazy figure now materialized. A cloud of dust washed over the group and two coughed.

"I-can-not-see-ve-ry-far. Please-de-scribe-them."

Rulf replied, "It's a tulka. That's all I can tell at this distance. Anyone else?"

Higg and Ida shook their heads. Roan remained still until the Allthame squirmed in its sling. "Wait here," she commanded and kicked her mount into a gallop.

The equine flew across the dusty, gray landscape. Roan clenched her jaw as an unnerving tickle climbed her spine. She couldn't deny the deep strangeness she sensed bleeding from the figure. Beneath her, the equine fought her for control. The beast wanted to divert its course, but she wouldn't let it. With a soothing word, almost too low to hear, she calmed the mount. The equine relented and allowed her to continue, to speed the animal towards the apparition.

Rulf was right. It was a tulka. A man. He wore a dusty brown robe that muddied his form, and his head was as bald as his face. Others wouldn't have noticed it, but Roan could see there was a faint disturbance in the air around the stranger, like the effect produced by flat rocks on a hot day. Her eyes bounced from the man's petite nose, large eyes, and finally to his notched ear. Greydal. She slowed her mount as her sometime lover approached on foot. The two met next to a withered bush, which at one time may have been green, now ossified and frozen in time.

"Hello, Roan."

Roan was silent. She searched the man's face. On her back, the Allthame shuddered and seemed to grow heavier. "You're not him," she told the stranger. "What did you do with Greydal?"

"It's me. Maybe more now than ever."

"No. Whoever you are, you got the foot wrong. Greydal's missing a leg."

"He's missing more than that. But I'm fairly positive I healed myself."

Roan blinked and stared at the rosy man. His brown robe was a tattered mess and looked as though it had been filched from a barn. "You're *him*," she told the imposter. "Bythos. Greydal's Interloper."

He shook his head. "I'm Greydal. I always have been. I just didn't understand what that meant."

Roan folded her arms. "No. Mabet said Bythos used Greydal like a mask. You're the wearer."

"Use your eyes. Do I look like I'm wearing anyone but myself? Bythos is just a name, an old one. Like Interloper or Old Man Moonlight."

"Hardly."

"Believe me. Marcos was more than right. It's *all* shorthand."

"*Don't* tell me what my father was," she hissed.

"He said our brains aren't tuned for it. Don't you remember?"

Roan's confusion must have shown on her face. The stranger explained, "I know this won't make sense, but I just got back." The man tilted his head towards the sky and continued more softly, "I recall parts of my time...away. A presence. But even those memories, I think, are only a story. A convenient lie."

"Are you truly telling me you're *not* the Interloper? You're plainly not Greydal."

The man said nothing for a moment. At length, he appeared to arrive at a decision and explained, "If you need an answer, I'm...the shadow cast by the Interloper, who no longer exists."

Frustration supplanted her confusion. "Wordplay, little god," she said and added, "The air writhes about you."

The sound of distant hooves reached her ears, and she glanced over her shoulder to see Ravobisob approaching on his equine. Then the stranger before her cleared his throat, and she turned back.

"Believe what you want," the man said, "but before the Ichablist gets here, why didn't you tell me?"

"About yourself?"

"That you were pregnant."

A dry wind drew dust between the two. Underneath her, Roan's mount whinnied and shifted its footing. "Of course, you would know, Bythos. Now, I'm positive you're not Greydal."

"Believe what you want, but I met our son."

As Ravobisob neared, Roan said, "That's a lark. The boy *vanished* just as he was being born. My pregnancy was part of why Mabet sent me away to begin with. She knew what Greydal was, what *you* were. And what my son might be."

The man smiled to himself before returning his gaze to her. "Well. He's unique, even more than you or me. Were you... Did you get a good look at him?"

She narrowed her eyes. "No. One moment, I was in labor, the next, I wasn't."

"I'm sorry. Did you name him?"

"What are you apologizing for?"

The stranger didn't reply.

Roan sighed and added, "I didn't get the chance."

"You should have. He's part Pneuma, part tulka, part other. That's a first to my knowledge. Granted, I don't understand how I know that." Roan's eyes widened at the use of her species' name.

Behind, Ravobisob arrived on his equine. "Ah! Woun-ded-one! Have-you-come-for-the-All-thame?"

The stranger smiled and replied, "Hey, Ravobisob. I have, and to bring a warning. When you arrive at the compound, you're going to be captured."

That was enough. Roan spoke in a high, clear voice, "You have *lost your way*, little god. The Allthame stays with me. And we are not waltzing into the Wyrm's compound like simpletons. So, no capturing. You have till I count to ten to leav—"

"You're wrong. Don't ask me to explain, but I know it," the tulka interrupted. "If you want to help our people, don't resist. You'll get a chance, after."

"You—" She struggled to contain her fury. "Speak plainly."

"He-sees-fur-ther. Can-you-not-tell?"

"Not that, either. I just remember how it goes. Allow yourself to be captured. It'll be the quickest way to the Sophites."

"You're not making sense," she said.

A deep silence held for several breaths. Then the stranger replied, "Please, give me the Allthame, Roan."

"No."

On her back, the Allthame slithered out of its wrapping, and then its sling. It hit the ground with a *thud* and swam toward the stranger's waiting hand. A faint reverberation sounded, like the noise of a physical blow, or impact underwater.

A staff of pure, clear crystal, as tall as his notched ear, refracted the light of the manmade sun. "This..." the stranger whispered. "You were right to keep this from me, before," he told her. He looked up at Roan and must have seen the fear in her eyes. "Don't be afraid. It was meant for me, I think. A gift from me to myself."

Ravobisob was silent as Roan's hand fell from where it had reached out to grasp at the escaping weapon. A small, blue vein was visible on her pale neck. It only appeared when she was deeply frustrated. "That..." she began, "that shouldn't be. *I'm* the one who called down the staff. Mabet meant for me to have it."

"Maybe she didn't know. I'll admit I don't fully understand it, either. I caused some kind of collapse—a change—when I stepped into that grove to look for you. You didn't always have blonde hair."

"You're not making sense."

"With-re-spect-En-chant-tress," Ravobisob interjected with a vague gesture, "he-is. I-was-wrong. The-in-stru-ment-shall-stem-the-cos-mos, true. But-look. The-Woun-ded-one-is-the-in-stru-ment." Roan looked, and at first, didn't know what the Ichablist meant. Before her, the man professing to be Greydal stood robed, holding the crystalline weapon to the side. The Allthame appeared born for his grip. Hadn't the real Greydal told her a tale like this once? Perhaps one of the nights they huddled together in the wagon, or high up in the kith's meetinghouse?

"I have to go," he spoke softly. "I need to get to the Mansions before you all."

"You can't just walk in. We're using hooks to descend the cliff face."

"I have another way down," he replied as the wind increased. Piercing insects of swarming dust pelted them and the two long-suffering mounts. The tulka turned and walked away. As the swirling dirt swallowed his figure, becoming one with that dingy, tattered robe, Roan decided who it was the imposter resembled. What had Greydal called it? The Tale of the Wizard, or Excondalt? Yes, that sounded right.

But for the life of her, she couldn't remember how that story was supposed to have ended.

INSTRUMENT

Even under the stark light of day, the Vog startled. It stooped low next to him, its saucer eyes glowing will-o'-the-wisps. If anything, the Calf-Ripper—*his son,* an unwelcome thought corrected—was more frightening when fully illuminated.

It was because the beast didn't look like it belonged, Greydal decided. In the uncertain murk of shady trees, his progeny could be mistaken for some terror sourced from a nightmare, soon to disappear. But under the bleak sun, with no cover in sight, the Vog forced the fact of its reality upon the viewer. It didn't disappear. It didn't evaporate with the sleeper's fitful awakening or the rubbing of eyes. It was simply there, as plain and matter-of-fact as the dead ground on which it crouched.

The substance Greydal could now only think of as hair still obscured the Vog's canine face. The obsidian filaments dragged across the ground, collecting dust on their tips. He sensed the beast was mirthful, though he couldn't decipher an expression beneath that bizarre nest. There was only the wide mouth and that lolling tongue, panting without noise.

Greydal severed his gaze to glance at the precipice. The wolf seemed to sense his intention, and turned to crawl on its hands and knees towards the Edge. He shifted the crystal staff he had taken from Roan to his other hand, and followed the hound to gaze over the cliff. Below, the face of the Edge plunged into the depths. Only the fractal structure of the Mansions broke what he suspected would be a very long fall. It was the first time he laid eyes on the monstrosity from the outside, the whole of the Bishop's complex. Sebastian had told him it would take a while to travel the Mansion's length, and Greydal could believe it. Far to the south, the structure continued until it became misty with distance. Despite the differences in opulence and scale, he could discern the hand of those who wrought the Rings in the structure's architecture.

Towers of silver-capped stone spun skywards from featureless blocks. Here and there, balconies and glass domes congregated amidst what he suspected were the long corridors through which he had once hurried. Beneath some of the glass domes, he saw what he thought were colorful shimmers, like sunlight beneath shallow water. Each disappeared when he looked at them, only to return when his gaze shifted. The structure in its entirety was mindless. It was as though the complex had been organized at random. Had the Bishop's machines simply gone mad when building the place? Surely no one could require a space of such magnitude. Unless this was where the man planned to spend eternity, should his plan prove itself doomed.

To his right, the Vog waited. One of its arms, almost fully translucent in the light, rubbed an inky chest. Greydal noticed how the limb's veins were pale within the taut sack of wolf-flesh. Not red-blooded, this hound. He stepped towards the creature. His arm resisted him, but he forced a hand onto the beast's back. Its skin purred. At once, his consciousness merged with the Vog's. But he nearly retched as he tasted the blood of children, his mind struggling for control as the wolf's memories surged. But the intense disgust allowed him to momentarily come to himself.

He was no longer standing on the cliff face. As his reeling gaze turned downwards, he screamed. The void flew towards him, and his stomach lurched. He was on the Vog's back, clinging beneath six feet of hair like tar-covered straw. The creature descended along a boundless rock face as Greydal's breath came sharp and shallow. He caught glimpses of the Mansions between the forest of filamented darkness.

The Vog's hooves, almost like a razorback's, plied at the stone. The creature's multiple arms moved like a juggler's, cycling through handholds which he could never have hoped to use in a hundred years of climbing. Despite the shock, he had to concentrate to stay aware. Continually, his mind threatened to sink and fuse with the hound.

Greydal strengthened his grip and looked past his feet. The gap vaulted upwards, and he became dizzy, but the fear let him remain himself. Holding onto the Vog was easier than he would have expected. The skin was soft and dry, but he was inexplicably stuck to it.

Maybe it was a fleeting madness causing him to release, or try to release, one hand from the back of the creature. Either the thing's flesh held him, or his arms refused his command. Then he registered what he *wasn't* holding. He swore. The Allthame was gone. Had he left it in the dust above? He hadn't meant to allow the wolf's memories to engulf his own, only to compel the horror to carry him down the cliff-face. The Vog's body shifted under him as he squeezed his eyes shut and reached out, searching for the keening of the crystalline staff. It was close. Very close. He could feel its thin ululation in his sternum as much as his thoughts. But where? Then, at once, the Vog jolted, and Greydal almost fell. He released an involuntary gasp only to find the wolf now stood on one of the domed, glass roofs, this one a tower built straight into the cliff-face.

A translucent arm reached behind the Calf-Ripper's back and plucked him from his perch, setting him lazily on the dome. Greydal crouched and placed both hands on the glass to steady himself. The material was warm, almost painfully so. Below his palms, on the other side of the barrier, a type of library or repository hid within a series of dark shadows. The shadows were cast in all directions by the roof's silver trim, which spread like rays from a circle at the rotunda's summit. The glass smelled hot, something he didn't know could happen.

Near him, the Vog's returned to its childlike pose on hands and knees. He watched the wolf's colorless fingers slowly splay across the dome until he shook himself and turned to scan his immediate surroundings, leaving the Vog at his back. The collection of silver and glass roofs fell in disorganized assemblies from his vantage.

Down and to the west, he thought he spied the protracted balcony where Sebastian had likely just finished showing the younger Greydal the expansive divide between Edge and firmament. It was hard to tell, shadows obscuring the finer details of the far parts of the structure.

Behind him, his son moved closer and a new, weaker shadow crawled from the beast, caused by the light reflected off the rock wall. The shadow blanketed him before it grew, and then reared upwards. When the shadow's mouth opened, wider than he thought possible, he blanched. Greydal spun. The Vog's mane had parted to reveal its muzzle, which spread towards the sun. The dark fibers sprouting from the animal's skull and face fell like rain, now shading the upper half of its body. With an audible *crack*, the beast's mouth opened further, almost horizontally.

A staff of crystal, covered in a milky fluid, rose skyward. The Vog's lower torso contracted, and the staff went higher. Then a pale arm grasped the crystal and pulled, unsheathing it from whatever unseen gullet had housed it. The Allthame's keening grew in volume as its faceted body met with open air. It seemed to twist like a serpent, the crystal. Then the Vog placed a second hand on the weapon, and it stilled.

The beast proffered the Allthame to Greydal. In its wide fists, the tool looked smaller than it should. Greydal reached out and took it. As he grabbed the Allthame, he suppressed a shudder at the feeling of the cool, white substance coating it.

"Thank you," he said after an awkward pause. The Calf-Ripper only stared. Greydal turned and peered into the library beneath his feet. "I'm guessing this will be the easiest way into the Mansions," he said after a moment. Fingering the Allthame, he whispered, "The best practice is practice."

He gripped the weapon with both hands and concentrated. For a breath, the staff shuddered in his grip but soon fell still. He frowned and tried again, holding the weapon tightly. Still, it didn't do what he wished. Frustrated, he took a sizable breath and closed his eyes. Come *on*, he told it in his thoughts.

A thin wire was there, the Allthame's representation in his mind's eye. It tugged at him, waxing and waning alongside that fitful keening. Reaching with his mind, he tried to take control of it. The faint wire dipped and dived, eluding his grasp. It was a little like trying to pick up a smooth river-stone too large for a single hand.

A sigh, and he opened his eyes. Next to him, the Vog sat in the same position as before, watching intently. For a ridiculous moment, Greydal felt embarrassed. Then, irritated with himself, he tried once more. He let his eyes fall shut and released his need to command the Allthame. Instead, he thought about the sensations of his body.

Beneath his stolen boots, the flaring glass of the roof emanated warmth, heating his feet. He focused on that before shifting his awareness to the sounds available to his ears. The whistling of the wind through the world-bordering canyon was a constant murmur. Behind it, there was a sound he couldn't recognize at first. A kind of buzzing, like distant bees. Then he recalled where he had heard it before. The starslipper, the craft the Bishop and his people had used to cross the void. Come to think of it, hadn't Greydal heard, or rather felt, a similar noise—a vibration—in the gray wastes surrounding the Rings? Perhaps the buzzing was from a type of engine like that of the rover. That was his best guess.

Realizing he had forgotten to stay with the sounds, he returned his attention to his body. He was hot under the heavy robe he had filched from an abandoned home just west of the town of Heron. The air around him was thin, making his breathing more labored than he liked. Though, perhaps that was just the fault of nervousness.

He flexed his toes within his boots, feeling the sweat between them. A mild urge to urinate presented itself. All these feelings and others swam together to form his understanding of his physical self. But, behind it or above, a greater awareness of a different sort of body hovered. Greydal pawed at it with his thoughts for a moment, receiving a glimpse of profound darkness and phantasmagoric lights.

Something he had once read vaulted into his thoughts: *It is indifferent to me where I begin, for to that place I shall return again.*

Greydal's consciousness seized the wire before him. The Allthame ignited and blazed in his mind's eye, the smooth surfaces of the staff making his palms tingle as he opened his eyes. The crystal staff was no longer clear. Within its depths a fire burned, at once polychromatic and no color at all. The flames moved with alarming speed as the tongues of that lunatic hue jumped and spanned the length of the staff. In the imprisoned blaze, he saw himself, the other piece of a greater whole.

Ravobisob had been right. The Allthame was a tool, a key to open and close. In the harsh light of the sun and the glare of the rotunda, the Allthame was a rainbow slit in space, lit as much within as from without. He couldn't see it, but his eyes reflected that terrible un-color that now danced and pulsed within the crystal. Though the flames didn't heat the weapon's exterior, the milky substance coating it bubbled. Smoke rose from the shining facets where the chalky oil cooked as the peculiar smell of burning leaves reached his nose.

Looking at the Vog, he smiled and said, "Alright. Let's try this again."

The wolf grinned.

NECESSITY

He crashed through the glass ceiling into the waiting library. The balls of his feet hit first, and he rolled as the crystal staff coiled with him. Above, the Vog drooped down and pulled itself through the hole made by Greydal's first use of the Allthame. The glass complained and further broke as the wolf-body slipped through an opening that should have been too small for it.

"Ah!" Greydal exclaimed. He beamed. In his hand, the Allthame dimmed, its bizarre, internal fire returning to a kind of slumber. He looked back at the Calf-Ripper, who waited, now cushioned between two towering bookshelves. "Did it," he told the animal. The Vog's pale eyes shined in the dark, and it nodded, or seemed to.

"What you have done," another voice said, "Is chosen grief."

Greydal and the Vog turned to see a small figure in a nearby doorway. The doorway itself was stretched tall and thin, as if to accommodate some species of insectoid life grown large and bipedal. Greydal's eyes widened. The figure in the opening wasn't there, not fully. Through its dark folds, he spied the hallway beyond, which spun deeper into the Mansions.

"Mabet?" he whispered. The tiny shape bobbed its head. He had to concentrate, but he could just make out the deep, onyx eggs that were the Pneuma changeling's true eyes. Clearly, she saw no reason to pretend any longer. "Are you really here?" No, he knew she wasn't even as he asked it. Some sort of projection?

"In the ways that matter, I am here," she answered in a low voice.

"I shouldn't be surprised," he said, shaking his head ruefully. "But I'm glad to see you. The Bishop, he's—"

"*I* am sad to say I am not glad. Not glad at all," the apparition spoke.

Greydal shut his mouth. The old woman's face, what he could see of it, was hard. He swallowed and replied, "Don't be angry. It's because of you I finally embraced myself. But—"

"You believe that is what you did."

"But," he repeated slowly, "even if I don't remember it all, I know it was my choice to make. Staying."

"Hm. You will stay for a long time, I fear," the Mabet projection murmured. The golden hallway beyond her form darkened.

"What?" Greydal asked. Behind him, the living hunger that was the Vog loomed nearer.

The witch sneered and replied, "*What?* That is what you ask me? Do not pretend you cannot sense it."

Greydal paused. "I feel nothing."

"Hm. That is evident."

"You're upset."

Mabet shook her head. "Foolish man. Foolish *revenant*. You may have doomed yourself in not accepting Bythos. This world is now in its final day."

He almost chuckled in spite of the circumstance. He countered, "You don't know as much as you think. And you couldn't possibly know that."

"Oh? I know the Wyrm as I know all men. This wide estate dies by midnight."

This wide estate? "The Mansions?" he asked.

She only stared at him. Her form vibrated as if it struggled to maintain its shape. "Not the Mansions," he whispered. She didn't offer any further information.

At last, he said, "If that's true, then we should do something."

"Fret for your own life and that of your copy," the shade whispered. After a beat, she paused, seeming to consider. "Perhaps one of my sisters will lead him out. They *are* smitten with the boy," Mabet said with a curious smile, and then crumbled. Bits of translucent shadow drifted to the floor, thin as fly wings. Behind where she had stood, the hall brightened.

He remained still. "Think she's telling the truth?" he asked the wolf. The Calf-Ripper only stared.

Greydal straightened, and brushed the stray bits of glass off his shoulders and the folds of his dirty robe. Stepping over the shards on the floor, he left the library the way Mabet had appeared, through the narrow archway, turning his shoulders to allow him and the Allthame through. The archway opened to a shining corridor, replete with faded paintings and other miscellaneous, framed art. Some clung to the silver walls of the corridor, others lay where they had fallen. In the corners near the ceiling, gossamer webs hung like corpse hair.

"This wing doesn't see frequent use, I'd say. But keep an eye out," Greydal said over his shoulder. He didn't mention the Friars. The creature needed no encouragement there. He continued forward, and then paused to look back. "Oh."

The Vog loomed behind the thin entrance as a solid wall of dry darkness, the gold trim of the aperture framing it. The beast's head was wider than the opening. "Sorry," he told the animal. "Can you find a way around?"

In response, the Calf-Ripper drew closer to the archway, and then pressed against it. The fountain of hair covering the beast's head masked its face, but Greydal had the impression of a gelatinous sliding as it thrust its skull through the gap. He backed in spite of himself as the Vog continued its work, a horrible parody of birth. The animal's face was nearly folded in half as it finally slid its skull through. Two of its translucent arms followed, gripping the edges. Then came the rest of its body as the trim of the archway groaned against the wall.

The Calf-Ripper flopped onto the ground, and then lifted itself as its canid snout resumed its previous shape. The beast shuffled towards Greydal, who forced himself not to back away. The beast's pale eyes found his.

After a breath he said, "Alright. That was horrible, do you know that?"

*** *** ***

They arrived at a dizzying staircase of burnished wood. Descending it took them to a continuation of the hall above, and they progressed through the new wing, more of a home to arachnids than any other life. Cobwebs covered the ceiling for yards at a time. At one point, Greydal looked up to see a small, eight-legged creature scuttle into a hole in the metal, though he wasn't sure if the face he saw was simply a pattern in the thing's furry body. He didn't tarry to investigate.

As they walked, he thought of what Mabet had said. What if she was right? He had sensed a sort of assurance or peace when he... Greydal fished for the appropriate term. *When he stepped down into a body.* That was close to what had happened, wasn't it? Would he have done that if he knew it would doom the Four Corners?

He glanced at the Allthame in his hand. It had burned with an inner fire while eating through the glass dome of the outer roof as quickly as the thought had entered his mind. But could it prevent the death of these people, the ones living in this manmade garden? Something in his gut told him the artifact didn't work that way. If only he had retained some of his knowledge, some understanding from his time as...

As *what?* Not Old Man Moonlight. Not the Interloper. Something outside the sum of those ideas. And now, he was an only an abstraction. The thought stilled his heart. Outwardly a man, but paper thin. His existence was as an insect, sitting on the surface of a vast pool of water. He was as much himself as anything his gaze happened to glance across. One day, he would tire and sink. His essence would run together with those coldest of currents, and he would be ferried to whatever expanse was there to receive him: absence absorbing, or an understanding home. A calming weight materialized within him, and he focused his thoughts through the lens of that calm, to break down what he knew: Mabet had said midnight. If she was right, that was when something dire would happen. But how, and by whose hand?

He had to make it to the cavity in the firmament before his younger self. Afterwards he could presumably do what he liked, aside from one other task. Would that be enough time to lead *some* people outside?

Greydal grimaced to himself. Who said the world beyond the Four Corners was any safer? All he had seen was a cavern and a single atrium. He searched the nebulous growths beyond his mind, which served as something akin to memories, the recollections of that thing he had once been. But the embers of his experience as *Interloper* told him nothing. His mind could now no longer make sense of the remains, the bizarre forms and shadows that were his old life. The reality was, he would have to do this as a man. His earlier choice now bound him.

Of course, had Mabet not been miserly with details, he might have had a better shot at comprehending the nameless threat which she had pronounced. Never explaining things—the old woman was worse than her protege in that regard. But the ancient witch had implied people would die. Was there something wrong with the Four Corners? Is that what she had meant Bythos to prevent? Or would a mortal Greydal's attempts to save people be the cause of some sort of doomsday? Hopefully not, unless the world secretly and truly worked like one of his father's stories. Then that kind of unwelcome irony would inevitably rear its head.

Greydal clenched his jaw. One thing he noticed was Mabet hadn't seemed too concerned with her own wellbeing. He wondered just how much she knew. Was she aware the Bishop's troops were almost certainly coming for the kith, that the location of their home was known? If she could prophesize a threat to the Four Corners, then why not that? In fact, why not Greydal's decision? Why would she do *nothing* but enable him to make the very choice he had, if she were so wise and far-seeing? There was no logic in it. Unless, of course, her thoughts were more alien than he had credited her. Or perhaps she simply didn't care.

He frowned. Behind, the Calf-Ripper continued its shadowing. "Did I do wrong?" Greydal asked the wolf, glancing over his shoulder. The thing's ears perked. "Why am I asking you? You don't know." He turned and continued striding along the well-polished hallway. Well, first things first, he mused. He had to take care of the most pressing threat: Michael Bishop.

"Maybe I should just kill him and be done with it," Greydal muttered to himself.

"Yes."

His eyes widened, and he spun to face his companion. The Vog stopped its infantile crawling and waited. Its cold eyes betrayed nothing.

*** *** ***

A series of wrong turns and dead ends followed. When he turned a corner, only to see the fourth archway in a row leading to an enclosed room, he swore, "How many libraries does he fucking need?"

Temporarily flummoxed, a kind of bored frustration made him step inside. He eyed the titles of the books on the nearest burnished shelf. All in the Old Folks' tongue. One was a faded red against a white background. Brown stains decayed at the edges like mold, and the title was dwindled and partially erased. *N-ur-mancer*. The author's name was there, too. Was this a book on magick? He supposed it must be.

He spoke over his shoulder to the monster waiting in the hallway. "It's odd. Despite the Friars and that golden suit of his, I didn't get the sense the Bishop was the type to traffic in actual sorcery. He seems..." Greydal fumbled for the right phrase. "When I was growing up, the Red Faith was strict. It's why Harlow disliked outsiders. The Bishop's the one who designed that faith, built it around himself, built it around that Legate persona of his."

Greydal left the books where they sat and returned to the hallway. The Vog eyed him with a stale curiosity.

"I guess what I'm trying to say is he seems traditional. He kept his—*our*—language alive over hundreds and hundreds of years with almost no change. You don't do that if you're the progressive sort." If the Calf-Ripper had thoughts on the subject, it didn't share them. After a protracted silence, Greydal relented and started walking the way they had come. "Come on," he told the beast. "We'll find it eventually."

They did. That evening the duo arrived at a familiar stretch of the Mansions, after further wrong turns and correct descents along precipitous staircases. Greydal wiped the sweat off his palms as he neared what he recognized as the corridor with the portals.

The Bishop's manmade gates. The opening was to the left. That meant the corridors to his right would lead to the shadowy hall, the one which confined the entrance to that vast space where his younger self was likely having a one-sided dinner with the man who had introduced himself as Legate.

Greydal cleared his throat and shifted the Allthame to his right hand. Despite the presence of the colossal hound at his back, fear licked his spine and left him feeling deeply alone. He pressed onwards until they neared the hall he remembered. The wall of black rebuffed his gaze as he squinted into it. He furrowed his brow. So, he could see in the dark, but *only* beyond the firmament? He supposed that tracked with what he had come to suspect about the nature of the cold iron the expedition crew once mentioned. The stuff was clearly the Bishop's attempt at forestalling any major disruptions born from the churning universe. Perhaps, at one time, that was needed, even if the substance barely worked. But now, it was an impediment to his task.

He filled his lungs, taking as much time as he could to stave off what he knew he had to do next. He exhaled. "Get ready. This is it," he whispered. His footsteps announced him as he walked towards the gloom, and he mentally urged them to silence. After several tense seconds, he glimpsed the choked outline of the towering doors to the dining hall. As the first chimes tinkled, much closer than he anticipated, he thought he saw a lone light in the distance, two blurry figures basking its glow. Then the tinkling grew louder.

The Friar never made it to him. Few did. The first one to close reached a glistening probe from one of the pits in its globular helmet. The corpse the Friar piloted matched it, straightening its arms as if to embrace Greydal. But without a sound, the Friar disappeared. Greydal's gaze tried to follow it upwards only to watch the shining coat vanish in the dark over his head. The muffled sound of rending metal preceded something viscous and heavy hitting the floor.

Others attacked. A chorus of jingling metal rose all around as the second Friar emerged from the dark to his right, its head low to the floor like a snake's. The golden thing hurried clumsily towards him. In a way, it appeared comical. Or would have if not for the thing's awful intent. As the monster loped near, Greydal's mind connected with that other self he had sensed on the rooftop, that place of darkness and lights. At once, the Allthame in his hand ignited, matching the surreal colors that now danced and chanted mutely behind his eyes.

The Friar was feet away...and closing.

OPEN. That was all he thought.

At once, the metal frame of the creature split apart, revealing a cadaver whose head had been replaced with something dark and red. As soon as he registered the sight, the body and red parasite unpeeled further, like a flower in bloom. The ruined figure fell to the floor with a *squelch.* To his right, a glob of sizzling muck fell from the dark over his head. Almost immediately, another Friar who rushed at Greydal flew upwards, pulled by translucent hands.

The rest vanished from memory. He would later piece together he had probably killed another Friar just before a different one reached him. He remembered seeing one of the things fall to pieces, followed by the sensation of his back on the ground. Panic. A golden figure sprawled over him. The Vog had gotten that one, he was sure.

When he eventually stumbled to his feet, the rest of the Friars were dead, and the Calf-Ripper uncoiled itself from the murk of the distant ceiling. Greydal blinked. Something was wrong. He tried to raise the Allthame but dropped it. The crystalline staff didn't so much clatter to the floor as flop onto it, as though he had released a python. At once, a terrible wetness in his shoulder announced itself. The pain was horrific. A scream bubbled towards his lips, but he knew he mustn't alert the two in the dining hall to his presence. He clenched his teeth together and surveyed his shoulder.

Things weren't so bad this time, a smile of open tissue stretched across the meat between his neck and his armpit. But he had all his limbs.

Greydal bent and retrieved the Allthame with his left hand as he shook, his adrenaline seeping away. In the dark, the Vog curled low and shoveled a bubbling soup that used to be a Friar into its maw. At least Greydal thought so. To him, the Calf-Ripper was only a muted torso and a series of pale arms.

"How can you eat that?" he tried to whisper. His jaw shuddered as the shock of his wound clawed away his words.

He held his eyes shut and tried to connect with the Allthame. The endless deep and the un-colors were still there, just at the edge of his awareness. *FIX. CLOSE.* He sent the thoughts like moths towards a lone candle. At first, the torment didn't cease, and Greydal feared he had failed. Then the wetness seeping through his robes dissipated. He opened his eyes only to watch the Vog swallow another deceased monster.

"Unbelievable," he murmured. Even the tear on his robe was gone. As soon as he realized it, the pain went as well. He flexed his right arm and rotated it. It seemed good as new. The Vog sidled towards him, and Greydal glimpsed the featureless disks of the hound's eyes peering intently, now only pools in the dimness.

"I'm fine," he whispered to it and reached up to pat the Vog on one of its shoulders. His stomach lurched, but he kept his awareness from tumbling into the wolf. "We've got to hurry. Can you find the rest of the Friars or any soldiers in this wing? The Bishop—" Greydal spit and took a deep breath to steady himself. "He can't see you if I want a decent shot at convincing him."

The Vog didn't nod so much as lower its heavy skull. Before Greydal could say goodbye, the hound melted into the glassy shadows. He stood alone.

Where was he supposed to go now? Sebastian had led them away before. But he was certain he was supposed to travel right from the unlit hall. Without much deliberation, he made his way in the direction he believed led to the corridor in the firmament. As he walked, an audient silence bathed him and the hall.

The Bishop and also the Legate. What kind of man was he, to devote his life and time to boxing up a world? When he had dined with the tyrant, the man seemed dead set on returning to the past. Pointless, but Michael didn't know that. Perhaps Greydal could tell him.

But again, what kind of man was he? Like many of the recollections of Greydal's young adulthood, his memories of Michael Bishop now were foggy with time's idiot slurring. But he could recall enough. The older Bishop, the one who called himself the Legate? That man had in almost all certainty used Elis' decapitated head and attached it to a suit of armor. Perhaps that act had been to extend the doctor's life. Greydal guessed the Bishop would, if given the chance, declare it was all for the greater good. But the act was deranged either way.

So, what would this deranged man who had stayed alive for a thousand years do when he was told that his quest was *pointless*?

Another memory: When Greydal was young, the village of Harlow Valley would, every three years, participate in the Pursuer's Fair. It was an event a bit like the Old Folk game of Hide and Seek, given new form and rules. Participants would draw straws, colored on the bottom. This decided who would be hunters and who would be prey. Any prey who lasted the night or hunter who caught three runners would receive a small bag of shavings and a slightly larger gift of food or fabrics.

As a boy, he had always wanted to be prey for one reason: his father. More specifically, his father's dead cats. The first time Tier had used the tactic, Greydal had been confused. Why had they collected a decaying animal from the woods? Why did his father stuff it in a large jar to keep predators from seeking the thing? On the night of the Pursuer's Fair, he had his answer.

Now, the village *didn't* allow those who acted as prey to take items into the woods. It wouldn't be fair, after all. Tier got around this stipulation by burying the feline corpse and its glass sarcophagus deep in the trees days before the night of the Fair. As Greydal and his father fled into the verdant twilight under the ten-minute head start, they would beeline for the hidden cat. Once retrieved, the animal and its awful stench became a short-term companion. Dragging the musty corpse behind them, Tier would use the cat to confuse the keen noses of the mutts, throwing them off the duo's trail (or sometimes *on* someone else's).

This idea brought Greydal to his current predicament. Despite all the otherworldly understanding he had relinquished, he knew the Legate's cave, the object of the man's fixation, was nothing more than a dead cat, though maybe an unintentional one. Stopping the place from being investigated, before or after it moved from the doctor's original home to Tehom, would do nothing.

Could he explain that without causing more violence? Probably not. Perhaps that was what Mabet had meant when she warned of apocalypse. But he couldn't avoid a confrontation. Not if he planned to blow open a hole in the firmament. Which he did.

***   ***   ***

The marbled room with the domed ceiling was unmarred by signs of combat. Above him the mural of the man and his shining jewel presented itself again, as it had last time. Though faded with age, Greydal could now identify the features of that ceilinged visage, having seen him in person.

The story of the mural made more sense as Greydal's eyes roved its frozen tableaus. Here, it showed Michael Bishop holding the Four Corners in his hand like a golden fruit or toy. Below the image was the word *Savior.* Later, the fruit became a pyramid, the one in the cavern. Now, the Bishop ogled that miniature world, not with longing as Greydal had first imagined upon originally seeing the mural, but with fear. The word beneath this image was *Guardian.*

Here, the Bishop, apparently dead, lay on a multi-colored mat. Maybe that was part of the technology used to transfer the minds of the Old Folk into the bodies of tulka. This section's word was *Sacrifice.* And at the far end, hidden behind a pillar, the mural showed the Bishop's transformation: An image of a pink head sat on a pedestal, eyes open. The art was faded, but the face appeared pleased. Wires or snakes sprouted from the head's neck, trailing until they united with a headless golden body. A suit of armor.

Below the image was a word that was too faded to read. But he could guess its meaning: *Immortal.*

Greydal strode towards the unlit corridor reaching west from the room. As he neared it, he paused. No wind this time, not yet. He entered the darkness and sent a thought to the Allthame. As his mind connected with the staff, it became excited, sparking with a convulsing luster. The indistinct firmament-rock mirrored the fiery lights falling from the weapon, evoking dreams the minds of men didn't contain.

His steps were quiet. As before, the corridor simply stopped, a door of metal fused shut blocking his way. Greydal's hand reached out and grazed the material. For a moment, he sensed the utter boundlessness of the world beyond, and his heart skipped a beat. Then the door returned to being just a door, and he stood in silence before the last and only barrier.

OPEN.

The Allthame shuddered as a pale keening rose in his mind. The door flared as a puckered gash in the shape of a circle disappeared from its center. Wind, old and cool, spilled into the shadowed corridor from the now-smoldering opening.

He had done it. But now, an alarm should be sounding in the dining hall. He didn't have much time. One last thing to address.

Again, he connected with the Allthame, feeling its kinship as a doorway between two alike spaces. Above them both, a wider province beckoned. He and the weapon pulled at that power, and it came readily, dripping into their bodies like rain.

They turned their thoughts outward, to the staggering universe past the firmament walls. The seams were still there.

CLOSE.

The Allthame wailed, and he joined it, that sound exploding from his throat. The power that the two shared ejected from them as the staff shattered, embedding crystal shards into the walls, the floor. He fell to his knees as his mind's eye showed him what he had wrought.

Out beyond the walls, eternity stretched. Trillions and trillions of leagues of city, wilderness, nations, and mystery. Through them all, unseen scars stretched, remnants of an ancient catastrophe. But now? Now, those scars faded. The rifts would close.

It would take only hours, maybe less. The younger one better hurry.

Beyond the hole in the door, a distant peal of thunder sounded, once.

CHAPTER

31

GEHENNA

The hiss of steam was the only sign Michael Bishop had arrived. Greydal inhaled and unsteadily rose, retrieving the remainder of the Allthame. The artifact was now a ruined handle of crystal, ending in a sharp edge. He took a second, deeper breath as black spots cluttered his vision. He spoke without turning around. "What am I supposed to call you? Legate? Bishop? *Mike?*"

A silence. And then, "*What have you done?*"

Greydal stared at the distant tower of wax. "Fine," he muttered to himself. More loudly, he continued, "The world was sick. It got... Well, it got fixed a long time ago. But as you yourself said, there were still tears, interstitial distortions I think you called them. I don't understand much about the lands beyond these walls, but that's no way to live. Here or there. People can't be worrying that one day someone will trip through a Type Two and kill a kingdom or reverse history. So, I healed the remaining bits. I closed the tears."

"*Closed...? Turn around.*"

Greydal turned. Without the lights of the Allthame, the cavity in the firmament was darker than before, but the guttering candle at the Bishop's feet made visible the emotion distorting the man's face. And, yes, behind him, the now-dwindling image of a dinner cut short. Then Michael's features calmed, recognition playing across them, and he nodded to himself. "*Inevitable, I suppose. My constant error, underestimation.*"

Greydal inclined his head.

A great bout of wind whistled from behind, fully dousing the dying candle on the tunnel floor. In the ensuing dimness, the Bishop buzzed, "*You look the same. But you* feel *as different from your clone as Peter was to his.*"

"I'm not a clone, and neither was the other Peter"

"*But you're acquainted. With the nature of your...corruption.*" The gust lulled, making Greydal's voice stark against its absence. "If you want to call it that," he said.

"*I do. You're aware the other one doesn't know?*"

Greydal folded his arms. "He will," he replied as his mind flicked to his memories of the black sea.

"*I was trying to illuminate him. He's the key. But, perhaps, I was hunting for the wrong tulka.*" The Bishop's dull form took a step closer. "*But, no, I can already see it, you're not going to come willingly.*" Thin spurts of steam leaked from the joints in the Bishop's dull armor. The man's brow was knotted.

Greydal shook his head and raised a hand in warning. "Michael, wait. You need to listen to me. It's not as simple as you—" A metal fist connected with his forehead. His skull snapped back, and he sprawled against the melted doorway. *So fast!* He waited for consciousness to slip away. But it didn't. Only a slight pain between his eyes presented itself.

"*Hm. Perhaps* tulka *was the wrong word.*" The man reached behind his back and pulled something small and black from somewhere out of sight. Another of the glass bricks? Greydal's eyes widened. He scrambled to his feet and threw himself backwards towards the opening in the door as the black object embedded itself in his shoulder.

He plummeted for minutes, long enough to realize he was going to die and make a sort of final peace with that knowledge, before landing on and rolling several feet. Red sparks leaped from the ground, and he glimpsed them fall to the substance underneath, causing ripples. That should have hurt more than it did. Maybe the table...?

A golden figure followed and tumbled down, closer to the tiny ladder. It then raced at him, threatening to achieve the same size. Greydal jolted as he understood his plight, and he rose to sprint towards the old, brown stain at the center of the table. Over his head, the cavernous chamber echoed with a distant rumbling. With each step, his surroundings grew smaller, and he made better headway. He didn't look to see how close the Bishop was to his heels. The sweat covering his hands made holding the Allthame shard difficult, but he feared dropping it for a reason he couldn't quite understand. Was the thing still alive? The numbness in his shoulder made it hard to concentrate. Based on what he could see out of the corner of his eye, the Bishop had thrown what appeared to be an obsidian knife into him. Greydal ignored it, closing with the center. The candle was two-thirds his height.

A wall of gold interrupted him. He bounced off the Bishop's oversized legs as a gout of steam obscured his vision. One of those giant feet arced, booting him in the chest with tremendous force. He gasped as the blow forced the air from his lungs. Greydal hit the table and rolled back, looking up to see that the Bishop was larger. No, *he* was smaller. The ex-doctor had knocked him closer to the edge of the table.

Greydal snarled and wobbled to his feet as Michael disappeared, only a man-shaped wisp of steam left in the demiurge's wake. Then a human-sized hand reached from behind Greydal's back and grasped his throat. He felt himself being lifted into the air, and then slammed to the ground. The red sparks of the table rippled outwards.

He struggled beneath the Bishop's grip as the ceiling changed, as if someone had quickly moved everything hundreds of feet towards the center of the table. *Oh*, a thought whispered. The Bishop picked him up again and bashed him against the ground a second time. Greydal's head lolled back, and he glimpsed the very normal-sized ladder only feet away.

"*We're going back inside.*"

The cavern disappeared. In its place, the elaborate mural of the pink, marble room reeled. A golden fist rained downwards towards Greydal's nose, and he twisted, pulling himself from Michael's grip. The golden comet connected with the marble and shattered it, leaving a round crater in the floor. The Bishop stood as more steam released from his body.

The man leaped, and a golden elbow hurdled towards Greydal's sternum. Greydal rolled twice. The first time, the Bishop's attack connected with the floor. The second time a kick, seemingly from nowhere, hit the ground and sent marble chips into Greydal's eyes. He clenched them shut as he stumbled to his feet and brandished the shard of the Allthame in a tingling hand.

"*Stay still!*" The Bishop produced what appeared to be a second black object, giving Greydal time to get a look at it. But his vision was blurry.

Why, the shrapnel from the floor? No, that wasn't it. He didn't have the time to examine the issue as a second obsidian knife hurdled past his head, nearly giving him a new notch on his ear.

"Stop," Greydal breathed and pulled the first knife from his shoulder, letting it clatter to the floor.

"*I'll stop—*" the Bishop threw a driving punch, which Greydal dodged. Michael's other hand caught his arm and threw him against a nearby wall. But the light had bloomed, becoming different. Harsher. Suddenly, Greydal registered it wasn't a wall into which he'd been tossed. A tree? He caught a quick glimpse of the Bishop looking in bemusement at the backdrop. But then more steam erupted from that golden body as the man turned and stampeded through a sapling, simply evaporating it. They were outdoors, a stray thought told Greydal as he jumped, dodging just in time to avoid being crushed by the Bishop's tackle.

The man stopped and rose, a strange look on his contorted face. "You're confused," Greydal told him between breaths. "Didn't mean to take me here, did you?"

What had the man once said? Something about the golden pack taking hours to be suitable for safe operation again? Presumably, the Bishop's golden body operated under similar limitations. Greydal bent and leaned on his knees, still gripping the Allthame shard in his right hand.

The Bishop rotated a shoulder and grimaced. *"By all rights you ought to be unconscious now. The toxin—"*

"I told you," Greydal interrupted as he eyed the encircling wilderness. It was a dense wood, though the trees didn't grow tall. Somewhere north or east, then. "It's not that simple. The problem was beyond you. But you can change the lives of everyone in the—"

The Bishop disappeared, and then so did the surroundings. A metal hand grabbed the back of Greydal's head and slammed it into what looked like a boulder, then an alloy wall, then a crumbling stone edifice, the light and environment altering with each strike. There was another jump. A shocking blow swept Greydal's legs from under him, and an aureate arm and knee pinned him to the ground. They were now in the Mansions, this time in what appeared to be a miscellaneous hallway, complete with suits of inhuman, silvered armor lining the walls.

"Peter..." Greydal tried. The arm moved, putting pressure on Greydal's windpipe. "Peter— He was right," he wheezed.

"*Be silent.*"

"He...was...right..."

"*About what, that the problem is too big? I'll grind it all down, then, until it's manageable. This won't end until we* make *it,*" the Bishop told him through gritted teeth. Steam spurted in rough gouts from the arm under Greydal's chin.

"You won't," Greydal whispered. "Nothing to fix—" he coughed.

"*There's* EVERYTHING *to fix!*" the man overrode. But the pressure under Greydal's chin abated slightly.

"Not— I'm not fooling... You...were never going to stop...it. Help what's left," Greydal choked out. For a moment, neither moved.

Then four translucent hands pulled the Bishop off him. "*Agh!*" Michael yelled in surprise. Greydal coughed and rolled unsteadily to his feet, only to see his son enveloping the Bishop, milky drool leaking from the hound's mouth as it made a child of the golden man.

"Wait," Greydal wheezed through his compressed windpipe. But it was too late. The Calf-Ripper strengthened its pale grasp on the Bishop and pulled. For a moment, Greydal thought nothing would happen. Then the Bishop's left arm disconnected from the shoulder. An explosion of steam followed, and at once, Greydal was in freefall.

He had enough presence of mind to realize there had been another jump, perhaps caused by the golden armor's rupturing. He spun, flashes of the faceted sky and the not-so distant ground displacing one another at greater and greater speeds. Below was what looked to be a—

Greydal slammed into the face of the basin rock and tumbled for several feet to an outcropping before his world went dark.

***   ***   ***

The sounds of the crowd shouting for his father to bring out the last of the Ague victims woke Greydal. He shook his head. Why didn't they listen? It wasn't his fault their kids had died, and he had lived.

A pain in his spine and shoulder caused him to open his eyes. The night sky greeted him as the soiled moon danced. He wasn't in the barracks. He moaned as he shifted his body and sent a bleary glance to the dry rockscape cradling him.

Even from his current perspective, his resting place looked familiar. Several feet away, the Allthame shard lay shining in the dust like a splinter of the sky. Had it followed him? He could have sworn he had dropped the thing. Greydal groaned as he lifted himself to a sitting position. His head reeled. Then, as he steadied himself, he found the shouts from his dream had followed as well. He stumbled to his feet and trudged forward, stopping to snatch the Allthame shard and nearly dropping back to his knees as he did so.

The night roared. The experience was so disorienting he almost didn't notice the golden lump crumpled on the far side of the mountainhead's lower scalp. He disregarded it for several breaths as he tried to obtain his bearings. He was near Mabet's home, that much was clear. Though he was certain he and the suspicious golden shape were both on the other side of the basin. This assessment was sourced solely from the position of the descending cliffs and foggy lowlands to their right. Time would tell, however. Greydal absently rubbed the aching spot in his shoulder as it re-announced itself.

The noises plumbing the darkness grew louder. As he meandered closer, the golden lump he had spotted before slowly became the Bishop, facing away and sitting down. The man's right arm was gone, a jagged shear replacing it. Intermittently, steam ejected from the gaping wound, and small and dark somethings appeared or disappeared around the man's stationary form. A portion of the night sky to the right detached from the horizon. Greydal ignored the Calf-Ripper as it calmly shuffled after him.

As he drew nearer, the roaring of the crowd became almost deafening, taking on the aspect of a collective moan. It was as if a great many people had only just heard the worst news of their lives. As Greydal continued, he recognized where in the kith's hidden encampment he had landed. That dip of shadow coming up on his left? That was the center basin. Soon, he should be able to see the twinkling outline of the great meetinghouse. That meant the mist-smothered lowlands to his right were the same ones he had traveled through so often. The Bishop sat on a rise of the divide, the veritable wall of stone acting as the south-facing portion of the basin itself.

Now oriented, the landscape resolved itself. And something stranger; the sounds he heard divulged their true nature. *Not* moans, or roars. Screams. Screams of abject terror, taken on a mindless reverberation, resounding among the countless rocky channels of the mountain.

The Vog had already identified the source of those cries. The beast's skin quivered with pleasure as it smelled the oceans of fear on the night wind. The wolf would drink deep from the vein of life tonight if given the chance. But not now. Now, the master neared the downed leader of the red filth. The wolf's shadow would be Greydal's until this was done.

Greydal looked down at the seated Bishop. The objects he had seen before, the ones winking in and out of sight, told of a horrific fate. As each appeared or vanished, the Bishop jerked almost imperceptibly. Greydal walked to Michael's right. At first, he made to check on the man, to determine his state. But upon seeing Michael's eyes, Greydal gazed out upon the sights below.

The scene was divided into two sections. The first was represented by the proceedings being conducted within the thick fog of the lowlands. Due to his current altitude and the density of the haze, all Greydal could identify with any certainty was that a great, *great* many glimmering figures convulsed in the gloom. The whole of the marshy waste was filled with them. These caperers appeared to be the major source of the howls of fright.

But the events occurring within the basin itself were what drew his attention. These were easier to see for the basin, even at its lowest depth, was not much more than several stories below where Greydal now stood. Here, the obscure figures from the low-lands were repeated, these men and women proving to be the soldiers of the Bishop. The Armargure.

Their varied arms and armors all gleamed in the baleful light of the moon. Despite the clarity with which he could spy these figures, at first, he couldn't decipher what it was he watched. Was it some sort of combat ritual? He blinked and looked farther. Beyond the throng, the meetinghouse was lit from within, every room spilling warm light into the bluish dark. Figures milled about in there, countless specters shuffling around and crowding every available window. They watched as the thousands (and it must be thousands) of soldiers filling the rocky bowl moved as if madness puppeted the whole lot.

No, not simply moved.

The rising and falling screams of terror made it hard to reconcile what it was Greydal's eyes *told* him. But it was plain, the soldiers danced. Every man and woman spun and twirled, some gracefully, some not. But all writhed to the rhythm of a silent melody.

Later, he would convince himself he had glimpsed the pleading eyes and open mouth of one dancer who had looked up to him as if for help. But all cried aloud as if the cruelest, the most grotesque crime had been done— No! Was *being done* to them. But all they did was...

Greydal's gaze traveled from the twirling participants and saw that the soldiers weren't the sole inhabitants of the basin. On an opposing ledge, overlooking the misty flatlands and thrashing bowl, a series of figures stood robed in darkness. Their exact number was hard to guess, but he identified at least fifteen or twenty. They congregated as a group, arms raised to the sneering moon, as if praying over the floundering soldiers. Greydal knew them at once. The women of the kith, a small portion of them. And one visitor, a short-haired girl who didn't join her companions' invocations. He thought Ida held a hand over her mouth. Though, whether it was in awe or horror he couldn't say.

To Ida's right, two of the assembled women stood apart. Queens next to handmaids. Even from his distance, he could tell how Roan's mane of blonde hair twisted in a breeze that wasn't there. To his lover's right, the small absence that was Mabet gyrated. The old woman danced, as if each and every one of the enraptured Armargure were her individual partners. Above their heads, odd sigils squirmed. Spirals within spirals.

Intuition told him they weren't looking at the moon—they focused on those glinting symbols.

Next to Greydal, the Bishop spoke, "*All for nothing.*"

He looked to the man. The liver perched on the gritty dirt between them evaporated, what appeared to be a lung replacing it. The Bishop quivered as more steam ejected from the tear in his shoulder. "*I-I-I,*" Michael tried to say. The man couldn't finish.

"Do you want me to kill you?" Greydal asked him as softly as he could. Below, the shouts and howls reached a new crescendo. Michael nodded imperceptibly.

With a flash, Greydal whipped his arm outwards, embedding the Allthame shard deep into the man's head. Or at least he tried to. The blow glanced off the Bishop's skull, leaving a hanging strip of flesh to mark the Allthame shard's wayward arc. Another gout of steam announced the arrival of a grease-stained heart.

"*Devil...*" the Bishop buzzed. Greydal tried again, this time succeeding in penetrating the man's temple. The man crumpled as Greydal withdrew the Allthame, now covered in sour blood.

A peal, like a great bell or glassy tolling, sounded.

Later, he would imagine he had heard that strange noise both echoing down from the skies, and, more quietly, from within the crumpled form of the slayed demiurge. As it was, he didn't know what to make of the sound, this knell accompanying the passing of Michael Bishop. A new development occured, which at first, he also didn't understsand. Far above him, a fundamental aspect of the sky changed. Had he never once left the confines of the Four Corners, Greydal would never have appreciated how the great prism of the sky, that marvel of architecture containing the burning light of the sun and the white-hot grime of the moon, had a glassy sheen. It was simply the sky.

But, from his time beyond the world and from his life as something more than a man, he found himself capable of addressing the fact that was now pressing itself into his awareness with an ugly urgency:

The sky had opened.

A luminous, milky substance descended like a raging, world-covering blanket. It announced the end of everything. There was no time at all and yet Greydal was rooted, staring upwards, and then at the horizon where, as far as he could see, the burning vitae that was the moon hurdled in uniformity towards the ground.

At once, a small part of him woke up, that place inside those who always search for the falling hammer, the pulled rug. *See!* it whispered triumphantly, *I was right!* And so, it may have been. After all, this was the fulfillment of old dreams, wasn't it? Nightmares he had suffered as a child about the end of the world, now come a-choking.

Something tickled his ears and neck. Despite the terrible spectacle of life's plummeting finale, Greydal looked away. A forest of hair blocked out the growing luminescence. A canine mouth, opened so wide as to be horizontal, descended first. But as the cave of wolf-flesh stole his consciousness, he had the time to decide one thing. The aspect that horrified him the most wasn't the *fact* of his devourment. It was that multiple, shining eyes lined the inside of the beast itself.

He lost himself before an audience.

*** *** ***

Blood tastes as sweet as candy to something starved of it. The woman's aureate plating was as paper or thatch. Nothing would prevent sharp teeth and lolling tongue from slurping at the exposed viscera. This one had evaded the raining fire. All the better, the wolf reasoned impressively.

It dug further into the still moaning victim. A *crunch*, and the woman was silent. Her dull eyes stared at the blackness overhead, never once glimpsing the horror that took her. The wolf felt itself reconstitute and was thankful. Its belly was pregnant with unmoving fare, and yet hunger coursed through its mind, pushing the wolf to gorge itself. But it couldn't partake of meat just yet. Blood would have to sustain it for the journey ahead.

Long-memoried, this old wolf. The beast didn't feel the creeping strangulation of age nor the weight of time, for it was as eternal as fear. And so, it dived into its far recollections, the redolence of the crimson broth coating its chops and locks recalling other, grander feasts:

Once, in the place men knew as the northern Drop, the wolf crept down a great, cylindrical cavern which housed millions of myriad trees, plants, and animals. People, too. At the time, the wolf had known but several hundred years and was still in the process of perfecting the hunt. The leader of the red filth had recently returned, capturing a section of the world in his gray iron box.

The wolf knew it would have to one day attempt an escape. Yet, there was no point in trying the snare so soon. Not when there was an apparently endless variety of prey trapped alongside it in perpetuity.

The beast drooped from branch to trunk to mud roof, each movement taking it further into the green depths. The beings it scented were little more than animals. But animals or not, a glorious convergence of entrails and fangs neared.

A small hamlet was discovered, built into the straining trees on the inner walls of the northern Drop. One hut stood separated and elevated from its neighbors. That homestead would be first. As the waning light from the newly installed sky cascaded through the endless boughs, the beast clambered towards the lone hut. There were at least four within by the smell of it. A woman, a child, and two men, though one had the scent of decay common to the elderly and infirm. It would only take the woman and child, the wolf decided.

Coming to the present, the undying hound considered its best route. The real landscape, the one not in its memories, was irrevocably changed, and the ancient paths would likely no longer be available. Had other beings survived? If they had, they would surely be attempting a similar exodus.

As with most concepts not immediately concerning the eating of flesh or supping of blood, the cur released its half-hearted musing to the molten wind. It continued its journey, both in memory and reality.

*** *** ***

Much later, the hound blinked its eyes and groaned. A burning numbness suffused its entire body, turning hands and feet to

| 434 |

a maelstrom of pins and needles. "Ugh," the wolf said, its voice a shattered grave. A sharp pain dug into the beast's ribs, and it rolled, causing it to tumble several feet to the mossy ground. Blinking in surprise, the wolf shot a glance to its damp surroundings. It had just fallen off a table.

The wolf attempted to raise itself but failed, its hands and arms deadened, rejecting any mental commands. The beast waited there for a time, the only sound the wheezing of its irregular breathing. After several minutes or hours, it perceived something interesting. Its hands were black. But with what?

Blood.

The knowledge came as a warm rain, and the hound smiled at the memories the concept evoked. The beast found it could lift itself to a sitting position and looked around, rubbing its body with stained fingers to encourage further circulation. It was in the cavern. The one housing the...

What was it called again?

Shaking its head, the wolf stood. Though the grotto was lightless, the creature could see the shining blood smeared on the table and moss-painted stone. It was fresh, much unlike the layer of old carnage covering its own body. Mingled with the newer crimson was a different, paler fluid. It smelled of burning leaves and reminded the wolf of something intimate.

But as soon as the beast mentally groped the dancing recollection, the thought dissolved. The wolf took a fumbling step, and its keen ears alerted it to a strange tinkling. Peering down, the wolf spotted the source of the noise. It had just kicked a small, crystalline shard. It bent to retrieve the strange object.

As his hand brushed the Allthame, Greydal flooded into himself with a scream. He soon found he couldn't stop the noise and fell to his knees as the past several months of his life returned, crystalizing in his erupting memory.

His robe was now a bodysuit, congealed to his skin with a layer of coagulated slaughter. He looked at his hands as he fought to stand. They were covered as well. All at once, he couldn't handle the smell of himself. The reek of butchery saturated, and he *knew* he would never not recognize that stench. It had seeped into his essence. But there was something worse, still.

Slipping as he turned, Greydal gazed on the corpse of his world. The Four Corners was a ruin. The lights he had once glimpsed swimming within that faceted pyramid were gone, replaced by smoked glass. Stumbling towards the artifact, he peered within, only to see his imparted wolf-memories told him true; there was nothing salvageable in that desolate landscape, that charred plate. Of course, his eyes couldn't distinguish details, not at his size. But, somehow, he knew it was true. If not for the Calf-Ripper, he would have perished under the falling moon.

A small moan escaped as he waited by the cadaver of his life. He was alone.

EPILOGUE

Greydal walked. He was following, or hoped he was, whatever path the Vog had carved after the beast deposited him in front of the entrance to the Four Corners. His son left no prints, and yet there was only one way to go from the cavern: The keep. Deathly light filtered through the shattered windows of the old hall beyond.

Rumpled carpets and fallen suits of armor mixed on the ancient floor along with other, and likely newer, artifacts. Lusterless screens long cracked sat in piles next to odd devices with many buttons like some child's toy. Disarray held sway. As he trudged, Greydal sent a glance towards the heavens behind the destroyed windows. All was white, as if existence had blotted itself out in respect for his mourning.

Slowly, he came to realize he was cold. The robes and boots that caked him acted as a second layer of leathery skin, but his head was frigid despite his mask of hardened blood. Glancing down at the dormant shard of the Allthame, Greydal wondered if he could make it warm him. He no longer knew, nor in truth, cared what the implement's current purpose or limits were. He would keep it with him anyway, just in case. Though, perhaps the shard would find him, regardless.

It didn't take him long to pass the spot where his younger self had gone through the rip in reality, the door to that glassy, white room. All was quiet now. Still, he walked because he didn't know what else to do. And so it was that, at length, Greydal came upon the end of the complex.

When compared with the Mansions, the fastness through which he had just traveled was a miniscule and paltry copy. He had no thoughts for it, though, only the gleaming wastes beyond. Squinting, Greydal wandered under an oppressive archway into a new world. As he stepped fully outside, incandescent light greeted him, burning away the comfortable and neutral darkness of the crowded keep.

At first, it seemed the fate of the heavens had been replicated against the landscape. All was white. Even the air. Tiny, colorless flecks like holes in the world drifted from the nothingness above. One landed on his eyelashes, and he blinked, causing something cool to mingle with his salty eyes. Water? A step on the whitened ground produced a muffled *crunch*. Greydal exhaled in wonder and a gout of steam like that from the Bishop's golden body coasted through the air. His eyes widened as he shivered. Where *was* he?

Greydal took another step, and his boot sank into the white substance up to his shin. Pulling his foot up, he smiled in spite of himself as the cold blankness fell in silence. Greydal stooped and grabbed a handful with his free arm. Sniffing the substance told him nothing. He took a bite and started. Coldness quickly became a lukewarm wetness, quenching an up-until-now unknown thirst. Whether the material was a kind of crushed ice or something else, Greydal didn't care. He shoveled it into his jaw by the handful, barely taking the time to warm it under his tongue before swallowing. After several moments of this, Greydal panted and smiled. Thirst extinguished, Greydal's belly rumbled. He needed more blood.

Blood? No. That wasn't right at all.

Greydal stood and looked around. The keep he had exited was nearly as white as the ground. And yet, beneath the substance, he spied old stones. They rose toward the top of the structure, only several stories above his caked head. They rimmed the shadowed mouth through which he had passed. Greydal thought for a moment in silence and strode away. The horizon beckoned.

*** *** ***

Hours of cold and an unceasing, sloshing trudge made a doll of ice out of him. Or so he felt. Fingers and toes numb, Greydal continued in what he hoped was the right direction, though what did that mean? The landscape around him bled upwards and into the sky, with nothing on the chalky horizon to tell him about his current location.

In fact, the only proof he had gone anywhere at all is that the Bishop's dilapidated keep was no longer in sight, despite the faint incline Greydal sensed he had climbed. Looking once more confirmed it; there was only a vague diminishing in the sensed slope, continuing the way he had come. No ruined citadel was within view.

And so, he continued, leaving an indented snail's path through the cold powder. Greydal lost track of exactly how long he had progressed. The white heavens closed with the ground as he made his tired way, and a cold wind whispered itself into existence, cutting into him with a surprising fierceness. His nose was wet, and he sneezed, once. Greydal's foggy breath heralded him as he crested what revealed itself to be a ridge. Below, a lake of swirling powder sprawled, becoming one with the blank horizon. Greydal squinted against the rising gale as bits of the white powder peppered his eyes.

And as though via magick, the wind changed course and parted the wall of white. Greydal blinked the ice out of his eyes as he tried to make sense of the mystery before him. A series of figures in a perfect line suspended in the air, roughly fifty yards up and away.

The women hung by their own power over the misty and whirling void. Of many shapes and configurations, these naked figures were somehow motionless despite the powerful breeze. Greydal's bleary eyes traveled from one to the next, baffled. Near the smallest of the women, a different, familiar face greeted him.

Greydal stared at the floating figure. Her mane of blonde hair whipped in the icy air. Though she was far from him, Greydal imagined he perceived a faint smile playing on those lips. The woman's pale arm rose slowly, as if underwater. She pointed down and to the left, towards the sea of whirling mist. It, too, parted, revealing a colony of ants.

They scurried with surprising lethargy between small, hide-covered mounds. All were alike in their bizarre, boxy form, except two who stood off to the side of the encampment next to a burgeoning blaze. One of the ants was large and the other small. Seeing them, he started. Not ants. People.

From his vantage, they were more distant than the hovering Pneuma, but he was just near enough to make out what seemed to be Higg smacking Rulf on the arm. Then the boy pointed upwards, towards Greydal's perch.

Carrion effigy emerged from ice, he closed his eyes and smiled.

He couldn't see it, but on the horizon, the winds parted the blankness further. There from the chaotic distance they leered: old patterns and new—limitless kaleidoscopes of plunging towers and living landscapes, wheeling nirvanas. The night was pregnant with music about to erupt within glades sourced from the deepest dreams.

Not only nightmares thrived—delights dwelt there, too.

Sometimes, these things were the same.

And maybe *this* is the answer to that other mystery, the hidden understanding passed down from weeping hermits and the fugitive dead: Terror is a path, an initiation. We might follow it and see.

CPSIA information can be obtained
at www.ICGtesting.com
Printed in the USA
LVHW081905210323
742176LV00013B/39